ALSO BY SCOTT REINTGEN

A Door in the Dark

A WHISPER IN THE WALLS

A
WHISPER
IN THE
WALLS

SCOTT REINTGEN

Margaret K. McElderry Books
New York London Toronto Sydney New Delhi

MARGARET K. McELDERRY BOOKS
An imprint of Simon & Schuster Children's Publishing Division
1230 Avenue of the Americas, New York, New York 10020

MARGARET K. McELDERRY BOOKS is a trademark of Simon & Schuster, LLC.
Simon & Schuster: Celebrating 100 Years of Publishing in 2024
For information about special discounts for bulk purchases, please contact Simon & Schuster Special Sales at 1-866-506-1949 or business@simonandschuster.com.
The Simon & Schuster Speakers Bureau can bring authors to your live event. For more information or to book an event, contact the Simon & Schuster Speakers Bureau at 1-866-248-3049 or visit our website at www.simonspeakers.com.
Interior design by Irene Metaxatos
The text for this book was set in ITC Veljovic Std.
Manufactured in the United States of America
First Edition
10 9 8 7 6 5 4 3 2 1
Library of Congress Cataloging-in-Publication Data
Names: Reintgen, Scott, author.
Title: A whisper in the walls / Scott Reintgen.
Description: First edition. | New York : Margaret K. McElderry Books, [2024] | Series: Waxways ; 2 | Audience: Ages 14 up. | Audience: Grades 10–12. | Summary: Seeking revenge, Ren Monroe teams up with Vin'Tori siblings Dahvid and Nevelyn to take down House Brood, the most powerful family in Kathor, but Ren's magical bond with Theo Brood complicates her plans.
Identifiers: LCCN 2023005199 (print) | LCCN 2023005200 (ebook) | ISBN 9781665930468 (hardcover) | ISBN 9781665930482 (ebook)
Subjects: CYAC: Magic—Fiction. | Revenge—Fiction. | Fantasy. | LCGFT: Fantasy fiction. | Novels.
Classification: LCC PZ7.1.R4554 Wh 2024 (print) | LCC PZ7.1.R4554 (ebook) | DDC [Fic]—dc23
LC record available at https://lccn.loc.gov/2023005199
LC ebook record available at https://lccn.loc.gov/2023005200

For Kristin Nelson.
My champion from the very start.

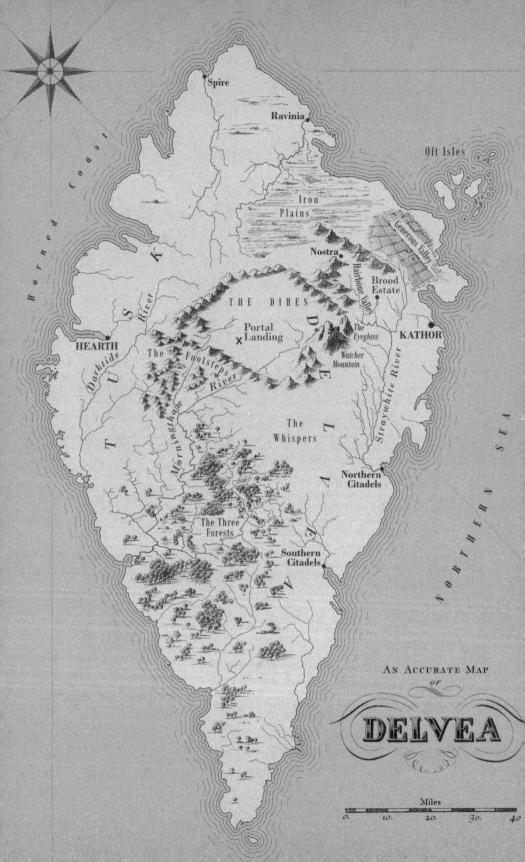

Spire

Ravinia

Oft Isles

Horned Coast

Iron
Plains

Generous Valley

Nostra

Harbone Valley

Brood
Estate

THE DIRES

Portal
Landing
✗

*The
Eyeglass*

KATHOR

The *Footsteps River*

Watcher
Mountain

HEARTH

Darktide River

T U S K

The

Morningthaw

Straywhite River

D E L V E

The
Whispers

Northern
Citadels

The Three
Forests

Southern
Citadels

N O R T H E R N   S E A

AN ACCURATE MAP

OF

DELVEA

Miles

0.   10.   20.   30.   40

CONTENTS

PART ONE

The Game

1

REN MONROE

It was hard to feel like an honored guest when no one would speak to her.

Ren Monroe found herself at yet another party in the Heights. Tonight she was a guest of the Grand Emissary of Kathor. His handwritten invitation had possessed more warmth than all the conversations she'd attempted thus far. She'd arrived an hour ago. Theo had been stolen away to a private room for an arranged meeting with the viceroy himself. The other Broods sought out their own comfortable circles, leaving her completely alone.

Ren tried not to feel bitter about Theo's absence. She knew tonight was important. The warden had announced his retirement. There were one hundred livestone statues scattered around the city, eagerly awaiting the command of a new master. It was possible the viceroy would even go as far as assigning Theo the post tonight. She remembered sitting by a fire, when they were lost in the mountains, and listening to Theo talk about this dream of his. He'd secretly been working toward it for years. And then she remembered who else had been sitting around that fire. Cora had been asleep. Timmons had been sitting close enough to Ren that their knees had been touching.

Before I let both of them die . . .

Ren shoved that thought back into a shadowed cage in the corner of her mind. She took a deep breath and tried once more to join the nearest conversation. Music danced in and out of their words. As she approached, however, the group fell silent. She received a polite nod, a quiet compliment on her dress, and then suddenly they had somewhere else to be. It was hard not to feel like this was an echo of the past. A year ago Timmons had forced Ren to attend another party in the Heights. A slightly wilder one. That night, Theo had been their host. Ren remembered sitting alone on a couch, sipping her drink and watching all the other students who'd already secured their bright futures. That version of her felt a world away. She'd gone through so much. Surviving in the wilderness. Escaping from a revenant. Bonding to a scion of a great house.

And yet here she was—alone once more.

As she watched the group depart, Ren spotted Landwin Brood. He was seated near the fireplace in the study across the hall. He caught her eye, raised his glass, and offered a satisfied smirk. Her social status was undoubtedly his doing. Similar obstacles had risen time and time again over the last few months. As she finished classes at Balmerick, she'd quietly probed for potential alliances. Classmates, teachers, anyone. But even the Broods' staunchest rivals—the Shiverians— refused her offers to meet. It wasn't exactly a problem that she could bring to Theo, either. After all, how would she explain the *why* behind her desire to make those new connections?

Well, I need someone powerful, who hates your family, to help me destroy your house. Any ideas?

It was already difficult enough for Ren to veil her feelings from him. Their bond offered emotional insight into each other. Brief slashes of raw *feeling*. Ren had gotten quite skillful at summoning new explanations whenever he sensed that slumbering rage that lived inside her.

Almost on cue, Theo came thundering up the steps. He nodded once to his father before turning to Ren, concern written on his face. "Everything all right?"

He can feel my frustration. "Yes, of course. I just got the wrong name for one of the Jamison sisters. It's nothing. I was just embarrassed. What about you? How was your meeting?"

"Confidential," he replied, then winced at how haughty that sounded. "For now. I'm sorry. It was just a preemptive conversation. He wanted to know about . . . what happened to us."

"In the mountains?"

It was a foolish question. That was all anyone wanted to know about her and Theo. The rumors surrounding their time in the mountains were many, a culmination of stories that were starting to edge into myth.

"Yes. More out of curiosity than anything. I . . . I think he might have been vetting my handling of Vega. Making sure I'd demonstrated clear skill . . ." He shook his head. "I don't know."

Theo was biting his lip. She did her best to focus—ignoring his father looming in the background—and set her eyes on the uncertain boy she'd bonded with. The boy to whom her entire future was now tethered. "Who else would they consider for the role?"

Theo's eyes darted nervously about the room. "The retiring warden has a nephew serving in the guard. He's not from a major house, but he's got plenty of actual experience. The Carrowynd family has a daughter—Zell—who has livestone training like me, but I'm not sure if they had the same intentions that I had when we commissioned Vega. Traditionally, the crown wants someone young who can fill the post for several decades. But what if they ignore tradition? There are generals from the War of Neighbors who would be very sensible choices. . . ."

"But you're the best fit?"

He blushed slightly. "Yes, I am the best fit."

That was good. Theo was already powerful, but she'd learned about the structure of his family over the past few months. He was a generation away from proper influence. If Ren wanted to destroy House Brood, she still had a lot of careful planning and waiting ahead of her. Being engaged to the new warden, however, would usher in a measure of influence that was not directly tied to House Brood. That might provide opportunities for Ren as well. She found herself nodding.

"Worrying won't help," she said. "Why don't you refill my drink instead?"

That earned an unceremonious snort from him. But Theo accepted the invitation, leading her into the next room, where an open bar was waiting. Ren caught a final glimpse of Landwin Brood. He was deep in conversation, but that didn't stop his eyes from flicking up as they passed. It was good to know that he at least thought she was worthy of his attention.

Theo procured a new drink for her. The weight of that cold glass in her hand brought on another echo of memory. Last year, she'd set down a glass just like it as Timmons drew her out to dance on the balcony. The revelry had paused when Theo took the stage. He'd performed his fateful party trick, which sent a massive instrument crashing recklessly down into the city. His worst hour had been an opportunity for Ren. A door opening in the dark. She had been brave enough to walk through it—and now she felt there was no turning back. She could only press on deeper into the shadows and hope there was some light waiting for her in the distance.

A dinner bell rang before they could take their first sips. Theo led them through the crowd, heading for the sprawling banquet table in the far corner. Ren paused at the threshold, eyeing the available seats, and was surprised when Theo tugged her on toward the staircase.

". . . what are you doing?" she asked.

"We were asked to sit up here tonight."

She raised a curious eyebrow. Theo grinned at her reaction. Clearly, he knew something was afoot. Ren felt a pulse of adrenaline. The upper floor was always reserved for the lords and ladies that ruled their city. At these obnoxious dinner parties, the heirs normally sat at a separate table, almost always a floor below. Ren and Theo had found themselves positioned that way at any number of parties this summer, fraternizing with the other young men and women who would one day be handed empires.

Now she allowed herself to be drawn up the stairs into the presence of true power. She had to remind herself that there was nothing special about the people in the room. No blood or magic that ran through their veins that made them any different—any better—than her father and mother. Still, it was hard not to feel the weight of their collective meaning to the city. Like entries from a history book that were stepping out of the pages, taking on flesh and bone before her.

There was Able Ockley, the most dangerous duelist in the city. He was lost in conversation with Ethel Shiverian—she and her sister had practically invented the levitation magic that was keeping them all afloat right now in the Heights. Not to mention a hundred other spells. Balmerick's headmaster—Priory Woods—looked red-faced and drunk, though that did not stop the grand emissary from sweeping over to pour more wine in her cup. Other members of the ruling houses were present: the Graylantians, the Proctors, and the Winterses. At the head of the table, the viceroy sat like a golden seal confirming their power. All of them chatted amicably as servants glided ghostlike in the background.

Theo guided Ren to where the other Broods were sitting. Landwin sat in gilded silence. His wife—Marquette—always seemed positioned slightly behind him, even when seated next to each other at the table. She kept her hair short, beautifully shaved on one side, and appeared to be uninterested in the conversations around them.

Ren's attention was drawn by obnoxious laughter to the eldest son and heir to their house: Thugar Brood. She'd learned that his great vice was the flesh, which meant he rarely took notice of Ren. He kept himself in prime physical condition, nothing wasted, and his wife looked like she'd walked right out of a drunk's fantasy. Ren thought if a single thread of her dress unraveled, she might come pouring out onto the table.

Beside them sat Tessa Brood. The girl waited, straight-backed with her hands folded neatly in front of her. Ren thought she was the most dangerous of the group. Quiet and intelligent. Tessa was a famous singer who had earned a permanent role in the city's finest acting troupe. Ren had initially believed it the result of nepotism. Most of their positions were the result of nepotism. But then she'd heard Tessa sing. Her voice was threaded through with gold. It might have been more moving if she hadn't heard Tessa use that same voice to skewer servants for even the slightest errors. She was tilted ever so slightly toward her mother, quietly commenting on something.

Theo and Ren took the two remaining seats. She felt a blush creep down her neck as their movement became some unspoken, final piece to the puzzle. As they sat—completing the table—the other conversations in the room fell quiet. Servants tucked away neatly into the corners of the room, nearly blending in with the wallpaper behind them.

The viceroy stood, tapping his glass with a spoon.

Delvean fairy tales were full of bumbling kings. They failed to do their duties and any number of wizards would arrive to save the day. The viceroy didn't fit into those old stories. His ability with magic had been unrivaled at Balmerick—Ren knew some of his records there had endured the test of time. That felt like an important foundation for the man who existed as the primary check on the influence and power of the five major houses. His gray hair was thick and long, brushed back artfully. He had high cheekbones and a narrow jaw, covered over by a neat gray beard. He'd risen through the government—a second son from one of the minor houses—and Ren marveled at his calm as he addressed the wealthiest members of their society.

"Good evening," he began. "I have several announcements that deserve your undivided attention—and then we will get back to the business of growing fat and happy. First, we've negotiated a new position with Ravinia. The recent sanctions against the free-port have been lifted. All of you may resume whatever trading you pretended to cease over the past three months. Everything can be out in the open again. Business as usual."

There were a few nods, a few raised glasses.

"Next, I would ask Theo Brood to stand."

A shiver ran down Ren's spine. It felt like her name had been called too. She watched as her bond-mate took his feet. There was a lesson for her there, written in his posture. Power in the way he lifted his chin, set his shoulders, and stood before the closest thing they had to a king.

"As many of you know, the defense of our city—and its interests—is paramount. For all the petty rivalries that exist between the great houses, we have always been unified by that common interest. If war knocks on our door, we all answer. If a plague comes, we all share the antidote. It has always been this way between us. In peace, the best are allowed to thrive and survive. But in times of trial, the city's livelihood is our greatest priority. Kathor comes first.

"As such, we take any appointment to the city's defenses very seriously. It is no small task to be one of the shields that stands between Kathor and its enemies. After all, there are many who would take joy in seeing us fall. Any person appointed to such a role walks out into the world bearing *our* seal on behalf of *our* people. Theo Brood, do you think yourself worthy of such a calling?"

Ren could sense the emotions that question stirred in him. This was a moment that he'd patiently approached for many years. Now that it was here, he showed no signs of nervousness.

"I am ready and willing. My worth will be proven in time, Viceroy."

She saw the viceroy's eyes flick briefly to the right. When Ren followed his gaze, she caught the most subtle of nods from Landwin Brood. A silent confirmation between them. Then the viceroy's attention swung back to Theo.

"Well spoken," the viceroy said. "It is my honor then, on behalf of House Brood, to approve you as the next watcher of the valley. I am sure you're familiar with this position. After all, a Brood has held the post—or a version of it—for nearly a century. . . ."

Ren might have missed what had happened if she didn't feel pain sear a path across their bond. Her stomach turned and it took all her self-control to *not* react to that sudden rush of emotion. Theo's pain dripped into her. His disappointment flooded her mind. She finally saw the error. He was not being named warden. The viceroy had used some other term.

". . . the watcher might be a family title—and the mountain castle might belong to the Broods—but it also acts as a functional piece in the armor that Kathor wears. Thus, it falls to me to give final approval for the man or woman who should claim one of the most time-honored posts in our city's long history. . . ."

She noted the others' reactions just as Theo's emotions honed into a fine-pointed shame. All around the table, smiles like daggers. The worst were offered by his own family. Thugar looked like he was barely keeping himself from laughing. His sister wore a condemning smirk. His mother's eyes were downcast. Landwin Brood did not bother with the effort it took to smile. He simply watched his son take in the weight of what was happening. Ren could not help admiring the way Theo kept his face neutral. Even as the entire table enjoyed some joke at his expense, he stood his ground and pretended indifference. Ren felt a fierce sense of loyalty to him at that moment. Completely separate from their bond. Her fingers itched to reach for her wand and wipe the smiles off their faces. She'd never heard of that specific title, but the expressions around the table made it clear: this was no desirable fate.

". . . you will take a few days, gather your possessions, and make your way to Nostra. You go with the full commendation of this city, the full support of your house, as well as the faith of your people. Everyone, raise a glass to Kathor's newest watcher of the valley."

A raucous cheer rang out, followed by the clinking of glasses. Those sounds could not fully hide the curious whispers around the room. Theo didn't react the way Ren might have. He simply bowed his head, rather than thundering angrily out of the room. She felt that pitted dread in his stomach begin to roil. It was burning a path toward something Ren found far more useful: anger.

Theo took his seat and refused to look at any of his other family members. She waited to ask him until the servants hustled out the first course, distracting those seated nearby.

"What just happened, Theo? Where is Nostra?"

She had a vague inkling of an idea. A memory from some corner of a map.

"Exile," he whispered back. "My father has exiled me."

As a plate appeared in front of her, Ren heard the unspoken words at the end of that sentence. Words Theo would never say aloud, because he cared too much for her, even if they were true.

My father has exiled me . . . because of you.

Ren didn't understand all the implications. She lacked context. Was it a true exile? Something else? For a while, the two of them sat there in silence, hating Landwin Brood in equal measure. They ate their food without a word, chewing like it was their only duty left in the world.

Topics that normally would have fascinated Ren made their way around the table. Magical theory and state secrets, all of it tangled with the light tinkling of silverware and glasses and laughter. Landwin Brood caught Ren's eye as the entrées were served. He raised his glass, ever so slightly. A clear taunt. She'd imagined her bond with Theo would open an entirely new world. A rush of resources and power and influence. Her chance to begin setting an empire on fire.

But now Theo was leaving. Would Ren be expected to go with him? Or would she be abandoned here—as she was earlier tonight—in this glittering circle of wolves? She could only imagine the strain of being separated in that way from someone she was bonded to. Maybe that was the point: to break them. Rather than show weakness, Ren met Landwin Brood's appraising stare. She lifted her own glass and offered a lifeless smile.

It turned out to be one of the best meals she'd ever eaten.

2

DAHVID TIN'VORI

He had blood on his boots and a hood over his head.

There was nowhere to look but down. The hood hung loose enough to allow him to breathe, and that looseness created a sliver of visibility. He saw the scarlet spatter on his shoes as they traversed the dunes. He could see dead reeds and choked grass and gray sand. Up one hill and down another. The biggest pity of the whole thing was being trapped with his own stench inside the hood. He'd not been afforded a trip to the baths after his victory in the gladiator pit.

The crowd noise still drummed in his head. There had been a roar when he let the other man spin unconscious to the ground. He'd fought the man straight up. Not using any of his tattoos. His opponent had been a classic brute. Strong as a bull elephant and with about the same level of footwork. Dahvid had danced in and out of the blows with ease.

Apparently, too much ease.

He'd recognized his mistake as soon as he looked at the hour-glass on the judge's table. Less than thirteen seconds had passed since the fight began. Afterward, in the training room, Dahvid had been unwinding his hand wraps when two men ghosted through the entrance. Both wore the emblem of Ravinia's most famous warlord. The taller of them had tossed a hood onto Dahvid's lap.

"Put that on and come with us, or else leave the city tonight."

An introduction to Darling was a part of the plan. The only problem was timing. He'd been hoping to make first contact a few months from now. He wasn't ready. Needed more time.

Dahvid felt the pressure at the back of his neck vanish. There was a tinkling rattle of chains, and then the hood was removed. Daylight blinded him. He blinked until there were shapes. He saw two figures in front of him, framed by a wine-dark sea. Distant waves gnawed on the shoreline, filling the silence. There was a sprawling villa on his right. As his eyes adjusted, he knew it was one of the finest houses he'd ever set eyes on. Far finer than the Tin'Vori estate had ever been, though there were many in Kathor who'd envied their family. Once upon a time.

Dahvid straightened, carefully pinning his gaze on the first man. His sister had prepared him for this moment. Darling was not one person, but two. The man standing in the fore-front was the most beautiful creature he'd ever seen. Eyes like slashes of river. A proud chin. Muscle rippled just beneath the surface of his clothing, though he was shaped more like a dancer than a fighter. The grand effect was marred only by black manacles attached to each wrist. Twin chains lagged across the sandy earth, connecting the first man to a second. Hidden in the background. Dahvid didn't look directly at that second figure, but when Darling spoke, he heard both voices.

"Do you know who I am?"

One voice was angelic, bright as a church bell. The other was hidden until the very last syllable. It sounded like stone scraping against stone. Dahvid nodded.

"They call you Darling."

There was another rattle of chains as the front figure started to pace. When the angle changed, he could have looked at the second man, who was seated, but he didn't.

"And you know what I do?"

"You run the gladiator pits."

"I run the *city*," Darling corrected. "I am the lifeblood that pumps through Ravinia."

Dahvid glanced at the villa on his right. "Pays well."

That dragged out a genuine laugh. He heard the deeper voice laugh first, followed by the tinkling laughter of the main speaker. "It does pay well. I run seven gladiator pits. We host ten thousand people a night. Our prizefighters make more money than tenured generals. Every detail is arranged. The fights are balanced. There is a system, because the system is what creates the demand. If I paraded out my best fighter every night, eventually no one would care to watch him. These are basic laws of commerce. And you? You produced an imbalance in that system. People attended that fight to see the Bearling. He's a crowd favorite."

Dahvid pictured the man he'd fought less than an hour ago. He recalled the broken nose, the eyes rolling before his body crashed to the arena floor. Dahvid replied, "Not anymore."

Another laugh, but this time only from the more musical voice.

"Surprises are good," Darling admitted. "But short fights? Those can be a nuisance. I'm sure you surprised them. No doubt they roared with delight. Expectations create a sort of magic all on their own. But then the crowd realized there'd be no more rounds, no more bloodshed, no more bouts. Their night was over, just like that. If I'd known you were that good, I'd have made other arrangements."

Dahvid nodded. "No one asked for my thoughts."

Neither Darling laughed this time. Dahvid's insides crawled as the silence stretched. The front man stood with his hands on his slender hips. Through the crook of one elbow, Dahvid caught a glimpse of the other face. A colorless circle. Not just pale but drained to a dying gray. His lips were chapped and broken. His eyebrows knitted together in a look of chronic pain. It was a spell that the rest of the city pretended not to notice. Those chains running between them were conduits for the passage of a soul. One man was slowly conquering the physical being of another. Such magic was forbidden. The Tusk people would view it as an abomination. Even Kathor, which prized innovation, would have condemned such a practice. Dahvid knew his people had always preferred more legal conquests.

"Would you submit to contractual fighting?" Darling probed. "Under my banner."

"Eagerly."

"Good. It can be arranged. If you satisfy one query."

"You want to know about House Brood."

Darling looked surprised by his frankness. "Yes. My associates have identified you as Dahvid Tin'Vori of the fallen House of Tin'Vori. You were one of the only image-bearers in all of

Kathor. It's a rare trait, even for someone with as much Tusk lineage as you. According to a great number of witnesses, you died seven years ago. Yet . . . here you are. Standing outside my villa."

"What is it that you want to know?"

"Is House Brood going to come sniffing around for you?"

"I think that would be likely, yes."

"And? Will they cause me trouble?"

"Less likely. When their spies come, they'll see a brawler. A man who makes his living day to day in the arena. Sure, one day I might make decent coin in your service, but they're coming to make sure I have no followers, no contacts, no possible incentive to return to Kathor and take my revenge. And I will make sure that's what they see. You've nothing to fear from them."

Dahvid could tell that last line annoyed the warlord, as he'd intended.

"I have nothing to fear from anyone," Darling answered. "Ravinia is mine. The Broods could sail their entire army north, and they'd be lucky to make it up the beach without getting slaughtered. I do not fear them, but I will not suffer lapses in efficiency. A house as powerful as theirs could inconvenience my business. You will put on a good show. Content their spies you've forgotten all about their precious city. Do that and you can make a name for yourself here."

Dahvid knew he could never truly forget Kathor. Not the way the sun struck the water outside the back windows of their estate. Nor the smell of cocoa and cinnamon as he walked through the streets in the Merchant Quarter. Bright memories came to him, waking or sleeping, of the only place he'd ever truly thought of as home. Nor could he forget that dark night all those years ago. Waiting like a coward in the escape tunnel. Hearing the swords scraping overhead as guards died to save them. Knowing his brother was already dead and his parents were already burning. He saw all this in quick, painful slashes of memory. But when he answered, his voice did not tremble.

"Consider it done."

"The contracts are on the table behind you," Darling said. "Sign them and go. My agents will be in touch. We'll have to figure out a good name for you. Build your reputation. People do not buy tickets to watch sacks of meat run into each other. They swarm through the gates to see men and women that we've convinced them are their dearest friends. We will do the same with you."

The warlord's eyes roamed Dahvid's body more openly, now that he imagined him as a possession. He'd grown accustomed to such appraisals as a boy. All his outfits were tailored—once by his mother and now by his sister—with his famous battle tattoos in mind. There were clever slits in the fabric where normal people would never bare their skin. Each displayed one of his tattoos, or at least made them accessible. It was especially necessary in a fight, as he needed physical contact in order to activate their magic.

"I've read that Tusk image-bearers can combine their tattoos. . . ."

Dahvid nodded. "They're called berserkers. I'm not one of those."

Curious, Darling pointed to the marking at Dahvid's throat. "What's that one do? The flower?"

Dahvid couldn't see the image, but every time he'd ever

looked in a mirror over the last decade, that flower had stared back at him like a third eye. He'd memorized the design over the years. Thirty-seven scarlet petals circled a golden center. Sunlight graced the right half of the tattoo, as if an unseen sun floated above Dahvid's left shoulder, casting its light across. It was the first one that his brother—Ware—had drawn. Before the Broods executed him.

"The flower is a scarlet traveler."

"I know what it is. I was asking what it does."

Each tattoo housed a powerful magic. Dahvid currently wore nine. The scarlet traveler was undoubtedly his most powerful one. "It allows me to exist outside the laws of nature."

Darling smiled at the vagueness of the answer. Both chains were drawn taut, forcing the pretty figure to backpedal toward the other. *Toward the master,* Dahvid saw. *The one who is conquering.*

"All magic is an abomination. Some spells are just prettier than others." Darling sighed. "I look forward to watching you fight. Sign the contracts. I'll see you in the pits." And then to his two attendants. "Pay the man."

Dahvid turned his attention to the contracts. Both of Darling's escorts came forward, making a lot of noise, guiding him through the details of the arrangement. One filled the sack they'd used to blind him earlier with a tantalizing amount of coins. A down payment for his services. He knew this was by design. They were enticing him, drawing his attention to hide their master's retreat. Against his better judgment, Dahvid risked a glance back. The dancer had picked up the smaller man. The man that he knew was the original Darling. He ferried his master across the dunes, carrying him like a child. The dark chains trailed them, kicking up dust. Before the escorts could scold him, Dahvid turned around and signed his name.

This was a beginning. Even if it was coming sooner than anticipated.

He smiled at the idea of blood.

"When's my first fight?"

3

REN MONROE

Dinner concluded.

Ren watched the others around the table rise, drinks in hand, conversations filling the air around them. She knew they were about to be subjected to even more mingling. Theo would be congratulated on his new post. Each repetition would be performed with the slightest hint of mockery. She caught his eye as they stood. It was startling to see the effect the news had on him. It reminded her of the way he'd looked right after he'd been gutted by the blade-sharp claws of a wyvern. After Cora's surgery had stitched him back up. Nearly all of the life drained from him.

It made sense. His confidence had always been rooted in his name. He was a Brood. An heir to one of the great houses. It was only logical that his father was the one person who could steal that from him and leave him looking so barren.

"I'll stay with you."

"No," he replied. "Not for this."

She didn't need him to explain. Sometimes, it was unbearable to have a witness to your greatest shames. He would be forced to smile and nod, all while the designs he'd made for his own future vanished into thin air. Ren would want to face that alone too.

"If that's what you want, I'll wait for you downstairs."

No one noticed her leave. Down a floor, she found royal cousins seated, laughing loudly at the far end of the table. Merchants with deep pockets discussed politics and shipping routes and trade goods. Ren hadn't thought about the fact that the other tables might still be dining. It made her feel even more out of place. She located a corner seat at the table and claimed it without a word.

The elderly woman on her right was little more than bones. An elegant bracelet of jewels dangled from one sparrow-thin wrist. She swirled her wine, inhaled the scent, and turned to Ren as if they'd been in conversation the whole time.

"As I was saying, it's *all* that anyone is talking about. Can you imagine? Dead for nearly ten years and suddenly the name just—*pops*—back up. The Broods pretend not to be concerned, but I have found that even the city's elite have a healthy fear of ghosts. No doubt they're wondering how he survived."

Ren sipped her drink to cover any confusion in her expression. What was the woman talking about? Her confidant grinned, a flash of wine-stained teeth, before plunging into a conversation Ren assumed she'd been having with someone else. Likely someone who looked vaguely like her. It became clear that the woman had been drinking for some time now.

"Dahvid Tin'Vori." The woman said that name, then shushed

Ren as if *she* had been the one to speak it aloud. "I know, I know. Don't say the name. Never fear. Thugar Brood is a floor above us. I have no doubt he's flirting with everyone except for his own wife."

Ren nearly spat out her drink. She knew there were factions and divisions amongst the upper class. Houses that naturally opposed one another. Minor houses striving to be more. Merchants who disdained the whole system, having succeeded on hard work instead of inherited pedigree. But she'd forgotten there were some who were bold enough to make fun of an heir so publicly. She supposed wine and old age were natural encouragements toward bluntness.

"Remind me," Ren said. "What happened?"

The name Tin'Vori sounded familiar, but she couldn't recall where she'd read it. One too many drinks had dulled her own senses. The old crone's eyes narrowed with delight.

"I told you. It was quite the scandal. Ten years ago . . ."

Before Ren had enrolled at Balmerick. Well before she'd have been in a position to hear the rumblings of the city's elite. She leaned in to hear the next part of the story.

"It started with the oldest brother, Ware Tin'Vori. He made the mistake of dancing with Brood's fiancée in front of everyone. When Thugar asked to cut in for the next dance, Ware Tin'Vori made his second mistake. He confused the Brood heir for someone with a sense of humor. The boy kept dancing with the girl. He claimed that it was a sin to stop in the middle of a song. A normal person would have laughed. Because it was a joke. But Thugar Brood? That is a man who brooks no trespasses. He vowed—then and there—that he would bury Ware Tin'Vori in his family garden. The famous threat was heard by everyone in that ballroom: 'I will plant you in the ground.'"

The crone waved a hand, jewels dancing farther down her wrist.

"Everyone thought they were empty words. Tall talk. After all, House Tin'Vori was a bosom-mate to House Shiverian then. One of the few houses that the Broods would not risk opposing. But there was the rub. No one knew the Shiverians had been eyeing the Tin'Voris' holdings for years. Thugar's anger was an invitation to act on that greed. A raid between the Shiverians and Broods was arranged in secret. Ware Tin'Vori was sketching down by the river when Thugar found him. The boy begged for his life as he was dragged through the Lower Quarter. No one intervened. They threw him in the back of the carriage and took him up to the old Brood estate. The two dueled. It was a long fight, but only because Brood made it a long fight. He broke that poor boy. Slowly. Then he did what he'd promised to do."

Now the woman looked down the length of the table before glancing back at Ren. For a moment, she narrowed her eyes, and Ren wondered if she'd finally realized that she wasn't speaking with the person she thought she was. Instead, she simply lowered her voice.

"Have you ever been to the Brood estate, dear?"

Ren nodded. "Once."

Landwin had invited her for a single family gathering. She'd been allowed on a small tour of the high-walled estate that was northwest of the city. Theo had delighted in telling her stories about his childhood. All Ren could see, though, as she walked from villa to villa was what she was truly up against. All of that wealth. All of those guards. An impenetrable fortress that had stood against its enemies for centuries.

"There's a tree with a black trunk. Bloodred leaves. Did you see it?"

Ren nodded again. Near the very heart of the estate. She remembered how Theo had fallen quiet there. He offered no anecdotes about that place. As they passed, Thugar had stopped in front of the tree while the rest of them continued through the gardens. Landwin Brood, who rarely displayed his emotions openly, had looked back at his older son with distaste. Ren hadn't understood the subtle expressions on the faces of the rest of the family that day. Thugar had bent a knee, his head briefly bowed. Ren had assumed he was praying. Now she had the real answer.

"That is the tree that grew, fed by Ware Tin'Vori's body. Only Thugar visits it. The gardeners aren't even allowed to prune the leaves. No one has properly mourned the boy."

Ren was surprised. "The family didn't ask for his remains to be returned?"

The old woman scoffed. "Haven't you listened to a word I've said, Isabelle? The raid was that night. The Tin'Vori estate was overrun in an hour. A single boat made it out to sea. It was believed that the other three children—and their parents— were on board. The Shiverians torched and sank the vessel. Everyone watched as boats circled the blaze. There were no survivors."

She swirled her wine again and accidentally sloshed some onto the table. It was a pause for dramatic effect. Ren didn't know the old crone's name, but she was a rather masterful gossip.

"At least that's what everyone *believed*. Until Dahvid Tin'Vori was spotted in Ravinia last week. Rumor is that he fights in the gladiator pits. I've no doubt the Broods will send their spies. Confirm whether or not it's really him. He's rather distinctive, though. Hard to miss."

"And why is that?"

"He's an image-bearer."

That snagged Ren's attention. The old crone looked rather satisfied by her reaction. Image-bearers were nearly as rare as enhancers. They were living vessels, capable of wearing magic directly on their skin. Magic that required no source except for the wielder themselves. She'd never seen someone with the specialized tattoos before, but she'd read about them in books.

". . . a far more common practice in Tusk, but not unheard of here. What I want to know, though, is how did he survive? And if he survived, what of the two sisters?"

The woman leaned back in her chair as servants set down a roasted shank of meat in front of them. Ren leaned back as well, her mind racing. She was so consumed by the story that she almost didn't notice Theo trying to get her attention. He'd come down the stairs, looking utterly drained.

"I need a bit of air," Ren said to the older woman. "Excuse me."

The old crone nodded. "Yes, of course. Go on, Isabelle."

Ren smiled at the thought of some confused girl reappearing at her grandmother's side, unaware that she'd just been briefly confused for a stranger. Ren could feel the relief from Theo as she crossed the room. He wanted to leave, and he wanted to leave with her. There was a subtle flicker in her chest at that realization. She quieted the feeling. Whatever his father's reasoning for the exile, Ren realized that the leader of

House Brood had made a mistake. His punishment was driving Theo away from House Brood and into her arms. She was the only one he could trust now.

"Take me on a walk," she said. "Let's look at the stars."

In spite of everything that had happened that night, Theo smiled.

They took a long, winding route back to his villa in the Heights. By unspoken agreement, they walked out onto the balcony. Stars glinted above like teeth in the dark. It was ironic that Ren found herself in this place. It was the exact spot where she'd first met Theo. She'd wanted to murder him that night. Now she was back—pitying him instead of despising him.

"Stop that," he whispered. "Please stop."

Ren's eyes met his. "What?"

"I can . . . feel it. You feel sorry for me. It's not helping."

A gust of wind swept over the balcony. Theo's blond hair tossed across his forehead as he turned away, eyeing the city below. Ren understood. In her lowest moments at Balmerick, pity had never done anything for her. Teachers had always bemoaned her situation. How unfair it was that a talented girl like her was not receiving proper attention. But they'd done nothing to actually improve her standing. Their pity was as useful as a threadbare coat offered in the dead of winter. Ren's thoughts returned to the old crone and her story about the Tin'Vori family.

"Let's strategize, then," Ren proposed. "How long do you think your father will keep you in Nostra?"

Theo sighed. "The last person assigned to the post was Uncle Lander. There was a party. All the people you saw tonight.

Lander was very drunk. His guard was down. A manipulator from one of the other houses cornered him. He foolishly revealed our family's designs for taking over a new business sector in Kathor. They took that information, used it to cut off our plans, and spoiled the entire enterprise. When my father found out the source of their information, he exiled Lander to the same post in Nostra. It was always . . . a joke. A good laugh for the rest of the family. 'Don't be like your bumbling uncle or you'll be sent to live in the mountains.'"

"And how long ago was that?"

"He's been in Nostra for twelve years," Theo answered in a dead voice. "I'm sure he will be very grateful to be returning to Kathor. Finally, another fool has arrived to replace him. . . ."

Ren's heart sank. "But you're his *son*. Surely he wouldn't keep you there. . . ."

"Lander is his brother. I think being his son makes it worse somehow. More shameful."

"And what about me?" She thought about the best phrasing for her question. "Do you think he'll allow me to go with you?"

Theo shook his head. "Tomorrow you will receive an invitation. An internship, perhaps. From one of our respected trade partners. He'll offer you something enticing to keep you here in the city. If you turn it down, he can use that against you. 'See? I offered her a place, and she would not take it.' But if you accept, he begins the work of separating us. I will be there. You will be here. My father is a thorough man. I learned long ago that if he ever offered me a choice, both possibilities had already been carefully curated by him. I was simply allowed to choose between *his* desires for me. It's always been that way."

Ren couldn't help thinking that Theo was edging into less

pitiable territory. What had those choices been for a child in his position? Listen to your priceless tutor or else I'll send you to a bedroom that's larger than most people's houses? A familiar anger curled to life in her chest. It never quite went away, no matter how much she'd come to actually care for Theo. The chasm between their lived experiences could not be forgotten. Theo was watching Ren. No doubt, he thought her sudden anger was linked to what he'd said about his father. About his own plight.

"I can't refuse. Not right now. But my father is a fool if he thinks he can keep me pinned in the mountains for a decade. I—*we* are meant for more."

His eyes locked on Ren's. She lifted her chin, meeting that stony gaze. This was the Theo she'd first started liking out in the Dires. The one who'd stood fearlessly before a wyvern, who'd fought shoulder to shoulder with her against a revenant. This was the version of him she needed if they were to carve a path forward in this world.

"We are going to change this city, Ren. He does not own Kathor. He does not own us, no matter what he thinks. Weather this storm with me. I will come up with a plan while I am away. There are gaps in my father's power. I thought the warden post would be the most natural path to independence, but there are others. We will discover them."

We could start by removing your father, Ren thought darkly. She buried those emotions quickly. Asking for that would be asking too much too soon. She needed to work with what was in front of her. Right now, Theo was burning with anger and indignation. It was possible that he would dare to plot a life apart from his family. His words tonight were a far cry from actual action, but they could be the start of something.

"I'm with you," Ren answered. "No matter what."

It frightened her to realize those words were at least partly true. Not just pretense. Not just a survival mechanism. Genuine feelings had started to blossom. Ren found there were two separate categories. First, there was the bond magic. She'd felt it on the bridge. Watching Theo bleed out, she'd briefly considered the possibility of not saving him. She could have returned home, demanded an inheritance from his family. Instead, her bond with him had roared to life and forced her to act. That initial impulse had only continued to grow. A deeply troubling development.

Would it go on like that forever? Increasing, year after year, no matter what? Would her feelings for him grow until they were something she couldn't override? She worried the bond might eventually outstrip her current purpose.

More disconcerting, however, was the other feeling. Separate from their bond magic. Not forced upon her at all. There had been moments, since they'd returned from the wilderness, where Ren found herself actually liking Theo. For no reason other than the fact that he was who he was. Those moments came in no discernible pattern. A glance of him reading by lamplight in his study. The subtle way he would redirect conversations back to her interests. Even the way he set his hand on the small of her back whenever they walked into a room, as if he wanted everyone to see her before they saw him. It was all annoyingly charming. And charm was a dangerous thing.

The simple truth was that Theo brought a certain level of unpredictability to the equations in her mind. Unpredictable. That was not an ideal word for someone attempting to execute a plan ten years in the making. Not ideal at all.

Theo waited a few paces away. With a sigh, Ren extended her hand. He accepted, tugging her up to her feet. Ren allowed his arms to curl around her until they were close. Less than a breath away. In the past few months, they'd not been overly romantic. Most of the time, they were called to public appearances and parties, and there'd simply been no room for privacy. Now she allowed it, knowing they were about to be separated for an indeterminable time.

A part of her knew that this was expected. Theo needed to cling to an image of his bonded sweetheart while he was gone. Creating that memory for him now would impact the coming months. Some other part of her, though, simply wanted the taste of his lips. She tugged him down by the collar. It was a clumsy, out-of-practice first kiss. The second was anything but clumsy. Theo shivered, and Ren answered by pressing her body closer to his. A third kiss, a fourth. As they tangled together, Ren felt a sharp spike of something entirely new. Her bond *pulsed*. Both of them broke away for a moment, gasping. She couldn't have said if it was pain or pleasure or both. All she knew was that they'd both felt it at the same time. It was like being burned. Like wanting to burn.

Neither one spoke after that. They did not try to kiss each other again either. Instead, they stood there, under the stars, eyes on the shadowed horizon. Ren knew all the tired metaphors about dawns and new days and fresh starts. For once, it felt true. Tomorrow would bring an entirely new world. Theo would leave for Nostra. She would be alone, surrounded by powerful enemies.

Unless she found allies before the circle closed entirely.

4

NEVELYN TIN'VORI

Nevelyn's exhaustion was twofold.

First, her fingers ached. A bone-deep pain that only faded when she was asleep. In her waking hours, she felt that subtle throb as she worked, practicing patterns or mending cloaks. Her brother insisted that she was pushing herself too hard, but Nevelyn knew their timeline. She knew the level of skill she needed for their plan to work. Nothing short of perfection would do.

Physical pain was one thing, but the frayed nerves from using too much magic felt even worse. She'd taken up the craft of weaving—braiding magic into the threads of garments. It suited her. A quiet and contemplative craft that relied on looking at the larger pattern of things. That was all in her wheelhouse, but actual weaving demanded hour-long spells. Each one was brutally taxing, difficult to sustain, and frustratingly subtle.

The approved artisans of the Weavers Guild could craft weightless cloaks capable of turning away arrows as effectively as plate armor. Nevelyn understood why warriors spent a fortune on such items. Not only because they were useful, but because the supply was limited. Even the simplest boons were immensely difficult. Magic that reduced sweat or lowered anxiety or increased one's strength. She'd successfully enchanted two items in thirty attempts thus far. Luckily, those had sold for enough to cover the cost of more practice materials and nearly half of their rent. Gods knew they had little enough money.

A floorboard creaked.

Nevelyn had drifted in her thoughts—somewhere between the dreaming and waking worlds—and now her vision of their little flat snapped into focus. She sat at the kitchen table. It was a sad circle of faded wood held upright by uneven legs. There was a bed in the far corner, sectioned off by a partition they'd salvaged from a nearby alleyway. Her brother's lover and artist—Cath Invernette—sat on the edge of that bed, her foot tapping out a nervous rhythm.

The poor thing.

She'd returned two hours ago. Alone. Dahvid had been approached after his recent victory in the gladiator pits. According to Cath, both guards had worn Darling's mark. Nevelyn had done her best to calm the girl down—after all, this was their plan—but even she had been unsettled by the suddenness of the invitation. It wasn't meant to happen this soon. Dahvid needed more time to train. She needed more time to hone her craft. The steps of their plan were moving along at too rapid a pace. Nor did it help that they were nearly out of money.

On the other side of the partition sat Nevelyn's lonely cot. Even in her current state of exhaustion, it hardly looked inviting. The sheets were harsh and scratchy. Her pillow looked like it was on the verge of unraveling if someone simply tugged the wrong thread. She had slept there for months, but only when she reached points of pure exhaustion, when her body and mind simply shut down from overwork. How long, she thought quietly to herself, could she go on like this?

There was a gentle click.

The lock on the door turned. Cath bolted to her feet. Nevelyn smiled as her brother entered the room. Dahvid offered her a quick wink. Always so confident. Like many of the Tin'Voris who'd come before them. Too confident for his own good.

"And?" Nevelyn asked quietly. "Did you meet him?"

Dahvid ignored her question, gliding across the room to Cath instead. He set a kiss on the girl's cheek, all while whispering reassurances. The sight brought out yet another ache in Nevelyn. She'd not been touched in what felt like years. There was no time—she told herself, on the loneliest nights— for such frivolities. Maybe one day. After they'd accomplished their revenge.

Her brother turned to her. "Yes. I met Darling. What a frightening creature."

"I warned you."

"That you did," he said. "But all our preparation worked. I'm his newest prizefighter."

Cath sighed. "Finally, some good news."

Nevelyn wasn't certain about that. She asked the question that would determine if the news was actually good, or if it was a fine wine laced with hidden poison. "Where's your first match?"

Her brother hesitated. She saw the way he shifted so that Cath couldn't quite see his expression, and she guessed the answer before he said it.

"The Western Pits."

She shook her head. "That place is *brutal*, Dahvid. It's too soon. We must delay."

"I'm ready. I'll be fine for the first few fights, at least. He'll want to display me, Nev. That's how it works. He needs to build my reputation first. A string of victories. A few easy wins. That'll buy me some time. At least a few weeks. And then . . ."

"He'll set up a title bout," she finished. "I know how it works. I'm the one who scouted the matches and cataloged the rotations, remember? I know Darling's whole system. He'll set you up against one of his best to draw a big crowd. And if he picks the wrong one? At worst, you'll be killed, Brother. At best, he'll force you to use some of the tattoos earlier than we'd planned."

Dahvid shrugged, like death was nothing to him. Like the murders of their parents and their brother were not the exact reasons they were here now, scraping an existence out of this hovel. Nevelyn let out a sigh.

"Cath, what about his next tattoo?"

There were drawings on the far wall. Several images they'd discussed at great length. The last couple of attempts had failed to properly settle into Dahvid's skin. It had created the first tension she'd seen between the two lovers. It was always easier to laugh when things were going well. Cath confirmed her guess.

"We might need more time."

Nevelyn cut a concerned look back at Dahvid. "You're not ready."

"Not ready for simple head-to-head matchups, but you want me to eventually win a gauntlet? Explain how that works, Sister."

"To win a gauntlet, you will have to guard your biggest secrets until the very last possible moment, Brother. A fight against one of Darling's handpicked champions will force you to reveal too much too soon. As if we haven't discussed this a hundred times. I will not lose another brother. . . ."

"Ease up, Nev."

This came from Cath. She was a bridge between them. Dahvid, headstrong and quick to act. Nevelyn, spiderlike and cautious. Whenever they could not find a middle ground, it was Cath who stepped forward to offer one. Much like Ava once had. Nevelyn softened at the expression on the girl's face.

"Fine. You've done good work, Brother. Father would be proud." She took a deep breath. "Ware and Ava would be, too. You know that I am just being cautious. It's all that I'm good at."

He grinned wildly at that. Cath smiled too. At heart, both of them were dreamers. Creatures of great optimism. They believed that they could leap off the cliffs the world offered and events would simply work out in their blessed favor. It fell to Nevelyn to actually supply the logistics that allowed them access to those bright, imagined futures. There were logical steps that needed to occur. Passion was not everything. Dahvid thought that emotion could triumph if you simply had enough of it. That was something their father had imparted to him, and that impracticality—that lack of looking at the larger picture—was exactly why House Tin'Vori was destroyed in the first place.

Not again. Not while she was in charge.

"Let's celebrate, then," Nevelyn sighed. "Down at the Severed Head?"

Dahvid looked surprised. "You're not too tired?"

Her eyes flicked over to the unwelcoming bed with its lackluster sheets.

"Not nearly tired enough. Let's go. Cath is right. This is good news."

Her brother hefted a sack of coins from one hip. Nevelyn recognized the fabric. It was likely the same sack they'd used to escort him to Darling. It looked like the cloth she'd often seen in the hands of pit masters, after a fight ended. They always slid them over the heads of the dead, not wanting the audience's stomach to turn when they saw the lifeless eyes rolling. People liked the killing. The startling color of blood leaving a living body. They didn't care for what came after, though. Corpses and shit and ruin.

She saw a brief and frightening glimpse of Dahvid lying on his back in the arena sand. A faceless pit master sliding a similar sack over his head. And then her mind flicked back to the present. The sack was just a sack. The coins inside sounded like they were laughing at her fears.

Dahvid was grinning.

"Drinks are on me."

5

REN MONROE

Theo's guess proved accurate.

A letter arrived in the morning. Ren was invited to work with a group of spellmakers. It was precisely the sort of work she'd craved in undergrad. Research and development. New spells that stretched modern thought about what magic could do. It stung that the invitation was a trap, but at least the bars of her cage were bright, golden things.

Theo read the letter twice. "I didn't expect my father to be this kind. Clearly, he thought you'd turn down anything less to go with me to the mountains. It's a compliment, I suppose. He thinks you're loyal to me. At least this means you will be happy."

Ren heard the bitterness in his voice. The implication was that he would suffer in exile while she went happily about her work in Kathor. She doubted that would be the case. She would likely be surrounded by men and women who were loyal to

House Brood. Her every move would be watched. Still, it was better than being shipped off to the middle of nowhere. She genuinely pitied Theo. This wasn't just their bond tugging at her sympathy. His family had gone too far. Bad enough to exile him, but to humiliate him in front of the city's most powerful people? She thought what they'd done was unnecessarily cruel, and that might be very useful to her.

"Are you traveling by waxway?" she asked.

Theo actually shivered. "After what happened last year? No."

"Carriage?"

"I'm not *that* antiquated. My father arranged a method of travel that I am far more comfortable with." He smirked. It looked like the expression she'd seen on his face out in the Dires—before everyone started dying. "I am traveling by wyvern to Nostra."

Ren actually laughed. "Really? You're not comfortable with the waxways, but you'll take a wyvern? After . . ." She gestured to the scars that barely peeked out above the V in his shirt.

"I doubt this one will attempt to kill me."

"You're a brave soul."

"It's not bravery. It's logic," he answered. "I haven't used the waxways because I still don't understand what happened to Clyde. It wasn't logical. How he died . . . it doesn't make sense. I have no answers to that particular mystery. That's why it scares me. The wyvern attacked because we were passing through its territory. It acted logically. Logic, I can handle."

Ren tried to rein her thoughts in. There were several secrets that loomed between them. Some that she would need to reveal eventually, if she was going to convince Theo to take up her cause and fight his own family at her side. But there were other secrets that she could never reveal—for fear of destroy-ing everything. It was Ren's fault they'd been pulled into the wilderness last year. Her spell had merged their distances and locations. It was also likely that her spell had placed Clyde at the mercy of the waxways. She'd effectively killed him. In a way, she was responsible for all the deaths that happened in the wilderness.

Theo was frowning at her. She'd given those thoughts—and the tangled emotions that went with them—far too much room to breathe. He was *feeling* those feelings across their bond. She snuffed them out before whispering, "It's just hard to imagine being alone again."

As always, he accepted her answer. Trusted her word.

"You won't be alone. Your mother is here. You'll have new work to focus on."

"You know what I mean. Your family hasn't embraced me. There's no help for me in those circles. Any event or gala or dinner they host—I'll be alone. I won't have you as my shield."

He warmed to that notion. She knew he would. Being painted as the hero always had its appeal. "I'll be working night and day to figure out how to solve this. And we can arrange for you to come out and visit. You won't be alone. I promise, Ren."

Outside, there was movement. Ren buttoned her coat and followed Theo. The wyvern landed with no more than a gentle thud. The quiet was a trick. As they walked forward, she saw the creature was nearly twice the size of the one they'd encoun-tered in the wild. A helmet had been fashioned on its head. Blinders, she remembered, to keep the creature focused on the intended destination.

The rider wore a thick coat, round-rimmed goggles, and the

padded leggings she'd often seen equestrians wear. He offered Theo a simple nod, like the two of them had met a hundred times before. Ren was even more surprised by Theo's casual approach. He went straight for the pouches dangling against the creature's flank. He stuffed his belongings inside, cinched each pack, and turned back to face Ren.

"Not your first time, then," she said. "Flying a wyvern."

He smiled at her. "I told you I wanted to fly them when I was a boy. My father permitted it, because he thought a real flight would terrify me. He was wrong. I only wanted it more after that."

Ren could see the parallel he was trying to draw to this moment, to his feelings for her. She didn't point out that his father had succeeded. Theo was not a wyvern flier. His metaphor did not bode well for their chances. Instead of speaking those thoughts, she did what was expected. She stumbled into his embrace. They held each other tight as the great creature shifted on its haunches. Theo pulled far enough away to kiss her forehead.

"I'm not leaving you alone."

She snorted, but before she could point out that he was *literally* doing just that, there was a flutter of movement in the air. Claws sank painfully into her right shoulder. Vega imitated a ruffle of feathers before going stone-still in her usual pose. Theo grinned at Ren's expression.

"You'll have time to get used to her landings. I decided that Vega will stay with you."

Ren stared at him. "Theo. No. Take her. You'll be without half your spells."

"So? I'm defending a mountain pass that has not been

attacked in more than a century, Ren. I am going to be *bored* beyond belief. I've already made a list. I'll work on adding those spells to my other vessel. Besides, this way, you're not alone. I'll feel better if Vega is here with you."

The bird's claws tightened on Ren's shoulder. It was a sort of confirmation. The stone creature had no intention of disobeying Theo's command. She felt an unexpected turn of emotions. He'd guessed her fear and had chosen to do the one thing he could to counter it. He was weakening himself to strengthen her. It was an unexpected boon. Ren nodded her thanks. Theo offered one more unreadable look before sweeping forward. He embraced her again, but before he could pull away she caught him by the collar. She kissed him. Normally, it was the other way around. Not this time. It was just a whisper of a thing, and then he turned around in a swirl of cloaks.

Ren felt absurdly like one of those characters in romantic novels as she watched the rider reach down. Theo accepted the offered hand, moving his feet along built-in footholds; then he was up on the creature's back saddle. He waved down to her like he was riding off to war. Ren couldn't help waving back. Why not? She'd already tied her entire future to him. Might as well send him off in style. There was a clinical nature to what came next. Compared to the wild creature that had attacked them in the mountains, this wyvern was a docile thing. It responded to every command with neat efficiency, turning, spreading its wings. Ren heard the sound of a tongue click, and they launched breathlessly into the air. She was gusted back a few steps, but she stood there, offering Theo one final glimpse, as the creature soared free of the Heights—beyond the city proper.

When she was certain he was gone, Ren marched back inside.

She had packed a bag too. She had a plan of her own.

Somewhere in the city below, there was a boat she needed to be on.

Her mother's house was the only place Ren felt certain that Landwin Brood was not watching. She'd set magical charms to monitor infiltration, and all of them were still intact. At least in here, she was free to act and speak without fear of being heard.

As she entered, she heard laughter. The sound had her pausing midstride. That was not her mother's laugh. Ren stood there in the doorway, unsure of how to announce her presence.

Eventually she decided on making tea. The kettle offered a loud clank when she set it on the stove. She got the fire burning. The voices—free and bright a moment before—were now hushed behind her mother's door. Ren let the tea start to scream before removing it, pouring two steaming cups. Ren had sent word ahead about this visit. The letter had included a few requests from her mother's contacts down at the docks. Had she not received the note? And if she had, why would she have someone over?

Ren hadn't thought much, over the years, about the company her mother might be keeping. It was only natural for her to seek companionship. Roland Monroe had died nearly a decade ago. It would be unfair to expect her to spend the rest of her life alone. Ren had spoken that very truth to her mother a dozen times. Still, when they emerged from the back room, Ren's mother looked embarrassed. The man she was with did not.

"Ahh. Here she is. Finally," he said, all confidence. "The brilliant daughter. Your mother speaks about you at all hours of the day."

"Surely, not *all* hours," Ren threw back, eyeing the bedroom door. "Nor in all places."

Her mother shot her a warning look. If she hadn't given up using magic a few years ago, Ren would have thought she'd just cast a spell. Under the heat of that look, Ren averted her eyes, pretending to stir her tea. "My apologies," she said stiffly. "That was . . . *untoward.*"

The man lifted one eyebrow at her use of that word. It was a handsome eyebrow. He was a handsome man. A few years older than her mother. Just as fit as her. Shaped by hard work, whether at the docks or somewhere else. He was slender as a knife. Ren hadn't realized how tall he was until he stooped into the living room and fell into an unceremonious sprawl on the cushions against the wall. He was too big for the space, nearly comical looking.

"Mother, I think our pillows shrank."

That had both of them laughing. Her mother rolled her eyes as she took the teas. Ren spoke in a quieter voice. "Did you not receive my letter?"

Her mother bristled. "Of course I did. Everything is arranged. Apologies for having a previous engagement. You know, I do have a life apart from you."

"You don't have anything to apologize for," Ren answered quickly. "Other than the fact that you're stealing *my* cup of tea."

Her mother grinned. "Guests come first."

Ren crossed the room, fetching another cup. She didn't

have time for lengthy conversations. She poured herself just enough to get through the morning and then crossed the room to join them. Her mother sat a respectable distance away, but Ren suspected the two of them would be cuddled together against the cushions if she weren't there. She saw it written in the way their bodies, even now, bent toward each other. A strange storm of emotions turned around in Ren's mind. Her mother deserved to be happy. Deserved to smile and flirt and do whatever she pleased. That did not change the fact that the presence of any man in this place would always point to her father's absence.

The guest offered his hand. Ren shook it.

"I'm Harlow. Your mother and I are friends."

"Good friends, I see," Ren shot back, making him smile. "It's nice to meet you, Harlow. I can't believe my mother has kept you a secret. You look rather hard to hide."

That earned another snort from him.

"If you don't mind, I need to speak with her. Alone."

He held up both hands to say, *Of course.* "I've got to get to my shift."

Ren watched as he leaned over, pecked a quick kiss on her mother's forehead, and then sauntered to the front door. She noted that he was comfortable enough to take the mug with him. No doubt her mother wouldn't mind him coming back to return it. Ren waited for the rattling click of the door before turning to her mother.

"Ren, look, I'm sorry . . ."

"Oh, I don't care about that. He seems handsome enough. I'm sorry to cut your morning short. I really do need to get moving. You've arranged everything?"

Her mother took a sip. "I have, but I need to know why you're traveling so far."

"I have to do some research in Ravinia."

"Research? Your letter said that you don't want to be listed on the ship's manifest. What kind of research would require such privacy?"

Ren had dreaded this. Her mother was no fool. She was, after all, the primary source of Ren's own intelligence. "Research that I don't want the Broods to know about."

Her mother pursed her lips—clearly disapproving—but nodded.

"I've set out a cloak in your room. Go and put it on. We'll want to make sure any of the Broods' spies mark your route."

Ren frowned. "We? Mother. Just tell me which ship to go on. You don't have to—"

"Please, I am not letting you travel *alone*. Not after what happened last year."

There was no room for argument in her mother's tone. This was not up for debate. And what, really, could Ren have said? *It's too dangerous for you to come, Mother.* That would only make her want to come even more. The truth was that Ren didn't know what waited for her in Ravinia. She had no idea if she could find the people she was looking for or if the old crone's rumors were even true. But she'd heard a story about someone who had a bone to pick with House Brood. Here, in Kathor, she'd found no such harbor. No one that dared to help. None of the major houses had even engaged in introductory conversations with her. Dahvid Tin'Vori might be her best chance to gain a proper ally.

"Fine," Ren said. "Does your suitor know you're leaving?"

"He'll survive," her mother replied. "Speaking of suitors, where is yours? Usually he's following you around with his tail wagging."

Ren sighed. "He left this morning. It's a long boat ride. I'll explain when we're on board."

"Explanations. Secrets. Yes, this all sounds very safe already."

She got that motherly touch of snark in before whipping back into her bedroom, gathering the necessities for travel. Ren obeyed her mother's instructions, sliding into the bright red cloak she'd set out. As she did, a gnawing discomfort began to grow in her stomach. She had the same feeling she'd had when she first landed in that dark forest. She'd rolled over on her side and found Timmons sprawled impossibly beside her. Even though she'd only intended to bring Theo and Clyde into the wilderness, her friend had been drawn in by the same spell. It was an accident, but it was Ren's fault. And that moment had wound inevitably to Timmons's death.

Most of the time, Ren could compartmentalize. Carefully set emotions aside in order to complete the task at hand. It was one of her strengths. But that did not mean the emotions weren't there. She felt them, pooling in the darkest corner of her mind. All of the grief and pain and shame over what happened last year. For now, her barriers were holding. She knew they would break, however, if she ended up drawing her mother into a similar danger. She'd have to move quickly in Ravinia, find out if the rumors were true, and return home before the Broods took note of her absence. She just hoped she'd chosen the right trail to follow. Her plans depended on it.

6

REN MONROE

Her mother's instructions were strange, but she knew the docks better than Ren. The two of them parted ways. Ren aimed for the larger market down in the Lower Quarter. She walked slowly, allowing any Brood spies in the vicinity an opportunity to collect themselves and follow her trail. Perhaps she was guilty of thinking too highly of herself, imagining that the Broods cared enough to waste such resources on her. But with Theo leaving for Nostra, she suspected that she'd be watched even more closely until her new work began. The Broods did not suffer lapses in concentration. She'd need to turn their focus against them.

Ren found the store her mother had noted. A simple apothecary shop. She paused by the windowfront, pretending to admire something, and then entered. Heavy-handed scents pressed forward against her senses. A wall of candles stood directly in front of her, all earthen, natural colors. Plants coiled down from the ceilings. The rest of the space was dominated by great cabinets that Ren knew were full of the powdered substances that guided different types of magic.

Before she could even step fully inside, the clerk gave a hand signal. Ren followed the directions, moving to her right, deeper into the store. In the very back corner, she found a girl waiting. She was a similar height and build to Ren. Her hair was the same color. Only her skin tone was slightly darker—as Ren had paled some during her time at Balmerick. The girl didn't bother speaking. She simply unlatched her cloak and held it out. Ren offered her bright red one in return.

The girl studied Ren for a moment. She turned to a hanging mirror and began adjusting her hair to match. She fastened the cloak, turned back, and nodded.

"Your mother said you should wait a few minutes. I'll lead them up toward Beckers Street."

"Understood. Thank you for your help."

"No need to thank me. I'd do anything for Old Agnes."

Ren nearly laughed. "I wouldn't let her catch you calling her old."

The girl frowned. "Everyone calls her that."

Before Ren could say more, the girl slid past her. She gathered up a prepared satchel, cumbersome and distracting, before backing through the entrance and rushing up the nearest street. If all went to plan, the spies would trail her for a while before they realized she wasn't Ren. Which left the real Ren waiting in that dark corner of the apothecary, alone with her thoughts.

Everyone calls her that.

She wondered when her mother had picked up a nickname:

Old Agnes. It felt strange. The idea that her mother might have carved some new identity in the world Ren had abandoned. Another reminder that while Ren maneuvered in the clouds— another world labored on below. She knew she would do well not to forget that. After all, her father had died for this place and these people.

A few customers came and went. Ren slipped quietly back outside. The market was churning to life. Ren had no idea if their ploy had worked, but she felt the slightest burden lift from her shoulders. It was nice to think that Landwin Brood didn't see everything that happened in this city. It breathed hope into what she planned to do next.

She aimed for the docks. The market spaces were welcoming. There were natural paths for customers, intentionally carved out to lure a person deeper into their chaos. Not the docks. This was not the place for a casual stroll. A misstep here would be punished. The bustle existed not as a show—but by design. Pure efficiency. Unwelcome guests earned cold stares or lowered shoulders. As a child, she'd seen more than a handful of people knocked into the water simply for standing in the wrong place at the wrong time. But Ren had learned the dance back then. She sidestepped a pair of haulers heaving massive crates onto an open barge. Around a trio of strong-armed deckhands who were executing timed pulls to bring a boat closer to the docks. Ren noticed a boy, no older than seven, sitting cross-legged on one of the thick pilings, fingers performing nimble work on a fishing net. Ren had sat there, once, though she'd always had her nose buried in a book. Her mother waited at the far end of the docks.

"We'll be aboard the *Transient*," she whispered. "Their captain owes me a favor. He's agreed to let us stow away. The crew knows to keep their mouths shut. No listing on the official manifest, but the cost is our comfort. There aren't any . . . suites on these ships."

Ren rolled her eyes. "Very subtle, Mother. Thank you for preparing me for dire conditions."

Her mother feigned looking around. "Oh. Dear. Did you forget to invite your butler?"

"I don't have a *butler*. Gods, Mother. You act like I *want* to live up there. As if . . ."

She trailed off. Her mother didn't know Ren's true goal. She'd never been brave enough to breathe it aloud to anyone else. The point of all this was not gold and luxury. It was about fire and blood. She was not simply advancing through the ranks of their society to secure some vain comfort for herself. The intention was to destroy the people who'd destroyed their family. Without that knowledge, Ren knew it might look as if she'd simply been lured in by the royal houses of Kathor, as if she simply wanted a pampered life.

"You forget whose daughter I am."

Those words drew a more serious look from her mother. "I could never forget that, but I am glad to know that you haven't forgotten. Come. Let's board."

The *Transient* was unremarkable. A single bright sail above a deck of long-faded wood. The crew had finished stuffing crates into the hold and now set to the task of unlashing the bone-thick ropes from the docks. The captain—short and round and talkative—greeted them in one breath and berated a lazy deckhand with the next. Ren found herself smiling. He was a lot like her father's friends. The men who'd come over to play cards and laughed long into the night. They were led with little ceremony to a closet. Someone had stuffed a single pillow and a set of tattered blankets inside.

"Oh," her mother said. "Well . . . this is . . ."

"What?" Ren asked, goading. "Something wrong, Mother? Is the suite not to *your* liking?"

That earned a withering look. Ever stubborn, her mother reached down and began fluffing the nearly featherless pillow. She spread out the blanket and sat, reclining as if they were on the verge of enjoying the finest picnic in the world.

"It looks comfortable enough to me. You wanted a ship. I got you a ship."

Ren could only smile at that. She took a seat beside her mother.

"Now that we're *comfortable*," Ren said. "Tell me all about this Harlow character. . . ."

As the winds howled against the closed door of their makeshift bedroom, Ren finally told her mother why she needed to visit Ravinia. And that revelation led to the heart of her plans with the Broods. After making sure they could not be overheard by a passing deckhand, Ren started at the beginning. The words fell out of her mouth—somehow made less dangerous by the dark nothing of their makeshift quarters. There was just enough light that Ren could see her mother's face and little else.

"You're being quiet," Ren noted.

"I'm thinking."

Ren would have paced, but there simply wasn't room to pace.

"How will Theo be involved?"

"Right now, he's not involved. He doesn't know about any of this."

"You're bonded. He's going to eventually figure it out."

"Agreed. For now, I'm nursing his distaste. He's wounded. His father humiliated him. I have to build a bridge from that feeling—that experience—to mine."

"Hatred isn't too long a walk from shame."

"I know that, but it can't just be hatred. Anger is a fire, and fires burn out. I don't need Theo to simply be angry at his father. I need him to move a step beyond that. I need him to rationally accept that his family deserves to be destroyed. I need him to choose me over them."

Her mother nodded. "That will take time. Years, maybe."

"Or a single moment."

They'd been speaking quietly in the dark for a while now. Ren wasn't sure how much farther they still had to travel, or even what the weather was like outside. All she could hear was the tossing waves and the hissing wind and the occasional thump-thump of deckhands passing their location.

"Do you remember the Tin'Vori family?"

Ren's mother nodded. "Their estate was near the harbor. We could see their children playing sometimes. From the docks. There were two boys and two girls."

"The oldest one was killed. By the Broods," Ren supplied. "His name was Ware Tin'Vori."

"I remember that. Everyone talked about it for weeks. Your Aunt Sloan claimed she heard the boy shouting as he was dragged through the Lower Quarter—the liar."

"Dahvid is the one who was seen in Ravinia. He's an image-bearer."

"Powerful magic," her mother replied. "But hardly subtle. You can't smuggle an image-bearer into Kathor. He'd be noticed everywhere he went. How can he help you? If he can't even return to the city?"

"I don't know," Ren admitted. "I feel like I have no other options, though. None of the major houses in Kathor will even speak with me."

Her mother nodded. "There were two girls in the family: Ava and Nevelyn. The younger one was a wild thing. We'd spot her climbing all the way to the tops of the trees. Sometimes she'd set things on fire and throw them into the harbor. The other one was more like you. Always reading books. What did the old lady say about them?"

Ren sighed. "She wasn't sure. It's like you said. Dahvid is easy to find. There aren't many image-bearers—even in a free port like Ravinia. But she thought if he was alive, it was possible they were too."

"What's your plan? When you find him?"

Ren did not answer for a time. She didn't actually have a plan. What do you say to someone who has the same hatred in their heart that you do? She couldn't imagine discussing the weather or magical theory with someone like that. It felt like the only thing that could exist between them was a mutual desire for destruction. It was enticing. The thought of having someone who understood. But that would only be true if he'd carefully grown his hatred over the years as she had.

"I suppose I'll ask him to destroy the Broods with me."

7

DAHVID TIN'VORI

I t began with blinding brightness.

Dahvid shielded his eyes as he walked into the room. The door closed behind him with a muted click. Everything around him dripped with cleansing magic. A pearl-white layer that looked like false snow. The room was furnished with a single table, set at the very center. Dahvid quietly stripped out of his clothes. He covered himself with a towel, then lay down on the table. Everything around him—the cushions and cabinets and walls—looked eerie for their lack of color, almost dream-like. Once he was settled and his eyes were closed, the spell began.

He could feel layers of dirt peeling off his skin. It always felt nice. At first. But then the magic would dig deeper. He gritted his teeth against that sharpness. He knew the pain was necessary. He'd visited cleansing rooms since he was five years old. Any time a new tattoo had been chosen for him. The part of his body that would house the magic needed to be a perfectly blank canvas. There was dirt, of course, that might make his skin less receptive, but there was also dormant magic. Residual traces that the naked eye could not detect. Removing that layer always felt like having hairs ripped from his body with hot wax.

Pain, his father's voice reminded him, *is a road to power.*

Dahvid tried to keep his breathing steady. Eventually the claws of the magic retracted. The cleansing spell faded. His chest rose and fell. When he opened his eyes, the room had lost its dreamlike color. The table beneath him was normal, gray stone. The cabinets and the door were a matching bronze. Cath didn't bother knocking as she entered.

"Ready?"

"For you? Always."

He loved how easily she blushed. How she came to his side without hesitation. Even as a boy, he'd grown accustomed to startling others. Living life as a spectacle. Image-bearers were, by their very nature, eye-catching. Most people had treated him as something to be enjoyed at a distance, like a painting on a museum wall. In truth, his magic wasn't all that different from other branches. More powerful, perhaps. Not sourced from government warehouses like most. But that didn't stop the majority of people from thinking of him as something dangerous or exotic.

Cath had spotted him across the room at a tavern in Peska. Before he and his sister had decided to come to Ravinia. All of the tattoos had lured her over. She'd joined them for a drink, and then a second. Sometimes it felt like she'd sat down that night and simply decided to stay for good. He thought he loved

her, but there was no one left to tell him what love was supposed to feel like.

Now Cath leaned over him, carefully repositioning his arms
and legs for the morning's work. She let her nails trail playfully along one thigh before turning to unpack her equipment.
He tried not to shiver, but goose bumps spread from the place
she'd grazed. It felt so boyish, this lack of control. The two of
them had been together for nearly a year now. He'd assumed
that he would grow accustomed to her and all the impulses she
drew out of him. The opposite had occurred. All this time, and
he felt more in her power than ever.

"Calm down, dear," Cath said, arranging her supplies. "We
only have the room for an hour, and it's not going to be that
kind of hour. . . ."

Dahvid scowled at her, adjusting his towel. He fixed his eyes
on the ceiling. A mirror hung there. He saw his entire body
reflected back like a painting. All the tattoos he'd gathered
over the years stood out, bright on his pale, muscled frame.
His body existed as a living, historical record. Three different
artists had made their marks on him over a little less than two
decades.

His eyes drifted to the first tattoo. On his right wrist, a sword
that shimmered with light. Martha had drawn it. His father
had hired the artist when Dahvid was just five years old. He
still found it remarkable that he'd been permitted to summon
a weapon at that age.

Martha's second drawing sat on his right shoulder. Three
golden circles, overlapping in such a way that the eye could
not tell where one began and the other ended. She'd etched
that just before Dahvid learned to hate her. Before he was old

enough to understand that the way she treated him was not tough love but a pattern of abuse. It was particularly ironic, because the golden circles she'd drawn remained one of his best protective spells.

Her third tattoo was the smallest one. A reflection of their shrinking relationship. The slender glass vial stood out on his right thigh, frothing with golden elixir. Designed as a protection against poisons. Smart, he supposed, for one of the heirs to a major house. He'd learned how to use the spell's power for quick healing in recent years. Far more useful to him. No one cared enough about nameless gladiators to actually poison them.

That was where Martha's drawings ended. He remembered finally feeling brave enough to walk into his father's study. How smoke had drifted in the air between them like a haze. Ware had stood a few steps behind Dahvid. His older brother's presence was the only reason he managed to speak in a steady voice. He told his father how Martha used pain to demonstrate her control over him. How easily she'd blurred the lines between discipline and abuse. His father had watched him with an unreadable expression. When Dahvid finished, the man crossed the room and cupped his son's chin in one hand.

"Why didn't you tell me? Did you think I would not protect you?"

In the years since, Dahvid had forgotten so much of his father. All the little details that made a person more than just a memory. He would never forget the fierceness in his expression that day.

"You are my *son*. I would fight the tides for you. I would

rip the moon from the sky. Mark my words, boys." He had looked back and forth between them. "The two of you—and your sisters—there is *nothing* I would not do to keep the four of you safe."

Dahvid never saw Martha again. As a boy, he'd assumed she'd been dismissed. Thinking back on his father's words— the fury buried in each syllable—he was less certain of her fate now.

As Martha's work ended, Ware's began. His brother had always been a fine artist, but he'd secretly been training to replace her. The proposal was accepted by their father, who liked the idea of his boys working so closely together. Ware was born a dreamer. Bringing strange spells to life through Dahvid suited the creative in him. Their first successful tattoo was the scarlet traveler—the one piece of art that caught everyone's eye.

The flower stretched from chin to lower chest, petals unfolding in the imagined sunlight. It was a credit to Ware that it still housed Dahvid's most devastating spell. Their second tattoo together was less useful. It ran down one bicep: a flock of birds taking flight. They looked like silhouettes against the pale sky of his arm. A natural choice for two boys who'd always pretended that they could fly as children. Even after years of training, the spell hurt more often than it helped.

Ware's final tattoo remained a mystery. Dahvid saw the edges of the image, beginning on his right hip, circling before vanishing onto his back. He never looked at it for long. He had never activated its magic, no matter how tempted or desperate. Ware had finished the tattoo and promised to explain how to use it. He never got the chance, because that same night the Broods killed him.

Dahvid closed his eyes. He heard swords scraping overhead. He smelled smoke as it started to filter down into their hiding place. He felt *fear*. Followed by cowardice. Then a sharp tug on his arm.

"Don't go there," Cath whispered. Her voice echoed in the small room. "You're thinking about your sister again. Stay with me, dear. There's nothing you could have done."

He stared back at her until his heart stopped thrashing in his chest. His hands had balled into fists. Slowly, he let his fingers uncurl. He hadn't been thinking of Ava, and he felt guilty for not thinking about her enough. His youngest sister. As lost to them now as the others.

Before his mind could stumble down those darker trails, his eyes sought out the newest tattoos. They always comforted him, because they were not drawn by a ghost. Each one had been created by Cath.

Martha's work had produced efficient, useful spells. Nothing that a wand couldn't summon. Ware possessed a rare ability to create images of great depth, which produced magic to match. Cath was more of a trickster god. Her artistic power rested in creativity and wickedness. All three of her spells had quietly become favorites.

On his left bicep, there were the twins. Two imps expelling mirrored blasts of frosty wind from their puffy cheeks. She'd also drawn the delicate rope that circled his left wrist. The pattern almost looked like it was weaving in and out—writhing over his skin—if he stared at it for too long. Finally, there was a perfectly drawn circle centered on his upper abdomen. A simple design that resulted in an equally simple but clever magic. Today, Cath would try for her fourth tattoo.

Again.

"What attempt is this?" she asked.

"It's our seventh try," Dahvid replied. "It will work this time."

"Don't make promises you can't keep."

He winced. That was one of Cath's only rules. Her life—at least from what he'd gathered—was full of little, broken promises. She'd made a point of calling out the quickness of his words early on in their relationship. He had a natural tendency to boast. A brashness that manifested from him. He knew it was a habit he'd learned from his father and his older brother. After all this time with Cath, he knew better than to claim something he could not actually guarantee.

"I am *hopeful* that it will work."

Cath nodded, bending over him. "You know what they say about hope."

"What?"

"It's the brightest bird in the sky and thus the easiest to kill."

Without further warning, she stabbed him. Just a pinprick, but the first one always jolted through his system. She moved methodically from there, poking and shaping and stretching his skin. He felt the area they'd chosen starting to go numb long before she even reached for the dyes. He truly was hopeful. Failure was so common. Not every image worked. His skin was receptive to magic, but it was a fickle judge of which spells were *worthy*.

Over the years, he'd learned his own opinion had no sway. It didn't matter how much he willed it to work. Sometimes, the more he craved the power of a particular spell, the less likely it was that the tattoo would survive the first usage. Martha had wasted a countless number of tattoos. It had been so painful to go through each etching as a child, only to watch the image fade from his skin the first time he activated the spell.

Cath hummed a song. Dahvid clenched his jaw against the occasional spikes of pain. He let out a ragged breath when she finally switched instruments. Slowly an image was taking form. A speckled hart that wrapped around his left thigh. Its head was raised. Two piercing eyes stared into the imagined distance. Only half the creature's head was antlered. Where the other half should have been—there was an echo, no more than shadows. Dahvid found himself staring into the hart's dark eyes, mesmerized.

"I am nearly done," Cath said. "Are you ready?"

This part was all superstition. Some believed a tattoo needed to be activated immediately. Others thought a year should pass, allowing it to sink properly into the skin. One could attempt the magic while holding a certain spice in their right palm. And of course, never activate it during a full moon. Countless methods, but Dahvid had not found any of them to be more certain than the next. Instead, he patiently watched Cath and waited for her signal. She finished a stroke, blew on the spot, and then set her instrument down.

"Now."

"Back up," he whispered. "All the way to the corner."

She moved obediently, clearing a space for him. Dahvid looked once more at the tattoo, taking in its beauty—imagining the possibility they'd discussed. He set aside desire and greed and all his other emotions. Reduced his thoughts to function and form. After a long breath, he took his feet. The cloth fell away. Dahvid settled into a fighter's stance. Magic flexed in the air around him—ready and waiting. He did not need a vessel. He was the vessel.

"Come on then."

With one fingertip, he grazed the hart's antlers. Magic hummed to life. He grunted against the onrush of power. It set his teeth on edge, raised the hairs on both arms. Dahvid ignored the discomfort and pressed that magic forward—forced it into being. He felt the weight of his creation a moment before he saw its reflection in the overhead mirror.

A great helmet crowned his head. Knife-sharp antlers extended out of one side. Shadows dripped out of the other. His eyes were no more than bright slits peering out from the forest-green, plated front of the armor. Dahvid could not help grinning. It looked wild and wicked. He cracked his neck, settled his feet once more, and pushed the magic a step further.

From form to function. The helmet's power hummed. A vibration that ran down his shoulders, his spine, through his legs. He was about to attempt the fullness of the spell when he heard it. A vague ripple became a resounding crack. Cath let out a cry as the helmet snapped in two. As if it had suffered a direct blow from an axe. Dahvid could only brace for impact as the material fell from his head. It crashed onto the floor, rattling for a moment, then dusting into inexistence.

The magic slipped away. His chest heaved breathlessly. He looked down and watched helplessly as the tattoo—all its bright colors and lovely details—vanished from his skin.

His eyes cut back to Cath. He already had words of comfort ready. They'd been through these failures so many times. But for a brief moment, she hunched over. A stray antler had broken off from the helmet. Launched across the room like an arrow. He saw it had pierced her stomach, deep and centered. A clear deathblow. There was a strange bruise on her throat. A great thicket of black-and-blue skin. There were smaller gashes on her thigh, her upper arm. Blood was pooling out. Cath's hands pressed to the wound, but nothing could staunch the flow. . . .

He blinked and there was no blood at all. Only Cath, whole and well, pacing the room with a thousand curses springing from her lips. He knew how hungry she was to get the tattoo right. Like Nevelyn, she believed this would be the tattoo that made the difference between surviving what was to come and dying an inglorious death. She believed she was leaving him vulnerable without it. Dahvid kept staring until he was certain the blood and the wound had been in his mind. All of it imagined.

"We will try again," he said.

There was the slightest tremor to his voice. He had not completely shaken that image of her away. It took effort to steel his thoughts again, before Cath noted the change.

"Again. Next week."

He kissed her forehead as she began packing up the materials. An attendant had appeared at the door. They would not be allowed a second more than what they paid for. That was how Ravinia worked. Everything a transaction. Everything at a price. Dahvid let Cath walk in front of him. The place where the tattoo had been was bright red and raw. He ignored the pain as they left but could not help pausing on the threshold. He looked back to where Cath had been standing. There was blood on the floor. A speckled pattern.

When the attendant activated the cleansing spell, however, the room took on its familiar white sheen. No matter how hard Dahvid stared—he could not see the blood. It was gone.

Never there at all.

8

NEVELYN TIN'VORI

Nevelyn did not enjoy the concept of bustle.

If it were up to her, she'd start walking into the mountains and never step foot in a city ever again. She dreamed of building a cabin in some remote place, growing a fine garden, and reading books on a wide, creaking porch. The place of her choosing would be nothing like Ravinia. Nor anything like what she remembered of Kathor when she was a child. It would be a place with more trees than people—a place with a blanket of stars overhead. . . .

Dreaming. She knew better than to dream. There was far too much to do. Nevelyn shifted her feet and craned her neck to see if the line had moved, quietly letting her imagined cabin slip from her mind. Which left her to focus too fully on the person who was breathing on her neck.

"Could you back up?"

The woman startled back a step. Nevelyn watched the small

ripple it created. She bumped the person in line behind her, who bumped the person behind him. On and on like that until someone shoved back, and then the line quieted once more. They'd been crowded in the shadow of the same building all morning. Each of them had arrived well before dawn to claim their spots. Nevelyn let out a chest-deep sigh as she turned back to the front. She was ninth in line.

"Who do you deliver for?"

It was the woman behind her. The breather. Nevelyn had apparently earned her attention. "I can't imagine how that would be any of your business."

"Oh? Everyone says that. At the start. All puffed up because they've got some important job for some important person. Don't want to spill their precious secrets." The woman paused, and Nevelyn could hear the smile stretching over her face without even looking back. "But we all end up chatting eventually. It's more fun that way. Trust me."

Nevelyn thought she'd already effectively communicated her position on the concept of chatting, but the woman was clearly in a mood to pester.

"Why?" Nevelyn asked, half turning. "Who do *you* deliver for?"

That was all the invitation the woman needed to lean in conspiratorially. It was as Nevelyn expected. She was bored or lonely or both. The woman had sun-kissed skin—someone who'd grown up working the docks down in the harbor. Other than a few tight creases at the edges of her mouth, there were no other details that betrayed her age. Nevelyn guessed she was in her fifties, but with no more than a passing glance, she might have been in her twenties.

"I run papers for some of the merchant lords in North End. You know the place?"

Nevelyn nodded back at the woman. When they'd first arrived in Ravinia, she'd become a scholar of the city. Studying every facet and detail. Any viable path toward power. Who could two stranded heirs cozy up with in an effort to make their way back to Kathor? All roads eventually led back to Darling and his gladiator pits—but the North End lords were a fine guild. A private club that pooled resources and information to benefit one another.

"The North End? That place where old men dress up in too-tight suits?"

The woman let out a great gust of a laugh. "Fair point. But those old men pay quite well. Who's your lord, then? Some old man who dresses more like an old man?"

Nevelyn returned a lifeless smile. "I serve only myself."

The words had the opposite reaction of what she'd intended. If there was no well-to-do lord waiting for Nevelyn's return, she'd hoped that would make her uninteresting. Instead, the woman seemed all the more curious. Nevelyn cursed her carelessness. This was only the third time she'd waited in this line. It was outside a building known as the Herald. She'd been lucky to discover the place at all. A well-kept secret that belonged to the higher-end clientele of the city—and their footmen. News washed up in the harbor every day. Boats brought word of this and that from the other major cities, but always on a delay. Days or even weeks in which that news might already have grown stale or useless for the everyday merchant. The lone exception to that rule was the Herald.

Once a month, a waxway runner would deliver a single

stack of newspapers. None was more highly prized than the *Kathorian*. Ravinia's wealthiest would pay top coin for the issue that had been printed that day. Less for yesterday's news, and still less for any copies older than that. The immediacy and breadth of that news allowed those who purchased a copy to react to the market before the rest of their peers. Nevelyn knew that was why most of the people waiting in line were there. They came with their master's coin, prepared to ferry back information that would line their pockets with still more gold. Nevelyn was an exception. She came here once a month and spent what precious little coin they had to continue their eternal hunt of the Broods.

The woman was still watching her closely, waiting for more of an explanation. Nevelyn glanced casually down at the charm on her necklace. A small heart-shaped thing. She confirmed it was turned the right way, before looking up and meeting the woman's eye again.

"I told you: what I do and who I am is of no concern to you."

Magic whispered between them. It would feel like the gentlest push. A light mental shove. When Nevelyn broke off eye contact, the woman would forget. She'd straighten, feeling slightly woozy, and wonder how the last few minutes could possibly have slipped through her fingers. Nevelyn stood rather still as she allowed the spell to run its course. She'd not used this particular magic in a few years. A drunk had trailed her home from work and she'd vanished from his attention in exactly the same way.

Dahvid had his gifts. Father had spent most of their young lives celebrating and honing her brother's magic. He'd never thought to ask if his daughter possessed any talents. Some-

SCOTT REINTGEN

times she wondered how skilled she might be if her gifts had garnered the same attention. But she knew that fell into the realm of dreaming, so she killed the thought before it could take a second breath.

There was commotion at the front of the line.

Finally, the delivery boy was arriving. It was always a bit jarring to watch. The Herald was a single-story building. Roofless and with its front doors thrust wide open. Inside, there was a single, unremarkable rug on the floor. Candles glinted in every corner of the space. A gentle flicker of those flames announced their guest.

The boy appeared. His mouth gaped open and his eyes were pinned shut. Each time she'd witnessed this, he appeared the same way, hovering slightly in the air. It looked as if he was still midstep. She'd learned that the boy traveled using consecutive waxways. A network that was arranged so that he could jump from location to location to location. All the way across the northeastern seaboard in less than the time it took to shake someone's hand. He hovered there before the crowd, looking almost lifeless, for what felt like the longest-held breath in the world.

And then he was shouting.

"All right! All right. Calm down. And have your money ready for once!"

He made the first exchange without so much as a glance. The line began to move. Nevelyn was pleased when the woman behind her made no more inquiries. She would suffer no more unwelcome interest today. She waited patiently for her turn to come and then stepped forward.

"I'll take your oldest copy," she told the boy.

"Fifteen mids, then."

Nevelyn hesitated, but only for a moment. The price had always been ten. She knew he was just pumping it up because he could. No one would be out here to regulate a trade like this. And if she made a scene over five mids—people in line would find that curious. Which master couldn't afford a slight increase in the price? And that would lead to unwanted attention. She slid a hand in her pocket, fetched the extra bills, and slapped them into the boy's hand. He smirked at her, because he knew he'd just earned himself a little extra money on the side.

Nevelyn answered in her own way, allowing her nails to dig down slightly during the exchange. The boy hissed in surprise at that pain, but Nevelyn was already moving away, paper tucked under one arm. She didn't have time for little boys playing their little games. Not today.

She started across town, aiming for the city's lowliest graveyard. Cheap land where they buried the coinless and bereft. She would find the headstone marked with their sister's name and sit in the shadow of the lily pines there. It helped her to read the stories from the paper aloud and imagine what details Ava would remark upon. Her younger sister had always been compulsively obsessed with the specific. Ever since she'd left them, Nevelyn had felt like she was overlooking some small but crucial piece of their plan. And so she read every single article, every scrap of news, and hoped that Ava's ghost would whisper some light over what she might be missing.

She smiled at that grim thought, tightened her threadbare coat, and walked back through the clogged streets. Busy as they were, no one seemed to notice her. Nevelyn smiled at that, too.

REN MONROE

R en watched impatiently as her mother separated from the others in line. She had a purchase tucked under one arm and an almost unreadable look on her face. When she finally spotted Ren waiting at the corner for her, she smiled.

"Got it," she said, untucking the paper. "This is the one you wanted, right?"

Ren frowned. "I don't care about the newspaper, Mother. Was it her?"

Their mark had just disappeared around the corner. This had all been her mother's idea. It was the only place in the city where a person could keep official tabs on the happenings of Kathor. They'd bribed the first few messenger boys who arrived that morning, showing them an old portrait of the Tin'Vori children. There was a girl, they said, who looked like one of the sisters, but they couldn't be sure. It was more than enough to convince Ren and her mother to wait around and see who showed up. They'd both marked the girl's arrival. She fit the description perfectly. A little tall. Her hair a nest of curls. Pretty, but always looking down to avoid eye contact. Now they were running out of time to pursue her. Ren just needed a confirmation of their guess.

"Was it who?" her mother replied.

"The girl. You talked to her in line. Were we right? Is it Nevelyn Tin'Vori?"

Her mother shook her head. "Ren. I didn't talk to anyone. I got you the newspaper. . . ."

But now she looked confused. Muddled. Ren was struck by the realization. *Magic. She used magic on my mother.* She thought back through what she'd witnessed from the shadowed mouth of the alleyway. Her mother had quietly taken her place behind the girl. Eventually she'd struck up a conversation. Their suspected Nevelyn had appeared closed off the entire time. A reasonable stance for someone who might want to hide their identity. Their conversation had ended rather abruptly, but Ren had been too far away to know the reason. She'd assumed it had simply run its course, but looking at her mother, she suspected that Nevelyn had used some sort of spell. Her mother was no forgetful crone. She was one of the sharpest minds Ren had ever met. But right now she was claiming she'd never even talked to the girl that Ren had clearly watched her talk to?

"You don't remember any of it?"

Another headshake. "Love, I'd . . . I'd remember if I talked to someone."

"Head back to our rooms. I'll meet you there in a few hours. Go. Quickly."

And Ren shot toward the distant alley. In pursuit once more. She heard a startled noise from her mother, but there was no time to explain. The messenger boy had given them a list—along with descriptions—of anyone in line who kept their identities hidden. Apparently, the crews that delivered papers back to their masters were all relatively familiar with one another. There were only a few outcasts in the group, and one of the women he'd pegged was the one who fit Nevelyn's description. Never spoke to anyone. Never revealed any details. Bought the cheapest papers, too.

Now that same girl had cast a spell on her mother.

Ren turned the corner, rushed down the length of the alleyway, and came shouldering out into a much more crowded space. She'd give anything to let Vega loose now. The bird would have found their mark in no time, but she'd left the bird back in Kathor, not wanting to risk such a visual display. If there were Brood spies in this place, they'd mark the statue instantly. No, she'd have to hunt with her own two eyes.

Her attention darted from face to face, outline to outline. Their suspected Nevelyn had been dressed so unremarkably, though. As if she'd intended to blend in with a crowd. All light browns—not a single color that might catch the eye. The only notable detail was a small, silver necklace.

Ren searched again. She cursed the busy, trafficked hour. On instinct, she pressed into the larger market square on her right, hoping the change in angle would offer what she needed. There was no sign of the girl. Ren knew the delivery boy would not return to the Herald for weeks. It could be just as long before they found her again if Ren did not find her now.

There was an alleyway on her right. Ren eyed the length

of it and saw another market in the distance. Maybe Nevelyn had gone that way. She started forward, so distracted that she nearly missed the distant call of her name. It wasn't her mother. A man's voice. Growing louder.

"Hey!"

Ren turned. To her utter surprise, Mat Tully was bustling toward her. He looked ragged, at least compared with the polished boy she'd spoken with at Theo's party last year. He was thinner and paler and looked as if he hadn't slept since that last conversation. Ren could feel a mental clock ticking as her chance to find Nevelyn continued to slip from her grasp.

"Mat Tully," she remarked dryly. It was too late to hide her identity. She didn't want a long conversation—especially not with someone from Kathor who could report to others that she was in Ravinia. "Apologies, but I can't stop to chat. I have an appointment. Perhaps we could catch up later? If you let me know where you're staying . . ."

She turned away, aiming once more for the waiting alley. Mat Tully sputtered out a warning, though. "Wait, Ren. This isn't Kathor. You can't just walk down random alleyways. That's a traveler's trap if I've ever seen one. Look."

He pointed. Ren had been so focused on the distant and glittering market that she hadn't taken note of everything between here and there. Stray crates stacked up in strategic choke points. The slightest movement in those nestling shadows. She looked back to Mat.

"Thieves?"

"Of course. There are crews running every quarter," he replied. "And they're not always content to pick your pockets.

The more dangerous groups will knife you first. Trust me, you don't want to go down there. . . ."

Ren let out a sigh. Any chance of trailing Nevelyn was gone. She eyed the surrounding crowds one more time before turning her full attention to Mat Tully.

"Why are you in Ravinia?" she asked. "I thought you were traveling to . . . distant villages? Studying alternative medicine, right?"

Their last conversation had been rather pivotal for Ren. After learning that Mat had been chosen by House Winters to conduct medical research, she'd decided to take the matter of her stalled career into her own hands. That had led to her decision to alter the portal spell, which led to the death of her friends, which led to the current bond she shared with Theo Brood. Her darkest shame and her greatest hope, spun from the same moment. It was hard to imagine it had all started with plain-as-rain Mat Tully.

"I thought the same," Mat replied. "The Winters family assigned me here instead. There were rumors about the healers who attended to the gladiators in the pits. Herbal remedies. Unique magic. I was assigned to make contact with them, study any unusual traits, and report back. I've been here for nearly half a year."

He looked like he'd been there for half a century. Ren didn't say that, though. She could see that he was itching to share more about his situation. As if holding his tongue was actually painful. Ren's mother had taught her there was wisdom in letting a fool run his mouth.

"And?" she asked invitingly.

"And this is also where they abandoned me." His cheeks

blossomed a bright red. "It's embarrassing to admit, but after Clyde . . ."

That name, mentioned so casually and in such a different context, caught her completely off guard. *Clyde.* She saw flickers of memory. Clyde sitting in the corner of her ethics class, offering up lazy answers. Clyde unleashing a spell, moments before the portal magic erupted. Clyde out on the river, no longer truly Clyde at all, snapping Avy's neck. And then up in the mountain pass, pulling Timmons down by her white-blond hair. Ren could see the way her best friend fell. She could hear the way she screamed. . . .

Ren's heart was thrashing in her chest. She forced her mind back to logic. Back to a separate set of facts. Disassociation. Mat had been one of Clyde's better friends at school. More of a hound, she recalled, always following at the wealthier boy's heels. But still. The closest approximation to a friend that any of the heirs could have at Balmerick. She'd been too focused on her own plight to think that his death might create consequences for others, like Mat Tully. Her heart rate was slowing, but she thought if she spoke, the words might come out strangled and wretched.

"Well," Mat went on awkwardly. "The Winters family severed ties with me. Sent a final stipend, and then left me here. On my own. My father isn't rich. Not like they are. I've been saving up money to try to get back to Kathor, but I owed rent, too. It hasn't been easy out here on my own."

Ren nodded, guessing his suffering was still rather limited to the kind of suffering that wealthy people experienced. A slightly-less-than-normal sort of suffering.

"I'm sorry about that, Mat."

He shrugged. "Anyways. That's a sad song. Not worth singing out here on such a fine day. What about you? Why are you here?"

Ren had been carefully considering what story to tell him. If he'd been here that long, it was quite possible that he had no idea about most of the current events in Kathor. He certainly wouldn't know about Theo's exile. He might not even know about the fact that they were bonded. But she also didn't want to overstep on the information she shared with him. It was possible that he was still connected with other Kathorians in Ravinia.

"I was sent by House Brood," she answered. "I am investigating a matter on their behalf."

His eyes lit up at that. "So, you found a house! I remember . . . at the party. Honestly, I was such a prat. You asked for help, and I just kind of . . . didn't help. Sorry about that. You clearly landed on your feet. What's your role with them? Are you working for one of the cousins?"

Now she had a chance to really impress. "I'm bonded to Theo Brood."

If Mat Tully had been drinking tea, he likely would have spat it out. She watched a run of emotions flicker across the features of his face. He landed on something between shock and elation.

"Good for you. Seriously. Good for you. That's a very nice upward move."

"Maybe you can help me," Ren said, leaning a little closer. "I have some money to spend on resources for the investigation. I could certainly pay you for your services. I'm not sure who your contacts are in the city, but I'm searching for a very particular person here in Ravinia."

Mat was nodding enthusiastically. "I've made some connections. It just depends on who you're looking for."

Ren knew it was a risk to say the name. Mat could take her inquiry back to someone else, but if she could really sell herself to him as the true envoy of House Brood, he'd have no reason to report to anyone except for her. This could be a very useful relationship.

"Have you ever heard the name Dahvid Tin'Vori?"

Mat's quiet smile faded. His face completely shut down. He no longer looked simply tired. He looked almost dangerous instead. A building fury. "Seriously? You know, you didn't have to backpedal into it like that. Pretending to be all friendly just to drive the knife home. That's some slick to pull. I know we weren't exactly friends or whatever, but I never treated you poorly. . . ."

Ren was completely lost. "What?"

"Come on. Don't act like you don't know. Why the hell would you bring that up if you didn't? It must be fun, now that you're established in House Brood, to kick a man when he's already rolling around in the gutters. . . ."

"Mat. Wait. I don't actually know what you're talking about."

There was an awkward silence between them. He was more red-faced than ever now, breathing raggedly. He stared at her long enough to get a proper read and realized she was telling the honest truth. "Really?" he asked. "That's just a coincidence?"

"Mat. *What* is a coincidence?"

"Dahvid Tin'Vori. That's the name you said."

"Yes. I'm looking for him."

Mat was actually pacing around. "Sorry. It's just . . . odd. It's odd. Fine. I've been telling people that the Winters family let me go because of Clyde's death. Selling it as . . . you know . . . them not caring to keep up with connections that no longer existed after he passed. That story allows me to save face. The truth is that I was removed from their employ because I informed on them. And a few of the other great houses."

That caught Ren's attention. "Informed how?"

He shrugged. "I don't know. I was drunk. They knew I was from Kathor, and they kept asking me questions. About the different houses. Who owned which properties? What businesses were thriving? How had the seats of power shifted over the years? I honestly didn't think anything of it at the time. I thought they were a pair of curious outsiders. . . ."

Ren took note of that detail.

"A pair? There were only two of them?"

He nodded. "Dahvid and his sister."

One sister was alive. But not both sisters? It took all of Ren's restraint to not smack Mat on the shoulder. "You mean you actually *know* them?"

"I really only talked to them one time. It's not like we're friends. . . ."

"Can you help me find them again?"

Mat hesitated. It was clear the first encounter had set him back, and he felt like he might be digging the hole even deeper. Ren followed her instincts. She went with the first lie that came to mind.

"There's money in it for you," she said. "And if the results are satisfactory, maybe there's even a position with House Brood down the line. What's the worst that could happen, Mat?

It's not as if the Winters family can end your contract twice."

Mat was slowly nodding. "How much money?"

"I can't guarantee it's enough to get you home, but it would be a start."

"Okay. I'll help you."

She gestured to the shadowed alleyway. "You already did."

"Right. Wait. Don't you need to get to your appointment?"

She waved that idea away. "You are suddenly much more interesting than the person I was intending to seek out."

He smiled at that, and Ren smiled back, happily pretending to be his friend for now. It would take some careful navigating. If Mat led her back to any Kathorians who were properly connected, they'd be able to figure out rather quickly that she hadn't actually been sent on behalf of the Brood family. For now, though, Mat Tully was a bridge, and she had every intention of walking straight over him and to the Tin'Vori siblings.

10

REN MONROE

After making arrangements for Mat to contact her, Ren headed back to the temporary quarters she and her mother had chosen that morning. She had not slept well on the voyage, and she'd risen early to search for Nevelyn. She could feel the exhaustion pressing in behind her eyes. A slight pressure at her temples. She needed sleep. Desperately. Ren knocked twice on the door of their room—already imagining herself vanishing under the covers.

Until her mother answered the door.

"What is that? Why are you bleeding?"

She had a folded towel pressed to her cheek. When she removed it, Ren's heart nearly stopped in her chest. There was a gash stretching from her cheekbone and nearly to her ear.

"Who did this?"

Ren's mother shooed the fury and the question both. The

same way that Ren had waved away Mat Tully's concerns. "Come in and calm down. I just took the wrong road home. I was . . . woozy. I should have said something before you went racing off, but I thought I could fight through it. Whatever happened this morning, it left my mind out of sorts. I got lost on the way home. One of the streets I took . . . there were men waiting there in the alleyway."

All of Ren's carefully maintained barriers broke. Like a chain spell leaping from one darkness to the next. Grief and guilt flooded through every part of her mind. Cora and Avy were dead. Timmons—her best friend in the world—was gone. Forever. They would never return home. Never enjoy a meal with their families. They'd never practice spells or raise children or take lovers or move to new cities or *anything ever again*. Ren had snuffed their lives out between her fingers, and in pursuit of what? A revenge that might never manifest? Fear began to weave itself through her guilt. What if she didn't succeed? What if she wasted their sacrifices? Everything Ren had been choosing not to feel came pouring out.

Her mother swept her into an embrace. She held her tight, and Ren sobbed into her shoulder, the way she might have when she was little. Over a skinned knee or a lost toy. This was so much more than that, but her mother's arms were the same answer they were then. A needed salve.

"There, there . . . ," her mother whispered. "I'm all right. We're all right."

Ren's mind began to reestablish order. She carefully set those feelings back on their proper shelves, turned out the lights, and locked the doors. When it was done, she released a ragged breath that sounded more like a whimper. "You were attacked, Mother."

"They struck first," her mother agreed. "But they weren't the only ones carrying knives."

Knives. Her mother had been forced into hand-to-hand combat in the streets. It pained Ren to remember that her mother possessed no magic to defend or heal herself with. She'd left magic behind long ago.

"It could have been worse," Ren pointed out.

"'Could.' That was your father's least favorite word."

Ren half laughed and half cried. She was right, of course. Roland Monroe had given many dissertations about his hatred for that word at family dinners. Thinking of him drew Ren's eyes to the bracelet he'd once gifted her mother. She worked it down her wrist and held it out.

"Mother, I know it's been a long time, but I want you to take this. At least while we're in Ravinia. Magic—"

"Has no use to me now." She gently pushed the bracelet back toward Ren. "I've built up a resistance to it over the years, Ren. That's the only reason I wasn't completely paralyzed by the first spell they hit me with. And truly, I'm not you, girl. I never was. I have no knack for quick-thinking spells. I am far better with a set of knives than I ever was with a wand. Magic wouldn't have helped me."

Ren scowled but knew better than to fight back on this particular subject. Her mother had given up magic when her father passed. It was a purely emotional decision. At first. Later, she found a group of dock workers who actively avoided magic too. Ren had never been able to get more than the vaguest details, but she knew the camaraderie her mother found amongst them had led to an entrenched view on the subject. She would not use magic. Better to argue with a wall than to challenge Agnes Monroe.

"Let me at least refresh your rag," Ren offered as a compromise.

Her mother relented. Ren took the soiled cloth and her stomach turned again at the sight of that wound. It was the most gruesome thing she'd seen since . . . Clyde. She shoved away that thought before it could knock on the door of any more memories. She could not spare a moment more for the past right now—not when the present required her fullest attention.

She needed to tend to her mother. And then she needed to figure out what to do about Mat Tully. Not to mention her best possible approach with the Tin'Vori siblings. It was a stroke of absolute luck that she'd found a contact who actually knew them. In a city this large, it might as well be divine providence.

She was reaching for the silver handle of the bath when a draft of cold wind buffeted her. Ren stumbled back a step, shocked by the sudden cold. Her eyes snapped to the right, searching for the source of the spell. There was only the bathroom wall. Ren stared at the patterned wallpaper, waiting for some threat to step free of the shadows, when a chest-deep tug pulled her. She felt a profound and painful sense of loneliness.

Reality flickered. The bathroom dissolved. Ren instinctively reached for the wand at her hip as the temperature of the air plunged. Her lungs constricted. Everything was too tight. It was as if someone were standing on her chest, pressing down on her ribs.

A new reality presented itself.

Snow. Every outline and angle glittered with snow. Ren found that she was standing in the great shadow of a building she'd never seen before. There were two towers. Each one clung to the side of a different mountain so that, connected as they were by a bridge, the entire structure blocked all entry into the waiting pass. The crowns of certain arches had crumbled. Maybe the stones had been a rich color once—but time and wind had warped them into the putrid brown scales of a great slumbering dragon. Both towers were fronted by a gigantic soldier, spear in one hand and shield in the other. Like the rest of the building, she was certain they'd once looked intimidating and majestic. Now she could not even make out their expressions.

The snow continued to fall. It dusted everything. Ren could not help shivering as the wind howled again. It was the kind of cold that bit through cloth and skin, a bone-deep sort of chill. Ahead, she saw a single path winding to a lonely draw-bridge. A lantern bobbed. There was a face, barely visible in the glow. Ren saw the person was making a line directly for her. She had no idea what was happening, could not tell if she was in danger. The figure finally drew close enough to make out. A girl, even younger than her. She was mouse thin with short hair that had been recently shaved. She had narrow eyes that narrowed further as she inspected Ren.

"Well," she said, sounding bored. "You must be the new one."

It took Ren a moment to notice that the girl was not looking at her. No, her gaze was fixed on a spot just to the left. Ren glanced that way and saw the reason for all this. Understanding clicked neatly into place, like a missing puzzle piece. Theo stood there in the snow. He was wrapped in thick cloaks to the point that only his eyes and hair were truly recognizable. As he took in the distant castle, Ren felt it again. A pulsing sadness. A looming sense of being alone and abandoned and lost. The strength of that emotion ran headfirst across their bond with so much force that Ren had to pull away. Their connection, which was usually a guilty pleasure, became pain.

As Ren flinched back, the snowy mountain vanished. The lonely keep disappeared. Ren found herself in the bathroom again. She was gasping for air. "He . . . he pulled me. . . ."

"Ren?" Her mother's voice sounded on the other side of the door. "Where's that towel? The blood is starting to drip on the carpet. . . ."

It took an effort to shake herself and focus on the task at hand. Her mind kept doubling back curiously. Theo had somehow used their bond to pull her to him. It was as if she'd actually been standing there in Nostra. She'd felt the cold like fingers wrapped around her neck. She'd breathed in that barren mountain air. Ren knew there were stories of unique magic between the bonded. Manifestations that were more fitting of the wilder magics that existed amongst the Tusk people. Still, she found what had just happened inexplicable. She had not *actually* traveled. After all, she was still here in Ravinia. But what would have happened if she had not flinched away from that feeling? What if she'd accepted Theo's pull? It was another mystery to be solved later.

Ren returned with the warm towel.

"Thank you," her mother said. "Are you all right?"

"I just experienced a magic that I've never encountered. If you hadn't given up your own spells, I imagine we'd have a great deal to discuss."

Her mother pressed the rag to her cheek. "I was attacked in an alleyway. Before that, I was bewitched by some kind of memory charm. We've taken a boat to pursue the long-lost survivors of a raid that happened nearly a decade ago and we're hoping to find them in a city with tens of thousands of people. And you think we have nothing to talk about?"

Ren couldn't help smirking. "Fair point. But not to worry, Mother, I already found them."

"Really? That will save a lot of time, I suppose."

Ren nodded, but a new realization struck her a second later. She was turning over the list her mother had just presented. All that had happened thus far. There was one thing Ren hadn't noticed until now. Nevelyn Tin'Vori had used a spell on her mother. Magic—and it had worked quite well.

"Mother, how strong is your magical resistance?"

She saw an unexpected reaction flit across her mother's face. A wariness. As if this were prized knowledge that she'd been keeping private for a long time. The expression vanished after a brief moment. She seemed to remember it was her daughter asking the question.

"I can resist most spells," her mother admitted. "It depends on a number of factors."

"Did you resist a spell when you were attacked in the alley-way?"

"Several," her mother said proudly. "I doubt any of them were quality casters, though. We're talking about a street gang—not trained duelists from Balmerick."

"Still, you resisted their magic . . . but you couldn't resist what Nevelyn did to you?"

Her mother saw what Ren was getting at. It was their first hint of the abilities Nevelyn Tin'Vori possessed, and Ren thought it was a rather promising sign. She still hadn't figured out what spell she could have used to wipe someone's memory with such specificity and efficiency. The mind was fickle, and even the strongest manipulators in Kathor would need weeks to pull off something like that. Ren felt a mixture of excitement and foreboding. There was strange magic forming between herself and Theo. There was the bright possibility of Mat Tully shortening her journey. And then there were the mysterious Tin'Voris. It seemed the two of them were more than dangerous enough to be useful, but she knew the same power that might help her efforts could also turn against her. She would have to move forward with all caution.

Fire could burn both ways.

11

REN MONROE

It took some convincing, but her mother agreed to stay behind in the safety of their room. Ren had located the neighborhood doctor, who dispatched a nurse for the purpose of stitching the wound. Ren oversaw the first half of the procedure until she was certain the nurse knew what she was doing. As she gathered her things, her mother offered one final piece of advice.

"Don't screw it up."

Ren rolled her eyes and left. They'd mapped a route to her destination that kept her on the main thoroughfares. She held no delusions that this meant she was guaranteed to arrive safely, not after what happened with her mother. As she walked, she kept one hand on the horseshoe wand tucked into her waistband. Ren Monroe had no plans of being caught off guard.

Instead of danger, though, the city offered its most enchanting self. The sun had just dipped below the shoulders of the nearest buildings. Street lanterns were being lit, one by one. No enchantments, as it was done in Kathor's Lower Quarter. Just an old man busying himself with a task that would charm a new world onto the streets for the evening. Ren navigated over three separate bridges before sensing a subtle shift in her surroundings. The call of hawkers vanished. The market sprawl fell away. Here, she saw couples on evening strolls. A mother was kneeling down, tending to a child who was eager to get back to his play. Ahead, she spied the crowded fish house that was her destination.

The place was known, rather charmingly, as the Severed Head. Mat Tully's note had boasted about the quality of their bread, and Ren saw plenty of seated customers ripping great chunks of sourdough to be dipped into a variety of spiced chowders. It all smelled delightful.

Ren did not allow such comforts to dull her senses. As Mat flagged her down, she eyed the rest of the restaurant, memorizing where people were seated and at what angles. She would not be taken by surprise if Mat Tully turned out to be less trustworthy than she hoped. Mat had already had a glass of wine and now he was sipping a second. Apparently, her poor contact had enough money for drinks.

"You came," he said with a wide smile. "I wasn't sure you would."

Ren shrugged into a chair. "I'm here. Did you locate them?"

Mat let out a laugh. "Gods. Always so serious. Yes. It wasn't easy, though. They'd left their last apartment for another. Pretty common around here. There's a lot of price shifting. Landlords will gouge someone if they feel like they've come into more money. It's not regulated at all. . . ."

Ren made a noise. "While I do find city ordinances fascinating, I'd like to remain focused on the task at hand."

That earned another laugh from Mat. "Of course, of course. I visited their old flat. For a small fee, I learned that a woman named Cath Invernette stopped by to provide their new address for . . ." Mat frowned midthought. He tugged a journal out of his breast pocket, flipped a few pages, and found the note. ". . . for a shipment of fabric? She wanted to be sent word if the delivery arrived at the old address."

While Ren would have preferred to make first contact in a public setting—a business or out for drinks at a tavern—she would certainly not turn up her nose at a home address. She also mentally noted the name Cath Invernette. Was that an alias? A contact? A friend?

"Is it far from here?"

Instinctively, Ren reached for the journal. Mat was quick, though. He leaned back in his chair and tucked the journal back in his pocket. A broad grin surfaced.

"Apologies. Nothing against you, Ren, but I need the money first. The Winters family has shattered my trust in the concept of future payments. I have no plans of being stiffed again."

Ren nodded. "Fair enough. How much?"

"Make me an offer."

It was an annoying tactic, even if it was clever. He had no idea how much money Ren had in reserve for this supposed mission with House Brood. Mat certainly knew just how deep their coffers were, but forcing her to make the first offer was a fine test. Too low and he'd never take her seriously. He might even doubt her story about working for the Broods. Too high, though, and Ren and her mother would be left with very little money to navigate back home with. She could not access all her accounts while in Ravinia.

"I can pay two hundred—but only if you escort me directly to the address."

His eyebrows shot up. "Really? That's all? You're about to be handed the actual location of the people you're searching for—and you can only spare a day's wage?"

"I have other means of finding them," Ren noted. "Dahvid fights in the gladiator pits. All I have to do is attend a match. . . ."

Mat's grin widened. "He's scheduled to fight two weeks from now. If you can afford to wait that long—and pay for room and board—then surely you can do better than two hundred."

"Four hundred," Ren said through gritted teeth. "Two days' wages should go a long way for someone without any prospects."

Mat threw a hand over his chest, pretending to be wounded. "I'll take eight, because I get the sense that time is of the essence. I am by far your fastest route to finding them. I can tell you're trying to get to them before someone else does. I don't know why, and honestly, I don't care. But if you want to win whatever race you're in—I'm the one that gets you across the finish line first."

Ren disliked being back in this position. Beholden to the Mat Tullys of the world. And yet, he'd pegged the situation rather perfectly. Besides, there was some small pleasure in spending Landwin Brood's money on his potential undoing. She reached into a pocket and carefully stacked the bills up, one by one. She stopped at six hundred instead of eight, though.

"Final offer."

Mat swiped the money so fast that it barely felt like it had been there at all. He nodded once, drained the last of his wine, and said, "Onward."

"Don't you have to pay for the drink?"

Mat winked at her. "Not if we move with haste."

As he slid out of his seat, Ren scowled. The last thing she needed was a waiter pursuing them through the streets. She set a much smaller coin on the table and followed her unlikely escort. Mat was taller than her, and at a glance, looked at least five years older, even though they were the same age. The city had truly worn him down to the bone, though he wore a fashionable scarf to ward off the growing evening chill, and his boots looked finely polished. The only memories she had to compare with this version were from their time in school. Back then he'd been full-cheeked, a bright and foolish kind of creature. This version had come face-to-face with the real world. It did not suit him.

"I think you'll like them," he was saying. "The Tin'Voris."

Ren frowned. "Oh? Why is that?"

"They're like you. Focused."

"You've managed to make that word sound like a curse. Do you see focus as a bad quality?"

"No, of course not. Obviously, you've ended up in a far better spot than I did. Cheers to you for that. It's just notable. I don't know how else to say it. You were that way in class. You're that way now. It's like you have one thing on your mind and nothing else matters. These two, the Tin'Voris, they're the same way. You'll see what I mean when you meet them."

Ren counted that in their favor and tried her best not to be too bothered by Mat's condescension. She was considering a new topic of conversation when he stopped abruptly. They'd crossed a single bridge and stood within shouting distance of the fish house. She could still smell the baking bread. Without ceremony, Mat gestured to a brown-stoned building on their right.

"That's the one. They live on the third floor. Western corner of the building."

"Seriously? Why'd you arrange our meeting so close to where they lived?"

Mat shrugged. "Why not? I thought it would save time."

Ren felt like that broke some protocol of espionage, though she couldn't logically explain why she was annoyed. It felt like something she'd read in old stories. Maybe she was just nervous. This was what she'd come all this way to do. She thought she'd have a long walk to properly steel herself, but now she stood on the precipice of what would either be a colossal waste of time—or an entirely new path forward. That thought had her heart pounding in her chest.

"Well," Ren finally said. "Lead the way."

Mat faltered. "Really? I thought . . . Don't you want to chat with them privately?"

"Proof of purchase. You can leave after I've seen them with my own eyes."

Mat dramatically adjusted his scarf.

"Oh, fine."

She found herself wishing she'd spent more time with him at school. If they hadn't both been desperately seeking the approval of the chosen ones at Balmerick, maybe they'd have become friends. Or maybe not. As a general rule, Ren didn't like people. She smirked before following Mat into the waiting building.

The interior offered no signs of wealth. The carpets were plain, discolored in places where heavy rains had caused substantial leaks or flooding. The place was almost pure functionality. Long halls that led to a series of separate apartments. Paint-peeling stairs led up to another floor that was an exact replica of the first. The only ornamentation that Ren saw were the knockers on the doors. They were small, made of an iron that verged on the black of night. Each one was a different animal. Hawk, dragon, mongoose . . .

Ren followed Mat to the third floor. All the way down a narrow, poorly lit hallway. He paused in front of the door that supposedly belonged to the Tin'Voris. Their iron knocker was shaped like a wyvern. Her breath caught at the sight. She knew it was unlikely that they'd chosen this particular room. Far more probable that they'd simply taken whatever was available.

But the wyvern felt like a wink of fate. Incredibly difficult to tame. Incredibly useful to the one who could. She'd witnessed the sheer power of these creatures the year before. Out in that wilderness, when Theo's mating dance had nearly worked. Ren remembered the way Theo's stomach had ripped open, all the blood gushing out. Was that how this encounter would inevitably end? Mat Tully was watching her, waiting on her. She quietly set the memory aside.

Reaching for the handle, she knocked.

12

DAHVID TIN'VORI

Dahvid was growing restless.

He recognized this as a quality he'd inherited from his father. As a child, he'd been tasked with observing his father's reception of the daily reports. It was a lesson on how to run an estate. The assumption was that Dahvid would eventually lead the family, even though he wasn't the oldest.

He used to watch his father's countenance as servants detailed the shifting affairs of their house and business. His father never sat for those meetings. Instead, he paced the length of his study. Sometimes, he would completely turn his back on the speaker, tracing an idle finger down the glittering spines of the books he kept in his personal library. No matter how distracted Dahvid's father appeared, though, he never missed a single detail. He used to say that he kept his hands busy to keep his mind still.

Now Dahvid paced their own cramped quarters. He tried not

to dwell on the fact that the three of them lived in an apartment that was smaller than his father's study had been. Cath and Nevelyn were bent over the kitchen table. Dissecting the most recent copy of the *Kathorian* with surgical precision. Nevelyn was the first one to find an article of worth. It detailed the casting choices of an upcoming opera in their old city. The name "Tessa Brood" stared up at them from the third line. Nevelyn carefully extracted the article, holding it out for him. Dahvid accepted the task gladly. He pinned the article up in the closet with the rest and resumed his pacing.

A knock sounded at the door.

All three of them went completely still. It was the natural reaction of prey, he realized. Like a family of deer reacting to the sound of a snapped branch. His jaw tightened at that thought. He hated the idea of them as thin-necked creatures with glassy eyes, simply waiting for their turn to die. That was not the Tin'Vori way, but a decade of surviving had reduced them to this.

Nevelyn nodded once. Cath hastily hid the newspaper as Dahvid glided across the room. He slid one hand through the false pocket by his hip, fingers hovering against the tattoo there just in case. The door opened with a groan. Two people waited in the hall. One was a previous acquaintance: Mat Tully. They'd gotten him properly drunk a few months before. He'd given up a great deal of information, and the rumor was that he'd gotten in trouble for it. Which had Dahvid curiously inspecting the person that Mat had brought with him.

She was short and thin. Her cloak was clasped at the throat by a silver leaf. Her hair stopped at the shoulders, perfectly straight, framing a hawkish face. Dahvid's eyes flicked to her beltline. A horseshoe wand hung in plain sight. And on her wrist, a dragon-forged bracelet. *Those are both vessels.* The silence stretched, and the only one who seemed uncomfortable with it was their old drinking partner. Mat's eyes were darting between the two parties. He was such an impatient creature.

"Dahvid," Mat breathed out. "Good to see you again. . . . I've brought . . ."

The stranger silenced him with a look.

"That's all I need from you, Mat. You may leave."

He slipped back down the hallway like a chastised dog. Dahvid was even more curious now, but still he waited for his sister. A chair groaned behind him. Nevelyn crossed the distance and took her rightful place at his side. Ever since losing Ava, she'd been forced to step into the role of spokesperson. Dahvid knew she didn't like it.

"Well?" Nevelyn asked bluntly. "Who are you?"

"My name is Ren Monroe. I am the enemy of your enemy. I came here to talk."

Dahvid felt a small thrill in his chest. They'd been waiting for this moment. Naturally, they'd formed and set their own plan into motion. But they'd also hoped desperately for some sign that there were others in their position. People who despised the Broods. Potential alliances. He glanced at Nevelyn. She looked far more skeptical. Of course. It could be a trap.

"Ren Monroe," Nevelyn repeated. "Are we supposed to recognize that name?"

"Maybe. Depends on how long you've been collecting those newspapers."

Dahvid fought the urge to look over his shoulder. He knew

the paper had been put away, so how could the girl know about their research? Ren's voice cut through his thoughts.

"But truly, no. I am no one of consequence. Most Kathorians had never heard of me until last year. I was one of two Balmerick students to survive a malfunctioning portal spell. Four others died. We trekked back through the wilderness. That is also when I bonded to Theo Brood."

The name drew out something visceral inside Dahvid. He felt his entire body constrict. This was not a casual reference. The stranger was claiming an intimate connection to the Brood family.

Bond magic. Which makes her one of them.

Nevelyn reached out just as Dahvid started to move. Her fingertips clawed into his left bicep. It was just enough pain to drag him back to the surface. Out from the blinding rage that was starting to color the entire room.

"You married a Brood?" Nevelyn asked. "And you expected what from us? Sympathy? I believe you've come to the wrong place."

"No. Not married. Bonded."

That was an odd distinction. Their parents had been bonded. Most bond spells were reserved for incredibly intimate relationships. Kathor might have changed in their absence, but he knew such pacts were normally rare outside of marriage.

"Explain," Nevelyn said.

"It's a long story. I know I'm asking a great deal to be allowed into your home and to have a proper audience with you. Let me make it easier."

Ren reached slowly for the wand at her hip. The girl carefully unclasped the bracelet too. Dahvid's finger hovered over his tattoo the entire time, but as they watched, she tossed her vessels onto the floor at Nevelyn's feet.

"There. I am at your mercy now."

Dahvid couldn't help smirking. This was either very clever or very foolish. He couldn't decide which. Nevelyn weighed the girl one more time and then stepped aside.

"Have it your way."

Ren Monroe didn't hesitate. She walked straight into the waiting jaws of the Tin'Vori family. Weaponless. The decision had shifted the dynamic. Now she was their prey. Nevelyn shot him a quick look that said: *Stay on your toes and quit smiling so much.*

They'd had a hundred conversations like this one. Former Kathorians who'd made a new life in Ravinia. Some were exiles. Others just preferred life in a free port that had fewer rules and less oversight. Together they had carefully extracted information from everyone they could. Even the smallest details might color in what the newspapers didn't. So far, this was their most dangerous visitor. Which made her the most intriguing to him.

"And you're the youngest sister?" Ren asked, her eyes on Cath.

Nevelyn bristled. "No. This is Cath Invernette. A dear friend. Our sister died when we first arrived in Ravinia. Another casualty of the Broods. First, they took Ware, and then they took her."

Ren looked shocked. "They killed her?"

"Not with a blade," Nevelyn answered. "Or poison. But they're guilty all the same. She was sick. We had no money. We'd been on the run for so long. We had no way to take proper care of her when it happened. . . . But that was not the topic of our discussion, was it? You were about to explain why we should let you walk back out of here alive."

Their guest didn't flinch at that threat. She appeared fearless. *She must know something,* Dahvid thought. *To walk in here with such confidence.*

"I am tied to the Brood family, but not without controversy," Ren began. "Last year, there was an accident at Balmerick. The public portal spell malfunctioned. I was one of six students who were lost as a result. In the Dires. We were hunted the entire journey home. Theo was one of the other six. We were the only two who survived."

"I read about that," Cath blurted out. "They searched the entire campus."

Dahvid saw Nevelyn set a hand on Cath's leg under the table. A quiet reminder to not give away more information than necessary. Dahvid shifted uncomfortably when their guest smiled.

"No one knew what happened or where we'd gone. We had to cross back over a mountain range to get home. I used all the magic stored in my vessels, but we were still being pursued. Theo had plenty of ockleys left. Before the final battle, he bonded with me. He needed my spellwork to survive what happened."

"So the bond was forced?" Nevelyn asked. There was a subtle note of disappointment in her voice. "You realize that bonds can be severed? That's what the Broods will do. Unless you come from a family of proper standing."

"I don't," Ren confirmed. "My parents lived in the Lower Quarter. Worked on the docks. I was a scholarship student at Balmerick. You're absolutely right. I am not a good fit for their family at all. Landwin Brood would happily get rid of me."

Nevelyn did not bother to hide her scowl. "Then what use are you to us?"

"He can't get rid of me, because Theo is in love with me."

Dahvid barely held back a smile. It was a rather fine turn in the conversation. He could tell their guest had been working up to that—and he could tell she had more secrets to share. It was hard to maintain a casual air when he knew this could be what they'd been waiting for all this time.

"Congratulations," Nevelyn said. "Theo Brood is lovesick over you. The two of you are bonded. It doesn't explain the only thing that matters: Why did you come *here*?"

It was the right question. If she was telling the truth, then she had a clear-cut path toward wealth, familial standing, and more. Why risk that by coming to see them? Dahvid felt desire burning in his chest. A fire that wanted to become a roaring flame. He desperately wanted her to give the right answer to their question. Ren Monroe offered another mysterious smile.

"I am here because I do not want to join House Brood. I want to destroy it."

13

NEVELYN TIN'VORI

Nevelyn thought it was too good to be true.

She could sense Dahvid's excitement. It was like a living thing, pulsing and hungry in the air between them. This strange girl had traveled up the coast, searched their city, all to find them. Now she was holding a mirror up to their deepest desire, perfectly reflecting back the very goal they'd been hoping to accomplish for over a decade? It was in Dahvid's nature to trust fate. He thought this was how the world worked—in spite of all the tragedies they'd suffered. Fortune favored the bold. Favored people like him. But Nevelyn was not so easily swayed. The curse of being the forgotten middle sister was that she'd long been a skeptic of the world.

This was all far too convenient.

"Why would you want that?"

"House Brood is responsible for my father's death," Ren answered. "He got in Landwin Brood's way, and he was killed for it. I was only eight. When I learned what really happened, I made it my life's mission to destroy them. It's why I went to Balmerick in the first place."

"What a story," Nevelyn replied. "It has just the right amount of drama. Believability. Most convenient of all: it is a story we have no way of authenticating."

For the first time, she saw hesitation. Ren Monroe had been so bold from the very beginning. Now she weighed something. An important decision was being made.

"Trust is difficult, especially when you've been running as long as the two of you have. I will not pretend to know what you've been through. My story is not your story, even if I believe we share the same goal. What if I tell you something that I've told no one else? Perhaps we can begin building a trust between each other."

Nevelyn could not help smiling. At least the girl was interesting.

"Try us."

"The portal spell . . . it didn't malfunction. I altered it. My original intention was to draw Theo Brood and Clyde Winters out into the wilderness with me. Two heirs of two major houses. I was hoping to demonstrate my abilities and earn a position. Once I had my footing, I could begin the process of tearing them apart from the inside out. But Clyde died inside the waxways.

"Theo became my only path forward. From that point on, I treated him like a mark. I carefully forced him to rely on me. I even persuaded him to bond with me. He thinks that I'm also in love with him. Landwin Brood rightfully suspects me. He has done his best to keep me isolated. I have money to spend, but no one I've met would dare challenge the Brood family. I need you as much as you need me."

Nevelyn turned those details around in her mind, attempting to fit them into the grand scheme of everything else they knew and had planned. "You assume a great deal."

"Do I?" Ren performed a brief inspection of their apartment. "I'm pretty sure I've made only two assumptions. The first is that you have very little money. No offense, but this is no summer palace. I don't see any paintings on the walls. No silk sheets on the beds. Unless you've found some other mysterious benefactor, you have nowhere close to the kind of wealth you'll need to take on the Broods. They're a centuries-old dynasty. Their estate is protected by every enchantment you could imagine. They have an army of guards at their disposal. Anger only goes so far without coin to back it. You need my money and my connections."

Nevelyn resisted looking around their dismal flat. She knew all the details confirmed Ren's guess. Her own jacket was missing a button. The partition separating their beds looked cheap and threadbare. Her first thought, upon seeing Ren at their door, had been: *Gods, that's a proper cloak.* There was no point in denying this particular claim. It was obvious.

"The other assumption," Ren continued, "is the more important one. I assumed that you were like me. That you carry what happened to you in your bones. It physically *hurts* me to know that Landwin Brood still walks this world. Sometimes I wake up and I can't breathe, because the only thing there's room for in my chest is hate. I will not stop until I've burned his entire world to the ground."

Nevelyn leaned back in her chair. It was strange to hear her thoughts spoken by someone else so clearly and with such venom. That was exactly how she felt about Thugar Brood. Nevelyn had killed him a thousand different ways in her mind. Watched him die over and over again. But dreams alone would not satisfy that sort of hunger. Blood was demanded.

"I want to believe you," Nevelyn finally said. "Dahvid. Let us test our new friend."

Her brother had been waiting for this moment. He strode to the center of the room. They all watched as he closed his eyes in concentration. He reached out and grazed the tattoo on his right wrist. Magic whispered through the air. Light formed— pulsing briefly—in the shape of a sword.

When Dahvid gripped the handle, it shivered from something gossamer into a hardened substance. He leveled the weight of that unnaturally bright metal and approached their guest. Nevelyn couldn't help smiling. She saw the way the girl's fingers stretched, eager to reach for that horseshoe wand that was no longer at her belt. Finally, proper fear. They might have a shared hatred—but Ren Monroe needed to know the Tin'Voris were not her pets. They would suffer no one else's rule over their plans, no matter how helpful they promised to be.

"Do you know what this is?" Dahvid asked. His voice always grew quiet when he was wielding a weapon. As if he was afraid of waking up the violence too soon.

"It's a sword," Ren answered.

"It is a *moral* sword."

Their guest let out an unexpected laugh. Nevelyn and Dahvid exchanged a glance as the girl covered her mouth. "I'm sorry. It's not you. A matter of personal irony. I had an argument with someone last year on the subject of moral swords.

There are some famous stories about them. The tale of Maxim and Rowan is a favorite of mine."

Dahvid nodded. "Perhaps you'll leave with a story of your own. My version of the sword is quite simple. I have channeled the concept of *truth* into the blade. It takes that concept and makes a god out of it. The metal bows only to truth now. It will obey no other natural law before that one. Nevelyn is going to ask you some questions. It is paramount that you tell the truth. After every answer, I will swing this sword. If you have told the truth, no harm will come to you. But if you've lied . . ."

He offered that famous Dahvid shrug. The one he used to say a thousand different things. This time Nevelyn knew his shoulders were saying: *We'll be cleaning your blood off the floors all night.* Ren Monroe surprised her again. She stood and strode purposefully into the range of his blade.

"Ask your questions."

The weapon's light pulsed in response. Dahvid looked back to Nevelyn for approval. She desperately wished Ava were still with them. Even if she was the youngest, Ava had a knack for reading people that both Dahvid and Nevelyn lacked. They'd both learned to lean on her charm after escaping from Kathor, and that habit had left them both unpolished for navigating the political. Nevelyn could only do her best. She tried to summon a confidence she did not feel.

"We'll start with a simple question. Are you truly bonded to Theo Brood?"

"Yes."

Dahvid brought his sword sweeping down in a diagonal blow that would have taken their guest's arm off at the elbow.

No blood spilled. There was no scream. The sword swished through empty air. Dahvid rotated the sword and carefully reset his stance.

"How did you first learn about us?"

"An old lady at a party told me the rumor of Dahvid being an image-bearer."

Another swing. The sword swished again.

"Are you a spy?"

"No."

Swish.

"Did the Broods send you here?"

"No."

Swish.

"Do the Broods know you are in Ravinia?"

"No."

But right before Dahvid could swing, the girl recoiled.

"Wait. I'm sorry. I don't know the answer to that. I believe that I left Kathor without their notice, but it's possible they have spies at the docks in Ravinia. I haven't led them here intentionally, but I can't answer your question with complete certainty."

Dahvid didn't swing. He shrugged over at Nevelyn instead. "The answer is too complicated. The sword might cut through her by accident. Ask something else."

What he meant is that even the smallest, most unintended lie would result in a lost limb. Nevelyn considered her next question. "What do you really want?"

Ren stared back at her. "I want to remove the Broods from power and take over their estate. I plan to use their wealth as a foundation for eliminating the other great houses. That includes the houses that helped the Broods raid your home and destroy your family."

Dahvid swung—and even Nevelyn saw the hesitation in the blow—like he was worried she was lying and this was all about to end in a bloody mess. But the sword hissed straight through the air again. Nevelyn took note that Ren's hatred extended beyond the Broods, to all the great houses. She did not point out that they'd once been exactly that.

"Why would you choose to work with us?"

"The Broods have mastered Kathor. It is their game board. They know all the players and control all the potential outcomes. But the two of you are pieces they aren't familiar with. You are unknown quantities with unknown abilities. Dahvid, of course, is an image-bearer . . . but Nevelyn, you possess powers as well. You used them on my mother this morning."

Nevelyn offered no reaction to that. No denial or confirmation. Her throat bobbed slightly, because it was a secret that even Dahvid did not fully understand about her. She'd been too cavalier if she'd allowed this stranger into some knowledge of her gift. Unlucky, really, that there had been a secondary witness to the small spell she'd performed this morning. The nature of her gift was that the person she used it on normally forgot, but she could not extend her spell to a party that she hadn't known was there. Clearly, she'd been too reckless.

Ren continued. "The two of you are my best chance at surprising them. I want to introduce an entirely new game. I want to make my own rules. I'm pretty sure that's the only way to beat them."

Dahvid didn't swing. He was too busy listening.

"Are you using us?" Nevelyn probed. "For your own benefit?"

"Of course."

Again, Dahvid didn't move. Her answer was clear, almost too blunt.

"Then how could we ever fully trust you?"

"You can't. I am going to use you," she said. "And you are going to use me. It's that simple. I don't think I can take down House Brood without help, but neither can you."

Once more, the answer was clear. It did not need to be put to the test. At the very least, Ren Monroe was good at making promises. Nevelyn had just one more question.

"Theo Brood. You said you don't love him."

Ren remained silent. At first, Nevelyn thought she'd finally trapped her. The one snag in this perfect presentation. But then she realized she hadn't actually asked a question. She turned over the words in her mind. She would have to frame it just so.

"Will you stand aside? If we have to kill him?"

"If it means the destruction of House Brood?" Ren said, altering the question slightly. "I will stand aside."

Dahvid swung his great sword one more time. Nevelyn closed her eyes. There was no sound of iron biting into flesh. None of the gut-wrenching noises she'd become accustomed to hearing down in the gladiator pits. Ren Monroe was telling them the truth. Finally, a proper ally. Dahvid let his sword whisper out of existence. Nevelyn blinked against the after-image of it hanging in the air. Ren Monroe allowed herself a triumphant smile.

"Now it's my turn. I have no moral sword to test you, but my concern has less to do with truth. I need to know you're the right investment to make. You both possess unique abilities. I am quite adept at magic myself, but talent will only get us so far. I would like to know what you were planning to do. What revenge did you have in mind?"

Nevelyn knew it was a fair question to ask them, but it grated against every instinct they'd followed over the past decade. Even Cath didn't know the entirety of their plan. Just the parts they'd allowed her to know. She felt goose bumps crawling down the back of her neck.

This path had been carefully determined. Years of painstaking effort. Starvation, sacrifices, and loss. Inviting someone else into those secrets felt like kissing disaster right on the lips. But she knew there were choke points in their plan where a lack of money could ruin everything. An infusion of capital would smooth those rougher edges, and Ren Monroe had just proven herself worthy of their trust. Dahvid usually left these decisions to her. She was the careful planner, their great architect. But this felt like a matter of the heart. All instinct. And that was his domain.

The two of them locked eyes. Dahvid nodded his approval.

"Follow me," Nevelyn said.

It was a short distance. She led Ren to the lonely closet on the other side of the flat. A variety of clothing samples hung there, on which Nevelyn had been practicing dyeing techniques. She shoved them aside and stepped back. Ren Monroe actually gaped at what she saw.

The wall was covered—floor to ceiling—with their research. Every article that had ever mentioned the Broods, carefully highlighted and organized. Maps they'd stolen from architects they'd gotten drunk. Sketches of family trees with each name written in Cath's precise handwriting. It was the collective effort of seven years of rigorous study. Nevelyn took a deep breath before crossing over to where a larger map of their continent hung. All of Delvea stretched out before them. She had to stand on the tips of her toes to set a finger on Ravinia, the northernmost port of the continent. Patiently, she began dragging it down and to the right. She paused before reaching Kathor. At nearly the halfway point between the two cities, slightly inland, sitting in the shadow of the great mountains there.

"Our plan begins here," Nevelyn said. "Have you ever heard of a town called Nostra?"

Ren Monroe surprised them with another loud laugh. There was a little madness in the sound. Nevelyn waited for the strange noise to fade. Dahvid didn't look concerned. He was grinning in the doorway as if he was already in on the joke.

"Nostra," Ren repeated, a little breathless. "It would seem fate is with us. As of two days ago, there was a changing of the guard at Nostra. A new watcher was placed there."

Dahvid and Nevelyn exchanged worried glances. She silently cursed their bad luck. They'd researched the old watcher of the valley extensively. He was the very fulcrum of their plan.

"Don't look so worried," Ren finished. "The new watcher is Theo Brood."

PART TWO

The Strategy

14

REN MONROE

Their plan proceeded like the first, gentle turnings of a set of carriage wheels. Ren's first duty was to do nothing. A most infuriating task. But she'd discussed this with the Tin'Voris before parting from Ravinia. She knew when she returned to Kathor, she'd be watched more closely than ever.

Landwin Brood reacted as expected. It was a great delight to realize that he didn't actually know where she'd gone. The Brood scouts followed her with a deliberate lack of caution as Ren led them on a rather boring hunt. Nothing she did connected to their larger plan. It was her mother who was executing the first crucial steps instead. Ren just hoped she was being properly thorough about it.

One of the other unexpected consequences of her brief disappearing act was a slew of invitations. A letter for this dance or that gala. A birthday party one night in the Heights, followed by a wedding the next day in Safe Harbor. Landwin Brood was clearly shifting his tactics. He would rather welcome her into those circles of power than lose track of her in the city at large. Ren would occasionally raise her glass from across the room, offering a smirk, just to screw with him.

She was also forced to walk right into Landwin's trap for her daytime hours. The invitation that had come before Theo left for Nostra wasn't one that she could turn down. It was a prestigious research position. Lacking any alternative, Ren accepted.

And so—two weeks after her encounter with the Tin'Voris— she found herself walking up the steps of the Peeress Observatory. She'd been here before. The entire first floor was a museum that cataloged the history of magic. Primary schools came here at least once a year. Ren doubted she'd have time to take a tour. Her lettered invitation directed her to the basement of the building instead. There were two paladins posted at the door for security. She saw the markings of the Brightsword Legion on their uniforms. Her papers were quickly checked and approved. The guard shoved open the looming double doors.

The hallway deposited her into a far wider room. The ceilings were relatively low, but the actual space was staggeringly large. Ren wasn't even sure she could see the opposite wall, which meant this underground wasn't connected only to the museum but to several buildings. The entire space could have comfortably fit several thousand people.

Her first impression was that it was completely empty. There were no walls dividing the room. Not even support columns to keep it from caving in. Just a great, vast emptiness. It took a few moments to notice the small displays. They were like odd little pieces of art. The nearest one was a single leather chair smattered with some kind of berry compote. Just beyond that, she spied a dozen ropes dangling from the ceiling. All of them were carefully twining together with the help of unseen hands.

Each new curiosity drew her deeper into the cavernous space. Only after passing a dozen similar oddities did she spy the other researchers. The group stood in the far corner of the room, all gathered around the base of a wide tree. Its uppermost branches brushed the low-hanging ceiling. As Ren approached, one of the figures detached smoothly from the others.

He was devastatingly good-looking. Nearly a head taller than her. The smile he offered was as sharp and pretty as any knife. Every angle of him was perfectly complemented by a tailored brown suit, which happened to match his eyes. Ren thought she was woefully underdressed in comparison.

"Hello. You must be the newest addition to the team." He sidestepped a small bucket that appeared to be filled to the brim with discolored forks. "I'm Ellison Proctor."

They shook hands. Ren recognized the name. He was the older brother of Ash Proctor. An image of Cora knifed through her memory with brutal quickness. She could see the girl walking beside her in the woods, shyly discussing her own opinions about the best-looking students back at Balmerick. Cora had claimed that Ash Proctor was one of the most handsome, but she'd taken him down a few notches for having small hands. It was the last time they'd all had a good laugh together, before all the dying. Ren swallowed once and slammed that dark cabinet of her mind shut.

She recovered just in time to shake Ellison Proctor's hand.

"Ren Monroe," she said. "It's a pleasure. I'm excited to work with you."

There was a small outburst from the group. Ellison grinned at her.

"Come on. I'll introduce you to your team. I'm more of a property manager here. Day-to-day magical maintenance. *These* are your fellow researchers."

He led her back to the waiting group. Ren quietly adjusted the collar of her shirt before following. It was a great relief to find that the others were not dressed in suits, or anything fancy at all. Ellison made a *Wait one moment* gesture as they reached the group. No one else looked her way. All of their attention was determinedly fixed on the tree. Ren spied traces of magic in the air.

The tree was being forced to blossom. She recognized the brightney apples that dominated the valleys south of Kathor. They started out small and bloodred, but as the spell accelerated their growth, each one colored in with the traditional white speckles. All but one.

Ren thought she saw the shape of the experiment. A single apple began to shrivel unnaturally. Far more rotten than normal. Red faded to brown, deepened to black. She saw it shriveling and twisting until it looked like a curse from a fairy tale.

"The moment of truth," one researcher announced. Ren noted the woman was by far the oldest in the group. "Time to see if you were worth the money, Pecking."

One of the other researchers snorted. Ren watched curiously. This wasn't a particularly new application of magic. The law of guided decay was very established agricultural magic. It channeled instances of rot from the collective group to a singular entity. Instead of twelve half-decent apples, an application from this category of spells would assure the harvester of one grotesque apple, but eleven others that were mostly flawless.

The common mistake, Ren knew, was in pushing the spell too far. That was on the verge of happening now. The spell had clearly been cast too wide. The decaying apple was preparing to hit a natural threshold. It was fully dead. Something so withered could not accept any more rot. Ren felt the subtle flick of magic in the air as a secondary spell activated.

Usually a severance charm came next. The apples would continue to grow naturally from that point on. A few of them might suffer the occasional imperfection, but most of the potential rot and disease would be mitigated by the first apple. Farmers had accepted this ratio as their standard for decades.

Except the second spell wasn't a severance charm at all. Ren heard an uncharacteristic pop. The apple directly above the first one started to fade and brown. As the process repeated, there was a raucous cheer from those gathered. The other researchers crowded around and slapped the back of the youngest-looking person in the room—just a boy to Ren's eyes. He couldn't have been a day over sixteen. His round cheeks blushed violently at their outburst.

"Great work," the older woman said. "Go ahead and get the secondary studies going. I want this to be foolproof before you present it. You've got something here, Pecking. Excellent work."

The woman's attention swung in Ren's direction. She had silver-streaked hair and her eyes narrowed to dark slits. She looked familiar, but Ren couldn't summon a name under such scrutiny. The woman didn't offer to shake hands. Instead, she gave a perfunctory nod.

"The Broods finally decide to come play," the woman said.

"And who do they send? Not one of the heirs. Not a prized cousin or a genius nephew. They send me *you*."

Ren had been prepared for any number of opening statements. This was not one of them. She felt a slumbering animal rise in her chest. All the years of anger and mistreatment back to a steady boiling. She set her jaw and said nothing.

"Tell me what you just saw," the woman demanded.

The boy—Pecking—was beside his prized tree, carefully examining the results. The other researchers, both older than Ren, waited intentionally in earshot. She saw the two of them exchange looks. They wanted to hear how Ren's first test went. Like most of her peers at Balmerick, they appeared all too ready to glut themselves on her failure. It only made her angrier.

"He used the common guidance spell for decay," Ren began. "Instead of using a severance charm, though, he added . . ." It had been some time since she'd done this. Class had kept her sharp and on her toes. Pressured her into being the best. She was rusty. "A proximity spell . . . with a directional overflow charm."

Pecking was watching her now too. The older woman's head tilted.

"My great-grandmother tried that combination," she replied. "Nearly a century ago. It didn't work then and it won't work now. Come on. Try harder. What's the missing spell?"

Ren felt like that combination of spells should have worked. Why wouldn't it be enough? Her mind scrambled for another answer. What else could there be?

"How about this," the woman said, cutting off Ren's thoughts. "You have until the end of the day to figure it out. If you give up, feel free to leave early and don't bother coming back. But until you figure out the answer, I won't take you on for this role. I do not have time to waste on the Broods' bottom-feeders. We all pull our weight here."

Ren tried not to be stung by that final accusation. The woman paced off in the direction of one of the other displays. The other researchers took that as a sign to scatter. Ellison Proctor hovered awkwardly beside her.

"Well. Good luck," he said. "I'd enjoy seeing you again."

He left her there, staring at the tree and the cherublike boy beneath it. Ren shook herself. It was like rattling a cage. Waking up some dormant creature in her chest. There was no time to seethe over being called a bottom-feeder. She'd learned this lesson at Balmerick. The only defiance that counted in their world was the sort of defiance that led to results. She thought back through spell combinations and possibilities. Truly, there were hundreds of categories of spell types—under which hundreds of subcategories existed. Even if she could research for months, it was possible she wouldn't stumble upon the right answer.

She waited for Pecking to back away from the tree before making her own approach. She half hoped there'd be some trace of his magic in the air. But whatever he'd done was far too complicated to parse. All she could do was examine the two pieces of rotten fruit. There were no real clues there, other than the fact that they were side by side, and the second apple had not rotted quite as extremely as the first. Ren circled the tree twice before realizing Pecking was watching her. His eyes flicked over to where the head researcher stood, then back to Ren.

"I could just tell you," he whispered, round face betraying no emotion. "The answer."

Ren snorted. She knew from experience that help like that would never come for free. There was also the simple and annoying matter of pride. If this boy could figure it out, so could she.

"No, thank you."

He blushed a little. Or maybe his cheeks were permanently that color?

"She just wants you to say that you don't know," he whispered back. "She gave us all a question like this. When we first came here. She wants you to say you don't know, because then she can begin teaching you."

Maybe he was really trying to help, or maybe he was doing his best to get rid of her. It was not a coin she could afford to flip. She sat down in front of the tree and closed her eyes. When Pecking sighed and walked away, she set to the task of solving the impossible. It was like unpacking old boxes, long covered in dust. All the information was still there, but that didn't mean it was sorted and set out quite as neatly as it had been during her school days.

As she searched the rows of her mind, the others went about their normal tasks. Nearly every experiment received a visit. At first, Ren had not understood their random array about the room. Ellison Proctor was the answer to that question. He spent most of his time along the exterior walls. He'd pause at very specific intervals and perform the same, repetitive spell, before continuing around the room. Ren had been idly observing him when the larger image fell into place. The room was one massive grid. There were no walls or corridors or hallways, but there was magic. Unseen spells sectioning off each experiment in its own tidy square. The perfect layout just made her want to be a part of all this even more.

The woman who'd assigned Ren her task vanished during the middle of the day. Ren had no appetite for lunch, but the head researcher's absence brought the other two circling back like a pair of curious vultures. Ren realized they were siblings.

"Any guesses yet?" the sister asked. "Or did Pecking already slip you the answer?"

The brother snorted. "Bet he asked her on a date, too."

"He didn't tell me anything," Ren replied. "I'm working it out myself."

That led to another exchange of grins. The sister twirled her hair with one finger.

"So. You're Ren Monroe."

Ren stared back at her. "I am."

"Heard you got lost in the woods last year."

The brother snickered. "Gods, Maryan. Have some manners."

"What?" The girl—Maryan—sneered back at him. "It's just a fact. It's not like I'm making fun of her or something. She literally *was* lost in the woods."

"Forgive my sister," the brother said, ignoring the explanation. "She's never been a very social creature. My father considered giving her away when she was young. No one would take her."

"Shove off, Flynn. She's not going to sleep with you just because you think you're funny."

Ren couldn't help smiling. She'd expected everyone in this place to be prim and proper. These two felt more comfortable to her than any of the others.

"Anyways," Maryan said. "The Broods picked you as their goat, huh?"

Ren frowned. "I'm not sure what you mean."

"This is the Kathorian Collective," Maryan answered. "A mutual research endeavor shared by all the major houses, without exception. Well, the exception *was* the Brood family. Obviously. Until you came."

"Right," Ren said. "The Kathorian Collective. So we're sharing our research with each other? Everyone's notes are public? How does that make me a goat?"

"She didn't read the fine print," Flynn said. He shook his head. "No one ever reads the fine print."

"How could you *not* read the fine print?" Maryan echoed.

"There was no fine print. I just had a standard invitation."

"The Broods probably signed the contract on your behalf," she said. "Can they do that? Who knows? Guess they can do whatever they want. Yes, it means we share research. New spells and all that. But the only reason all the houses agreed to participate was through a contractual obligation of mutual exposure. Which means you can be interrogated by the other major houses, whenever they want, and they're allowed to ask you anything. They can even use manipulators to extract the truth from you. Anything short of literal torture."

Flynn was studying Ren. "She still doesn't get it. Maybe she's not that smart?"

"And you said I don't have manners?" Maryan scowled at him. "Gods, Flynn. I'm sure the Broods sold it as some kind of honor, but you can say goodbye to being involved in any important house functions. As long as you're contractually working here, it means they're not going to let you in on any other private affairs, because that would risk something secretive coming out in an interrogation session."

They heard the distant sound of a door opening and closing. All three of them looked back, across the vast and open space. The head researcher had returned. Ren could hear her shoes click-clacking across the stones in the distance.

"Back to work," Flynn muttered. "Sorry to be the bearers of bad news. But really, you should have asked to read the contract. Who doesn't ask to read the contract?"

Maryan shoved him away. "It's not that bad. All the magic is brilliant down here, at least."

The two of them shuffled off, leaving Ren alone once more. The news should have been a bigger blow, but she'd already been ostracized by the Brood family. This move was a simple act of solidification. A far more official and logical reason to keep her isolated. She thought it quite clever.

But the more fascinating detail was that the Broods had not been participating in this so-called collective. They'd held out until her arrival. Which meant she would exist in this space unobserved. Unless one of the others spied for them? That felt unlikely. It was a small taste of freedom, but it shivered pleasurably down her spine, nonetheless.

Work resumed. The others orbited the room. She continued to hunt for the right answer until she felt like she'd exhausted every option. Sighing, Ren flagged down the older woman. She crossed over to Ren with a look that could have withered every flower for sale on Market Row.

"What? Quitting already?"

Ren shook her head. "I've arrived at my best possible guess.

I didn't think it made sense to delay. I am not going to think of a better answer."

The woman crossed her arms. "Go on, then."

"He used all the spells I mentioned earlier. Everything would be corded together. And then . . . I think he would have had to use a veracity altercation spell. Kind of like the one they used when they moved Balmerick University. I think he needed to lie to the second apple."

"Expand."

That was one of Ren's favorite words in the entire world.

"The second apple would have sensed the flow of decay entering the first apple. There was an established magical direction. Health comes this way. Rot goes that way. The original versions that attempted to expand on the spell didn't work, because the second apple *resisted* the fate of the first one. Not necessarily because it's sentient but rather because there's an established magical flow. It would recognize any attempts at redirection and reject them. Adding a veracity spell would convince the second fruit that the rotten flow . . . will be good for it? I don't know. That's the best I could come up with. . . ."

Ren knew it sounded absurd, but then the wizards who'd first suggested using that same spell for Balmerick's foundations had been greeted with doubt too. The woman snorted in response.

"So . . . you're not just the dregs of House Brood."

Ren lifted an eyebrow. "Was I right?"

"It took Pecking a whole damn year to figure that out. What a colossal waste of time. Gods. All right, be back here tomorrow. I want three new spells you'd like to work on—and the coinciding experiments that might help test them." She gestured around the room. "I can get you just about any imaginable material, but you can see our testing sites are limited in size. Unlock your imagination. Bring me something with teeth. My name is Seminar. Welcome to the Collective."

Ren's brain stumbled to a halt before she could properly celebrate her own success.

"Seminar? Wait. Like . . . *Seminar Shiverian?*"

The older woman nodded. "Do you know anyone else who's been saddled with that atrocity of a name? If you do, let me know. Maybe we could form some kind of support group."

"But . . . I mean . . . you practically *invented* the structural magic systems. I've read so much . . . We studied your spells in all of my advanced classes. . . . You're a legend."

"Right. I always forget about this part," Seminar said. "The glow you see emanating from all of my various orifices right now will eventually fade. I work my research team to the bone. We push the limits here. You'll forget all about the fact that I invented the modernized stun spells. Trust me."

Ren's mouth was still hanging open. "I did forget that you invented those. You've invented so many spells that I actually *forgot* you invented modernized stun spells."

Seminar smiled. "Get here on time tomorrow. Good work today."

Ren felt giddy. She knew this entire process was a glittering trap. The Broods were intentionally luring her to some version of a life without Theo, but she was literally researching spells under Seminar Shiverian. She and Ethel Shiverian *were* modern magic. It was an unthinkable honor. Her new advisor paused only long enough to speak with Pecking.

"She figured it out. Took you a bloody year. She figured it out in an afternoon."

Seminar glided past him. Pecking's cheeks colored a violent shade of red. He slammed his tray of instruments down. It was awkward, though. The room was too large. There was no exit nearby. No doors to slam behind him. Instead, he thundered off to the northwestern corner in the most pitiful, prolonged display Ren had ever seen.

She'd managed to impress one of the most accomplished wizards in Kathor. She'd found three new potential friends—none of whom should have any ties back to House Brood. She'd also found a new rival. The last detail was almost comfortable. Like slipping on a pair of old shoes. Her father had once told her that if she had no enemies, she was being too quiet. Ren walked over to Pecking's tree and plucked the finest-looking apple from the bunch. She found she was ravenous after skipping lunch. It was just the thing for the long walk home.

15

DAHVID TIN'VORI

Dahvid wasn't losing exactly.

He just wasn't winning, either.

A hundred hands hung down, banging against the upper walls of the pit. That disgusting mixture of spitted meat and sweat and blood hung in the air. The crowd was growing restless. He could hear that unsatisfied muttering underneath the normal cheers. There'd been excitement at the start, when Dahvid first summoned his sword. And again, when his opponent landed a massive blow. The rest of the fight had been boring and technical and bloodless.

The crowd always preferred to watch someone die.

Dahvid's opponent stood in the very center of the arena. He was a proper paladin. Great footwork. Defensive techniques. Military-trained. He'd clung to the same strategy for the last five minutes. His shield was enhanced by a divinity spell. Even when Dahvid was quick enough to strike past the actual metal—his blade would deflect off the golden light that encircled the shield. It reduced his target zones to almost nothing.

Even the golden spear his opponent wielded was a defensive measure. Every strike he'd made so far was designed to keep Dahvid from getting too close. Throughout the entire fight, he'd unleashed only one truly offensive maneuver. A powerful blow of light-magic that had knocked Dahvid completely off his feet and slammed him into the circular barrier enclosing the pit.

It had been an extension of the divinity spell. Dahvid knew enough about them to know that each person manifested the spell in their own unique way. His opponent had been absorbing each of his blows. After harnessing all that energy, he'd unleashed it back at Dahvid in a single, violent burst.

The fight was veering back toward boredom. Dahvid began a sequence. *Centered downstrike. Rotate to backhanded swipe. Lunge low. Spin out of range. Backpedal.* Each new swing was met by the enhanced shield. His opponent circled calmly. He was clearly waiting for a chance to unleash that absorbed magic a second time. Dahvid couldn't let it continue on this way. Eventually he would tire out and his opponent would go on the offensive.

The restless crowd was his fault. Darling had been advertising his status as an image-bearer ever since Dahvid signed the contract. They'd come here to see him use his tattoos, and Darling had been clever enough to pick an opponent that required him to burn one of them. Everyone knew he was an image-bearer. That was no secret. It was impossible to look at him and not notice the etchings that covered his body. No, the true secret was what was housed inside each tattoo. The kinds of magic that Dahvid could summon. No one but his sisters knew that.

But if using one now was the price of victory, he would pay it.

Dahvid backpedaled to a safe distance and tossed his sword to the side. It stuck in the dirt, point down, well out of reach. His opponent still did not break from his stance.

"Fine. I'll come to you."

He reached through the exposed slit by his stomach. His fingers brushed the perfect circle Cath had drawn on his skin. Magic rippled outward. The ground beneath their feet shook as Dahvid stepped forward into the spear range of his opponent. A perfect circle was forming around him. He saw a hundred different cracks etch in the dusty nothing at their feet. Rippling out in indecipherable patterns. The paladin eyed the spell uncertainly. Dahvid kept closing in on where he stood.

His sword was still plunged in the dirt. Well outside the extending circle. Dahvid stomped his right foot and the spell sealed. The circle was complete. He and the paladin stood perfectly inside it—just a few paces apart.

That's when the actual magic activated. Dahvid felt the spell hit him like a backhand. The paladin took the worst of it, though. The golden light of his divinity shield was snuffed out. His gilded spear flickered to a lifeless gray. Dahvid had cast a null zone. Inside this circle, magic could not exist. It was just the two of them now. Just flesh and bone and metal.

The paladin reacted as expected. A sudden lunge. Dahvid ducked beneath the strike and brought his left fist crashing into an exposed armpit. His opponent cried out, trying to backpedal, but Dahvid seized the top of his shield before he could get outside the circle.

The two of them wrestled over it, adjusting their positions, when Dahvid shoved the metal straight down into the ground. The paladin was so focused on keeping his grip that he didn't brace for Dahvid's headbutt. His opponent's nose broke with a resounding crack. The crowd roared at the sight of blood finally painting the sand. The paladin's arms pinwheeled as Dahvid tossed the shield uselessly aside. The end of this sequence was clear now. Like the unfurling petals of a flower. He could see it all unfolding, as if he stood outside time.

Another desperate stab of the spear. Dahvid sidestepped and broke the paladin's nose a second time. Blood was everywhere. The features of his opponent's face slipped away. Dahvid saw Thugar Brood standing across from him. The taunting leer and the thick beard and the forest-green eyes. That was who he was about to destroy.

He landed blow after blow after blow. Until Thugar Brood was on his knees in the sand. Dahvid's chest heaved. He reached down and dragged the pathetic wretch to the edge of the circle. He tossed him to the ground. Dahvid's sword was waiting there—outside the null zone.

He reached for the handle. It weighed almost nothing. Blood pulsed in his ears. The roar of the crowd thumped in his chest like an anthem. All he could see was Thugar Brood, begging him for a mercy that he'd never shown to Ware. Dahvid licked his lips, set his feet . . .

Reality flickered.

It was not Thugar. It was the paladin with the shattered nose and the wrong-colored hair. A stranger. Dahvid stood there as the crowd chanted for the killing blow. He was about to oblige them when the paladin collapsed sideways. Unconscious.

A few of Darling's medics darted out of one of the entrances. Sometimes a death was necessary to sate the crowd. Most of the time, though, Darling liked his challengers to stay in the rotation. Dahvid allowed his sword to flicker out of existence. He'd given away the knowledge of one of his spells. He knew Darling's people would take note. Likely they had a carefully maintained file on every gladiator, all their strengths and weaknesses and tendencies.

Good, he thought. *Let them believe they know anything about me.*

Dahvid rubbed the dirt and dust of the arena between his hands and left.

As they entered their apartment, Dahvid's eyes flicked over to the left corner. No sarcastic comment issued forth. No raised eyebrow awaited him. Nevelyn was not there. They'd removed her bed to make space for Cath's artwork and Dahvid's morning stretches. Nevelyn had also taken all her cloth materials with her. Every experimental weaving. The absence he felt was more than just a physical one, though.

Ever since their escape from Kathor, Dahvid had always had one of his sisters to guide him. It had been hard enough to lose Ava. She was easy to miss. Bright and cheerful and wild like him. They'd always had a lot in common. Losing Nevelyn was more like losing the functionality of an organ. Something vital ripped out of him. In the past few weeks, he'd found himself turning to ask her opinion—only to realize that she wasn't there. He forced himself to believe they would see each other again.

Before leaving, Nevelyn had also taken all their research on the Broods. She'd left only the information that was relevant to Dahvid's assignment. A list of Darling's favorite gladiators. Notes from fights that Nevelyn had scouted on his behalf. This part of their research would help him in his own impossible task: winning a gauntlet.

Darling's gauntlet was famous in Ravinia. Anyone who came to the warlord and requested to run a gauntlet could not be denied. He welcomed all challengers. The rules were simple. The challenger faced five opponents of Darling's choosing, one at a time. If they made it past the first opponent, they had exactly five minutes to recover before the next fighter entered the arena. If they won all five fights—they could make a single request of Darling. Only three people out of hundreds had ever survived one. The first victor was Agatha Marchment.

A world-renowned blade master who'd made a name for herself in the War of Neighbors. She swept through her gauntlet without taking a single hit. The next day, Darling announced her as the head general overseeing all the gladiator pits. Marchment's one wish had apparently been a percentage of Darling's earnings. The two had worked together for nearly a decade now.

The second was Able Ockley. Dahvid still wished he'd been there to witness that one. The best magical duelist in Kathor. He'd been sent on behalf of the viceroy. Apparently, he hadn't used a blade at all. No shields. No weapons. Only his wand. Long-range spellwork was crucial in larger battles and open warfare, but Dahvid still couldn't imagine how a wizard had navigated close-quarters dueling like that with nothing but a wand. After winning, Ockley had negotiated a very favorable trading partnership for Kathor with the growing freeport.

Finally, there was a brutal giant of a man who went by the nickname Creasy. He won his gauntlet the year before—and Dahvid had been in the crowd to witness it. Creasy had pounded his way through the early rounds, then caught some unbelievable luck in his fourth match when one of Darling's best wizards tripped on his own cloak midspell. The magic backfired and Creasy ended him with a casual stomp of his right boot. What made Creasy's gauntlet unique was that he beat the final opponent—and died mere minutes after. Bled out before the medics could save him. It was a surprise to many when Darling honored the victory. Creasy's sister had been granted a single wish, though no one had ever learned what her request was.

Three victors in all that time. The rest of the challengers were dead. Dahvid intended to be the fourth champion. He would win a gauntlet. He would make his one request.

"Distracted?"

It was Cath's voice coming from the corner of the room. She was seated, working on her sketches. He had drifted again. Drawn through time like a grain of sand in an hourglass. He looked down and realized he was washing his hands in their water basin. Who knew how long he'd been standing there?

"Just thinking."

"You revealed your null spell," Cath noted, eyes back on her art. "Interesting choice."

He grunted in return. "I was just following a hunch."

"You don't think Darling will use a proper wizard? That spell would be very useful against a pure spellcaster."

Dahvid dried his hands on the waist of his shirt. "I don't think he will now. He knows I can eliminate their magic with a single spell. Besides, most of his elite gladiators are brilliant in hand-to-hand. Casting the null circle would limit me, not them. It was the right move."

Cath nodded. "I trust you, Dahvid."

She was focused on her drawing, so she didn't see his entire body shudder involuntarily. *I trust you, Dahvid.* Those had been Ware's last words to him. His brother had looked back over one shoulder with a mischievous grin. Ware had always been such a helplessly restless creature. That night he told Dahvid he needed to get some air. He was walking down to the Lower Quarter for a drink—even though their father had ordered him to stay off the streets. At least until the controversy with Thugar Brood died down. Ware was trusting Dahvid not to snitch to the guards.

He could still imagine his brother's long hair, tossing bright over one shoulder as he turned the corner and slipped out of sight. No one—not even his sisters—knew that Dahvid had secretly followed him through the busy streets of Kathor.

Thugar Brood had come from nowhere. That's what it felt like. One second Ware was alone and happy and nodding to every person he passed. And the next second there was a wall of a human being standing before him. Thugar's foot soldiers fanned out in a half-moon before Dahvid realized what was happening. Ware stood there, completely alone, because Dahvid had kept his secret. None of the house guards had any idea they'd left the estate.

I trust you, Dahvid.

All the stories got it wrong. All the rumors they heard over the years. Ware was no coward. He did not run. He did not cry out or beg for mercy. Instead, he took up his fighting stance.

SCOTT REINTGEN

Dahvid knew that Thugar would have beaten his brother in a fair fight, but it had never been that. One of the foot soldiers came in from Ware's blind side. Another and then another. They rained blows on him until he was sprawled and unconscious in the dust.

Most of the witnesses had fled. Thugar came forward to bind Ware, patiently working the rope around his legs and his feet. Like an animal. Dahvid remained hidden the entire time, too afraid to move. There were too many of them. He was too small. He did not have enough magic. A hundred reasons kept him in the shadows.

I trust you.

"Come," Thugar Brood had said. "I've found the perfect place to plant you in the ground."

A carriage pulled around, kicking up dust. That was when Dahvid finally started forward. Instinct outpaced fear. They were taking his brother. To a place where no one else would witness what they were going to do to him.

Ware was thrown in the covered back of the wagon. There were eyes in every window of every shop, but all of them were cowards like him. Dahvid was halfway to the carriage when it happened. The final guard climbed inside. The driver shouted. The horses all shoved into motion. He started running, but deep down, he didn't really want to catch them. He was so afraid of being thrown in the back of that carriage with Ware. Afraid he would not survive.

He watched them drive around the corner and he knew the only way to save his brother's life was to go back to their father. He would know what to do. Dahvid sprinted the entire way. He had arrived at the Tin'Vori estate, breathless and unprepared for what he saw at the gates. A group of hooded figures were beginning their raid. Fire was everywhere. . . .

"Come back to me, love."

He felt Cath's gentle arms wrap around him from behind. She pressed herself to his back and kept whispering in his ear. Dahvid realized he was standing over the washbasin still. He had been idly rubbing at the bloodstains on his right wrist. Trying and failing to get out the last dark blots. He saw that the sun had quietly set while he'd been lost in memory. Cath held him there until he released a haggard breath. It was like someone who'd been underwater for several minutes and now finally found the surface again. His chest heaved against her grip. Still she held him.

I trust you.

Dahvid allowed Cath to lead him over to the bed. She kissed his cheek. And then his forehead. Kissed until he kissed her back. Until the past was driven out by the taste and smell of the here and now. Until the only fire was between the two of them. Dahvid's lips slid down her neck. She whispered in his ear, "Stay with me. Right here."

He sank back into the pillows, hands grasping at Cath's hair. Nails digging into her shoulders. They pressed against each other, and it felt a lot like he imagined dying would feel. An intensity that destroyed all else—a shattering of time itself.

Here, there was no revenge plot. No shadow waiting for him at the end of the road. Here, there was no blood streaking the sands. No crowd roaring for his death. Here, there was no boy racing through the labyrinth beneath his family's estate with a cloth over his mouth to keep out the smoke. Here was so much better than *there*, even if he knew he could not stay forever.

16

NEVELYN TIN'VORI

The seamstress room was exhausting.

It had nothing to do with the actual work. Nevelyn's fingers were quite deft. Her skill perfectly adequate. Years of practice in Ravinia had more than prepared her for the actual alterations they made. She realized on the first day that the advanced patterns she'd been using were too complex here. Their work needed to be fast and brutal and efficient. A pace that matched the frenetic world of an opera house that doubled as a theater. Most of their costuming was not inventive or new. The seamstress team built the wardrobe from what already existed in their closets.

What made it so exhausting was not the work but the continuous chatter. Five of them packed in a cellar room the size of a large closet, bumping elbows, gossiping about absolutely nothing. She'd only been working there for a week and already she'd reached her limit on banality.

"I just don't know what to do," Edna whined. She was the youngest girl in their crew—and the assistant directly ahead of Nevelyn in the pecking order. "If he liked me, why wouldn't he just come out and *say* that he liked me?"

That received an infamous tongue click from Kersey. Their overseeing seamstress seemed as if she'd been born right there in her corner of the room. The woman looked at Edna over the rim of her spectacles, but her wrinkled hands kept moving, perfectly rethreading a jester's cap.

"Gives you all the power," Kersey said. "Men can't stand the idea of being at someone else's mercy. No offense, John."

Nevelyn's eyes darted that way. She double-checked John's attire to make sure Kersey wasn't being rude. She'd only known them for a week, but they'd alternated their expressed gender several times. She'd seen them in a range of lovely, self-tailored dresses. Today's outfit was a checkered cardigan with cloud-white slacks. Regardless of which gender John presented as each morning, they always arrived immaculately dressed. Nevelyn supposed that was a natural byproduct of being the child of the city's most famous seamstress.

Faith DuNess sat at the corner of the table closest to John, occasionally offering up small squares of completed fabric. The woman lacked Kersey's longevity with the opera house, but she was the unquestioned head of their flock. If the papers ever praised the cast's wardrobe in their reviews, it was always for some clever decision Faith had made. She'd been teaching John the same techniques for nearly a decade now. Nevelyn recognized the pair for what they likely were: her most challenging obstacle.

Faith commented on Edna's debacle without looking up. "I

can't imagine what power you think a busboy actually possesses."

"But that only proves my point," Kersey replied. "A man like that has even less control over the rest of his life. Which means he'll cling tighter to what he *thinks* he's got."

Edna looked quite annoyed by the turn in the conversation.

"It's not like he plans to be a busboy permanently. He's got dreams, you know."

"All men's dreams sound bigger when they whisper them in your ear," Kersey replied tartly. Then, to prove her point, she leaned closer to an unsuspecting Edna and shouted, "Edna! Oh, Edna! If you love me, I'll sail to new lands. I'll invent new magic. I'll lead armies for you, Edna!"

An absolutely violent shade of red colored the young girl's cheeks. Faith and John snickered delightedly, which made Kersey laugh with even more self-satisfaction. Nevelyn watched in silence.

"I'm sorry I brought it up."

The younger girl slammed down her pattern and stormed from the room. Kersey called after her, but only half-heartedly. Nevelyn saw an opening. She'd been doing her best to develop a friendship with Edna ever since arriving. Small bits of conversation. Now she set down her work and glided after the girl.

The costume room was like a small country nestled inside a much larger, much more chaotic continent. It was easily the most boring part of the Nodding Violet Theater. Nevelyn spied Edna disappearing around a distant corner and rushed to catch up with her. She was nearly leveled by one of the stagehands for her effort, who managed to curse her entire family tree by the time they got past one another.

The labyrinth underneath the stage was vast and complicated. Nevelyn had already committed most of it to memory. Edna and John were both fine with needle and thread, but one of their primary functions was running outfits from the costume room to other specified destinations in the theater. If a seam ripped in the middle of a show, they'd be on hand to rush it downstairs for a quick fix. It was a task she needed to be able to do with her eyes closed if she wanted to replace either of them.

A small staircase led out of the darker basement. Here, lights twinkled softly overhead. She heard singers and actors rehearsing in their rooms. The effect was a garbled, fever-dream version of the play they were putting on that night. Her eyes drifted, as always, to the second room in the hallway to her right. The name TESSA BROOD glinted on the wall there in silver letters.

Focus, Nevelyn thought. *She's not your quarry today.*

She spotted Edna crossing the massive backstage area, past the mail wall with its slotted cabinets, and she doubled her pace to catch up. The girl paused before the playhouse's rickety dumbwaiter. There was a table there with two stacks of costumes set out. Nevelyn heard Edna curse under her breath as she began rifling through them.

"Edna. Are you all right?"

The girl's jaw tightened. She glanced back over one shoulder, eyeing Nevelyn from head to toe. "I'm fine."

"They were out of line," Nevelyn said. "I know what it's like. To not be taken seriously."

"I don't doubt that." Edna gestured to her entirety. "Look at you. You're a slob. The missing button. That small grease stain along your collar. It's a wonder they hired you at all."

Nevelyn was shocked back a step. It was like being plunged into cold water. That tightening in the lungs and chest. Her entire body constricted. Edna's lip curled up even more at that reaction.

"Look at you. Such a mousy thing. We are *not* alike. I need no sympathy from a useless creature like you. They only hired you on to see us through the production date. And then they'll be rid of you, and I'll be rid of you. So the next time you get it in your head that we are friends, remember that you work *beneath* me. If I want your thoughts, on any subject, I'll request them. If I don't, feel free to keep your mouth shut on matters that have naught to do with you. Understood?"

A decade of survival and scraping forced Nevelyn to nod. In the back of her mind, she knew that Edna held no true power over her. But anytime someone had taken this tone with them, she'd learned subservience. Resistance caused a scene. Raised voices drew unwanted attention. It had always worked out better to simply nod and avoid eye contact. She did that now.

"Gods," Edna cursed. "You look like you're going to have a cry. Do it somewhere else."

Obediently, Nevelyn turned to leave.

"Wait. I didn't mean you could take a break. I just don't want to be around to hear your sniveling. The crow's nest technicians forgot these outfits." Edna patted one of the stacks of clothing. She carefully lifted the other set of costumes in her arms. "They need to go upstairs for the play tonight. Be sure they get there, and don't let any of the fabric snag on anything."

Nevelyn kept her eyes low as Edna marched past, heels clicking along the hardened wood. She looked at the dumbwaiter mechanism. It had been some time since she'd used one, but she'd need to figure out how to work the levers. . . .

"Oh!" Edna called back over a shoulder. "The dumbwaiter is broken. You'll have to walk them all up. Thanks for being *such* a dear about everything."

Nevelyn thought she heard a fading snicker. Her hand drifted silently to the spot on her collar. She'd seen it that morning. A grease stain from weeks ago. The rest of her clothes were drying, though, and she'd already been running late. Her hand fell back to her side.

She'd hoped to win Edna over. Become fast friends. She'd wanted someone trustworthy inside the playhouse. Now, however, she felt no qualms in executing the other version of her plan. She and her siblings had met hundreds of Ednas in their travels. Base creatures who wielded power in their small kingdoms with unfortunate brutality. Experience had taught her exactly how to handle such people.

Nevelyn reached for the stack of clothes. She could only manage to carry half of them, pressing the bulk against her chest and starting up the winding steps. It would have to be two trips. The crow's nest was used in a number of the plays and operas. Gods would descend from the heavens on nearly invisible wires. Crooning lovers would sing to each other— one in the tower above and the other in a garden below. She'd never actually walked all the way to the top.

The steps turned in tight circles that had her feeling claustrophobic, not to mention sweating profusely. She passed several platforms, each with windows that could be opened or closed depending on what the current play demanded. The crow's nest was at the very top of the tower. Nevelyn arrived short of breath. An older man was there, leaning unceremoniously over a set of gears and cranks. He wiped the back of his nose with a sleeve before turning to her.

"Damn. Forgot those, didn't I?" He thumbed behind him. "Leave them with Garth."

Nevelyn frowned. "Garth?"

She followed the old man's gaze to a figure in the most shadowed corner of the room. He was so deeply asleep that she hadn't realized he was there. Nevelyn thought he looked older than her, though it was hard to tell. She'd never seen someone who looked more like a bear. Broad shoulders, thick limbs, a round stomach. A dark beard only added to the effect. Nevelyn set the clothes down in a pile beside him and turned to leave.

The old man clucked his tongue. "That other stack needs to go down. For mending."

He was pointing at the clothes *beneath* the slumbering man.

Nevelyn frowned. "I have to wake him up?"

"With a kiss, if the plays are to be trusted." The old man offered a wink. "Garth. You sack of shit! Wake up. We've company!"

This shout was paired with the old man tossing a literal metal wrench across the room. Nevelyn gasped, but thankfully the metal struck the wall above Garth and rattled harmlessly to the floor. The noise was enough to bring him back to life.

"Did you just throw a wrench at me?" He blinked, smacking his lips slightly, before spying Nevelyn. His entire face transformed. "Sorry. Gods, I thought you were Edna."

The old man laughed. "Edna would have kicked you in the stones already."

There was an awkward silence while the bearish Garth

lumbered back to his feet. Nevelyn wished she was still holding the stack of clothes, as she had nothing to do with her hands, nothing to hide herself behind. She didn't know why she felt so exposed before the two of them. It did not help that Garth now towered over her. Nor did it help that she'd been very wrong about her guess. The beard made him seem older than he was. There was a boyishness beneath that made it clear they were the same age. His eyes were deep and dark. His smile stretched as wide as the rest of him, and she'd never felt so comfortable and uncomfortable at the same time.

"I'm Garth," he said. "And you're . . . new?"

Nevelyn imagined he'd been about to say another word. Something else entirely. After a moment, she nodded. "My name is Nan. I work in the seamstress room."

The older gentleman snorted. "Gods. Who stuck you with that name? Even I've never dated a Nan. Thought they all died out last century. . . ."

"That's rich coming from someone named Daft," Garth cut back. His eyes never left her. "How do you like it . . . down there?"

She wasn't sure how to answer, or why he cared? None of her plans involved a stagehand up in the crow's nest. But even if it felt like a waste of time, his honest question lured an honest answer from her. "I find the seamstress room to be a little stuffy."

That drew out a laugh from both men. Garth looked especially pleased with her answer.

"They're not the kindest folks. If you ever need a break . . ." He gestured around the room. "You're welcome to visit the two of us. It might not be much to look at, but hey, at least it smells like sweat and failure up here."

She could feel her lips tugging into a smile, but the moment stretched and began to feel awkward. Nevelyn quickly pointed to the stack behind him.

"The clothes?"

"Clothes?" Garth echoed distractedly. "Right. The clothes. Here."

He bent to scoop them up. It was a surprisingly gentle motion from such a big man. She watched as he carefully folded them over one arm. Nevelyn took a single step forward to accept the offering, and their hands brushed beneath the fabric. A slash of unexpected warmth. Nevelyn tried to tug the clothes away, but he held tight to them.

"Wait. I was heading downstairs. Why don't I just carry them for you?"

Nevelyn couldn't help blushing slightly. She didn't bother to point out that when she'd arrived, he had not been heading anywhere. He'd been fast asleep.

"Well, if you're certain. There are more clothes downstairs that need to be brought up."

"Of course. Sorry for not thinking of it sooner. I'm still half dreaming."

I'm still half dreaming.

Nevelyn was not normally sentimental, but that's what Ava had always called it. That curious existence between waking and sleeping. Whenever her sister made a morning mistake, she'd claim that she was still half dreaming. It was an echo of memory that Nevelyn was not prepared to face this morning. She awkwardly allowed Garth to take the clothes back, ignoring the raised eyebrows the old man was shooting in their direction, and started down the stairs.

"So, Nan, are you . . . do you live nearby?"

Garth's voice echoed in the narrow stairwell.

"That's a rather personal question."

"Oh. You're right. I just like your accent."

Nevelyn frowned. "Accent?"

"I thought I heard something. You sound like you're from up north."

"I grew up outside of Peska. We lived on one of the farms there."

The fabricated story rolled easily off her tongue. It was built around just enough truth to make it easy to talk about—and just enough falsehood to keep a wiser soul from actually tracing the tale back to her and her siblings. "My uncle was born there. I guess I picked it up from him."

They'd reached the first landing.

"And what brought you to Kathor?"

"Work," she answered. "The pay here is better than up north."

That was true too, even if it was only a fractional improvement.

"That's interesting. You hear about folks leaving Kathor to travel north. Always talking like it's some big opportunity for them. Like they're striking it rich or something. I wondered if it was true. I guess people always think things can be better somewhere else."

Nevelyn made no reply to that. She was not prepared to philosophize with a stranger. They rounded another landing, and another. All in silence. Garth broke it with an echoing laugh.

"Gods, you're the quietest seamstress we've ever had."

She nodded. "I like the quiet."

"Me too."

That surprised her. He'd barely stopped talking since being woken from a dead sleep by a metal projectile. A final turn brought them to the base of the stairs. She was forced to turn and accept the clothes back from him. Garth offered her a smile when their hands brushed again.

"Well, that was a better start to the day than I'd imagined for myself."

Her cheeks flushed. She adjusted the weight of the clothes.

"Have a good morning," she said. "It might help if you fixed the dumbwaiter."

He eyed the contraption. "Right. I will. But I'm glad it was broken. For today."

Nevelyn started moving before he could turn back and study her again. *Missing button. A stain on her collar. Poorly matched clothes.* She felt if she stood there for too long, Garth might see those things too. Not that it mattered. She didn't care what he thought in the first place. She walked across the dark backstage area. Garth didn't follow, though she could feel him watching her depart.

She risked a quick glance over one shoulder when she reached the distant curtains. Garth had turned away. She smiled, though. He was fussing over the dumbwaiter. Trying to fix it.

Down in the dark beneath the stage, Nevelyn found herself smiling.

17

REN MONROE

R en began to imagine a normal life.

One in which she did not exist in the shadow of House Brood and all their sins. The weeks passed with Ren focused on whatever spells interested her most. Seminar Shiverian pushed her harder than any teacher ever had. The head researcher was demanding but fair. She never held them to a standard that she was unwilling to meet herself. No matter how early Ren showed up, Seminar was already there, tinkering with one of her ongoing projects.

Ren also got on well with her colleagues. Ellison Proctor stopped by to charm her once or twice a day. He was delightfully shallow. He cared nothing for the magical conversations happening around the room and had accepted this role purely for its simplicity. As far as she could tell, he was tasked with performing the same repeating spell over and over again.

The siblings—Maryan and Flynn—were equally fascinating

to Ren. Both of them turned out to be devilishly smart. Top of their class at Balmerick, in the year just behind her. At first, Ren had been confused about why they were both allowed to research there. If this was meant to be an equal distribution amongst the great houses, why would the Winters family be gifted two positions? It turned out they were not twins, but half-siblings born less than a week apart. One a proper-born child of the Winters family and the other a bastard born to one of the Graylantian princesses. They'd made it all the way to life at Balmerick before discovering the other one existed, and after that they'd been thick as thieves, with their father's infidelity as the binding between them.

The only person Ren struggled with was Pecking. He'd been recruited from House Shiverian by Seminar herself, because he possessed a rare gift. He was fully synesthetic. He could literally see magic in the air. While Ren could sense formations and patterns, she had no idea what it would be like to constantly watch magic manifest around them—especially in a city so full of magic that it was on the verge of bursting at the seams. This talent gave Pecking an advantage few possessed, though Ren had not been able to pick his brain on the subject. He'd refused to speak more than two words to her since the initial embarrassment.

Ren enjoyed all of it. A rival, colleagues, the nature of her work. There were a few times when she slipped fully into that version of herself. Someone who had no revenge to carry out. No bond with a boy in a distant castle. She was just a girl who wanted to explore the world of magic and was beginning a brilliant career as a spellmaker. It was always Theo who unintentionally pulled her back. She would *feel* him across their bond, and then she'd be imagining his tapered jaw and his narrow eyes and his golden hair. With that glimpse of him came all the truths she could not simply wish away.

One evening, Ren returned home from work. She was primarily living in Theo's abandoned apartment in the Heights. It was a sort of guilty pleasure to enjoy the comforts she'd once counted as sins against the Broods: silk sheets, first editions, a balcony with a view.

Two steps inside and Ren felt it. That subtle trace of magic in the air. She paused on the threshold, still half in shadow, trying to determine the source. Only in complete silence did she hear the distant, trickling sound of music.

Ren slid her horseshoe wand from her belt and cursed the fact that she'd sent Vega elsewhere in the city. She carefully slipped out of the buckles of her shoes, then silently padded forward into the unlit house. The sound of the music grew louder. Ren's eyes traced every corner and shadow. The noise was coming from the balcony. She saw the door was cracked open.

Landwin Brood sat outside in the dying light.

He was playing a seventeen-string. She had no idea when he'd had it delivered, but she knew it had not been there that morning. The sprawling instrument normally required three players—one at the neck, one at the legs, and one at the arms. Landwin was running a razor-thin bow across the neck. Ren was not musical, but she knew that was the most delicate of the three. Without the others, it sounded high and ethereal, almost painful to listen to.

He did not move or look up as she walked halfway across the spacious balcony. She felt certain that he'd sensed her presence. Likely he'd only begun playing when she opened the front door. That long-forming anger started to burn in her chest again. Here was the person she'd spent half of her life plotting against. And he was alone.

Ren felt an irrational urge to cast a spell. How many lethal combinations had she rehearsed over the years? But she knew he would never expose himself so easily. She sensed spellwork layered over his clothing. An invisible suit of armor. Knowing she could not strike now—that she needed him weakened and vulnerable—only fired her anger even more. And as it roared in her chest, there was an answer across her bond. It was like the bridge spell she'd performed out in the Dires to help their group across the river. When the magic finally touched down on the other shoreline and solidified. She could not explain the feeling in words, but she knew in that moment, she and Theo were more bound to each other than normal.

She set her mental hands on that spot and *pulled*.

The answer was instantaneous. She could not see him, but the air around her felt thick with his presence. Ren knew this was a rare opportunity. Theo was watching. A witness to this moment, and Landwin Brood had no idea his son could hear him. She strained to maintain the balance of the magic that kept Theo with her as Landwin finished the last note of his song. A single slash across the instrument's stringed throat. The sound trembled and died. Only then did he look up.

"Ren Monroe. You've been busy."

She kept her breathing steady. Her expression unreadable. What did he suspect? Had he learned about her visit to Ravinia? She stood there in silence, waiting for him to speak.

". . . all your work down in the underground." A smile crawled over his face. "How are you liking the Collective?"

Ren didn't even need to lie. "It's exciting work. I enjoy it a great deal."

"Oh good. How wonderful. Yes, Theo shared with us that you were interested in spellmaking. Seminar is the very best. Some would say Ethel is better, but I think Seminar is the greatest spellmaker of our generation. Who knows? Maybe you could be the greatest in yours."

He allowed that thought to hang in the air above them. Ren realized she was still clutching her horseshoe wand. She hastily tucked it back into her belt. If Landwin Brood meant to duel her, he'd have brought an army with him. No, this was something else. Ren just wasn't sure what.

"Well, Theo was right," she said. "I enjoy the work. Thank you for arranging the position."

Landwin Brood watched her carefully before nodding. His eyes returned to the seventeen-string. "Do you recognize this instrument?"

Ren frowned. "It's a seventeen-string."

"Not just *any* seventeen-string." He stood and circled. His fingers traced the wooden frame. "This is the same one that fell on that tavern. We purchased it from the wreckage at a local auction. For the past three months, a mender has been working with the wood. It's very difficult work. Low success rate, really. But our house has some of the best craftsmen in the world. What do you think? Looks brand-new, doesn't it?"

Ren felt another surge across her bond. Theo's pain, bright and hot beside her. She knew he was still there, watching the scene unfold as she'd watched the moment of his arrival at Nostra. His emotions darted from embarrassed to furious. Ren lifted her chin ever so slightly before answering. "Teahouse."

Landwin lifted an eyebrow. "Pardon?"

"It fell on a teahouse."

"That's right. My mistake. And you were here that night? When my son attempted the magic."

Ren's throat bobbed. "I was."

"Let's see where he erred."

Her breathing hitched. Landwin Brood performed the same spell. He adjusted his stance, altered his footing, and began the *exact* casting Theo had that fateful night. "The Winter Retreat" echoed out again. The instrument began to float. Ren could see the magic was properly tethered to the stones this time. Not the awning. She still struggled to breathe as she watched it float recklessly out—following the same path it had before. Landwin observed the instrument with casual disinterest.

"I'm sure you're wondering why I'm here."

Ren said nothing. She'd been wondering exactly that.

"I've been . . . retracing Theo's steps. That's what you do when your children leave the careful paths you've set out for them. You try to figure out where they strayed, how far they walked, and what might be the best way to get them home again."

He looked back to Ren. She worried his lack of concentration would send the instrument plummeting to the city below for a second time. More, it felt like Landwin was using the instrument as a threat. Listen to me—drink in every single word—or I will ruin even more lives.

"I was hoping some time in Nostra might . . . have an impact on Theo. But he seems stubbornly intent on following this course."

This course. Meaning a relationship with her. Ren felt an odd surge of pride hearing those words. This was no bond-born feeling either. It was a fierce pride that echoed in her chest. Theo was loyal to her—and she felt a surge of loyalty to him. The seventeen-string was passing the point where Theo had lost control. The song continued on, sad and heavy and full of meaning. Ren watched as the instrument began to rotate back. She was not sure what correspondence Landwin had been having with his son—but now she knew Theo had rejected his offers.

He'd chosen her instead.

"Which brings me here," Landwin concluded. "I have an offer for you."

Ren could not believe how direct he was being, after so much subtlety. Always wielding his influence behind the scenes to isolate her. This was either a sign of desperation or a sign that he felt as if he had something to offer that she wouldn't dare refuse.

"I have been approached by Seminar Shiverian," he said. "She thinks highly of you. I confess I was surprised. Theo talked you up, but what boy doesn't feel that way about a first love? I knew you were talented. Your record at Balmerick reflects that, I suppose. But you must be rather gifted if Seminar would come to me directly."

Ren couldn't help feeling a subtle thrill. It was not an emotion she could completely contain, and she knew Theo would sense it building inside her. This was a confirmation. She was *good* at magic. Not just at school and books and research but the kind of magic that might matter in the real world. It was validation, even if it came from the lips of her sworn enemy.

For a moment, she'd lost track of the seventeen-string. She glanced over and found it was crossing the lawn again. Nearly back on the balcony.

"She can't officially offer you a contract," Landwin said. "After all, you are technically the Brood representative in the Collective. But our houses can make arrangements. You could join House Shiverian when that agreement ends. You would be Seminar's understudy, guaranteed a position as a spellmaker with them. And as a show of good faith, I would also give you the deed to this."

He gestured to the apartment. Ren was astonished. It was nearly enough to knock her off her feet. The deed on a property like this would be unthinkably valuable. Something she would not have been able to purchase in her lifetime, no matter how successful she might be. Not to mention the stability of an understudy position reporting directly to Seminar Shiverian. It was nearly perfect. Quite the gilded cage. Beside her— still invisible to them both—she could feel Theo's agitation. Almost as if he were pacing.

"In exchange for what?" she asked.

The great seventeen-string finished its final rotation. It floated flawlessly back into its original position. Landwin Brood waited for the instrument to settle fully before turning back to her.

"Sever your bond with my son."

Pain coursed across their bond. She could feel Theo's retreat. She wasn't sure if it was the pain of his father's betrayal—or a deeper fear that Ren might say yes. Landwin's offer was clear. Abandon Theo. In doing so, Ren knew she'd also be abandoning her best chance of revenging her father. She was already inside. Like a whisper in the walls. The plan unfolding at this very moment—if it worked—would bring House Brood to its knees. More than that, Ren could sense a subtle ache in her own chest. To accept this would be to depart from Theo and she . . . she wasn't ready to do that. That truth felt like a betrayal of sorts, but it was right there, needling into all her other thoughts. She might actually want to be with him. Especially if her plans worked.

But at her very core, Ren was a logical creature. She knew there were a hundred very difficult steps between here and there. Everything would have to go right for their plan to come to fruition. Dahvid Tin'Vori would have to perform a miracle. Nevelyn Tin'Vori would need to do the same. What Landwin Brood was offering her now was dreadfully real in comparison. An actual guarantee of the kind of life her mother wanted for her. Ren felt Theo's absence. He was no longer there. Almost as if he was hiding from the answer she might give.

She decided to ask a question instead.

"If I am so talented, why would you not want to keep me as a match for your son?"

She already knew what he would say, but it bought her time to think. It was obvious that the easiest life for her waited down the road where she said yes. Abandon the Tin'Voris to their own plot. Take the position. Bid farewell to Theo and House Brood and go about living a normal life. Would her father's ghost come back to haunt her if she chose that path? If he visited her on some lonely night decades from now and found her living out her wildest dreams, safe and happy? She thought that might actually be enough for him. But she knew it would never be enough for her.

"Regardless of talent," Landwin answered, "you are not the right person for our son. There are politics involved in every decision. Theo has known this since he was a small boy. His life is not completely his own. We have alliances to consider. Previous promises to honor. Theo cannot marry someone simply because they dazzled him with a few spells while he was lost in the woods."

How easily he reduced her accomplishments. Ren marveled at how outdated his words sounded, even if they were utterly unsurprising. This was more evidence that the old houses weren't powerful because they possessed unique imagination or creativity. They were powerful because they'd been the first ones to arrive in Kathor. It was that simple.

"And if I do not accept your terms?"

Landwin set a hand on the instrument again. "I imagine life would be rather unpleasant for you. Theo would remain in Nostra. Permanently. And if you marry him, your life would be spent there as well. Away from Kathor. No spellwork. No magical research. From what I understand, there is not even a proper archive room there. Your life would be reduced to that of a steward. You would care for a lonely building, and a lonely man, for the rest of your days. And if I might be perfectly frank, that is the best-case scenario."

He shrugged, as if these consequences required no more than a snap of his fingers.

"Because that charming, sad little life relies on several factors going right for you. It depends on Theo not growing bored with you, or bored with Nostra. If the day should come when he wants to be restored to his rightful position, I would gladly help him. But Theo would know the price. He'd have to be severed from you. And then? You'd go back to having nothing at all.

"That life also depends on what I find in the coming months. As I said, I am following my son's footsteps. I've interviewed people about the party that night. Learned everything I could about what happened. My next stop is the portal room. Did you know that Balmerick's top researchers are still at a loss about what happened? No one's used the room since your incident, because they can't figure out why the magic failed. I plan to make my own inquiries. I wonder what I'll find. . . ."

Landwin Brood lifted both hands, mimicking a scale. He was weighing these imaginary options for her life in his upraised palms.

"Spellmaker. Head researcher. House Shiverian. The freedom to live however you want. Or . . ." He slid the opposite hand slowly downward. "Housewife. Exile. An unremarkable existence." Landwin considered her with those narrow eyes. "Do you truly love him that much?"

No, she thought. *This is not about love. It's much more to do with hate.*

That familiar fire roared back to life in her chest. His words would not douse it. The pretty baubles he was dangling before her would not distract her. Ren felt the surge of emotions pouring across her bond, reaching for Theo. He'd somehow cocooned himself. Like he was behind a door, and her rage was knocking again and again. He might not witness this directly, but she desperately wanted him to feel every pulse of what she felt now.

"I will not abandon Theo for you," she said boldly. "I am not your plaything. Neither is he. We are bonded, and that is the way of it. I will not be severed from him, no matter what you offer."

Landwin's playful smile faded. "Ren Monroe," he said. "A name that history will forget."

And with that, Landwin Brood walked past her. Right through the spot where she imagined the ghostly version of Theo had been standing before. Ren's fingers went numb. She wanted to reach for her wand. Begin casting the spells she knew that could unmake another person. She wanted to hit Landwin again and again until he was nothing but bones at her feet. Ren did not strike, because she knew now that time was on her side. Theo had witnessed some of their exchange. He would have questions. There was an equal fury building on his side of their bond for once. Landwin Brood had unwittingly given Ren an unbelievable gift. She would use it against him, because she needed a version of Landwin that wasn't protected. She wanted him vulnerable and at her mercy. And that Landwin Brood?

He would die at her hands.

Ren had never been so certain of anything in her life.

18

REN MONROE

Ren thrived on pressure.

At Balmerick, she'd loved deadlines. Exams. Anything meant to push someone to the very edge of their limitations. Landwin Brood should have done his research. He'd made all the wrong moves, and now Ren hastened to punish him for it. The next evening, she descended from her minor kingdom in the clouds and into the Lower Quarter. Her mother was waiting. A scheduled dinner that would also serve as a rendezvous. Her mother just happened to be the primary informant on all things Nevelyn Tin'Vori. Ren was eager to hear everything, especially given her own shifting plans.

The exterior door of her mother's building offered an absolutely ghastly groan as it opened. She was pleasantly surprised, though, to find her mother's apartment locked for once. She knocked three times. The door opened. Her mother was in a breezy dress, dark hair curled down past her shoulders. The tempting scent of pan-fried fish dominated the small apartment.

"You look nice," Ren noted. "And you cooked? I didn't know you still cooked. . . ."

"Please. I cook all the time."

Ren raised one eyebrow.

"Well, I didn't cook this. But I do cook. You're just never around. Harlow was here. Trust me, you'll prefer his recipe to mine."

"Harlow again . . . is he turning into a permanent guest?"

"Regular is not the same as permanent, dear. I live my life a day at a time. Let's eat."

The two of them quietly went about the business of filling their plates. Besides the fried fish, there were buttered rolls and spiced cucumbers. Ren felt famished, stretched as thin as she was by everything that was happening. She could barely restrain herself from eating as she crossed the room to sit at their knee-high table. Her mother settled in beside her and let out a pleasant sigh.

"You're right," Ren said, mouth full of food. "This is better than your recipe."

"The fisherman knows fish," her mother said. "Guess I shouldn't be surprised."

"That's what he is? A fisherman?"

Her mother shrugged. "He has a number of occupations."

"How vague. But he's good to you?"

"Of course. I don't have patience for anything less at my age." Her mother looked her up and down. "I'm getting you more fish. You're nothing but bones."

Ren could only smile as her mother went to grab another

plate. It was nice to have someone fuss over her needs like this. Her mother returned with the rest of the scraps. Ren reached across to pick at them, her own plate already clean.

"So . . . how is Nan?"

Their chosen pseudonym. Ren had thought it too old-fashioned, but her mother had insisted that the older names were always cycling back through. "Nan is settling in," her mother answered. "I saw her at the market the other day, buying rice. Our contact at the playhouse said she's doing fine. A good worker."

"*Our* contact? You mean Harlow?"

"Of course. Who do you think secured Nan's apartment? And who do you think pulled the strings to get her hired by the seamstresses in the first place? That's all Harlow's work. You told me you didn't want anything traced back to you. How else was I supposed to get it done?"

Ren only nodded. "No, you're right. I wasn't criticizing. I just want the circle to stay tight. No one else should know about her. The last thing we want is for someone to recognize that she's one of the missing Tin'Vori children."

"Who would? She left when she was a girl. She was how old? Seven? And it's clear life hasn't been kind to her since then. I doubt that even their dearest servants would know who she was. Besides, the rumor is that the Broods butchered most of them. Trust me, Nan's secret is safe."

Ren rolled that around in her mind. It all came down to trust. She might not know Harlow, but if her mother said they were squared away—they were squared away. The rest of the plan relied on Nevelyn's abilities. Could she navigate the politics of the seamstress room? Their plan required her to advance quite a bit past her current station. They'd given her mechanisms for making contact if it was not proceeding quickly enough, but so far, Ren had heard nothing.

"It's interesting," she said. "Harlow helping us so much. Why would he do that?"

"Because I asked him."

It took a lot of effort to not roll her eyes. "Come now, Mother. You're obviously a delight, but what's the real reason? He's sticking out his neck by involving himself. If the plan works . . . there could be some serious consequences. The other houses might retaliate. He's risking a lot."

Her mother nodded. "We aren't the only ones who hate the Broods, Ren. There were other men and women on that bridge when it fell. People in the Lower Quarter don't forget. They might not be able to do anything about it, but they don't forget. All I had to do was hint at what you were planning and Harlow agreed to it. He knows what we all know: if one of the great houses can really fall, there's hope that the rest of us can rise."

"Fair enough. I just—"

"—don't trust him. That's good. We taught you to question everything and everyone."

They most certainly had. Agnes and Roland Monroe had not raised a fool. The silence between them stretched, until her mother went on.

"But Harlow is one of us, Ren. He's Lower Quarter through and through. He was born in their shadow just like you were. If we can't trust each other, we'll never beat them."

Ren had no answer to that. She was about to bring up her work and the offer she'd just received from Landwin Brood. At the last second, though, she bit her tongue instead. She was afraid that her mother might like the idea too much. What if she pushed Ren to accept that offer of a normal life? Ren didn't want another fight. Instead, she reached for more fish. The two of them made small talk about the docks and pretended like nothing else existed outside these walls—like this was their normal day-to-day. When the evening had run its course, Ren cleaned off the plates with her mother at the washbasin. Her voice was quiet.

"I need to leave Kathor. An opportunity has presented itself."

"Going to Nostra?"

Her mother was too clever by half. Ren nodded.

"The Tin'Voris have their tasks and I have mine. I need to sway Theo."

Her mother asked the question Ren had been avoiding.

"What if he says no?"

She sighed. "What if he says yes?"

"That's not an answer."

Ren reached for a dishrag. She started drying off plates. Her mother hummed a song under her breath. It wasn't an answer, because Ren didn't know the real answer. The Tin'Voris had asked her in Ravinia about Theo. She'd spoken boldly, but she'd also contorted her answer just enough to avoid suspicion. The moral sword had not harmed her, because in that moment, she had been telling the absolute truth. If it came down to her revenge or Theo's life—she would choose revenge. The fall of House Brood, above all else.

But her mother had touched on her greatest fear. What if Theo weighed everything—his father's sins against him and against Ren—and still said no? What if blood ran too deep? She had been clinging to the belief that he would accept her plan. He would choose her. Of course he would.

Her next step was to travel to Nostra. Ren had already requested time off from Seminar, who was so delighted by her work that she granted it—though with the understood promise that Ren would use her time away to brainstorm even cleverer spells. Everything was settled, but Ren knew that her mother was right. She was avoiding the real answer to the question at hand.

What if Theo said no?

If he says no, Ren thought, *the Tin'Voris will kill him.*

19

DAHVID TIN'VORI

Once more, Dahvid had a hood on his head.

He held tight to Cath's hand as the two of them stumbled on, shoulder to shoulder. A pair of guards was either leading them to a party or an execution. It all felt a bit theatrical. Dahvid had wondered this before his first meeting with Ravinia's famous warlord. If Darling had one of the largest estates in the city, why bother with hoods? It seemed likely that people knew where his home was and how to get there. So why the need for secrecy? He thought it might be an exercise in power. One more way to remind everyone of their standing before Ravinia's uncrowned king.

A rough hand slid the hood away. Night had come in earnest as they walked. There were stars overhead, countless in number. The only other lights were twinkling along the exterior of Darling's estate. Bodies moved in the darknesses between each of those glinting, amber orbs—and music trembled across the dunes to them.

"Just follow the path," one of the guards said. "It's safer if you're quick about it."

Dahvid wasn't sure if that was a real warning or more exaggeration. He did know there were sand prowlers and horned crabs that preferred the rockier coastlines in the north. It would be quite a spectacle if their great scheme ended with him getting speared on the dunes by an aggressive crustacean. Cath slid her arm through his, and they started through the shadows together. They did not speak, except to point out their favorite constellations. The two of them had already established a strategy for how they'd act if they were invited to a function like this one. There were four rules:

Do not leave each other's sight.

Do not mention the Broods.

Do not talk about his tattoos.

Flirt with each other as much as possible.

It was Dahvid's choice to add the last one. He thought it was important. They ascended a set of wooden steps and found themselves on the first of a series of sprawling balconies. The connected platforms formed a sort of blockade between the actual estate and the distant ocean. Each shadow took on a face in the flickering torchlight. Dahvid spied other gladiators, politicians, escorts.

At the very heart of their current platform, there was hired entertainment. A man and woman were twisting around each other—their clothing tight, their movements sinuous. It looked strange until he and Cath stepped a little closer. Music flickered to life. A perfect beat that matched the rhythm of the two dancers.

Dahvid took a step back and the music faded. Now, that was

clever magic. A proximity charm of some kind. Anyone who cared to enjoy the music only had to step forward, but if they preferred a quiet conversation, they could move to the railing, out of range. He thought it was the kind of magic that Ware would have loved.

Cath tugged him away from the dancers, up another flight of stairs. The second platform was long and narrow. More walkway than gathering space. Along the oceanside railing, a number of looking glasses had been built into the metal bearings. Each one appeared to be a different size and shape. Dahvid and Cath followed another couple, leaning down to glance through the lenses, one by one. The first took Dahvid's breath away.

He witnessed a fast-moving sequence. The dunes and the ocean and the sky before him now, but in reverse. Stars faded. The sun rose and fell. The image cycled back through time, revealing storms and quieter days and ships passing off the coast. He witnessed what felt like several weeks, all in less than a minute. Dizzied, he followed Cath to the next looking glass. This one offered the most beautiful sunrise he'd ever seen. Colors so bright that they didn't even look real. He watched the waves retreat soundlessly before moving onto the third.

His heartbeat doubled in his chest. It was a bright, clear day. Out over the water, dragons. The extinct gods of this land. He knew they were all dead and buried. But for a moment, Dahvid watched them live again. Their glittering wings beat the air before widening back out to glide over the water. If not for Cath's touch on his shoulder, he might have sat there watching their graceful flights forever.

The last one. Dahvid expected this looking glass to somehow usurp the others. A challenge, no doubt, after traveling back through time and witnessing dragons. He bent down and was rewarded with the exact same view he could see with his own eyes. He squinted for some time, trying to discern what unique image was on display, but there was nothing.

He frowned at Cath. "What is this one?"

"It's just the stars," Cath replied. "I'm not sure. Maybe that's the point? They're magical in their own right."

There was one more staircase to climb. The two of them found the main balcony waiting for them at the top. It was three times the size of the other platforms, and far more densely crowded. Dahvid saw, too, that it was where the brightest stars in Ravinia orbited one another.

On his right, Agatha Marchment was in conversation with one of the city's dockmasters. Her figure was slight and unsparing. She did not look like the most vicious creature in the northern hemisphere, but Dahvid knew better. Even after a cursory inspection, he saw eight different weapons arranged neatly about her person. He could trace the potential movements—and attacks—that would force her to reach for each one. Dahvid knew she was older than she'd been when she won her gauntlet, but Darling's head general was likely one of the few gladiators that he simply could not beat in a duel. He quietly hoped that she'd retired from brawling.

It was hard not to notice the other legendary gladiators in the crowd. There was Little Ben, who'd famously died three separate times in the arena—only to drain his opponent with a final spell that brought him back to life. Next to him, Dahvid spied Beatrice Lively—who rode a livestone warthog into her duels. Even the Bearling was there, sipping a dark beer in the shadows. That was a surprise. Dahvid had left him for dead on the arena floor. He was glad the man had pulled through. He wore his graying hair slicked neatly back and respectfully raised his glass in salute when he spotted Dahvid.

As Cath led him deeper into the crowd, they finally saw the evening's main attraction: a fighting pit. Of course. The circle was carved out of the wooden beams with great precision. About twelve feet below them, two creatures kicked up sand as they probed at each other's defenses. Dahvid could hear the clacking jaws and pincers. He moved close enough to get a proper angle on the action. Two armored crabs. By far the biggest he'd ever seen. Both the size of full-grown dogs, their claws extending out from hardened carapaces. As he watched, the larger one bull-rushed the other.

There was a resounding clank. The crowd roared as the smaller crab skidded back through the sand. It barely kept its footing. The big one backpedaled, gearing up for another charge, when Dahvid finally spotted Darling. The warlord sat directly across from him—or at least the beautiful version did. His face was bright and oiled. His dark curls were arranged neatly. He looked like a painting in the dying light. Dahvid resisted looking just over the man's right shoulder. He could sense someone watching him from that darkness, and he saw the linked chain running in that direction. That was where the real Darling sat, a god in the shadows.

The big crab committed to another bull rush, but at the very last moment, the smaller crab darted to the right. Dahvid saw a claw shoot out beneath the other's carapace. There was a painful hiss as it found its mark. The iron claws clamped down tight on the back leg of the larger crab and started to twist. No matter how much the bigger one writhed, it wasn't fast enough to free itself. Everyone was shouting. Darling's proxy smiled down with satisfaction. Dahvid guessed the smaller crab was their champion.

The fight ended with a sickening crunch. The back leg had been severed, and the larger crab slumped to one side. There were shouts to finish the creature that turned Dahvid's stomach. All of it felt too familiar. How long before it was him down there? Facing his own life and death?

"I'm going to go look inviting," he whispered to Cath. "Stay here."

He grabbed a drink from a passing servant. There was an empty space by the railing. He leaned against it and sipped, hoping the reason he'd been invited tonight would appear. He did not have to wait for long. There was some satisfaction in watching Darling's handservants cross the distance to join him. Just like his first visit, the pair made a great show of wanting to talk, but it was all an effort to veil their master's approach. One complimented him on his recent victory in the Western Pits. The other asked if there was anything that they could arrange for him before his next battle. All pointless chatter. A suspicion that was confirmed by the fact that as soon as Darling arrived, the servants melted back into the crowd as if they'd never been there at all. The beautiful Darling leaned almost flirtatiously against the railing, perfectly blocking Dahvid's view of the other one. He raised his glass to the warlord.

"To your health."

Amusement flickered over Darling's pretty face. He raised his own glass with the barest of efforts. "And to yours. I was not present at your recent match. How did you like Golden?"

"I nearly fell asleep fighting him."

That dragged a laugh from both Darlings. "Paladins aren't very interesting. Effective but boring. That's why I like them, though. I've found if you set them beside a proper fighter, it draws out the colors even more. I'm told the crowd was pleased with you."

Dahvid nodded. "In the end, yes."

"The end is all that really matters," Darling noted. "They only ever talk about how it ended. Not the feint you made at the start of the fight. Not the strategy that positioned you to make your killing blow. No, all they'll tell their friends the next day is which fighter is still breathing."

"Sounds like you're speaking from experience."

The pretty face stretched into a too-bright smile. "Once upon a time. Now that we've displayed you, it's time for a proper title bout. If you want to be paid like a champion, you have to beat a champion. Look around. All my best are here tonight. You can be one of them."

Dahvid followed the gesture. His eyes located Cath first. She was standing right where he'd left her, sipping a drink, watching the next fight. Then his eyes were moving from gladiator to gladiator to gladiator. This was what Nevelyn had warned him about. Her fear had been that he was advancing too quickly and would be put to the test far too soon.

"Normally, I would choose someone that I felt was a perfectly balanced match for you," Darling said. "I like a coin flip as much as the next person. Maybe you win. Maybe you die. It's the kind of fight that separates the wheat from the chaff. All of my favorites face a test like that."

Dahvid was listening closely. "You said 'normally.'"

"Yes. I did." The chain rattled as the pretty Darling shifted his stance. "The Broods have increased their presence in Ravinia. If they'd come to my city making threats, I would have shoved my boot straight down their throat. But they didn't make threats. . . ."

Dahvid sighed. "They offered money."

"They offered money," Darling confirmed. "A onetime payment, but that's not all they offered. They wanted to send their own fighter. Someone they knew would draw a crowd."

For a brief moment, Dahvid allowed himself to believe that they were sending Thugar Brood. He wanted it so badly. He'd hungered for that fight for so long. But that didn't make sense. The rest of the world had not survived by feeding on this hatred. Darling couldn't possibly know about it. And Dahvid suspected the Broods would not be foolish enough to send their heir to fight in a gladiator pit. There were other, more rational answers.

"I do not like being ordered around," Darling said. "I serve no man. But their offer was tempting. Too tempting for me to refuse. We have agreed to terms. You will duel Able Ockley."

Dahvid's entire world spun. Until now, the concern had been preserving his secrets. Nevelyn had known that a champion duel in the Western Pits would force him to use several key abilities. He also knew that some of his tattoos took longer to restore than others. He could summon his sword once every five minutes, as needed. But the scarlet traveler? He could use that tattoo once a month, at best. Burning one of his tattoos in a match had meant potentially not having it for his gauntlet attempt—which then meant not having certain abilities for his showdown with the Broods.

Able Ockley changed everything. Dahvid would be lucky to

survive the fight even if he burned *all* his tattoos. The man was notorious. By far the most respected duelist in living memory.

"Well," Dahvid finally said. "That is unfortunate."

Not just unfortunate. It was a death sentence. At best, it would ruin their plans entirely. He could not hope to defeat Ockley and then turn around and win a gauntlet within their desired time frame. Darling's decision would ruin them. Dahvid turned back to look out over the ocean, leaning his forearms against the railing. His eyes traced the barely visible waves—brief slashes of white against the endless black. Darling unexpectedly grabbed his forearm.

"I don't want to die," the pretty man begged. *"I don't want to die."*

There was a sharp pull on the chains. The dancer's entire body was dragged back a few steps, stumbling away from Dahvid. The desperation on his features smoothed out instantly. Dahvid could only stare in shock as the bright smile was forced back onto that pretty face. What was that? Had Darling's spell faltered for a moment? He stared until the two voices spoke, and he could hear the gravelly voice more audibly than ever.

"My apologies," the warlord said. "You've stirred my emotions. Please know you fascinated me. I was eager to work with you—and to work with you for a long time. I truly hope you have enough to beat Ockley. We will make sure you have everything you need between now and then. There is a detailed record of his duels from the last time he visited the city. I'll make sure they're sent to you. It would be a fine coup if one of our own defeated Kathor's golden son. Please ask anything of my servants, and I'll make sure they attend to it. I wish there was some other way forward, but it always comes back to money.

In this case, your life isn't worth nearly as much as your death. I do hope you'll survive. But if you don't . . ."

He shrugged those pretty shoulders. The chain rattled slightly.

"Enjoy the rest of your night."

It did not take long for Cath to notice that Dahvid was alone. He was still too shocked to move. When he did not move from the railing, she slid through the crowd to join him. Her dress billowed behind her. He thought he'd never seen someone quite so beautiful as her. Or maybe that was the inevitable thought of his own death talking.

"Well?"

"Change of plans."

She frowned. "What?"

"I'll be right back."

There was no other way. He needed to act now. Before it was too late. There'd been no public announcement yet. He felt quite certain that Darling was entrusting this information to him because of some misguided sense of sympathy. A warning shot to help Dahvid start mentally preparing for what was to come. The gambling halls had no idea of the news. Likely they wouldn't until morning. It gave Dahvid the smallest window in which to intervene. He secretly wished Nevelyn were there to confirm his decision. He hoped this was the wisest route, but deep down, he knew there was no route left to him that was wise. All of them were perilous.

Darling was back at the front of the crowd. He was watching some petty fight unfold below him. Dahvid pushed forward and raised his voice to a guttural, rattling shout.

"Darling!"

Everyone fell quiet. There was a small buzzing down in the pits, but every other sound died away. He saw hands drifting silently to weapons. Agatha Marchment was shadowing over to his position without making a sound. Dahvid raised his voice again.

"Darling. I challenge you. A gauntlet!"

His words echoed over the dunes.

"My name is Dahvid Tin'Vori. Before all of these witnesses, I challenge you to a gauntlet. I will defeat five of your champions. And when the last one takes their final breath, I will make my demand of you. Do you accept my challenge?"

He saw a run of emotions on Darling's face. Surprise, anger, humor. Eventually the pretty man settled on a grisly sort of smile. Dahvid already knew what he would say. They had studied all the rules. Darling's system worked because he was an immovable object. Always, he responded in the same way. Everyone waited for the warlord's answer, but there was only one possible response.

"Challenge accepted," Darling called back. "Let there be a gauntlet."

There was a great roar from the crowd. Champions were already clamoring to their lord, asking to be one of the chosen five. He saw one final look of annoyance cross Darling's features, and then Dahvid turned away from the scene. He reached for Cath's hand. Together, they glided down the stairs. Past the glittering eyeglasses and all the pretty things, back out into the waiting jaws of the night. Cath kept asking what happened. Why did he do that? It was far too soon.

Dahvid offered no answers. There were guards waiting for them with hoods. Ready to escort them back to Ravinia. He dipped his head down, and the world went completely dark once more. His stomach turned as he stared into the disorienting black.

He could not help wondering if this was what death looked like.

Like nothing at all.

20

NEVELYN TIN'VORI

"So much for visitors," Nevelyn whispered to herself.

She climbed down a step stool, waiting until her feet were solidly on the ground to inspect her handiwork. She was standing in the center of her apartment. It consisted of three very small rooms. A decent-sized living room that Nevelyn had not bothered to furnish. A kitchen that was cramped and tiny, which led to a bedroom that felt even more cramped and tiny. It had already been difficult to imagine ever inviting a guest here, but her newest addition eliminated the possibility entirely.

Nevelyn had installed four identical hook rings. Each one glinted on a different wall, set just a hand's length lower than the ceiling. From each ring, a black rope ran to the center of the room, each stretched taut. They all attached to the dangling beginnings of a magnificent black dress. Nevelyn had measured everything, considered each angle with meticulous care. If someone were to slide into the finished version of the dress with the help of a footstool, they would remain suspended in midair, unable to touch the ground below them. She circled once, testing each rope, but even her full weight was not enough to make them do more than tremble. She'd used most of her money on these particular ropes. A vendor had promised they were the strongest ones.

In that morning quiet, she heard a low moan. Nevelyn's eyes swung from the dress to her apartment's interior wall. She padded over on bare feet and set her ear to the cracked plaster. There was another moan. Followed by a lower voice. The distinct groan of a bed. Nevelyn sat there listening to her neighbors. Her own loneliness loomed then. Like an empty stomach that had gone days without food. She stood in a state of paralysis for several minutes.

Her mind was the only thing that could free her in such moments. *Alter the paradigm.* The sounds were not a reflection of her own loneliness—but rather a way to measure the current effectiveness of her magic. Yes, that was a better way to view it. When she'd first moved in, the noise of their lovemaking had been echoing and everywhere. There'd been no room in her own apartment—no combination of shut doors or well-placed blankets—that could fully keep out the sound. Now, after just a few magical applications, she had to strain to hear them through the wall.

Nevelyn knew that was not good enough. She needed this entire room to be completely soundproof. It would require even more of her precious magic. Ren Monroe's contact had provided what they could. A vessel and the name of someone who never collected their magical stipend. Nevelyn had stood in line on the first day of that month and been awed as someone casually handed her free magic to use. That was unthinkable back in Ravinia. Everything there had a cost. Kathor, though, was rich with spells and enchantments. She'd learned that in just a few weeks living here. A person saw magic everywhere they walked.

Based on the current schedule, she'd have one more chance to refill her magic before their plans were fully in motion. That final stipend would need to go almost entirely to preparing the room. She could not afford to waste any of it—that much was certain.

Outside she spied subtle traces of red shooting through the endless gray. It was nearly sunrise. Time to go. She left the couple to their fun and got dressed. There was a forged letter sitting on the kitchen table between two bottles of wine. Nevelyn folded the letter carefully before placing it and the bottles into her satchel. Determined to win the day, she trotted down her steps into a side alley and walked with her head high. She would look the morning right in the eyes, as her father used to say.

There was a great deal of work waiting for her at the playhouse. Several ripped seams from the evening's performance. Nevelyn arrived first. It allowed her to get in extra work, but it also guaranteed she would not miss any gossip. Her plan would not work if there'd been a change in Edna's relationship status.

Faith and John arrived next—quietly debating something they'd read in the morning paper. Kersey came after them. Nevelyn was so focused on the pattern in front of her that she didn't even see the woman enter. It was as if she'd used the waxways to port there.

Finally, Edna arrived. The girl was always quite put together. Her hair was neat and curled. She'd shadowed her eyes, colored her cheeks, plucked her eyebrows. For all that, she was not a very pretty creature. Maybe Nevelyn's opinion was soured by the treatment she'd received, but there was a pinched quality to the girl's appearance. It reminded her of someone who'd just sipped curdled milk.

The group worked and chatted, worked and chatted. Edna offered no revelations about her situation. Apparently, she still liked the man she'd been dating. Nevelyn waited an hour, long enough for any proper news to surface, before excusing herself for a break.

In the dark of the underground labyrinth, she removed the small letter from her pocket. Her fingers traced the words. It had taken quite a bit of practice. She'd found a single note in one of Edna's pockets from her current love interest. It had only been one sentence long, but that had been more than enough to rehearse his handwriting. The way he darted too far down on his *t*'s and the rather strange loop he made whenever he scribbled the *S* in his own name: Saul Bathlow.

She'd kept her forged letter brief and to the point. She didn't want eloquence to throw Edna off the trail. Upstairs, Nevelyn glided across the backstage area. With such a massive work crew—and so many shifts involved—the mail wall served as the main source of communication. There were small, open compartments for every worker that ran from floor to ceiling. Nevelyn found the slot that had been marked with Edna's name and slid the letter carefully inside.

Most of the correspondence was between crew members. A note to remind someone on the next shift of what work someone had or hadn't done. But Nevelyn knew outsiders used the wall to leave notes for busy spouses or friends. She just needed Edna to see the letter.

There was movement on her left. She looked up in time to lock eyes with Tessa Brood. A shiver ran down Nevelyn's spine. She'd been so focused on her current task that she'd nearly forgotten her true enemy was in these same halls. Living the life that Nevelyn had been denied. Tessa looked away first, inspecting her own mail slot. The girl's bright hair was up in a tight bun that drew out the sharpness of her cheekbones. She had a pointed chin and narrow eyes. She was beautiful in the same way that most predators were beautiful. A luring that brought its prey in just a step, close enough to kill.

Not yet. I will face you soon enough.

Nevelyn knelt down and pretended to inspect her own mail slot. She heard Tessa leave and was about to leave too when she saw a slash of bright ribbon. She'd never inspected her own mail slot carefully. Only a passing glance, because the seamstresses rarely communicated in that fashion. She reached inside and found there were several notes piled on top of each other. All for her.

"What in the world . . . ?"

There were four folded slips of paper. All identical, except the newest one. Someone had taken the time to punch a hole in the paper and tie a lovely red ribbon through. Nevelyn realized this was likely because she'd missed the other notes. She unfolded the first slip, thinking certainly it was from Ren Monroe. The handwriting was cramped and messy and signed by another name:

Do you like coffee?—Garth

She could not help smiling as she unfolded the second, hoping she had them in order.

Gods, you must be a tea person. I've obviously offended you.—Garth

And then the third:

Or maybe you're religious? And my use of the term 'gods' has offended you. Lovely. I'm off to a horrible start with all of this, aren't I?—Garth

Finally, she opened the one with the ribbon.

I've figured it out. You don't know how to read! Which means I could write anything here and not even be slightly embarrassed about it. For example, I could write that the first time I saw you . . . I nearly called you beautiful. I could write that I wish I had been brave enough to just come out and say it. I could write that I'm afraid I won't get the chance to say it again, even if it's true. Anyways, it's a shame you don't know how to read. If you find someone who can read, please tell them to not say any of this out loud. I'd like to be the first one to tell you.—Garth

Nevelyn felt like her face might go numb from smiling. It was delightful, unexpected, and utterly terrifying. She read them one more time from beginning to end and fought the urge to clutch them to her chest. The last person to call her beautiful had been her father. Some small part of her had imagined she'd never hear the word applied to her again. Surely, this was the first time in her life that anyone had ever written a note to her. There was no ulterior motive either. No game behind what he was saying. He'd written these purely with the hope that she might write him back.

"Gods, what has you grinning like such a fool?"

Edna appeared at Nevelyn's shoulder. She was glancing nosily down, but Nevelyn had already folded the slips back up. She shoved the notes in her pocket and fought the blush that was rising in her cheeks.

"It's nothing."

"Nothing," Edna repeated. "What a fitting word for you."

The line was delivered so casually that Nevelyn almost missed that it was intended to be cruel. Her eyes flicked to the forged letter and back to Edna. She left the room, continuing to play the part of the mouselike creature Edna wanted. There was some small satisfaction in hearing the noise of delight the other girl made when she found a waiting letter in her mail slot.

A normal workday followed.

Edna had returned to the room buzzing about going on a date that night. Nevelyn's forged letter had instructed Edna to wait after work. Saul would be coming by to pick her up and escort her to one of the finer restaurants nearby. The others hooted and joked, but Edna's shallow joy filled the room like sunlight all afternoon.

One by one, their crew departed. There was no show tonight. Once every ten days, the entire playhouse emptied itself out. An actor might stay behind to rehearse lines—but Nevelyn knew it was by far the quietest the Nodding Violet ever got. She had been waiting for this specific day, counting on a mostly empty playhouse.

Edna took a small break. Nevelyn could tell she was starting to grow restless. She took advantage of the girl's absence. There were two wine bottles that had been stowed in her bag all day. She took them both out and used a small knife to remove the first cork. The stuff smelled cheap, but that didn't matter. Nevelyn found the spare glasses in a corner cabinet and set them out. She poured a rather healthy measure of wine, poured less in her own, and waited for Edna's return.

Eventually the girl's shoes came clicking down the wooden floors of the labyrinth. Nevelyn heard her enter. When she spied the wine, Edna snorted. No doubt she had some sort of insult ready on her lips, but Nevelyn was quite done with that part of their relationship.

Before the girl could speak, Nevelyn turned the charm on her necklace. She set the golden side facing out and drew on her magic. This was her true secret. Ren Monroe had only witnessed half of her gift. Certainly, she could vanish from someone's attention and memory. She could make herself into nothing. But her power ran in the other direction too. There was a push and a pull. She could also force someone to behold her, to prize her above all else. That was what she did now.

The spell struck Edna with full force. Nevelyn watched the girl's face twitch unpleasantly. Her lips curled into an unnatural smile. The girl's eyes lit up at the sight of Nevelyn. She slid into the seat across the table like a fish falling into a barrel.

"There's wine?"

"Just for you," Nevelyn intoned. "Go on. Have a drink."

Edna eagerly obeyed. It sloshed down her chin a little, but she took two healthy gulps. Her lips smacked together before she sighed delightedly.

"It's delicious. Where did you get it?"

"Have some more. I brought plenty."

Obediently, the girl tilted back again. She kept drinking until she'd finished the entire cup. As soon as she set the glass back down on the table, Nevelyn filled it to the brim. Edna was staring at her with open fascination.

"You have nice hair," she noted. "I like the little curls."

"Thank you," Nevelyn said. She was carefully maintaining the spell. It was always a delicate balance. She'd learned this lesson as a girl. Her father had taught her that magic craved order until it was ordered, and then it craved release. To keep Edna within her enchantment took more than a smile. "I don't like your hair. I really don't like anything about you."

Edna wanted to frown. She wanted to offer her own insult in return, Nevelyn was sure, but the power of the spell was too strong. Instead, she raised her glass.

"Cheers to that."

Another huge swig. And another. Nevelyn allowed the moment to stretch. She could see Edna's discomfort growing. The girl tried to fight that feeling off by drinking more—sip after desperate sip. The glass emptied again. Nevelyn opened the other bottle and quietly poured. Edna reached up and scratched at her collarbone. The spot was growing more and more red. There was no poison in the wine. Nothing so crass as that. Her twitches were growing more frequent because the spell was keeping her bound, and she wanted nothing more than to dismiss Nevelyn entirely.

"Something wrong, Edna?"

The girl twitched again. "My . . . well . . . I'm not sure."

She drank another healthy measure of wine. Her lips were starting to purple. Like bruises. The stain had dried along her chin, too, which had the unhappy effect of making her look a touch feral.

"You're wondering why you can't leave," Nevelyn offered.

Edna itched the spot on her collarbone again. Her words were starting to slur.

"Yes. What . . . why can't I leave?"

"The door is right there. No one's forcing you to stay."

Edna heard her but didn't move. Her fingers were tapping nervously on the table.

"Saul was coming to meet me."

"Was he?"

Edna nodded fervently, though she seemed to doubt her own words now. It was almost as if nothing outside this room existed anymore. There was only Nevelyn.

"Your hair is really pretty."

"You already told me that."

"Did I?"

The girl blushed at her mistake. Nervous, she reached once more for the wine. Nevelyn had never experienced magic like this herself. She did not know if anyone else possessed a spell quite like hers. She suspected, though, that it was rather unpleasant. Likely, the girl felt like crawling out of her own skin. Instinct would tell her to leave. Get up and go find out if Saul was waiting by the back door. Edna knew she did not actually want to be here with this girl she despised. But Nevelyn's magic was impossible to resist.

"Here. Have one more glass."

The girl's hands were already trembling. Her eyes looked unfocused. One thing that could be said for such a small girl, so slight of frame, was that it wouldn't have taken much more than that first glass to get her drunk. Nevelyn thought one more pour would be enough for her purposes.

"I'm . . . I'm going to be late."

"No worries there," Nevelyn replied. "Saul isn't coming, Edna."

Wine sloshed out of her cup. Edna hissed a curse before drinking deeply again.

"Not coming? But he wrote a letter . . . the sweetest letter . . ."

"I wrote that letter."

Edna's face looked stricken. Only for a moment, though. She fell back to adoration a breath later. "You won't remember any of this tomorrow," Nevelyn informed her. "Not a word of it. The amount of wine you've had? It could knock out someone twice your size. But the others will remember that you stayed late. They'll remember you were meeting your friend here. It won't be hard for them to piece it all together. Saul arrived. The two of you looked around the empty playhouse and thought it was a fine opportunity to be alone together. A little drinking. A little fun. If only it hadn't gotten so out of hand . . ."

Edna set the empty glass down on the table. "The . . . the world is spinning."

Nevelyn stood. She offered one final push of magic.

"Come with me. I know where you can lie down."

Edna agreed. She followed Nevelyn up the stairs. She paused briefly to listen for noises before aiming her ward toward Anna Mata's dressing room. The unquestioned star of their current run.

"Why don't you go to sleep?"

Edna agreed again. She set out her own cloak, curled up like a baby, and fell asleep in almost no time at all. Nevelyn released the magic. Her hands were trembling with the effort. It was by far the longest casting she'd ever done. Suddenly she felt an enormous thirst. Her throat was a desert. Her lips cracked. There was a half-filled cup on the nearest table. She gulped down the entire thing.

Edna was already snoring. Nevelyn looked down at her.

"You poor thing," she said. "At least you deserve this."

And then she set to work. It took the better part of an hour. She patiently removed Edna's clothing, trying her best to keep the girl covered. Anna wore a lovely white dress for the opening scenes. The material was gossamer and delicate. She slid Edna into the dress before taking the rest of the wine and creating stains all along the front.

Next, she set out several coats, stacked neatly in one corner, and constructed a makeshift bed. She didn't want Edna waking in the middle of the night due to discomfort. She might flee the scene. Far better if she remained comfortable. Far better if someone found her here in the early morning hours. After finishing that task, Nevelyn went back to the seamstress room. A quick rinse of all the glasses. She stole back the letter she'd forged and headed upstairs. Nevelyn glided through the shadowed backstage with a smile on her face.

"One down. Two to go."

The back door would be locked on the outside, but magicked so that she could still leave. She gave the door a shouldering heave. It felt cool and lovely. Night had come, bringing a fine breeze with it. She turned back to close the door and jumped out of her skin. A man was moving toward her through the shadows. She let out a clipped scream.

"Whoa. Gods! I'm sorry, Nan. I was just . . . It's just me."

It was Garth. Nevelyn's heart was thundering in her chest. She couldn't have been more scared. Worse, now there was a witness. Someone who'd seen her leave the scene last. If it came down to questioning, would Garth give her away? She forced those thoughts carefully aside.

"What are you doing here? Stalking me?"

He sputtered at that. "No. Well, I . . . I wrote to you?"

Nevelyn remembered the slips. She'd tucked them into the front pocket of her jacket.

"I know. I found them today."

He offered a hesitant smile. "You didn't think they were funny?"

Nevelyn snorted. "No. I mean, yes. They were funny."

"Oh good. So you *can* read."

"Of course I can read, you prat."

He laughed. "Well, that makes one of us. I had to get Daft to write all of those for me."

"Oh. Is that so? Well then, why isn't he here? Seems like he should be the one to take me to dinner. . . ."

Garth startled. "To dinner?"

"Gods. Please don't tell me you waited here this whole time and still aren't going to treat me to a proper meal. I'm famished."

She started walking away from the back door of the theater. Garth trailed her. He was smiling to himself. In truth, Nevelyn didn't know what else to do. She would have preferred to walk straight home, close the door to her apartment, and anxiously await the morning. Garth's presence complicated things. Her best strategy was to keep him close. And what was closer than a date?

He was rattling off suggestions for where they might go. Nevelyn half listened but could not help glancing over her shoulder one final time. The playhouse door was shut. No sign of Edna. No hint of a stagehand who'd witnessed her dark deed. Nevelyn had always had quite an imagination, but she supposed real life was not like the stories she'd grown up reading. Full of spies and romance and foul magic.

Lost in thought, she almost failed to notice the way Garth kept letting his elbow bump into hers as they walked. It was so obvious that she finally slid her arm through his. He looked as if he'd been waiting for that. The arrangement felt comfortable, natural. The two of them settled into a rhythm as they walked through the streets.

Well, she thought. *Maybe there is a little romance after all.*

21

REN MONROE

Nostra had once been relevant.

Nearly a hundred years ago, before the Broods made their famous pact with the Graylantians. The dispossessed northern settlers were having a lot of success raiding Kathor. Their forces moved with a fluidity that baffled the Kathorian generals. The northerners had a habit of slipping behind enemy lines and brutally punishing any company that marched too far north.

Until the Broods intervened.

One of Theo's ancestors was the first person to map out the entire area. There were two regions north of Kathor. On the coast, a sweeping valley full of rolling farmlands known as the Generous Valley. That was where the majority of the battles took place. Deeper inland, the Broods began scouting a narrower region known as the Hairbone Valley. Kathorian forces had practically ignored it to that point in time. The land was not fertile and the route scraped inward, up toward the mountains, which were still the rumored home of the last dragons. Too dangerous to bother with.

But when they charted the valley for the first time, they discovered a pass. The trail provided access to the northern shelf of the continent. Their enemy had been using the Hairbone Valley to maneuver around Kathorian advances, positioning soldiers and supplies behind them with ease. Gunner Brood built the fort that would eventually span the entire pass. Nostra bloomed in its shadow. A town to feed and entertain the soldiers who were assigned to defend the valley against northern incursions. Nostra became famous for turning around the war. It forced their enemy back onto the open plains to the west— where Kathor's numbers and magic proved overwhelming.

After the peace treaties were signed, the Broods continued to man the fort. After a few decades, though, they realized no armies would ever march that way again. The northern tribes of old were just farmers. There was no practical route to any major city or population—at least at that time. The fort's resources were redistributed until the castle became what it was now: a ghostly building watching over a corpse of a town.

Ren's back thumped against her seat inside the packed carriage. There was no established waxway route to the town, which left her rag-dolling down a poorly built valley road. At least it afforded Ren time to settle her thoughts. The next few days would be the most important of her entire life. Theo had no idea she was coming. The visit was meant to be a surprise. She needed Theo in a pleasant mood. The time had come for him to choose. He had witnessed his father's attempts to separate them. Now it was time for him to hear her story. All the sins his father had committed against her family. Ren would tell him what she'd told almost no one else. And once it was all out in the open—every secret laid bare—she hoped Theo would do the unthinkable.

Turn against his family. Choose her instead.

It was well past noon when Ren finally saw her destination. In the distance, the fort the Broods had built to watch over the Hairbone Valley all those years ago. The dueling spires looked like scabs growing up the side of that marbled mountain backdrop. She could just make out the two faded soldiers that stood as guardians on either side. There were still several hours left in her journey, but if Ren squinted, she thought she could see the famous beacon on the western tower. Historically, the watcher was charged with lighting that beacon if an enemy army approached the castle. There was a second beacon, back in the valley Ren had left behind, that could be seen from Kathor's highest cathedral. The beacons were lit once a year—for ceremonial purposes—but no watcher had lit them to announce an enemy in the last century. Ren would ask Theo to keep that streak alive and well.

She arrived at Nostra just before sunset. The carriage drivers had traded out somewhere down in the valley, which meant an unfamiliar voice called for all riders to disembark. Ren and an elderly woman were the only two left. Everyone else had gotten out at the previous stops.

Her feet set down on a cobbled central square decorated by a light frosting of snow. It wasn't winter yet, but Ren knew higher altitudes maintained colder temperatures far earlier in the season. Any precipitation would freeze, and rare were the days warm enough to fully melt that frost away. In a few months, the entire place would be locked in winter's embrace and the carriages would no longer be able to traverse the established paths between towns. She remembered Landwin Brood's promise that this would be her fate if she chose to stay with Theo—and she could not help shivering at the thought of living in this desolate place.

Ren tightened her cloak. The town of Nostra fanned out from the central square where she stood. There were dozens of rooftops running in every direction she looked. Once, the town might have boasted a thousand occupants. A thriving military base. Now most of the homes appeared to be abandoned. Ren turned back to find the carriage driver fussing over the horses.

"If I have the coin," she said, "can you take me up to the fort?"

The woman shook her head. "It's not a matter of money. There are no paths wide enough for a carriage. That's a journey you can only make on foot—and a journey I wouldn't make at night."

"There's no waxway station?"

"Only works if you've been there before. Have you?"

"No, but I can see the towers from here. Surely it's safe. . . ."

"The buildings are warded. You can port to the courtyards outside, but again, only if you've seen them before. Besides, it looks like the young lord is on his way down." The woman pointed to the shadowed hills. "See there?"

There were two slashes of color in the thicket of white and brown. She thought she was seeing the brightness of Theo's cloak, perhaps, but it was hard to make out from here. There appeared to be two people coming down the mountain. Far faster than should have been possible.

"Are they using magic?"

"Sleds. The two of them practice a couple nights a week."

Nearly everything about that sentence baffled Ren, but she asked about the part that concerned her the most. "The two of them?"

The carriage driver's eyes swung back to Ren. She seemed to realize for the first time that she was speaking with a stranger—and offering up information with each breath. Her fingers tightened on the reins as she turned away.

"Best ask him directly if you have questions," she said. "And you best get a room at the inn before dark. There's plenty available, but Hurst goes to bed early. Good luck to you."

Ren knew it was a dismissal. She turned back, watching the distant figures follow some predetermined path down the mountain. Ren remembered that first tug across her bond. When Theo arrived at Nostra, she'd witnessed a young girl there to greet him, and that had to be who he was with now. Ren watched their descent until the rooftops blocked her view. Not knowing what else to do, she headed for the building that looked like the inn.

She was given a key to a room, at a rate that was even cheaper than a typical Lower Quarter hostel. Ren set her things in her room and circled back to ask where the sledding path from the fort fed out. The innkeeper offered her directions.

"Right at the old clock tower, left when you pass the house that looks like a fishtail."

Armed with that odd knowledge, Ren pulled up her hood against the growing cold and headed outside. She was grateful to find the directions were quite accurate. They led her to an empty field. Across the way, two figures exited the woods, both dragging sleds behind them. Ren felt a flicker of unexpected jealousy. She'd never seen Theo with another woman. It was a strange taste on her tongue, but she could not deny that was what she felt as she watched Theo walk so easily at the other girl's side, their shoulders touching slightly. He was so lost in conversation that he didn't see Ren waiting for him in the distance. She couldn't help herself. She took that slight feeling of jealousy and gave it a proper shove across their bond.

Theo looked up instantly. He stopped in his tracks when he saw her there, shoulders dusted with snow. Ren felt a thousand different emotions as he abandoned his sled and sprinted across the snowdrifts. Here was the boy she'd tethered all her hopes to. Here was the son of her greatest enemy. Here was someone that, for better or worse, she'd started falling for. All those thoughts ran through her mind in the time it took Theo to reach her. He swept her up in a hug that took them both to the ground. She couldn't help laughing—even as the cold bit into her neck. Theo was as breathless as she was.

"You're here. How are you here? Is this a dream?"

She watched him for any sign of disappointment. Any sign that he did not actually want her to be here, but there was only excitement on his face. That look of pure delight remained until the interloper arrived. Ren saw that the girl had dutifully grabbed the rope of Theo's sled and patiently hauled them both across the snow. Her first impression of the girl, in Theo's vision, had been that she was plain. Now she saw that wasn't quite right. The girl had shaved her head sometime recently and allowed it to grow out naturally. The shorter hair emphasized round eyes that were a pretty shade of blue. And the cold drew out the roses in her cheeks. If she had looked mousy, it was simply because she was young. There was no doubt that she would be devastatingly pretty in just a few years. Too pretty for Ren's liking, but that didn't stop her from offering a hand.

"Ren Monroe."

"Dahl Winters."

Her last name surprised Ren, but the girl was quick to explain, as if she always had to explain. "Not those Winters," she said. "Everyone thinks I'm some distant cousin. But the name is common in the mountains. I'm no kin to any of them."

"Dahl grew up in the north," Theo explained. "On the other side of the pass. It was Peska, wasn't it?"

The girl nodded. Ren could tell Theo was trying to sound uncertain, as if he hadn't memorized her hometown. She realized that the two of them had likely been alone in that snow-covered fort for the past few weeks. How had she not thought about that reality until now?

"Dahl was appointed to my uncle's service right before I was assigned to replace him," Theo explained. "Really, she's been indispensable. Knows the castle in and out."

Indispensable. That was not Ren's favorite choice of words, but she smiled like nothing could have pleased her more. "How lovely."

"And very much beside the point," Theo said hurriedly. "You're here! You're *actually* here. Come on. We can talk about everything over dinner. Hurst makes the best soup."

Ren took his offered arm. They trudged back through the city streets, and it took Ren exactly the amount of time to get back to the inn to realize that he meant all three of them would be dining together. She'd traveled all this way to visit the boy who'd been exiled—to whom she was bonded—and he did not think that warranted some measure of privacy?

She shoved those thoughts back, hoping they didn't sit along the surface of her mind long enough for Theo to feel the emotions that went with them.

Dinner was in a back room of the inn. Apparently, Theo was staying there that night as well. Ren took a small comfort from the fact that he'd arranged separate rooms for himself and Dahl. But she also realized this was a regular occurrence. Sledding down from the fort, dining with some of the locals, sleeping here for the night. The two of them had formed habits together.

"I'm supposed to practice," Theo said, dabbing a piece of bread in some kind of corn chowder. "It's one of the mandatory requirements of the watcher. Even if this post is completely pointless, I thought I might as well do my best. In the case of some imaginary attack, my first task is to light the beacon. If I can't do that, I travel the waxways to Nostra. And if that isn't possible, I'm supposed to take one of the sleds down. The first watcher had them carve trails through the forest—all the way down from the fort to the town. It's already iced over. Really, it's kind of fun. Dahl and I have been trying to improve on our times."

The girl offered a tight-lipped smile but said nothing. Theo seemed to realize that he was, once again, focused on the wrong person.

"Anyways. I wasn't expecting you to come. Not so soon."

Ren lifted an eyebrow. "Should I leave and come back later?"

"No," Theo fumbled. "Absolutely not. This is the best news. Trust me. You're a far more welcome guest than my last one."

Another surprise for Ren. She kept the emotions off her face.

"Who was the first?"

"My brother came."

Ren felt a shiver run down her spine. Thugar Brood had traveled through the Hairbone Valley? He'd humbled himself enough to come to this remote place? Ren remembered the look on his face when Theo had first been exiled. The unmasked smugness.

"That's surprising. I didn't realize you two were so close."

Theo actually choked on his soup. He hacked a cough into the back of his hand for several seconds. "Close? We're not close. Do you not remember Thugar?"

"Of course I do. You're right. I guess he's not like you."

"Not at all. He's a walking mimicry of my father," Theo said. "Just take away some of the cunning and replace it with brute strength. We've never gotten along. We never will."

It felt like Theo was chastising her for what she'd said, but Ren realized he was partly speaking for Dahl's benefit. Distancing himself from his awful brother. Maybe something had happened during Thugar's visit to the keep? She had a hundred questions that she didn't feel like she could ask, so she settled on a more reasonable inquiry.

"Why did he come?"

Theo shrugged. "Why do you think he came?"

Ren knew the answer. An extension of Landwin's desires. He would have been sent to speak sense to his brother. Let go of this random girl. Abandon this course, and we'll bring you back where you belong. The fact that Theo was still in Nostra was a good sign.

"They seem very determined," Ren said.

"And I am more than a match for them in that regard."

He smiled, and a brightness filled the space between them. Across their bond. An emotion so pure that Ren could barely stand the way it felt. The way it coursed through the darkest parts of her heart, the emptiest spaces in her chest. She did not like the way it held up a mirror to her deepest desires—how it confirmed there was more to all this than pure strategy. This was a pleasure on the verge of pain. She was forced to look away. The intensity vanished, but the feeling did not entirely fade. Ren guessed it would never entirely fade. She liked him. It was as simple as that.

Which only made the presence of a guest even more awkward. Ren turned to Dahl.

"So, you're new to Nostra? Who did you replace?"

"Sonya served before me," Dahl answered, spooning a bite of soup. "She was quite old. She left to be with her grandchildren, but not before training me. I learned a great deal from her."

"Meaning you weren't a castellan before now?"

Dahl looked surprised. "No. There are only so many opportunities for someone as young as I am. I served as a housekeeper in my town. I hope you don't think me above my station. I'm grateful for my position, my lady, and I work hard to make up for any inexperience."

"That's not what she meant," Theo said, cutting in on Ren's behalf. He looked surprised by Ren. She realized that she wasn't playing her expected part. Maybe he'd assumed a kinship between them. After all, she'd grown up in the Lower Quarter. Her parents were from a lower station. If anyone could sympathize with a young, working-class girl, it would be Ren—not him. Dahl's use of the term "my lady" only emphasized how Ren was coming off. She adjusted course.

"Merely curious. You seem quite capable."

There was some friction across their bond. Theo clearly didn't understand what was happening, and Ren was not sure how to make him feel comfortable. She finally turned back to him.

"You seem at home. Are you? Doing well here?"

A shadow crossed his face. Again, she managed to feel as if she'd insulted him.

"I am in exile." He set his spoon down. "Away from the only city I've ever known. Away from friends. Away from my family. Away from you. No . . . I do not feel at home."

Dahl was watching them. Ren felt the heat on her neck. All the things she wished she could say would be best said in privacy. Instead, she had to make her apologies in front of a stranger.

"I just meant that you're in better spirits than I expected. I'm sorry, Theo."

He waved the apology away. "I'm just tired. I can never seem to sleep enough up here. Who knows? Maybe I'll get used to the cold one day."

"Maybe you won't have to," Ren said.

She meant the words to be hopeful. Instead, that looming sense of disconnect yawned across their bond like an unexpected shadow. Ren could not determine its source and knew she would not find out more until they were alone. She resigned herself to eating her soup, tearing off chunks of stale bread. Time felt like it was crawling. The end of dinner could not come soon enough.

22

REN MONROE

Ren waited that night for Theo to knock on the door to her room.

Every time she shifted, the bed's coils groaned beneath her. She waited for several hours before sleep took her. In the morning, she bolted upright. Squares of golden light were sneaking between the gaps in the blinds. Ren sat there, rubbing a sore spot on her side, trying to figure out why Theo hadn't come. It was disconcerting. Was Dahl the reason for this change in him? Or had something been said during Thugar's visit? Ren could not help considering the possibility that Theo might actually abandon her. It was possible that her arrival was simply making him feel guilty over a decision he'd already made.

Breakfast was meager. Boiled eggs, stale bread, dried meat. Ren saw Dahl out front through one of the windows, loading the sleds up with various goods, but there was no sign of Theo. She worked her way through the tasteless meal, hoping they might talk while Dahl was indisposed—but Theo's arrival was perfectly timed with the girl's return.

"How did you sleep?" he asked.

"I slept fine," Ren answered. "You?"

"Better than I have in weeks. Come on. We should start up to the castle."

She noted the way he avoided eye contact. That strange disconnect loomed again. Ren almost demanded an audience with him right then, but Dahl was on the move and Theo followed on her heel. It would have to wait until they reached the castle.

Outside, the sun was bright but did little to actually warm them. She set her luggage on the sleds, only to have Dahl immediately rearrange them. Ren tightened her scarf, pulled up her hood, and followed Theo up the mountain.

He turned into a guide once more. Pointing out distant peaks. Talking through old historical battles. She loved that he'd studied all of this, but the history lesson was tainted by the strange gulf between them. The path itself was not particularly daunting. Still, Ren saw why her carriage rider had suggested waiting until the sun was out. It was not hard to imagine a misstep in one direction sending wayward travelers skidding over the side of any number of dangerous precipices. Dahl forged ahead, pulling the heavier of the two sleds, while Theo hung back with Ren. It was not quite enough privacy for her to broach the more serious subjects, though.

Halfway to the castle, Ren started to sweat. She wasn't even pulling anything, but the sunlight had intensified and the wind from the valley had died. It was quiet, too, with nothing but their breathing and the distant calls of wheeling hawks to break the silence of the mountain pass.

It was a relief when they reached the flattened tier of land fronting the castle. The building looked uglier in the morning light. She could see great gaps in the stones. All of the crumbled arches. It looked like a piece of armor that time had knifed through in certain places. Even the two soldiers looked like they'd suffered through one too many battles. As if they'd rather limp home than keep defending the castle beyond. And this, she realized, was Theo's home. Not just for the last few weeks. Likely, he'd begun imagining his life for the next few years happening here. Maybe this was the source of his frustration. A reality that Ren had not had to wrestle with.

"I'm sorry, Theo."

He frowned back at her. "For what?"

"You've been alone out here. I'm sure it's been difficult."

"Oh. Right. No, it isn't a very charming place. Dahl has been here. Sam and Mather rotate the kitchen work. I haven't been completely alone, but . . ." He trailed off as he looked at the daunting spires. "You're right. It's a lifeless place. I feel like I've been trying to draw a pulse back out of a corpse. The only thing there really is to do up here is read."

Ren smiled at him. "Not the worst activity."

He smiled back, but the expression was flicker and gone. They trudged around the larger snowdrifts. Dahl pressed ahead with her load. Ren saw the growing gap as her chance.

"Theo. We need to talk. Just the two of us."

His eyes flicked back to her. There was such pain on his face. She'd never seen him look so uncomfortable, and she felt that echoed across their bond. What was happening?

"Of course. I was hoping later today, but I suppose there's no point putting it off."

And with that ominous beginning, he led her into the waiting castle. Dahl set to the task of unloading. Theo guided Ren through abandoned halls, full of morning light. It might have been charming if it didn't show off all the gathered cobwebs and dusty corners. Theo gestured.

"Dahl cleans a different wing each morning," he said. "But it's impossible to keep the entire place in good repair with a staff this small. Can't afford to put enchantments on everything either, since there's not a magic-house to refill vessels in Nostra. I decided to focus on the rooms that we spend the most time in."

Ren was led through another hallway—the windows stained and putrid—and up into a library. This room, at least, was in pristine condition. Books ran in a circle around them, reaching from floor to ceiling, and Ren could see why Theo would choose this room to be his refuge. There was a rolling ladder for the upper shelves, chandeliers dangling above a desk and several reading chairs. Even the windows offered a sweeping view back toward Nostra.

Yes, this room would have been her choice as well. Theo closed the door behind them and gestured to the waiting armchairs. Ren took her seat, and the irony of this moment was not lost on her. She was sitting inside a literal piece of history. One of the buildings that had carved the Brood legacy into the history books. If this conversation went the way she hoped it would, she'd take one more step toward dismantling that legacy.

Theo sat down with a heavy sigh. He'd always looked pale, but there was a hollowness to his features. The slightest thinning in his cheeks. A discoloring beneath the eyes. A part of her instinctually wanted to pull him across the room into her lap, to hold him for a while and stroke his cheek and tell him it would all be okay. But she knew she'd come here to ask even more of him.

"I needed to tell—"

"I know why you're—"

The two of them cut off. It almost helped Ren's nervousness, this fumbling start.

"Why don't you go first?" she said.

Theo bit his lip. "I know why you're here. It's hard to explain, but I saw you. Speaking with my father. At the apartment in the Heights. It was like I was standing there with you."

He was clearly expecting her to be shocked. Ren nodded instead. "I know. I felt you there."

"You did?"

"Of course," she said. "You pulled me once, too, Theo. The day you arrived in Nostra. I witnessed your first glimpse of the castle. It was the same magic. Across our bond."

He leaned back in his chair. "Fascinating. I didn't realize it had happened before."

"It had. So, you saw that conversation. . . ."

Theo nodded. "I heard what he offered you. Not just a normal life. A position with one of the great houses. A position you've always wanted. And then you arrived here without any warning. . . ." He shook his head, struggling to maintain eye contact. "I know you've come here to break the news to me. I just . . . I thought I'd make it easier on you. You don't have to ask, Ren. I'll absolutely release you from our bond. If that's what will make you happy."

His words were a shock of cold water. They ran down through her skin, past her bones, straight to her heart. She hadn't realized how much she felt for Theo until this moment. She sank back into the cushions of her chair and could barely keep from laughing.

"You think I came here to break up with you?"

Theo frowned. "Yes?"

Now Ren did laugh. The rest of the conversation would not be humorous for either of them, but at least this part was funny. "You didn't witness the whole conversation, did you? I thought I felt something. Almost as if you . . . pulled away. You didn't see my response?"

He shook his head. "No, I retreated. I'm not sure how to explain it. Maybe you felt the same way. Being there was . . . too painful. It was like I was *inside* your feelings. The emotions were too raw. It hurt so much that if I didn't leave, I felt like I might die."

"Then you don't actually know what happened," Ren said. "I told your father no, Theo."

The sudden brightness on his face was unmistakable. All the pieces fit together. No wonder he'd been so eager to avoid a private moment. It made so much sense. Witnessing his father's offer but not seeing Ren's response. And then her sudden arrival. She would have leapt to the same conclusions. It nearly broke her heart to think about.

Quietly, Ren stood. She crossed the room, following her earlier instinct. She placed a single kiss on his forehead. When he looked up, she leaned down just far enough that their lips could brush together. Once, twice, three times. Theo shivered, and Ren knew he'd gone weeks without any kind of physical touch. Isolated in this place. She kissed him one more time for good measure and then took her seat again.

"I'm not here to break up with you, Theo."

Theo's expression faltered. "But Ren . . . my father's offer . . ."

"I know, Theo. He was awful. As awful to me as he was to you at that dinner party."

"I'm not talking about that," Theo replied unexpectedly. "I've known that side of him my entire life. I was talking about Seminar Shiverian. My father's offer was . . . good for you. Timmons said last year that your dream was to be a spellmaker. You could start an entirely new life. Away from my horrible family. I don't want to be the one thing that's binding you to House Brood. If you secretly want that life, I'll still agree to it. We can be severed—and at least one of us would be free."

Ren saw he was trying to sacrifice himself. It was noble. If her affection for him was their only link, it might even be the right choice. But he didn't know the rest of the story. And how could he? She'd never been brave enough to tell him.

"You do not know my dreams."

He stared back at her. "Tell me, then."

She settled deeper into her chair. A quick glance to the entry confirmed the door was still shut. They were alone. "Are you sure you want to know?"

He didn't hesitate. "Of course."

"My father's name is Roland Monroe. Does that sound familiar?"

Theo shook his head.

"It should. He is the man your father's hound is named for."

She could see the gears turning in his mind. The impossibility of her words. Likely, Theo was trying to recall some employee that his father had been fond of. Imagining some charitable reason for naming a dog after a human being.

"My father worked in the canals. I used to visit him. My mother would send me there to bring him lunch sometimes. I'd watch the workers. Each day they labored to build your father's dream. Their conditions were poor, though. My father . . ." Ren fought for the right words. "He was a leader. If others were afraid to speak, he'd be the first to raise his voice. He organized a union. It undermined your father's efforts, but it would have benefited all the workers involved. As I understand it, my father won. The union succeeded in halting the progress of the canal. Your father called a meeting to concede to their demands."

Ren's breathing slowed. Her heart barely felt like it was still in her chest. How many times had she relived these memories? And always alone.

"You saw what happened. During our encounter with Clyde. That was the day. My worst memory, and it was all arranged. Your father asked him and the other union leaders to make an appearance at the unfinished bridge. It was where they were going to officially shake hands—but when they posed for a picture, the bridge collapsed. Everyone said it was so unlucky that they were standing there when it happened. Except it was no accident, Theo."

She could see him trying to piece together everything.

"It was your father who arranged their death," she said. "He invited them all there. Some of his own personal inspectors were seen that day, 'examining' the undergirding of the bridge. A hundred different people confirmed the rumor, even if there was never enough evidence to prove it. Not that it would have mattered. What judge would prosecute the head of one of the five great houses? You found that out last year, didn't you? After you almost killed the people in that teahouse.

"This is the unfortunate truth, Theo. Your father murdered mine. Roland Monroe got in his way—and he was killed for it. Not because he wronged your father. Not because he insulted your family name or committed some unspeakable crime. He was killed for asking that people like us be treated with decency."

Ren saw a hundred questions waiting to burst out of Theo. He was chewing on his lip, drinking it all in. She went on before he could speak.

"I was eight, Theo. Just eight years old when I attended my father's funeral. Your father came too. I always thought that was his final insult to my father's memory. One last chance to spit on his grave. The authorities who investigated the situation found your father innocent. Everyone called it a tragedy, but a few of us knew the truth. It was murder. But the worst part is what you told me last year, Theo. Attending the funeral wasn't his final insult, was it? What's your dog's name?"

His voice ghosted out. "Roland."

"Named after my father. I imagine he took a lot of pleasure from that. Watching a creature skulk around your estate, always underfoot, bearing the name of the man he'd just successfully buried. I might have never known that part of the story. Not without meeting you. But you wanted to know why I'm here. Aside from my affections for you, this is the answer. I am here to avenge my father. I'm here to seek justice for the man responsible for his death."

The room fell silent. There was only Theo's chest, rising

and falling. Ren's hands shook slightly at having finally confessed all this to someone. They stared at each other with the weight of new truth sitting on their shoulders. Theo broke the silence.

"You're certain?"

"I am certain, Theo. As certain as I could be about anything."

He bit his lip again. "That's why you didn't like me."

Ren couldn't help snorting. "I avoided you for that reason, but come on, the party? I had plenty of reasons to dislike you, Theo."

He nodded at that memory. Ren could feel the slightest rumbling across their bond. She'd been waiting to see what emotion would come out of all of this. Pain? Embarrassment? Instead, she felt the beginnings of rage. White and hot and glowing from the very core of him.

"Tell me what you want me to do."

The moment had arrived. Ren had dreamed it might come decades from now. If her original plan had worked, she'd be serving time in House Shiverian or House Winters, quietly working her way up through the ranks, positioning herself to strike back at the people who'd taken her father's life. Instead, the moment was here. In this mountain pass, sitting across from a boy who could either unlock every door for her or slam the gates in her face.

"I want you to choose me."

"I have chosen you."

"Then choose me again. Choose me forever. Do you really think I could suffer to live out my years as Landwin Brood's daughter-in-law? Imagine what that existence is like for me, Theo. Sitting at the same dinner table. Having to exchange words with him at every party. I will not live the rest of my life in the shadow he's created for me."

"So what are you saying? What do you want me *to do*? Kill him?"

"That would be a fine fucking start."

Her words echoed off the walls. There was enough light that she could see dust motes floating in the air between them. Theo shoved to his feet. He didn't turn to leave, though. He started pacing. Back and forth. Ren knew she was walking a narrow path. A tightrope that would require all her focus to cross.

"You've never imagined it?"

Theo shook his head, not looking back at her. "Of course I've imagined it. I *hate* my father, Ren. But there's a large gap between hating someone and killing them. You're talking about—"

"Justice."

Theo turned back. "I was going to say murder."

"It would be both," she replied. "Who else could make him answer for what he did? What he's done to you and to me? All the hundreds of sins that no judge or god will ever punish?"

Theo's face looked wretched. "You're talking about my *family*, Ren."

"Yes. Your family. The people who grinned as your father sent you into exile. As you were forced to come to this godforsaken place—for the great crime of stooping to love me."

She saw how that wounded him. The truth always struck the deepest.

"You didn't hear the end of our conversation," Ren said. "On that balcony. After I rejected his offer, your father threatened me." She weighed how much she should stretch the truth. "He told me that I would be sent here to live with you. We would spend the rest of our days in Nostra. Exiled. And he told me that was the best possible scenario. That I would be lucky to make it out here in the first place. 'Those mountain passes are tricky,' he said. 'Accidents happen all the time.'"

Ren felt how that stoked the flames within Theo. The way his rage continued building and burning across their bond. Theo was pacing again. He looked as ready as he'd ever be.

"But he would never actually . . ."

"Kill me? Listen to yourself, Theo. He *killed* my father. Why not me as well?"

Theo lashed out at one of the porcelain bookends on the nearest shelf. He sent it flying across the room. It struck the wall, shattering into pieces. She saw his hands were shaking.

"Even if I wanted to do this. Even if I agreed to kill my own father. How, exactly, do you propose to do that? He's the head of House Brood. Every asset we possess is at his disposal. He has defenses that only the great houses know about. Our estate . . ." He trailed off, gesturing wildly. "Gods, Ren. The estate is nearly impossible to breach. They took away my access before I left. Those walls are so deeply enchanted that they could hold off entire armies. It's not just that this would be difficult for me. What you're asking would be difficult for anyone. We could have Able Ockley with us, and he'd tell you the same thing. My father is one of the most protected men in all of Kathor. What, exactly, is your plan?"

Ren answered. "I have thought about this for the last decade. Every action I've taken. Every move I have made. All in service to this task. Do you think I would do all of this without a plan?"

Theo didn't smile. His eyes, though, were cold and calculating. She saw a confirmation of what she'd secretly been hoping for all this time. All she needed was for Theo to believe this was possible. That Landwin Brood was not a god. She knew it had started at the dinner in the Heights. In front of the city's elite, Landwin Brood had humiliated his own son. He'd exiled Theo to teach him a lesson, but now all it meant was that his son was far enough away—filled with enough rage—to actually imagine a future without him.

Ren waited for Theo to sit back down. "I am not the only one who has been wronged by House Brood. About ten years ago, there was a smaller house in Kathor that was destroyed. All of the members of that house were executed. It began with a minor offense to your brother. Do you remember that family's name?"

Theo's face went pale. This all would have happened when he was a child, but that did not mean he didn't know about it. His voice was quiet, distant.

"House Tin'Vori."

Ren quietly began explaining what would happen next.

23

REN MONROE

The next morning, Theo took Ren by the hand and led her carefully up the western tower. They skirted loose stones and sprawling cobwebs, arriving just in time to watch light crawl over the empty plains. Sunrise patiently carved mountains into the empty nothing. The two of them wrapped themselves in extra blankets, curled around each other, and watched morning take its first breath.

"You're quiet," she noted.

"The whole world's quiet up here."

He kissed the back of her hand. Ren could feel herself slipping. It had been such a gradual slope, her affections for Theo. Maybe that was why it actually ended up being so dangerous to her. She would have resisted a quick falling in love. Some nonsensical, butterfly feeling. Falling for Theo had been more like walking slowly down a hill and finally realizing she was in a new place, breathing in an entirely new air. She knew this moment—wrapped in his arms—was only uncomfortable because it was like nothing she'd ever felt before.

Theo had made a liar of her. The promise she'd made to the Tin'Voris was on the verge of collapse. What would she do? If she had to actually choose? Would she save Theo or take her revenge? The thought made her stomach turn. It would be far more preferable to arrange events so that no choice would have to be made. The two of them would burn House Brood to the ground—and then they would make their own house from its ashes. That would be the way of it.

It had to be the way of it.

"Now you're quiet," he noted.

"What else is there to say?"

She turned back. Their eyes met. Theo leaned toward her. Ren felt a bright thrum across their bond just before their lips met. He tugged pleasantly on her bottom lip. She reached up and ran a hand through his golden hair, pulled him closer, kissed him harder. All the emotions running across their bond flared in a white-hot instant. It felt like the world was on fire, like it should be. The two tangled together beneath those blankets for a long time—the sunrise forgotten.

The waxway candle was almost done burning.

Ren sat there, quietly focused on an image in her mind. An empty field outside Morningthaw. It was a small town that her carriage had stopped at on the way to Nostra. She'd purposefully walked out and memorized an abandoned stretch of grass, as well as the delicate flowers that bordered the field. Every detail she needed to travel back along the waxways now.

Theo was there. He sat behind her, humming softly. She'd

almost told him to stop being distracting, until she realized that she actually liked the sound. It was calming.

Down the hall, she could also see flashes of Dahl performing her various duties. The girl had been scarce ever since Ren's arrival. An incredibly hard worker, but rarely visible. Ren would find her bed made or her towels folded, without once spotting the girl inside her quarters. All of her initial fears about a forbidden romance felt foolish now. She saw how Theo saw her—like a little sister. Their kinship was wholly derived from a shared loneliness. Who else did they have up here besides each other? Ren hoped Dahl would continue to be useful when Dahvid Tin'Vori arrived. She knew it would be no small task to smuggle hundreds of soldiers through the mountain pass in the middle of the night.

Don't race ahead, she thought. *Take it step by step.*

Dahvid still needed to win his gauntlet. Ren would need to check in on Nevelyn Tin'Vori's progress. If there was even a hint that their plan was going awry, she and Theo would fall back on their own contingency plans. They would not waste their one shot at House Brood on a crumbling strategy.

She kept expecting her bond-mate to balk. Instead, he'd been the steady, driving force of all their discussions. Ruminating on every possible strategy. Offering up family secrets like they were the cheapest currency in the world. Ren had learned so much from him in their brief time together, but she suspected there were secrets Theo didn't know about his father's power. Secrets that would only come out when they truly put him to the test. They'd find out what those were soon enough.

"The candle's almost out," Theo whispered. "Last chance to join House Shiverian."

A smile ghosted on her face. "I prefer the sound of House Monroe."

"Honestly, I do too."

There was quiet. Ren watched the wax continue to melt down the side of the candle. The time was coming. She did not want to leave but knew it was necessary. They must part now if they hoped to survive together.

"The last time we traveled the waxways," Theo said, "you saved my life."

Ren nodded. "I don't like to think about that."

He'd looked so pale. So very on the verge of death.

"I think about it all the time. I wouldn't be here without you, Ren."

She waved it away. "It was nothing."

"It was everything."

He kissed the side of her head before rising. She watched him circle around the other side of the candle, and a sharpness filled the space in her chest. Was this truly what people spent their lives chasing? Why did love feel so much like a knife that had been sharpened and plunged in far too deep? She swallowed once before looking him in the eye.

"Promise."

He frowned. "Promise what?"

"Promise you're with me."

He held her gaze. There was a great burst across their bond. It felt like a thousand ropes were lashing themselves to her, invisible hands tying each one. It felt unbreakable and vast. Theo whispered the words into that waiting power.

"I promise."

The magic sealed his words. She knew he would not waver,

no matter what. Ren felt like she might cry if she kept looking at him, so she fixed her eyes on the flickering flame instead. She drew on the image of that empty field again. Her breathing slowly calmed. It had always been Ren's preference to snuff the candle herself. Her hand was steady as she reached out to pinch the waiting flame. Just before the spell activated, she heard a final whisper from Theo.

"I love you, Ren."

Magic pulled her into darkness before she could answer. Ren shoved forward through space and time. Her chest tightened uncomfortably, unbearably. Then her feet set down. The world colored in around her. She was in the empty field. Ren stared at the trees and the flowers and the distant town that was just waking up. She had a feeling Theo had waited until that final moment to say the words so that she wouldn't have to decide whether or not to say them back. Ren found it much easier to whisper the truth to the trees.

"I love you too."

She patiently set out the next candle and followed the rituals, lighting it and picturing the next location. She'd need to travel through the waxways twice more to get back to Kathor. It would be the work of just a few hours, though, instead of a full-day carriage ride. Ren's first priority back in the city would be to meet with Nevelyn Tin'Vori. Hopefully, the girl had made fine progress in Ren's absence.

The second candle burned down quickly. Ren echoed the same process and appeared on the edges of an abandoned farm. Candle, light, repeat. It was only noon when the third and final candle burned down to nothing. Ren had intentionally picked the location for its elevation—which she felt was close enough to the Heights to work. With the balcony of Theo's apartment centered in her mind, she made the final leap through time and space.

Pain.

Ren dropped to her knees. There was a pain in her neck so sharp and so piercing that she felt like screaming. Instead, she gritted her teeth, blinking down at the sun-brightened stones. Had something gone wrong with her jump? Was she in the wrong location? It took nearly a minute for the sharpness to fade. When Ren was finally able to raise her head, she saw the answer.

There was a full-sized stone gargoyle on the balcony. No more than a few paces away. He would have been several feet taller than Ren if he stood upright, but his posture was slumped so that his great stone fists knuckled down on the floor to keep him upright. The reason for Ren's sudden pain was struggling beneath the creature's left foot. Pinned to the ground.

"Vega!" Ren said. "Let her go!"

She reached for the horseshoe wand at her belt, but the gargoyle only offered a nasty grin. Ren saw the creature's eyes flick up, looking beyond her, when something struck the back of her head with force. Darkness threaded the light, consumed it entirely, and the world faded.

24

DAHVID TIN'VORI

Dahvid's training sessions had an audience now.

Every time his boots crunched down on the arena sand, Darling's observers were already there. They would take meticulous notes as he stretched, as he moved through swings and stances. When he began the walk home, a new set of observers would trail him through Ravinia's streets. Dahvid knew every breath he took from now until the day of the gauntlet would be counted, every gesture weighed. Darling was searching for weaknesses. Anything that could be exploited in the duels to come.

Cath eagerly worked to give him a new strength instead. She had been sketching day and night to perfect the next potential tattoo. Today's session in the cleansing room might be their last chance. Out of superstition, Cath had not allowed Dahvid to see what she'd been working on. While he wouldn't mind another weapon in his arsenal, he thought the session would be far better if they used it to smuggle her out of the city.

"We'll have an hour, Cath. There are passages below the parlor. I can have you on a ship before Darling's crew even knows what happened. I'll fight better if I know you're safe."

In answer, Cath slammed down a set of brushes.

"And what about me? I get to sit in some foreign city, waiting to hear if the man I love is dead? No. I will not leave you. Quit asking."

She returned to her sketching and refused to speak on the subject again. Dahvid came behind her, gave her shoulder a light squeeze, then began his ritual stretches. The two worked in mutual silence until it was time to leave. The cleansing room awaited them.

He let his fingers tangle through Cath's as they navigated the busy streets. He did not bother pointing out the man and woman who both neatly folded the papers they were reading and began following them some fifty paces back. Cath still spotted them.

"He's afraid you'll win," she whispered. "If he's watching you this closely."

"Very few people win," he corrected. "*Because* he watches this closely."

The two of them turned a corner, skirting a few of the larger markets. Darling's spies could follow him every hour of the day, but there was some pleasure in knowing they could not unearth the only secret of his that mattered: the tattoos. All of that hidden magic pooled in his veins. They were his only advantage in what was coming.

They arrived at the cleansing house. Cath set a hand on the small of his back. She was giving him the lightest of pushes. "Go ahead and lie down. I'll be in in a minute."

The stone table waited for him. The spell had not been activated. Not yet. Dahvid moved inside the room and began undressing. He was on the table, towel covering in place, when the magic began the way it always did. He felt it digging down—half pain and half pleasure—into his skin.

And then the lights flickered.

Every muscle tightened. Dahvid's eyes snapped open. He was not alone in the room.

"Hello again."

The beautiful Darling strode out of the shadows. He looked even more eerie in the strange white glow of the cleansing room. Every feature slightly askew. A perfect mockery of beauty. Dahvid saw the chain trailing from his wrist, winding over the stones, and vanishing through a door in the dark. He'd had no idea there was a second entry to this room. Darling paused at the edge of the stone table, eyes boldly wandering Dahvid's length. Even hooded and bound, he had not felt so vulnerable before the warlord as he did now.

"Hello, Darling."

"That was so very clever of you," Darling replied—and Dahvid could just barely hear the scraping voice echoing from the shadows. "The other night. Acting before I could announce the match with Ockley. My own mistake, really. I shouldn't have given you the chance. It was clever and daring and very much on the verge of rudeness."

"I thought it was gracious of you to accept the challenge."

Darling snorted. "As if you gave me a choice. You knew what the rules were. Alas, here we are. The gauntlet is set. I will make nearly as much money on that event as I would have on the other one. Still, gauntlets are nerve-racking. There's always the potential cost of losing, isn't there? That tantalizing prize. A single wish. Ask *anything* and I will grant it. Gauntlets are especially worrisome when a mysterious little creature like yourself is involved. . . ."

His eyes roamed again, gliding from tattoo to tattoo.

"I'll admit I find it titillating. I've hosted hundreds of gauntlets, dear boy. I began hosting them before you were born. And I have predicted—with absolute certainty—which challengers would win . . . and which would lose." He leaned forward, hands pressed to the stone mere inches from Dahvid's bare feet. "But you are the first real mystery of the last few decades. It is going to be so delightful to see how it all unfolds. Before we get to that, however, we need to have a discussion."

Dahvid wished he could sit up. He wished he had clothes on. He wished he knew how many guards were waiting in the dark behind that empty doorway—ready to intervene.

"A discussion?"

Darling nodded. "I need to know what your request will be."

Dahvid couldn't hide his surprise. In all their research, he'd never heard of challengers being asked to make their request in advance. He'd always imagined it more like a scene in a play. The victor heaving a great breath, wiping blood from their hands, bellowing out a demand.

"What if I haven't decided?"

Darling shook his head. The chain attached to his wrist rattled slightly. "That will not work for me, and it will not work for you. We are beginning a negotiation. You can have *anything*—within reason. The conversation starts here and now, because I need to make sure that we can actually come to terms before the gauntlet occurs. You will tell me what you want, right now, or I will make sure there is no possible chance for you to survive the fights to come."

Dahvid's surprise edged into shock. He stood for a long moment, unsure what to say. In the silence, he heard the slightest hiss. The sound was impossible to ignore. On the ground, the chain linking the two Darlings was beginning to smoke. Dahvid realized the white magic in the room was attempting—and failing—to cleanse the spell written in those chains. A dark passage of souls, an unholy conquering. It was a small reminder that this man did not operate within any set of rules besides his own. Dahvid would do well not to challenge that now.

"Fine. I want an army."

Darling's eyes narrowed. "An army. How many soldiers, exactly?"

"I want a thousand men. Your third and fourth company would be my preference. We watched all of their training sessions—down by the beach. Those are your best soldiers. Good generals too. I would like to borrow them for one month. Not so long that you'll be exposed without them."

Now the warlord's eyes glittered.

"That is a very interesting request. Would it have anything to do with House Brood?"

Dahvid shrugged. "I just like the sound of boots marching."

That earned a rare laugh from both Darlings. Both the musical and the guttural, weaving in and out of each other. Dahvid watched as the warlord began to pace.

"That is quite an expensive request," Darling said. "Maybe the most expensive, with the exception of Agatha, but she's more than earned her keep over the years. I highly doubt you intend to remain in my service. When you march south, you won't be marching back, correct?"

Dahvid nodded. "Correct."

"And my soldiers . . . if they don't return? That would be very costly."

"What if I offered them a percentage of spoils? The soldiers remain on your bankroll, but they can benefit from my . . . conquest. Would that work?"

Darling considered that. "It might, but there are other costs to discuss. What do you think will happen when you march an army south? You might just end up starting a war."

"Remove your insignias," Dahvid suggested. "Let them march as mercenaries. Then all responsibility would be set at my feet. If I fail, none of this will matter. If I succeed, well, I doubt you'll have to fight any wars. There won't be any retribution."

"Is that so?"

"Yes. Because if I succeed, one of your great rivals will be wounded."

Dahvid knew the truth. Nevelyn had walked him through the economics. Ravinia always benefited from a weakened Kathor. Historically, if the larger city struggled, it invited an opportunity for other powers to rise. Ravinia had grown twofold during the War of Neighbors for exactly that reason. If he could destroy House Brood, he would be doing the warlord a grand favor. Darling surely understood that, even if he was pretending to muse over the subject. There was nothing but greed in his eyes.

"An army," Darling said. "Very interesting indeed. I will take all of this into consideration. It is not out of the question. I needed to see if we were close enough on terms to proceed. I'm sure you can understand. There have been challengers in the past who demanded vaults full of gold. Asked me to bring dead dragons back to life. Such men cannot be reasoned with, but you are what my scouts have all reported you to be: measured. A man who appears entirely in control. We shall see how long that quality lasts once your gauntlet begins. Enjoy your session."

He glided out of the room. The chain rattled twice before vanishing after him like an iron snake. When the door slid shut, Dahvid watched as the edges blended perfectly back into the wall. No wonder they'd never noticed it before. He sagged back on the table. His chest heaved with each breath. The cleansing spell had been waiting all this time, distracted by the darker magic in the room, and Dahvid surrendered himself to it now. The pain was a welcome distraction. For a time.

Eventually fear returned. It was no small task to stare this city's god in the eye and speak as he just had. It was not easy to admit what they'd been planning for the last seven years to a man he did not trust at all. He could tell, though, that he now possessed something very valuable:

Darling's curiosity.

Cath's tattoo failed again. Dahvid told her not to worry. It was not pivotal to their plans. She seethed for the rest of the day, until they tangled together in bed, both eager to help the other forget the day's events. Long after she had fallen asleep, Dahvid found himself turning restlessly. Sleep eluded him.

He went to the window. The place was too poor to afford

proper balconies, but when he shoved the window open, a breath of night air rushed in that was equally satisfying. He could hear movement below. Shadows moving between circles of lamplight. Conversations echoed up to him. The passing scent of flavored cigarettes. Dahvid stood there for a long time, listening to the world.

After a time, his naked body began to shiver. It wasn't winter yet—but the nights in Ravinia were brisk, and on the verge of true chill. Goose bumps ran up his thighs, down his arms. He looked at the tattoos stretching over his skin. For the first time in years, he allowed his eyes to linger on the edges of Ware's final tattoo. The one that Dahvid had never used, never called upon. He reached out and shut the window. In the reflection, he turned so that he could inspect the whole image.

A hand was reaching down, from his shoulder blade to his lower back. The stretching fingertips fell just short of a body of water. Ware had rendered the surface dark—a sort of muddled swirl of shadows that ran horizontally, from the middle of Dahvid's back to his hip. As he stared into the depths of the tattoo, he thought he could see another hand—beneath the surface—reaching up. He could almost convince himself there was a fingertip breaching the surface of the water and that the two hands were separated by the smallest strip of his own pale skin.

Curious, Dahvid reached back and let his thumb hover there. Just above the surface of the tattoo. He could feel immense power pooled there. It had continued growing all this time. That wasn't true of every tattoo, but it was true of this one— and of the scarlet traveler. Not using them was like allowing a tree to keep growing to its fullest height. Dahvid had used the scarlet traveler two or three times a year, though not once since arriving in Ravinia. But the reaching hand? It had never been activated. Its power had been growing for nearly a decade now.

As his thumb hovered, he could sense qualities in the magic as well. It wasn't an exact science. Truly, he never knew how a tattoo would manifest until he actually activated the spell and watched it take shape. But every single one of his tattoos had a *feeling*. A core quality. He could tell this one was an exchange. He had no idea with whom or for what. He simply knew that if he activated the magic, there would be a trade of some kind.

Dahvid had memorized Nevelyn's plans for them. Every careful step that would lead from this lonely, claustrophobic apartment and to the Broods' estate. Plans were all well and good, but if life had taught him anything, it was that something would go wrong. He saw Ware's two tattoos—the flower and the reaching hand—as last resorts. If the plan failed, he'd need their power.

He moved his finger away from the tattoo. The underlying hum of magic faded. He could hear Cath stirring in her sleep. The room felt cool enough now for him to lie down without sweating. He settled back in beside his love, but his mind was far from that bed, that place. His thoughts raced ahead. He was dreaming of the gauntlet—and eventually, the Broods. He imagined Thugar Brood broken before him, begging and at his mercy.

It was that image that finally put him to sleep.

25

NEVELYN TIN'VORI

Nevelyn was promoted.

Poor Edna was gone. Such a shame. The others in the seamstress room were all chatting about it. For all their supposed loyalty, they now eagerly ripped the girl apart, like dogs gorging themselves on the first scrap of meat that hit the bowl.

Her work increased, but she was more than up to the task. It actually helped to keep her calm. Focusing on the mundane. There had been a certain pleasure in destroying someone. A feverish feeling that echoed her desire to destroy the Broods. But Edna was not her true enemy. No one in the seamstress room was. They were obstacles. The real enemy was pacing one of the rooms above them, quietly rehearsing her lines. Nevelyn needed to adjust her aim. It wasn't long before she had her first opportunity.

"Girl."

This was Kersey's favorite summoning for her. Nevelyn

knew the cast split between the two senior seamstresses. Half of them were under Kersey's province, and the other half belonged to Faith and John. With Edna gone, Nevelyn would have more direct contact with the players.

"Take this up. The brat demanded changes. *Again*."

Faith made a tongue-clicking noise from across the table but didn't comment beyond that. Nevelyn knew she was referring to Tessa Brood. Even if she was not the most famous actress on set, Tessa was easily the most highly ranked person at the Nodding Violet. Second in line to the Brood throne. All that power didn't matter to the elder seamstresses. The girl had become Kersey and Faith's target for derision because of her excessive wardrobe requests. Neither of them would have ever dared to speak this way to her face, but they felt they were the masters of this small corner of the universe—which loosened their tongues regularly.

Nevelyn collected the black dress and headed upstairs. Her stomach turned uncomfortably as she walked. She'd seen Tessa Brood several times already, but this would be her first face-to-face confrontation with the enemy. Not some imagined encounter or a fever dream. This would be terrifyingly real—another person, speaking and moving and breathing the same air as her. Nevelyn steadied herself before heading upstairs. Her next maneuver required perfect timing. She lingered in the common rooms of the backstage. Checked her mailbox and delightedly saw a note from Garth. She did not reach down for it, but the thought of opening the note later had her smiling.

Every now and again, Nevelyn's eyes would dart to the second door, down the hallway on her right. She was waiting for Tessa Brood to depart. After thirty awkward minutes, she was rewarded. The Brood heiress appeared. She was straight-backed, her hair pulled up in a flawless braid, her chin jutting out—pale and beautiful. She wore the most fashionable leggings Nevelyn had ever seen. The fit ran loose down her legs but fell well short of her ankles, displaying a pair of lovely red shoes. Her top was black, the fabric crossing from hip to opposite shoulder on both sides, leaving plenty of that nearly translucent skin on display. Nevelyn knelt down, pretending to inspect her mail slot, as Tessa passed by. There was a fine tap-tap as she walked across the hardwood. Nevelyn waited until the girl vanished into another actor's room.

And then she was moving.

Tessa's door was still open. This was common. No one really brought valuables to the playhouse. Too many people and moving pieces. It was impossible to account for lost items. The lights were on, glowing too bright. There was a standing wardrobe to the right of the mirror. Nevelyn reached up and hooked the prepared dress's hanger on the highest latch, letting the fabric dangle down the front for a proper display. She quickly smoothed out any creases and stepped back. All she could do now was wait.

A hundred different sounds reached her ears. She heard actors in the two neighboring rooms. On her right, someone sang a lovely melody—bright and hopeful. On her left, there was a garbled growl. It sounded like someone attempting the same line over and over. Twice she heard footsteps, but she knew they weren't the right ones. Too soft or too slow or too padded. Each time, she stepped forward and pretended to be in the middle of the act of hanging up the dress again.

The interlopers passed the room without comment.

Finally, she heard the slight tap-tap of Tessa Brood's shoes. Nevelyn steeled herself, stepped away from the dress once more, and pretended to be assessing it one final time. She tilted her head ever so slightly. She also kept her back to the doorway, so it would look as if she had no idea that Tessa Brood was behind her. She waited for the moment those tap-tap sounds faded. She could feel Tessa paused at the threshold, noticing someone else was in her space.

Nevelyn let out a dramatic sigh and delivered her line.

"Such a shame."

She turned to find Tessa Brood with one eyebrow raised like a knife.

"Such a *what?*"

Nevelyn feigned surprise and embarrassment. She didn't need to pretend to be afraid. She *was* afraid. This woman was a part of the family that had ruined hers. She was also the key to their revenge. So much was tangled in her words that they came out with all the proper emotion.

"I'm so sorry, my lady. I was just delivering Kersey's dress for you. I didn't say anything. I was just talking to myself. She made all the necessary alterations. Begging your pardon."

She set chin to chest, all subservience, and tried to slip back out into the hallway. Tessa Brood was far too proud for that. "Wait, girl."

Nevelyn stopped like a fish with a hook through its lip. She hunched her shoulders as she turned, putting on a polite but trembling smile. "Yes, my lady?"

"I heard you. You said the words 'such a shame.' What did you mean by that?"

Nevelyn shook her head like a nervous hen. "Oh, it's really not my place, my lady. I'm an assistant. I really ought to be getting back to the seamstress room. . . ."

"I have asked you for your opinion. You will give it before you leave this room."

Flawless. Nevelyn took a step closer to her enemy. She swallowed theatrically before gesturing to the dress—allowing Tessa Brood to see the way her hand trembled.

"It's just . . . My lady, I'm *really* not comfortable making comment."

"You already commented. Finish the job."

"It's old-fashioned," Nevelyn sputtered. "Even with the requested alterations—which certainly helped—it's simply not suited to you, my lady. I've seen some of the rehearsals. This dress. It just doesn't fully capture your character in the opera, nor does it display your beauty properly." She quickly set a hand over her mouth, as if she'd uttered something forbidden. "Oh, please don't tell Kersey I've told you that. I'll be skinned alive, my lady."

Tessa Brood had turned back to the dress. She was making her own careful examination. Nevelyn saw the way the girl's lips pursed with dissatisfaction.

"Opening night is nearly upon us," Tessa said, more to herself. "It doesn't help to hear this now."

"My apologies, my lady. I really didn't mean—"

"It is not a critique of you. It is a critique of your predecessor. Stop sniveling. You aren't in any trouble."

Nevelyn went silent. She kept her eyes pinned to a small square of fabric on the floor. She was doing her very best not to smile at how well all of this was going. The seed had been planted. Now all she needed was to be dismissed. Allow the natural momentum to run its course.

"What's your name, girl?"

It was hard not to flinch. First, at the fact that she kept calling her *girl*, even though Nevelyn felt certain they were only a few years apart from each other. She knew it was less a measure of age and more a measure of power. Tessa Brood was dealing with someone *beneath* her, and that was how people like her talked to people they thought were beneath them.

But she also flinched because she'd been so close to answering that question with her true name. Some small part of her wanted to say it out loud, bold and bright. *I am Nevelyn Tin'Vori, and I have come to kill you all.* Pride burned in her chest for a brief moment. But now was not the time.

"My name is Nan, my lady."

"Old-fashioned. You should know with a name like that," Tessa Brood said, smirking slightly. "All right. I will wear this dress for the first run of private shows, but tell Kersey I demand an alternative *before* the full house shows begin. That's when the reviews happen, and I'll not be caught in the wrong dress for the write-up. That should give her ample time to reconsider my wardrobe."

Nevelyn bit her lip nervously. "I'm sorry, my lady, but you want *me* to tell her? She's my superior. I'll be fired if I suggest . . ."

"Oh, very well." Tessa Brood sighed. She ran a finger along one of the dress's laces. "I will be the one to inform her, so that you can save your precious skin. I suppose you've been help enough. Though, I might have gone on thinking this was pretty if you hadn't opened your mouth."

"Of course, my lady. Apologies again. I didn't know you were there."

"And yet," Tessa Brood noted, "that is when we are most honest, is it not? When we think that no one else will hear us? I will always appreciate someone who tells the truth."

There it was. The first small sense of trust between them. Nevelyn stood there until Tessa Brood waved her away with one of the most demeaning gestures she'd ever seen.

"Out. I've rehearsals."

Nevelyn fled, back into the dark labyrinth below the stage. She could feel the quiet rush of what had just happened snaking over her skin. There were goose bumps running down both of her arms. She had to take a moment to collect herself outside the seamstress room before entering. John and Faith were arguing about some new book that was being published. Kersey glanced up briefly as Nevelyn took her seat.

"Well? Was the priss satisfied?"

Nevelyn nodded. "No complaints, madam."

That earned a snort. "Give her a few days. I'm sure she'll find something to whine about."

"Wine?" Faith added from across the table. "I'm pretty sure Edna drank it all."

That had the group howling with laughter. Even Nevelyn smirked. The next part of the game was already in motion. She had Tessa Brood right where she wanted her.

Now it was time to attend to Kersey.

Nevelyn had never been a spy. She was no trained rogue. But it wasn't all that difficult to avoid Kersey's notice. The old crone lived in her own, very specific world, and rarely engaged with anything that existed beyond that scope. For the next few days, Nevelyn observed every action she could. Kersey walked home at the same time every afternoon. She paused at the same three stalls, bought the same food, the same candles, the same everything. Not once did she depart from her routine. It was like watching someone who'd figured out what they liked about the world a few decades ago and now went about the business of only enjoying those things.

The woman lived in a basement apartment, adjoined to a much larger house that apparently belonged to her nephew. The nephew was a successful sea trader who'd been kind enough to take in his old and widowed aunt. Nevelyn did not have the time to look through public documents, but she suspected that Kersey paid a reduced fee to live there. Her interactions with the family living above her were minimal. Her nephew appeared to be very busy with work. His wife did not care much for Kersey. Only their daughter visited, a small girl with bright red hair. She'd talk a little each day with Kersey before fleeing back to the comforts of the house above.

Nevelyn noted each interaction and found the visits annoyingly inconsistent. There was no way to predict when the girl might come. It seemed that only the hours after bedtime were safe, and Kersey's own bedtime was not much later. A small window of opportunity, perhaps?

At night, Nevelyn used her magic to avoid notice. Turning the heart necklace to the shadowed side, she would cast her spell out in every direction; then she set herself up in the alleyway across from Kersey's apartment and watched through a small, square window. Kersey would always read two chapters of whatever book she was enjoying. She would listen to a bit of music, and then she would tuck in for the evening. Again, the routine did not vary. Every night was the same.

Nevelyn only unearthed something useful by accident.

On the first two nights, she abandoned her post to return home. There wasn't much point to watching an old lady's bedroom door—knowing her to be asleep. And she knew the suspended dress in her apartment would not finish itself. Both nights, she'd needed to cast soothing charms on her wrist joints. The amount of work was starting to wear on her bones, but a little boon of magic allowed her to press on past the pain. She was satisfied with her progress.

On the third night, however, she unintentionally fell asleep in the alleyway. Exhaustion swept her into dreaming, in spite of the discomfort and the danger. She'd woken up in the predawn hours, startled by her lapse in judgment. There was no point in rushing home. She'd likely be made fun of for wearing the same clothes, but at least it provided an opportunity to follow Kersey's morning routine.

The woman got dressed. She drank tea. She returned to her bedroom. And she never came back out. Nevelyn sat there, growing more and more uncomfortable with each minute that passed. The sun was rising. The streets to her left and right stirred to life.

Where was the old crone?

Enough time passed that she simply had to leave. She could not afford to be late herself. Nevelyn hurried through the streets, trying to ignore the slightly stale scent of her clothing. She arrived breathless and a little late at the playhouse. Thankfully, John and Faith were standing over by the mail wall, bickering about something. Nevelyn took advantage of their distraction, slipping downstairs. She turned the corner into the seamstress room and nearly leapt straight out of her skin. Her heart raced double. Kersey looked up in surprise.

"Gods, you look like you've seen a ghost, girl."

Nevelyn tried to recover and ended up stammering. "I'm . . . I'm sorry. I just didn't mean to be late, and I didn't want you to be mad."

Kersey frowned. "You're just a few minutes late, girl. Just because you work in a playhouse doesn't mean you have to act all dramatic about things. Go on. Grab your needles."

Nevelyn obeyed. She could not understand how this was possible. She'd watched the woman return to her bedroom. There hadn't been any sign of departure at all. No one had come or gone through the front door to her apartment. So how had she beaten Nevelyn here?

Her mind raced as she worked. Was there a secondary door inside the bedroom? Maybe a basement stairwell that led into the actual house? Nevelyn thought if that was the case, the little girl would use that route as well. And perhaps that would be too little privacy? Still, what other answer was there? Determined to learn, Nevelyn set up again in the early-morning hours.

Kersey woke at the same time, prepared the same tea, and returned to her room. Once more, she didn't reappear. Nevelyn angled herself so she could see both Kersey's alley entrance *and* the front door to the actual manor. No one came out of either. Nevelyn watched and waited until she was certain the woman wasn't coming—and then she raced to work again.

Kersey was already there.

Nevelyn paced through the dark labyrinth of the underground until the answer hit her right in the chest, like a stun spell. Of course. There was only one possible explanation. Clues had been sitting there all along too. She'd never *really* seen Kersey arrive at work, had she?

"You're using the waxways to get here," she whispered to herself.

Nevelyn smiled. She could work with that.

Over the next few days, she abandoned her spying, refocusing her efforts on the dress in her apartment instead. It was a patient and deliberate process. Weaving thread and then magic and then thread and then magic. She kept walking back over to her inspiration—a very old picture of a very lovely dress—in the hopes of making sure she was maintaining the integrity of the project. She worked until her bones felt like dust and her eyes had grown so heavy that they might never open again.

She slept better than she had in months. All of her nervousness siphoned away. When she finally finished Tessa's dress, Nevelyn opened her alley-facing window. She set a piece of red ribbon there and closed it—so that the fabric would dangle down, visible to anyone who passed.

This was their prearranged signal.

It was time for one more meeting with Ren Monroe.

PART III

The Execution

26

REN MONROE

An incessant whisper brought her back to the waking world.

Ren groaned, turning over slightly, too weak to really push back to her feet. It was a surprise to find herself unbound. The ghost memories of her time being tortured on that remote farm last year threatened to surface, but this was not that. Still, unbound did not mean free. There were others in the room with her. At least six livestone creatures by her count—and their master, seated in the center of the room.

She'd never met Zell Carrowynd in person. Really, she'd never heard of the woman until Theo mentioned their family at the same party where he'd been exiled. Afterward, she'd been handed the post of warden instead of Theo. All so that Landwin Brood could publicly spite his own son.

Zell's family was a minor house connected to the Graylantians. Ren's research had turned up little beyond that. No romantic relationships. No close friends. She knew the woman was quite cautious, though. After all, Ren had been expecting this meeting weeks ago.

"Ahh," Carrowynd said, leaning forward in her chair. "She lives."

Zell was one of the tallest women Ren had ever met. Even seated, she appeared to be a giant in comparison with Ren. This effect was emphasized by a trio of stone mice that skittered around her ankles, fussing over the shoelaces of her boots. The gargoyle was there too, perched in an open window well above their heads. The last two livestone statues present were the tigresses. A younger version of Ren would have thrilled to see them. Now they looked a bit too menacing for her liking. The two guardians had prowled the docks all her life. Watching as boats loaded and unloaded. Ren remembered there was a running dare amongst Lower Quarter kids to see if anyone was brave enough to tug their stone tails. She'd never met someone foolish enough to try. It took Ren a moment to realize that the whisper that woke her was not from anyone—or anything—in the room.

It was coming across her bond. Theo had felt Ren's absence. That sudden departure from awareness would have been quite startling for him. She tried her best to communicate a feeling of comfort back to him. She was alive. She was all right. At least for now.

"You're Zell Carrowynd."

"And you're Ren Monroe."

Ren nodded, and immediately regretted it. Wincing, she touched the back of her head. The source of all that throbbing pain was there—though the blood felt like it had long dried.

"How long was I out?"

"A few hours."

"Did you really have to hit me on the head?"

Zell shrugged. "I'll only feel bad about that if you have the right answers to the questions I'm going to ask you."

Ren almost nodded again but caught herself. "Ask them."

"I was . . . approached. By an heir to one of the great houses."

Approached. Ren could tell that was a very carefully chosen wording. The warden of Kathor could not be *hired* or *requisitioned*. It would be illegal to ask an official servant of the city to serve the interests of one specific house—though Ren knew it happened all the time. She also knew exactly who had approached Zell. None other than Thugar Brood.

Ren felt the great satisfaction of a correct guess. Landwin Brood wasted nothing. He did not rule one of the great houses because he was a fool. Theo's appointment as warden would have extended their family's power to an entirely new sphere of influence. Ren knew he wouldn't sacrifice that entirely. It was clear to her then that he'd cut a deal with the Graylantians. He would deter Theo so that one of their candidates might replace him, but only if the Broods had access to them. It fit their family's cutthroat business mentality. Sacrifice a child's happiness for the family's greater gain. Ren was starting to enjoy how predictably conniving they were.

"And what was it that Thugar Brood wanted you to do?"

Zell's face gave away nothing. Her little mice had skittered all the way up one leg and were now racing one another across the straps of Zell's leather jacket.

"He asked me to destroy your bird."

Of course he did.

Ren felt indescribable satisfaction watching another piece of the puzzle click neatly into place. She'd researched Zell rather thoroughly. There really was so little on paper about her. Almost no news clippings at all. Balmerick had next to nothing in its records. The only real point of emphasis, then, was how disconnected she was from the rest of the world. Ren had figured out what Landwin Brood simply couldn't imagine: Zell loved stone more than people. She'd grown up training with statues—as Theo had with Vega—but her only friends had been the three mice who were now playfully looping in and out of her loose hair. Men like Landwin Brood saw the livestone creatures as tools. A number of previous wardens had seen them that way too. Not Zell Carrowynd. These were her friends.

"Which you didn't do."

Carrowynd sighed. "Of course not. The only time a livestone being should come to harm is in defense of the city—or if it goes feral. We've had to put them down before, but only as a last resort. Which brings me to my first question: Why would they want to kill your bird? Most houses view a livestone creature as a prized possession. Like enhancers. It gives them an edge over the others. So why would they make that request of me?"

"The answer is simple: Landwin Brood does not approve of my relationship with his son, Theo. He approached Theo about breaking our bond—and Theo refused. Then he offered me a position in another house to sever the connection—and I refused." Ren was providing these details because she knew it would make everything feel more despicable to Zell's sensibilities. "Killing Vega was the only other way. After all, she was the conduit for our bond."

Understanding dawned on Carrowynd's face. It was a shocking revelation, but not to Ren. She'd seen this moment coming like clockwork. Landwin Brood was too cunning not to notice. His scouts would have observed her usage of Vega. From there, Brood would have realized that the reason they shared a vessel was that it was used to perform the ceremonial bonding spell. A person could not fully destroy livestone. Banish it, perhaps. Wound it, yes. But only livestone creatures could kill other livestone creatures. Landwin Brood had followed all of this to the inevitable conclusion: he could command Carrowynd to order her statues to kill the bird on the Broods' behalf.

"I hope they at least told you a good lie," Ren said.

Carrowynd nodded. "They said you stole Vega from his son through dark magic."

"Dark magic," Ren repeated, smiling. "I suppose love can feel that way sometimes."

Hearing that, Carrowynd took her feet. She looked incredibly annoyed.

"Well, this was a colossal waste of my time. If you bonded through Vega, that means she chose you too. She's a living creature. It would have been well within her rights to reject your request. Which means Vega trusts Theo—and she trusts you. I refuse to destroy a living creature solely because it suits the whims of House Brood. You are free to go."

The gargoyle had watched in silence, motionless. Now it swooped down from the rafters. Ren watched the creature unfold its wings. Vega came tumbling out. Ren heard a mournful cry as the hawk righted itself and fluttered up to her shoulder. She couldn't tell if she'd forgotten the pain of having the bird there or if it was clutching tighter out of fear.

"You're safe now," Ren whispered. "Welcome back."

The gargoyle had trundled over to the door. It was reaching for the handle when she spoke.

"Wait. I have more to discuss."

Carrowynd turned back with suspicion. This was always going to be the delicate part of their transaction. Ren needed to ask something of her without appearing to be just like the Broods. Once more, she planned to appeal to the woman's sensibilities.

"What is it?"

"I want to make a trade."

"Oh? And what could you offer me that the Broods did not?"

"A livestone statue."

That drew a sharp look from Carrowynd. "But you can't give Vega up. Unless you're willing to sacrifice your bond?"

"No, I won't do that."

Ren fell briefly silent. She was surprised by the strength with which she'd said those words. She realized they were utterly true. No matter what happened, she was not willing to leave Theo.

"I'm not offering Vega."

Carrowynd looked even more curious. She sat back in her chair and signaled to the gargoyle. It took up a guardlike position, leaving the door shut to the outside world.

"Go on."

"I need information from you. In exchange, there's a statue that the Broods use for entertaining their guests." She'd seen it once at Theo's party—and again when she'd visited the Brood estate. "I've witnessed the abuses personally. If you filed the right petition, you could have that livestone's memory examined. There's a bylaw . . ."

"I know the law. Those petitions never work. The great houses wield too much influence."

"Because no one within the family is ever willing to admit malfeasance."

Carrowynd considered that. "You would go on record?"

"Happily, if you give me what I want in exchange."

The three mice were starting to titter and grow impatient. Ren saw that same impatience written in Carrowynd's expression. This was not a girl who suffered the company of humans very often. Ren needed to get to the point. Luckily, she'd been thinking about how to frame this question for a long time. Livestone creatures enjoyed riddles, and she had a good one for them.

"Ask your creatures this. Where does Landwin Brood *not* go? What stones has he built but never visited?"

The woman leaned back in her chair. Ren did not see her mouth move, but there was a whisper on the edge of hearing. An answering sound filled the air. Like feet shuffling over stone. Ren watched in fascination. There was all kinds of lore surrounding livestone creatures. Bonded as they were to the city's defense, Ren knew they could all communicate with one another. It was also rumored that they were bound, in some deep way, to every stone in the city. Not just the enchanted stones that walked and talked. They knew every building, every bridge, every tower. Her mother used to say, "If these walls could talk," and Ren suspected they could, and did.

After a time, the strange whispers ceased.

Carrowynd's eyes narrowed. "47 Farthing Road."

Not one of the Broods officially registered addresses. How very curious.

"And I trust that address will not be mentioned to anyone else?"

"If you give me the details about that statue, I will keep your secret."

Ren could not help smiling. It wasn't her secret. It was Land-win Brood's secret.

"Deal."

27

DAHVID TIN'VORI

D ahvid sat alone in the dark—beneath the arena.

His armor was fitted perfectly to his body. Leather straps cinched tight enough that the armor would not slip in a key moment, but not so tight that he lacked mobility. He had already examined each of the specially designed slits that allowed access to his tattoos.

All that was left now was the killing.

The entire room vibrated. All the noise from above funneled down into that dark space, echoing until it sounded like the rumbling footsteps of a god. He rubbed his hands together and tried to keep his breathing steady. It would not do to work himself up before it all began. Most potential champions weren't defeated by clever swordplay but by the exhaustion of their own limbs. As the fights went on, their footwork got sloppy. Their movements grew haggard. It was already easy enough to die in the arena, even when you were at your very best.

Dahvid sat in perfect stillness, wasting nothing, until a lone voice echoed down the hallway, calling his name.

He stood. A quick crack of the neck, and then he was walking. The great doors protested as they were thrown open. Two guards stepped aside. Dahvid came striding out into the lights and the noise and the chaos, sand crunching with every step. He saw Darling first—seated like a king. His attendants were all there, and then a sea of faces fanned out in every direction. More people than Dahvid had ever seen in his life.

He felt some small relief when he spied the woman next to Darling. Agatha Marchment wore a dress. No armor or dueling attire. At least he would not have to face her. Most of the other gladiators looked ready, though. Dahvid knew that Darling was showing off his great arsenal of options. They'd spent so long wondering who he'd fight. The time had finally come to find out.

He turned his attention to the landscape of the arena.

Each gauntlet unfolded on a slightly different course. The makers had likely spent day and night shaping this particular arena with magic. Darling's gladiators would have been permitted to come early, assessing each feature, while he was only allowed to see it minutes before his first fight began. A small advantage for them. There was a central circle of normal sand. Identical to all the other arenas. Encompassing that, however, were added features. A downhill slope that led to a series of tight turns with high walls. A labyrinth of sorts. Those paths fed into a section that was decorated with dangerously sharp spikes. At least twenty of them, protruding from the ground like half-buried dragon teeth.

Finally, on the far left, Dahvid saw the ground was built like a puzzle. Interlocking pieces of stone that—he guessed—would shift if the fight took him in that direction. After memorizing the obstacles and spacing, Dahvid walked to the very heart of the arena. He shouted out the words he'd been instructed to say.

"I set my life down here before you. Come. Take it from me if you can."

The crowd roared and the earth shook and Dahvid felt death in the air, thick as smoke. Darling held up a hand. No one else could quell a storm so quickly. All the voices fell away.

"Five rounds. For each round you survive, you will have exactly five minutes to rest and recover before the next round begins. You are allowed no other respite. You are not allowed an attendant. You are not allowed to accept anything from the crowd or receive any magical boon from anyone besides yourself. To break these rules is to forfeit your life. Understood?"

Dahvid squared his shoulders. "Understood."

"Your request for a gauntlet is accepted. Call the first!"

The arena filled with a rhythmic drumming. The onlookers pounded their hands against their chairs or the stones or their own bodies. A great rolling tide of angry noise. Dahvid fed off that energy, allowing the rage to pool inside his own body. He settled into his stance.

Before the first challenger came, he found Cath in the crowd. Darling had honored her with a seat on the same row. Their eyes met. As he prepared to knock on death's door, he finally felt certain that he loved her. This was true love, and he did not need his father or mother or Ware to tell him it was true. He only wished he'd said something earlier. Now he could only stare the words at her. She nodded once, as if she could hear his thoughts, and that was enough.

The gates opened.

Dahvid let everything slip away. The faces of the crowd did not matter. There was no past. There was no future. Only the now. Dust spewed from the entrance as a man trotted out in steel-thick armor. There were slits for his eyes and mouth, but other than that, he was fully encased in the shimmering metal. The tactic was obvious. Protective armor intended to draw Dahvid into a prolonged fight. Darling had chosen this man for the purpose of dying a very slow death.

"I am the Harbinger!" the man shouted defiantly. "Fear the Harbinger!"

The crowd roared back. Dahvid pitied him. Calling out his own name so that they might know who he was. All so that he might die moments later. The man paused at the opposite edge of the inner circle. They both tensed, waiting for Darling's signal. In that stretching silence, Dahvid reached for the tattoo at his wrist.

His sword. It was likely his most versatile spell, because it was a spell that no one expected to be versatile. A sword was a sword. Unless it wasn't. Dahvid made a slight alteration in the summoning. He used his nail to dig into the skin of his wrist. Enough to draw blood. When his finger lifted, the magic of the spell released. Dahvid sensed the slightest manipulation nestled within the normal casting. Light pooled in the air beside him. Too bright to look at, until his hand found the grip of the sword. The crowd had reached a fever pitch. Ravinia's king stood and gave his signal.

The fight began.

Dahvid snaked forward. No hesitation. The Harbinger settled into a defensive stance. He was not as technically sound as the paladin. Dahvid could tell by his footwork. He was just a man trapped inside a big metal suit. He had a buckler and a pathetic-looking short sword. Dahvid picked up his pace. Their collision became inevitable. His upper body twisted to the right. A full-shoulder turn that exposed his own left flank but allowed him to take a massive, two-handed swing at his opponent. The kind of swing that could fell a tree. The Harbinger raised his shield, heels dug in, bracing for the first ringing impact of metal against metal.

But there was magic in the blade.

Dahvid's sword whispered straight through the metal shield. It did not rebound against the thumb-thick armor of the man's breastplate. It hunted what Dahvid had magically commanded it to hunt: flesh. He felt some resistance as he found exactly that, but his swing had been a brutal one. The blade came out the other side, splattering blood in a terrible arch.

The crowd stared in confusion. There was no mark on the metal. No sign that Dahvid's sword had passed through armor at all. The only sign that the fight was over was the way the Harbinger sank to his knees, then slumped sideways. Blood started pouring out of every opening in his armor. When they took him back below, they'd open him up and see his body cut in two.

Dahvid quickly dismissed the enchanted blade. He needed the full rest time for the tattoo to properly regenerate. There was finally a roar from the audience as they realized he'd won—as they understood death had come far quicker than they'd ever imagined possible. Whispers were running up and down Darling's row. He couldn't hear the words, but he knew what they were saying. What had just happened? How had his blade passed through the metal? Dahvid smiled to himself, then sat back down in the sand, eager to conserve his energy.

The magic was a trick he'd learned as a boy. An alteration—like the moral sword he'd used with Ren Monroe. He could bind the sword to certain laws and logic. If he asked, it would ignore metal and seek flesh and bone. Dahvid knew he couldn't use the trick again. The rest of the challengers would be warned and ready. But once was enough. He'd wasted no energy. Burned none of his tattoos. One down. Four to go.

Waiting was an unexpected annoyance. He had never been good at meditation, but he sat there with his eyes closed and legs folded as the crowd began to chant his name. He knew later that these five minutes would not feel like nearly enough time. Best to savor them while he could.

The crowd was beginning to grow restless when Darling took his feet. The warlord was preparing to signal for the second fighter. Could it really have been five minutes? Dahvid's eyes darted down to the tattoo on his wrist. It hadn't quite fully regenerated. Not yet.

"Call the second!"

Dahvid stood. His eyes kept flicking down to his tattoo. It was nearly restored. Another thirty seconds, and he could summon the sword again. A woman was walking out of the opposite entrance. He recognized her from Nevelyn's notes. They called her the Ravinian. An everyman champion who'd risen through the ranks over the years. Her weapons of choice were a pair of boxing gloves with steel-enforced knuckles and iron spikes along the wrists. Dahvid was trying to remember their notes about her fighting style when Darling's voice echoed over the crowd.

"Begin!"

He glanced down and saw the final lines of color filling in the edges of his tattoo. He needed ten more seconds. The Ravinian was too smart for that. She saw that he hadn't called the sword. Her eyes narrowed and in the space of a breath she was on him. He narrowly dodged a gut punch. The spikes on her gloves scraped against his stomach armor. A second punch nearly caught his jaw. He'd never backpedaled faster in his life.

She punished his retreat. Two more strikes—testing jabs—and then she unexpectedly went for his legs. A savage kick that nearly buckled his right knee. He dropped down, blocked a second kick with his hands, but that defense blinded him just long enough for the Ravinian to snake behind him. He found himself in her embrace. A tightening forearm that ran from his right shoulder to his left armpit. She squeezed so hard that the arm was trapped there, flopping helplessly.

Dahvid felt like every attempt to free himself made things worse. She snaked a leg through his, tightening, until he had no choice but to drop to the sand. The pressure was too painful. They rolled twice, but nothing could shake her grip. Too late, he remembered Nevelyn's notes about her.

Dangerous in close combat. Keep her at a distance. Incredibly strong upper body. Former wrestler.

Nevelyn's idea of what was dangerous had been far easier to shrug off when it wasn't choking him to death. The pressure under his chin was so intense that he couldn't even get loose enough to bite the exposed flesh of her forearm. He attempted another roll. Nothing. His chest was starting to protest from the lack of oxygen. Even the crowd noises had faded. The drumming in his ears was too loud. He tried everything. Driving his right elbow into her hip. Squirming. But she'd managed to pin his arms so that the only tattoo he could easily reach was the null spell.

Don't panic. There is an answer to every question. A counter to every strike.

His father's voice echoed in his mind. It had been so long since he'd heard it that clearly. Dahvid took an internal breath, and then he started to laugh. He knew what to do. He rolled again, but this time he timed the roll with a second movement. An inward hunch that allowed him to swipe his right hand across his left bicep. The winged birds were there. His utterly useless flying spell. The spell activated at his touch. Great wings burst out from his shoulders.

The Ravinian didn't panic. She kept her hold on him. Dahvid knew if she let go, he'd begin floating up into the air. He fought for position, knowing he'd only have one chance. A quick outward flex of his legs broke her hold on his lower body. It was a brief, scrambling moment that lasted just long enough for him to drive both feet deep into the sand. With that leverage, Dahvid kicked off as hard as he possibly could.

His tattoo's magic answered.

The two of them took flight together. It was a wild backward burst of movement. The Ravinian wasn't expecting it. Instinct forced her to tighten her grip, but they were both helpless as they vaulted through the air with uncontrollable velocity, blind to what was behind them.

A jarring collision shook him free. They'd hit something. Hard. Dahvid felt it knife through the armor of his lower back, just missing his spine. He let out a clipped shout as the arms holding him went limp. He fell to the sand. Half of the crowd roared with delight. The other half were booing. Their long-beloved champion—the Ravinian—was speared through the stomach on one of the waiting spikes.

Dahvid reached back to his own wound. His fingers came away bloody, but he could tell it wasn't deep. With a mental push, he cut off the magic of his flying spell. The crowd roared for him to finish her, but looking up, he knew she was already dead. He crossed the distance to stand in her shadow, lowering his voice to a whisper.

"I am sorry. You fought well."

Attendants hurried out moments later. Dahvid walked back to the same spot in the sand, chest heaving slightly, and sat again. This time he did not wish away the seconds. He held the hourglass to his lips and drank each one eagerly. Time had never tasted so precious.

"Send out the third!"

Darling was smiling down. Dahvid took up his stance as the gates opened. A man Dahvid had never seen before came striding out. He was shirtless. While Dahvid didn't recognize the stranger's face, it was impossible not to recognize the art decorating his body. There were tattoos everywhere. Darling had somehow found another image-bearer. But the true shock came as the stranger reached the edge of the center circle. Close enough that Dahvid could finally see the details. They were not just tattoos.

His eyes flickered over to where Cath was sitting. She looked like a ghost. One hand was raised to cover a gasp. They both knew why. All of the art was hers.

Every single tattoo on the stranger's body bore a resemblance to her style. Dahvid remembered her mentioning another relationship. Someone before him who didn't matter to her now. She'd never bothered to tell him that the man was an image-bearer, though. Clearly, it was a secret that only Darling had been able to unearth. Designed to unnerve him. And it was working.

Dahvid couldn't seem to settle his heart rate. His breathing was coming too fast. He felt like he'd been sprinting through Ravinia's hilled streets all morning. He fell back into his stance, but he could not help eyeing each tattoo and wondering about the story behind each one. How long they'd been together. Whether she'd loved this man the way she'd claimed to love him.

Darling signaled.

The fight began.

28

NEVELYN TIN'VORI

Her tasks were complete.

The black dress hung ominously in the center of the room. Finished, it looked like a fancy shadow ready to drape itself over a queen. She'd also continued layering the walls of the room with magic. The spells were so thick now that the sounds of the lovers next door hadn't been audible in days. None of the evening foot traffic in the nearby square could be heard.

It was as silent as a tomb.

There was evidence of her last craft project as well. The wax shavings littered one corner, but the results were worth the mess. Dozens of candles, all cut down to stubs. It hadn't been easy to find the right pearl-gray foundation, but once she had them, it had been a simple matter of painting on the midnight-blue veins that shot through a typical waxway candle. She'd held up a real one and her fakes in the light and could scarcely tell the difference.

Now all she needed was a knock on the door of her apartment. She'd been waiting for three days. The red ribbon dangled limply in the window, obvious to anyone who passed. And yet Ren Monroe had made no appearance. It was starting to unnerve Nevelyn. What if their partner had abandoned them? Worse, what if she decided to hand them over to the Broods? It was a logical move. One that would nestle the girl deeper into the bosom of their wealth and power. Nevelyn could almost imagine a team of guards surrounding her apartment and crashing through her door to find a poor girl with a strange dress dangling from the ceiling.

"What a disappointing treasure I would make," she said to no one.

There was a knock at the door. Finally. Nevelyn cast a glance around the room, making sure all was in order, before rising. She opened the door—no more than a crack—and was shocked to stillness. It was not Ren Monroe. It was not the Broods or their henchmen.

"Garth?"

"I am so sorry to visit uninvited. I know . . . I know it's not . . . This is all rather uncouth. I haven't had the chance to see you. Not since our dinner. I walked you home that night. . . ."

"And I specifically had you leave me in the square. A square that is surrounded by ten different apartment buildings. Hundreds of possible living spaces. There is a reason that I did not invite you to the place where I lived, Garth. What did you do? Follow me?"

She was angling the door to keep his view narrowed to the blank wall behind her. Any wider and he'd have a visual of one of the dangling black cords that connected to the dress.

There was the natural instinct to hide her plans from him, but there was another truth buried beneath that one: she liked Garth. She wanted to remain Nan to him, for fear that if he knew her as Nevelyn—he might decide to ignore her like everyone else did.

"No!" Garth said, blushing with proper embarrassment. "I mean, of course not. That would be awful. I just . . . I asked around about you. I really didn't mean to be creepy. It's just . . . I like you, Nan. I can't stop thinking about you. I guess I just wanted to spend more time with you. I knew this wasn't the right way—"

Nevelyn could think of no other course of action. She slid boldly through the crack in the door, shut it behind her, and reached up to kiss him. It was fumbling and awkward and she felt like she caught more beard than lips. Garth corrected that. He bent down to her. A warm hand found her cheek. There was something about the way he pressed forward that wasn't forceful, but inviting. Nevelyn did not mind the way his hands tangled in her hair. She did not mind that he smelled like sweat and burned cocoa and rain. She realized, as they pulled away from each other, that she'd been waiting to kiss him for years—even if she had only met him weeks ago.

"So . . . you're not mad?" Garth whispered.

"Of course I'm mad. You stalked me!"

"Right. Yes. I'm sorry. But . . ."

"But I kissed you. And I think I will again."

Garth smiled and she made good on her word, standing on tiptoes so that she could peck his cheek. She found herself half wishing there was not a strange dress dangling from the walls of her apartment. But to wish that away was to wish away the entire revenge. It was to pretend there had never been a House Tin'Vori or a brother named Ware who their enemies had planted in the ground. It was to pretend they'd not lost everything and that she was only a peasant girl named Nan with nimble fingers. She could not bring herself to do that, even if Garth was warm and kind and a fine kisser.

"You can't come in. It would be . . . uncouth." She used his word, which made him smile. "But I do like you. And I do want to see you again. For now, go home."

He did not mind being dismissed. She'd given him the confirmation he'd wanted. It made her own heart sail, to see someone so taken with her—in a way no one else had ever been taken with her. Garth leaned in to kiss her forehead, the softest brush of a kiss she'd ever felt, and then he was walking back down the steps that fed into the alleyway.

"I'll see you at the opera house," she called after him.

She'd never seen a man look so delighted with himself. She watched him walk back toward the market. It was a struggle to not go running after him. Before she could retreat back inside, she spied another figure, striding with purpose across the opposite end of the square. It was impossible not to recognize Ren Monroe. The girl kept her head down, trying to be circumspect. Nevelyn watched her make a show of examining the nearest market cart. After a few seconds of eyeing the wares, Ren slipped down the alleyway.

"What are you doing out here?"

Nevelyn frowned. "Am I to be locked away at all hours?"

Ren rolled her eyes before making a shooing gesture. Nevelyn obediently cracked open the door and the two of them vanished inside. There was a satisfying *oh* sound as her visitor spotted the waiting dress. Nevelyn had already been quite proud of her work, but compliments never hurt.

"Do you think she'll go for it?" Ren asked.

"Yes. I've positioned it well."

"Good. It's nearly time. Dahvid's gauntlet is tonight."

Nevelyn's eyes snapped in that direction. "What?! How do you know?"

"My contact in Ravinia," Ren answered. "It was scheduled for tonight. We'll have word in the morning about the result."

Nevelyn couldn't help it. She slumped into the only chair in the room. Her face fell into her hands. They'd spent so much time working toward this moment. Dahvid was as prepared as he could be. And truly, she believed in his skill. But she still felt a bone-deep fear come over her. What if she lost him, too? The way she'd lost Ware and all the others? If it worked, the other pieces of their plan would snap into place shortly after. If it didn't work, she'd be without yet another family member, living in a city she barely remembered, with no viable path to taking revenge against the people who'd taken everything from her.

"He'll win," Ren Monroe said, breathing hope back into Nevelyn's mind. "We have to believe that. If he does, will you be ready?"

"Go stand outside the door."

Ren frowned. "What?"

"Just do it."

Ren obeyed, slipping out and closing the door behind her. Nevelyn waited for a moment, and then she channeled all her fear and rage and terror into her chest. She let out a scream that could wake the dead. A long and terrible note that shook through the entire room. When she was done, she reached out and opened the door.

"Did you hear that?"

Ren Monroe frowned again. "Hear what?"

"Good. The room is ready. All we have to do now is get the timing right."

"You're certain? There's nothing else you need at the play-house?"

Nevelyn smiled with satisfaction. "No. I have it all under control."

"Fine. I won't be visiting you again. I will send Vega instead. If Dahvid wins, I'll send her to the corner building. Across the square. That will be the sign to begin your part in the plan."

Their partner and confidant hesitated.

"I thought . . . Was there a man just now? Leaving your apartment?"

"A drunk," Nevelyn confirmed, her face betraying nothing. "He stumbled down the alleyway and took a piss outside my window. This really is a charming place you've put me in."

"Free and charming are rarely bedmates," Ren answered. "You won't be here much longer."

"No," Nevelyn answered. "Regardless of what might happen, it is not my fate to scrape out a living in a hovel like this. We were meant for more than that."

Ren quietly crossed the room. She stood in the shadow of the black dress. Nevelyn watched the girl trace the intricate laces with a finger.

"My mother used to tell me that no darkness lasts for long."

Nevelyn nodded. "I used to tell my sister the same."

"But beautiful things can come from darkness. Can't they?"

"Beautiful," Nevelyn agreed. "And dangerous."

There was nothing left to say. With a quiet nod, Ren Monroe departed. As soon as the door closed, Nevelyn slumped back into the chair. Her thoughts were for Dahvid, and Dahvid alone. Who was he fighting? Did any of her research help him? She fretted and fretted until sleep claimed her early in the morning. Her dreams were shapeless, colorless, barely dreams at all.

29

DAHVID TIN'VORI

D ahvid quietly reached for his sword tattoo.

Again, he altered the summoning. Swiping two fingers across the tattoo instead of one. His sword manifested in the air. His opponent watched him, still smiling at their private connection. It took all of Dahvid's concentration to not look at Cath. He did not want to think of the world this man had shared with her, their secrets and their dreams. Darling gave the signal.

The third fight began.

His opponent wasted no time. He reached out with a thumb and ran it down the tattoo centered along his chest. It was a great bear drawn midroar. Only the colors betrayed that it was one of Cath's creations. She'd only ever attempted to draw one creature on him, and maybe this was why. The air rippled with magic—something that felt hungry and ravenous—but nothing manifested. And then his opponent reached for a second tattoo. A third. A fourth.

The man grinned as the tattoo on his chest shifted. Dahvid could only stare, along with the rest of the crowd, as the bear on his opponent's chest stood on its hind legs. The other tattoos were migrating across the man's skin. And the bear began to eat them. One by one. Every tattoo had been activated and now was swallowed in its waiting jaws. Dahvid had never seen anything like . . .

There are Tusk warriors who are image-bearers, Ava had once told him. She was nestled in the very corner of their cramped room, her nose in a book. She'd been sick all week. She'd looked frail because of it, her large eyes even larger above hollowed cheekbones. *This book says they link their tattoos together. Feeding the power stored into a single tattoo. And that tattoo defines them. Their battle style, their temperament.*

Dahvid had nodded back to her. *I know. They're called . . . .*

"Berserkers."

Dahvid sprinted forward. It felt like he was running in slow motion. His opponent's weapon fell to the ground with a clatter. Great tremors seized every muscle. The man lifted his chin, his jaw clinched, veins protruding from his neck. The power of all those tattoos was filling him from the inside out. Dahvid knew he had mere seconds to strike. He swung his sword in a brutal downward arch.

The blade struck right in the center of the image-bearer's neck. It should have taken his head clean from his shoulders. Instead, the weapon rebounded with so much force that Dahvid nearly cut himself. He was too late. Dark laughter filled the air.

The berserking rage had begun. An anger burned inside the man with such force that it enveloped his skin entirely. He was immune to blades—immune to almost all damage. Ware had told him about this, long before Ava had read it in a book. Darling had inquired about it too, during their first meeting. He'd asked if Dahvid possessed this skill, but he'd never wanted to learn it. He did not like the idea of losing control of himself.

The rumor was that Tusk warriors entered so fully into their fury that they could not tell enemy from friend. The combat style offered unthinkable power as long as the rage lasted—but was always followed by impotence. A weakness so debilitating that berserkers had to partner with other warriors who could drag them off the battlefield when the fury faded.

He remembered his reply to Ava, all those years ago.

What does the book say? How do you kill them?

She had smiled at him and pumped her arms dramatically.

It says to run away.

The other image-bearer straightened. His eyes were shot through with a terrifying red color. He was the bear on his chest. He was a thousand furies, ready to be unleashed. Dahvid saw how he'd grown taller. Each of his muscles had doubled in size. He was no match for a creature like this.

"Clever trick," he said. "Let me show you mine."

Dahvid drove his sword into the sand. It looked like a potential countermove, but really, he just couldn't bother with the weight. He followed Ava's advice, and he ran. He knew he would be lucky to survive the next few minutes, but he also knew that if he did survive, he'd be facing an opponent that could barely lift their own sword. An easy victory. He just had to stay alive.

He ran down into the waiting labyrinth. There was a great roar from behind him, something guttural. The crowd groaned in response, but he didn't care at all. There were great crashing sounds as his hunter reached the labyrinth. The walls started shaking. Dahvid moved swiftly through the passages until he came darting out the opposite side. There was another hill waiting for him. He sprinted up in time to glance back over one shoulder. His pursuer was gaining ground. It must have been the extra muscle in his legs. He wasn't just stronger—he was faster. Dahvid considered his options.

There were spikes on his right. The interlocking field on his left. The spikes, he knew, could only hurt him, not his opponent. A split second passed, and he darted left. He ran past where he'd left his sword and plucked up the blade in one smooth motion. He considered activating the twins but wasn't ready to lose that power. Not this early in the gauntlet.

Dahvid darted through the interlocking field, making sure his feet touched down on as many of the stones as possible. Quick moments of contact that he hoped would activate whatever mechanisms existed beneath.

His opponent barreled up the hill he'd just left behind and began stalking across the sand. Dahvid had reached the back corner of the puzzle. There was a subtle rumble from somewhere below. He was raising his sword in defense when the earth beneath his feet gave way.

He leapt to his right just in time. The larger square he'd been standing on plummeted. His arms pinwheeled slightly as he looked down into what seemed like an endless, black pit. He looked back up in time to catch a lowered shoulder to the chest.

The blow sent him into the back wall. Almost cracked his skull. Spikes of pain ran down his spine. He barely rolled away in time, dodging a second strike. Dahvid rolled once more and then leapt over a second missing square. It put a little distance between him and his opponent. The other image-bearer just smiled at him.

"Tricks will not save you, little one."

But luck might. Dahvid heard it a second before it happened. The square under the giant's feet gave way. He saw shock in those red-laced eyes. Then that massive body was swallowed by gravity. Into the darkness. Dahvid thought he'd won, but a single hand lashed upward.

The tips of the man's fingers caught the edge of the stone. He was hanging there—mere inches from falling to his death. Dahvid attacked. He swung with his sword first but forgot the blade wouldn't pierce the skin. Next, he went with his boots. Stomping as hard as he could.

His enemy roared back in defiance, feeling none of the pain. Dahvid was helpless as he watched the man patiently swing his other arm up. Those fingertips caught the edge as well. He began to pull himself out of the shadows.

There were more rumbles all around him—and Dahvid knew more squares were threatening to fall. He fled back to the safety of the arena center. His opponent was already half-way out of the hole. The power of his berserking spell was still pulsing.

Just one more minute. Survive one more minute.

His opponent was back on his feet, much to the delight of the audience. Dahvid could not spare glances at their reactions, but he did not doubt that a battle between two image-bearers would be talked about for years to come. It had likely never happened in Ravinia's history.

He considered another flight into the labyrinth but worried about what might happen if he was caught in the tighter spaces there. Better to make his final stand here in the open. He squared up—and dodged the first bull rush. He swept through trained stances, all with perfect footwork, but he was no match. The power of the berserking spell had reached its peak. He'd never seen someone move with such speed or strike with such strength.

When the other image-bearer finally landed a blow, it punched all the air from Dahvid's lungs. A second shot hit his shoulder with so much force that it nearly popped out of the socket. Dahvid tried to run, but the man seized him by the neck of his armor. He was pulled back with force, his legs taken out from beneath him. And as he fell backward, the man brought an absolutely crushing fist down on his nose.

Everything shattered.

Dahvid was on the ground. Blood was everywhere. He'd been hoping to save his other tattoos for the next fights, but Cath had already told him the truth about hope, hadn't she?

It's the brightest bird in the sky, and thus the easiest to kill.

Before the image-bearer could strike again, Dahvid swiped desperately at his shoulder. His fingertips grazed the golden rings there. A golden circle inside a golden circle inside a golden circle. And Dahvid inside all of them. The protective spell shoved his opponent back, strong enough to have him skidding over the sand. A translucent, gold-tinged sphere formed around Dahvid. There was a slight pop as all the sound muted. He could not hear the crowd. The grunts of his opponent went silent. For a time, he was completely alone.

Dahvid sat. His chest was heaving. He did his best to dab

at the blood running from his nose. It was still too painful to touch. Definitely broken, but that was fine. For the next thirty seconds, no harm would come to him. He sat there, counting each breath, and knew it would be just enough time.

His opponent's face contorted with rage. He battered into the sides of the sphere with great, furious blows. The magic shivered slightly, but it would not give way, and that made the man even angrier. As his fury grew, he burned even faster through the berserking magic. It was only a matter of time.

Dahvid had a spare moment to look over. Cath was seated there, still half a ghost. She looked like she wanted to leap over the barrier and run to him. Explain everything. He nodded once before turning back. The other image-bearer was still trying to break through the barrier. Dahvid took his feet. He adjusted his grip on the handle of his sword.

It was subtle, but he saw the power waning. A tiring in his enemy's arms. That bloodshot red in his eyes slowly retreating. Dahvid took a deep breath, settled into his stance, and when the golden light vanished, he drove his sword upward with perfect precision.

The strike was true.

It cut through the other image-bearer's chest. Right through his heart. Dahvid slid the blade back out, ducked a final swing, and shoved the helpless creature to the ground. His enemy collapsed in the sand. Dahvid very deliberately retreated to his usual spot. He sat down in the dust.

When he looked up, Darling was staring hungrily down at him. Dahvid knew how he must look. Bruised and beaten and weak. After a few seconds of holding the stare, he reached for his elixir tattoo. With great concentration, he channeled the magic into the places that felt the worst. The nearly broken rib. The bloodied nose. The gouge in his back. It was not a fix-all healing spell, but it could treat minor wounds easily. When the magic had run its course, he blinked at the adrenaline it offered him. He felt brand-new.

Dahvid looked back up at Darling—nearly as fresh as he'd been for his first fight.

"Bring your fourth!" he called.

And the crowd roared.

30

REN MONROE

Ren never thought she'd write a letter to Landwin Brood.
She penned each word carefully. The same way she
might have approached a question on an exam. Thinking about
who her professor was, what kind of answers they preferred,
and how she might use the knowledge she had to best fit their
standards. It was not a dissimilar process.

I have come around to your position, but I feel we are still not
settled on the terms of our arrangement. . . .

She knew she needed to be both appealing and appalling.
Luring him in with the promise of what he wanted, while
simultaneously enraging him with the size of her request. A
delicate balance had to be struck.

If you are inclined, I would meet you at the Brood estate. Let
us discuss these matters in private and come to an agreement that
would suit us both. . . .

Vega cooed from a corner of the room as Ren signed her

name. She sealed the letter with dripping wax, pressing the borrowed emblem of House Brood down as hard as she could. On the desk, there was also a note from Seminar Shiverian. A weekly review of Ren's spellmaking work. It praised certain projects and critiqued others. Ren's eyes traced over the words once more. The review was a glimpse into the world that could have belonged to her—if only she'd chosen it.

But she'd chosen vengeance instead.

Ren held her own letter up. Vega swooped down. It was too perfect to not have the livestone bird deliver this final letter to her enemy. She wanted him to know that his gambit with Warden Carrowynd had failed. The great lord of House Brood would never admit to backpedaling, but Ren knew she had him in the exact corner she wanted him in. It would look as if she'd waited all this time to leverage her position for the best possible payout.

"Happy hunting, Vega."

The bird swept through the open window with the letter clutched in its talons. Ren did not have any time to waste. There was a candle burning in the corner of the room. The wax had dripped down to the golden plate beneath. She knew the only way she could travel without the Brood scouts follow-ing her was by waxway. It was possible they had ways of track-ing her movements, magically determining which direction she'd traveled, so they could follow her whenever she surfaced elsewhere in the city. Fortunately, she had just one more place to visit. Ren reached out and snuffed the flame between her fingers.

There was a whisper in the dark—and then she was else-where.

31

DAHVID TIN'VORI

Darling was no longer playing games.

His fourth champion walked out through the gates. The man did not smile. He did not wave to the crowd. Dahvid knew him on sight. He had seen the man at Darling's parties, even watched him fight in some of the marquee showdowns. Everyone in Ravinia knew the Whisperman.

The man's name was born from his habit of leaning down and speaking with the dead after killing them in the arena. They said corpses from his fights would mutter aloud in the morgue, supposedly repeating his final words in a garbled tongue.

Dahvid didn't care about any of that shit.

His mind trimmed away the rumors and focused on facts. All the notes Nevelyn had made. Her research on the Whisperman had been thorough, because she'd imagined him as Darling's most obvious choice against Dahvid. They used to make bets on who the fifth gladiator would be in his imagined gauntlet. She'd been off by one. He'd have to remember to make Nevelyn pay up the next time he saw her. Just the thought of that had him smiling.

Across the sand, the Whisperman settled into his stance. Dahvid could not help admiring the sword he unsheathed. He was a fine duelist who'd been made into something more by an absolutely legendary blade. One that had been crafted by Maxim himself. It was a manipulation sword. Dahvid had witnessed its effect on a number of gladiators. The way they'd stumble the wrong way or swing at nothing but air—all because their opponent's blade was casting an illusion. That was the trick of it. Sometimes, the real Whisperman was rushing forward to cut them in two. Other times, it was an illusion of him that veiled the real attack. No one could truly know the difference.

Unless their sister had studied the patterns. Learned every possible combination. It helped, too, if the opponent had magic that matched the Whisperman's skills. As Dahvid did.

The warlord gave his signal. Dahvid reached for his twins tattoo. The two imps that Cath had etched on his body. This was still his favorite spell. Cold air gasped out from him. A great exhalation. He always imagined it sounded like a first breath.

Dahvid stepped to his left. A mirrored version of him matched that movement, stepping out to the right. His twin hefted the same sword, took up the same stance. They both smiled at their opponent. A perfect replica. Dahvid knew no one in that arena could tell them apart.

The Whisperman hesitated for only a moment, assessing

them both, and then he began striding purposefully forward. His first attack was for the real Dahvid. A lunging strike that would have caught his upper chest. Dahvid battered the sword aside with a quick parry.

The first one is always real.

Whisperman spun away from him, preparing to swing at the conjured twin. But Dahvid knew the pattern. *Real, fake, fake, real.* Sure enough, the actual Whisperman blinked back to life in front of him, his swing already halfway to Dahvid's neck. Any other person would have been cut in two. It was impossible to match that speed—unless you knew it was coming.

Dahvid turned the blow away and then parried a second. He was pressed just enough that he had to backpedal a few steps. The Whisperman used his retreat to swing his attention back to Dahvid's twin. Or at least it appeared that way.

But that's fake too.

Dahvid made a gut call. He swung his sword where the Whisperman had been a moment before. And he very nearly took off the man's head. His opponent ducked at the last second, forced into a backpedal by the unexpected strike. Dahvid took advantage, pressing him in return, aiming blow after blow after blow. The shock on his opponent's face was utterly satisfying.

I know you, friend. I know every combination you will try. All thanks to Nev.

His twin joined the fray from behind. Together they forced the Whisperman into a frantic retreat. His illusions would not serve him now. The fight was coming too fast and from both angles. He was lucky to avoid their blades as he danced and backpedaled, danced and backpedaled.

Nevelyn's notes continued to guide his attack: *Agatha March-ment disarmed him, because she kept him on his heels the entire time. His sword works best when he's on the offensive, so remember to keep pushing him.*

Dahvid and his twin had never trained together—but they didn't need to. The twin *was* Dahvid. They fought the same, thought the same, killed the same. His twin scored the first blow. A slit on the Whisperman's upper bicep. Dahvid landed the second, a gash that bit through the armor on their opponent's upper leg. A sequence of combinations drove the man back, step after step, toward the puzzle section of the arena. By now most of the stones had fallen away, leaving only a few platforms on which to stand. It had created several pits at the edge of the central circle. With each swing, they backed him closer and closer to those waiting, shadowed jaws.

Dahvid could feel the end coming. Sweat ran down the Whisperman's normally blank face. This was a man who knew he was about to die. In a final desperate move, he battered both their swords aside. It gave him just enough room to turn, building a few steps of momentum. He shocked Dahvid by leaping through empty air. The gaping hole was the length of a man. A difficult jump. Dahvid got caught watching the impossible attempt. How he glided through the air. The way the Whisperman's feet scraped that distant edge. His arms pinwheeling to keep him from falling back into the pit . . .

. . . and then there was a blade in his gut.

The real Whisperman was beside him. He'd never jumped at all. That had been the illusion. Thin fingers tightened their grip on Dahvid's shoulder. His voice was as quiet as a dream.

"Found the real one, didn't I?"

He'd never been in so much pain. Nothing so awful in all his life. The Whisperman held him tight to the sword, and he could feel the world starting to slip through his fingers. Until his twin beheaded the man.

It happened faster than an indrawn breath. Dahvid saw a final flash of surprise, and then he was gone. A soul leaving a body. Dahvid thought it was a fair mistake to make. The Whisperman had assumed that his twin would vanish if he killed the real Dahvid. The way his own illusion disappeared. He'd turned his back on the danger, because he thought there was no more danger left. But Dahvid's magic was stronger than that. He let the Whisperman's body collapse into the sand.

The victory was a hollow one. As he stumbled to the center of the arena, he nearly collapsed. His current spell felt like it was draining him. He banished the twin, who faded like smoke in the air. Dahvid reached down and carefully removed the sword from his own gut. A scream clawed up his throat. It felt nearly as bad coming out as it had going in. He tossed the blade aside and sank to his knees in the sand. It felt better to lie down, so he did, stretching out on his back as the crowd watched.

One more fight.

He still had one more person to beat, and he would have to do it like this. He knew the grains were already slipping through the hourglass. Five minutes to rest. It felt like nothing at all now. Dahvid ripped fabric away from his undershirt. He balled the material up and stuffed it into the gaping, bloody hole in his armor. Anything to staunch the bleeding. Even that slight movement had him hissing with pain. For a time, he simply lay there, staring up at the dizzying lights above. If he

SCOTT REINTGEN

could just sleep for a moment, just close his eyes, maybe he could stand back up. . . .

"Bring out the last!" Darling's voice cut through the air. "Bring out the fifth!"

Dahvid grunted with pain. He pushed back to his feet. His sword was waiting nearby. He stumbled over, blood still flowing from the wound, and lifted his weapon from the sand. The passing seconds only sharpened the pain. His eyes flicked up to Cath, and he could not help the pleading look he gave her.

Save me. Stop all of this. Please. I don't want to die.

And then his eyes drifted over to Darling. The gates were still closed. Dahvid saw who his final opponent would be just before the guards could shove them open. The seat beside the warlord was empty. Dahvid could not help laughing. As the gates groaned wide, Agatha was there, wearing her battle leathers. He wondered when she'd gone back to change. He had been too busy almost dying to pay attention. His end had finally come. He could not beat her. Not like this.

He let loose a scream. The collective frustrations of a decade came rolling up his throat and off his tongue. He could not put into words how terrible it all felt. Not that he might die. He'd accepted the possibility of his own death a hundred times over.

It was that he would die without burying Thugar Brood in the ground first. Ren Monroe had been right. She'd said that sometimes it was hard to breathe, because there was so much hatred in her chest. He felt the same way—and would go on feeling that way until the end.

Dahvid shook himself. He adjusted his feet and quieted his mind. Darling still hadn't given the signal. He was baiting the fans. Giving them a few more moments to enjoy the hero who'd made it through four rounds of a gauntlet. He would stretch it out until the old hero who'd won all five rounds put an end to the fairy tale. It was very nearly poetic.

Dahvid had three tattoos left. The null zone. Useless against Agatha. There was Ware's final tattoo. Unused all these years. An exchange of some kind. The optimist in him wanted to believe he would trade his condition for hers. Maybe the magic would hand Agatha Marchment a gut wound and leave him whole. Maybe that would be enough to sway the odds between them. He couldn't be sure.

The last option was the scarlet traveler. Thinking about it made him laugh. Was it too late to use it? He'd been saving it all this time for Thugar Brood. It was the only magic he possessed that would guarantee the death of his greatest enemy. What was the point of beating Agatha Marchment? If he went south to be buried next to Ware all these years later?

"They took him," Dahvid said to no one, to everyone. "They took him from us. They dragged him back behind their pretty walls, and they buried him in the ground. I never . . ." He trailed off, unsure what the point of all of this was. "I never got to say goodbye."

Darling gave the signal.

Agatha Marchment strode forward like an inevitability. He had no other choice.

"I'm sorry, Brother. I failed you."

He swiped his thumb across the scarlet traveler Ware had drawn. The flower rose from his skin, floated before him in the air, and he watched as a thousand petals unfurled in a dizzying pattern, far too fast for his eyes to follow. Time fractured. Bent and shaped into a thousand possibilities. He saw them all like little miniature worlds. As if he were a god, looking down on a universe full of half-glinting stars. In that endless cosmos, he began his hunt.

Every world he saw was different. He was being shown every possible combination, every possible outcome of the fight between himself and Agatha Marchment. What would happen if she struck first? What if Dahvid threw sand in her eyes? What if someone from the crowd leapt to their death and interrupted the fight? What if he parried first and dodged second? What if he swung a fraction of an inch lower in this one particular sequence? The scarlet traveler granted him access to every possibility that existed, across every timeline that existed.

Dahvid took his time searching. Time in this world and the real world were not the same. But the problem he faced was exactly what he'd guessed. As he picked up each potential world, examined its outcome, he kept finding Agatha Marchment standing over his corpse.

A gut wound here. Severed hands there. Sometimes he died of exhaustion or from losing too much blood. She was that good and he was that weak. World after world. Possibility after possibility. The results were all the same. He was meant to die in this place. His fate had already been decided.

"Not yet. Please. There has to be a way. . . ."

Another and another and another. If he surrendered, Agatha executed him. If he fought, Agatha beat him. If he ran, Agatha caught him. She killed him a thousand different ways in a thousand frightful sequences. Dahvid was starting to give up hope when he found it. In the darkest corner of his shadowy universe, a small star winked up at him. He knelt down in that imagined vastness and began to weep. Thousands of possibilities and just one way he could win.

Dahvid scooped the little world up with great care. He held it to his eye once more, watching for confirmation, and then he set the world between his teeth. He knew the consequences of this magic. He'd felt it happening for years. The way he drifted sometimes. How time bent and fractured around him. That subtle untethering of his mind. He'd not used the traveler much for that very reason, but now it was his last hope.

He bit down. Chewed and chewed. It was a thick possibility, though. A rubbery texture. He gagged a few times before swallowing the future whole. Dahvid braced himself for the pull. Out of this world of endless possibility and back to the limited one. It always felt like traveling through a too-narrow door. Time unwound.

He did not experience the sequence the way everyone else did. He did not see their exchange of blows or the stunning way Agatha disarmed him. He missed their dance through the spikes and the desperate finale that left him flat-backed on the ground. The crowd would witness every move.

Not Dahvid. The magic always took him straight to the end. Later, his memories of the fight would be gray and dull and incomplete. Dahvid regained consciousness at the moment that Agatha Marchment stumbled away from him, hands clutching at the knife buried in her chest. It was her own blade, the one she kept at her ankle. He slumped back in the sand, blood rushing out of his wounds.

When his opponent finally fell, he was left with a clear view of Darling. He would never know the sequence, never know how he beat her, but he didn't care. The gauntlet was finished.

He'd won. The crowd stared down at them in stunned silence. Both Darlings had taken their feet. Even the real one, who'd come forward into the light, shock bright and visible on that hideous face.

Dahvid was finally bold enough to look that version of Darling in the eye.

"Bring me my army."

And with that, he left the waking world.

32

NEVELYN TIN'VORI

Two days passed. Every minute was excruciating, even with Garth leaving her notes and doing his best to make her laugh. Nevelyn felt physically ill as she waited for some word of her brother's fate. Ren Monroe was too cautious to pass her a note, and Nevelyn cursed the girl for it. Hated her for it. A brief but consuming anger that ran deep through every muscle and bone.

Until the third morning.

Well before dawn, Nevelyn walked out to the square. Vega was there. Perched on the building just as Ren had promised. She let out a triumphant shout that startled a few birds into flight. Dahvid had done it. He'd actually won his gauntlet. Ren had clearly been waiting for confirmation that Dahvid's newly acquired army was on the move. If she sent Vega, it meant Dahvid would be in Nostra soon—in striking distance of the Brood estate. Nevelyn couldn't believe how quickly the moment had arrived. She felt a bit breathless as she stalked back down the alleyway.

Inside, the black dress was waiting for her. She folded it neatly into a large box. She had one stop to make before heading to work and little time to make it. When she had all her materials ready, she set out. Not for the opera house—but for Kersey's apartment.

The lights of the alley were dim. There was no sign of movement inside the apartment or inside the larger home to which it was attached. Nevelyn crept down the stairs. The door was bolted, but there weren't any extra enchantments barring entry. Nevelyn performed a practiced spell and heard a satisfying click.

Inside was quiet. The windows kept out a great deal of noise. There was a snoring sound from the back bedroom. Nevelyn tiptoed forward. The occasional creak would have her freezing in place, but she made a mostly silent path through the home. Inside Kersey's room, she began her search—always listening for that slight snoring in the dark shadows of the bed.

She found what she was looking for in the far corner of the room. There was a basket on the ground, full of the prize Nevelyn sought. Small waxway candles. Cut down perfectly to size. Each one was just large enough to whisk a practiced traveler from her home and to the opera house she loved more than anything else. Nevelyn paused to listen, making sure Kersey was still asleep. When she was certain, she started placing the real waxway candles into a satchel, one by one. Then she carefully replaced them with the false ones she'd crafted.

There was a slight hitch in Kersey's breathing. Nevelyn held still for a moment, then positioned the basket back in the corner. She tiptoed out of the room, catching one bad board as she went. Her breathing was reduced to soft, wheezing gasps. She'd never done anything so nerve-racking in her life. She'd paused at the door, gathering herself, when a voice echoed out of the dark.

"Nan?"

Kersey was standing at the entrance to her bedroom. Nevelyn cursed as she turned, as the old lady took in the strange impossibility of a colleague inside her home. Without permission no less. Nevelyn's reaction was all instinct. She turned her necklace charm to the darker side. Her secret magic pulsed outward. She cast the opposite spell that she'd used on Edna.

Ignore me. Do not behold me. Forget I was ever here.

Kersey stumbled back from the force of the magic. Nevelyn felt guilty as the old woman's eyes became unfocused. Kersey stared blankly at the wall. Nevelyn turned, made quick work of the door, and shut it behind her. She sprinted up the stairs, more terrified with each step, but knew when she rounded the corner that it had worked. Kersey would think she'd seen *something*. Maybe even *someone*. But when she went to check her door, she'd find it locked. There would be no sign of theft. Maybe it had all been a strange dream.

A giddy smile broke out on Nevelyn's face. Dahvid was not the only capable sibling after all. Her next challenge would be more difficult. She'd gotten rid of Edna. Kersey would be gone all morning. Nevelyn guessed that the old woman would attempt her normal waxway travel. She'd be confused when the candle didn't work. She'd likely light a second candle, maybe even a third. Each one would burn its way to nothing, buying Nevelyn valuable time, before Kersey would realize she'd bought a bad batch. At that point, her walk to work would take another half an hour. Combined, it would be more than enough time to execute her plan.

Next she had to face the DuNesses.

She was the first one to arrive. Before heading downstairs, she placed the black dress in Tessa Brood's changing room. She set it out as artfully as she could. It would be pitiful if Nevelyn had put all this time into the work, only to have Tessa think the piece ugly. When she was finished, she went downstairs and began her normal work. Luckily, the basement was always cold, otherwise she might have been sweating with nervousness.

John arrived in a golden dress with lovely sequins. Their mother wore her traditional business suit, crisp and refined. The two of them frowned over at Kersey's absence but did not comment. Nevelyn focused on performing the most basic tasks. Her hands would not stop trembling, and that made some of the harder patterns too difficult for her. An hour passed before Simon arrived. The house manager. Nevelyn had been waiting for him.

"Really?" Simon said, all attitude. "A *brand-new outfit*? You didn't notify *anyone*?"

Faith looked up in confusion. John was already grinding their jaw. The two of them had a long and enduring feud with Simon, who was in charge of everything that wasn't costuming.

"I have no idea what you mean," she said.

Simon snorted. "Really? Tessa Brood's new dress? It's a *completely* different design."

"I do not manage Tessa Brood's wardrobe. . . ." Faith trailed off, eyes drifting to Kersey's empty seat. "That wasn't in any of our discussions. What does the new piece look like?"

"It looks dark. It's very dark. Far more intense than the last one. I'll have to change a *lot*."

"Come on, Simon. Brood must be attempting a rebellion. Smuggling in her own dress or something. I would know if we had plans to change an entire outfit. This wasn't a part of our weekly summary at all. Kersey hasn't mentioned it." Faith's eyes swung to Nevelyn. "Nan. Do you know about this?"

She'd been waiting to be asked. "Tessa Brood. Which one is she again?"

They all rolled their eyes. Of course the new girl didn't even know the actresses.

"Tessa plays the role of Westchester," Simon replied. "Blond hair. High cheekbones."

Nevelyn frowned with false concentration. "Oh. Yes. Kersey was working on something more modern for her. Tessa was displeased with what she debuted in. Called it old-fashioned."

Faith sputtered. "Did you say *old-fashioned*?"

"Oh." Nevelyn threw a hand over her mouth in embarrassment. That had been, as intended, a critique of Faith's work. "Not my words. The old dress is really pretty. Very classic. Kersey said something about just wanting to keep Tessa happy? That there had been threats before? I can't remember. I only worked a little on the dress. Kersey stayed late to finish it last night." Nevelyn cast a look around, as if she'd only just now realized the old woman was absent. "Maybe that's why she's not here?"

Faith was shaking her head. "That overriding, conniving little . . ."

John set a soothing hand on their mother's shoulder. Simon watched them warily.

"I want to see it," Faith announced. "I want to see it *now*."

Nevelyn could not have asked for a more perfect result. Simon led the charge back upstairs. She waited for them all to file out of the room before trailing after them. Their ascent drew attention. Heads turned to watch. Nevelyn could not help admiring how easy it had been to set all of this in motion. Now for the finale. She just hoped Kersey was still at home, trying to figure out why her candles weren't working today.

Tessa Brood turned as they entered her room. She was already in the dress, though the back wasn't fully laced. She looked breathtaking. Nevelyn had tried it on a few times, but she'd not felt very comfortable in the tight fabric. Tessa could not have looked more at home. The Brood heiress glittered in the bright, reflected light of the mirror.

"Gods, you can't be serious," Faith began, gesturing wildly. "It's the wrong era. The fabric and the make and all of it. This doesn't actually fit with the rest of the play!"

All of this was aimed vaguely at Nevelyn, who supposed she was a stand-in for Kersey. Tessa Brood raised her chin in response. "This is the dress I want to wear."

John tried a more subtle approach. "What if we go with the original—just for the first run—and when we're a few weeks in, you can—"

"Absolutely not."

A sharp red color was forming on Tessa's cheeks. Nevelyn didn't think she was embarrassed. It looked more like anger. She was not accustomed to being challenged. The intensity she threw back at John and Faith made them seem more like mortal enemies than colleagues.

"I'll not suffer through another poor review. I want an outfit that matches my skill. This dress works for me—and you will *make it work*, or we will begin a very different conversation."

Nevelyn piped in. "Might . . . might I just make one suggestion . . . ?"

Faith rounded on her. "You allowed this to happen without telling me. You conniving, baseless creature. So *no*, you may *not* make a suggestion. Find your voice when it counts next time."

"On the contrary," Tessa Brood snapped. "I would hear what you have to say, Nan."

The room fell silent. By now there were likely others gathered in the halls and backstage rooms to listen to the drama of the day. Nevelyn wrung her hands, pretending to be the fretful creature they all expected. She knew, though, that Faith would never dare to override someone as well positioned as Tessa Brood. After a moment, the seamstress conceded.

"Fine. Out with it, girl."

"Why not try it out today? The dress? Run this through rehearsals. If it sticks out like a sore thumb, you'll have your answer. But if it *does* work? Well? Wouldn't it be better if Miss Brood was happy? Temperament impacts performance. Aren't they always saying that during the lessons?"

It was the most reasonable possible compromise. Both sides would see it as a victory. For Tessa, it would be a chance to prove the dress's merits. For Faith, an opportunity to point out just how poorly it fit with the rest of the play. The gathered parties exchanged glances.

SCOTT REINTGEN

John spoke when their mother remained silent. "It's a good idea. We'll try it for today."

Tessa turned back to her mirror, looking as victorious as Nevelyn felt. Faith was still seething, but she stormed out of the room without another word. Simon stalked in the opposite direction, consulting Tessa over possible eye shadows and other alterations. Nevelyn quietly trailed the DuNesses. When they began the descent into the under-stage labyrinth, Nevelyn saw her chance.

She darted straight toward the backstage exit.

It would be a near thing. If Kersey arrived too soon, all would be spoiled. If Tessa Brood decided to take off her dress for some reason, the plan would fail. Nevelyn had a short window of time to get home. She burst through the back door and hissed with pain when the force of her lowered shoulder made the door rebound on its hinges. It gashed the side of her foot as it slammed shut. A cut that started bleeding immediately. She ignored the pain and sprinted down the alleyway. Which is where she nearly leveled Garth.

She crashed into him with enough force to offset their size difference. It had them both pinwheeling to stay upright. Garth cursed before realizing it was her. A smile broke out on his face.

"Nan! Are you all right?"

She did not have time to talk. Not now.

"I'm very sick. Please move."

She shoved past him. In her rush, she could not make out the words he called after her. Nevelyn Tin'Vori had never won a footrace in her life. All of her siblings had been faster. Dahvid and Ware were older and stronger. Even little Ava had been far more athletic. Now, though, she ran like a wolf through the streets. A huntress in pursuit. She took every corner at speed and didn't stop until she'd reached her apartment door. One fumble of the keys, and then she was inside.

The black dress hung like a shadow in the middle of the room.

A perfect twin to the one she'd just handed to Tessa Brood. She'd patiently stitched them with great precision. Each night, she'd make the same amount of progress on both dresses. Weaving interlocking magic between them, one spell at a time. Over the course of those weeks, Nevelyn had bound the two dresses together. Her secret spells, manipulated and coaxed and guided into something more.

Now she moved the ladder over beside the dress. She carefully ascended the steps until she was standing high enough that she could look down through the unlaced top. It felt like she was staring into the throat of a nightmare creature. All shadows and teeth. There was magic pooled inside the dress that whispered to her—desperate to be loosed. Nevelyn took a deep breath.

And then she lowered herself into those waiting jaws.

33

REN MONROE

Earlier that morning, Ren had woken up and vomited.

It was unlike her. She'd never reacted that way before exams or practicals. No amount of pressure had ever impacted her physically. At first, she'd assumed her body was finally suffering the physiological burdens her mind refused to feel. But then she'd realized the turning emotions were coming from Theo. A pulsing nervousness was feeding from him, threading in and out of her own thoughts. A few minutes later, she felt that manifest into more. A steady *pull* across their bond.

Theo was summoning her.

She accepted. It was like allowing herself to be swept away on a wave. The magic ushered her across space and time. Her feet set down on the familiar ramparts. She was not looking down at Nostra—but the opposite way, at the northern pass. Cold wind nipped at her too-thin clothing. In the distance, she saw the reason for Theo's anxiety. An army was marching across the once-empty plain. No attack had come from this direction in a century. Squinting, she saw Dahvid Tin'Vori riding at the head of their party. He looked smaller than he had the first time they met, though Ren suspected anyone would look small across that endless terrain.

As she watched their approach, she knew exactly what it meant for Theo to be standing on the ramparts, unmoved. His familial duty, however embarrassing, was to run up the western tower. He should have been there already, preparing to light the ancient beacon. The signal that would warn his family—and all of Kathor—that an enemy was coming. But he remained at her side like a statue. A harbinger of a new era. He watched that distant army for a time; then he looked right over to where Ren was and wasn't standing. She looked back at him.

"I'm doing this for you," he whispered.

Ren felt his emotion—raw and untethered and wild. It was like setting her hand to the sun. She retreated before it could burn her, and the vision vanished. Their bond continued to thrum with that wild energy, but Ren found herself back in the safety of the bathroom—vomiting the rest of last night's dinner. Not the most romantic bookends for such an important moment, she knew, but beggars could not be choosers.

An enchanted carriage arrived in the morning. Ren delayed slightly, pretending to run back inside and fetch missing items. She could not arrive too early. Vega settled on her shoulder as she walked outside. Her chosen outfit was a two-piece charcoal dress. The jacket had padded shoulders and a thick collar, with midnight-black buttons running down to a cinched waist. Her skirt matched, though the fabric was patterned with distinct creases. She looked like a huntress.

She accepted the driver's hand as she stepped into the carriage. He smiled politely, making small talk, entirely unaware of her purpose. She knew it was likely he knew nothing about her at all. It was his job to escort her to the Brood estate—nothing more. Landwin had eagerly accepted her invitation. The letter had succeeded. Now she had one last performance to give.

Her role today was to keep Landwin Brood on his estate. At least until the attack began. She knew Dahvid's location, thanks to Theo, and knew exactly how long it would take the army to reach the northwestern woods that overlooked the property. She had used Vega that morning to notify Nevelyn, but she'd have no way of knowing if the girl's part of the plan succeeded until everything else was already crashing together. All she could do was perform her part in their grand play.

The carriage passed through the weather barrier surrounding the Heights. A light rain began pattering against the roof. The driver aimed for the western gates. She'd only flown in a carriage like this one other time. She felt the same dizzying feeling she had then. It always startled her to see Kathor spread out. All the houses, and all the people who quietly existed in their own worlds, never once brushing up against her own life.

As they passed over the city gates, Ren felt like she really did know the people down there. She'd lived amongst them, suffered with them, fought quietly on their behalf. She could only hope that the end of the Broods might mean a beginning for others. The first balancing act on scales that had been so imbalanced for so long that it made her sick to think about.

The city vanished from sight.

Great rolling hills ran into a scattershot of forests. She saw rivers and roads winding through the land like the veins of some great, slumbering beast. The trees eventually cleared, and the Brood estate came into view. A city in its own right. Pristine walls circled around a stretch of land that was as large as the entire Lower Quarter. From above, Ren had a perfect view of how the ancient Broods first divided their estate. In that era, the great measure of a house's wealth consisted of the four ideals: family, sustenance, strength, and rule. Two roads ran through the estate. One east to west, the other north to south. They created four equal sections—each one a nod to those original tenets.

The southernmost section was family. There were three lifeless, gray castles there. Each building was linked with the next by a series of glasshouse bridges. There were countless rooms in each one. Large enough to shelter thousands. These were the longtime dwellings of the Brood family, and the current residence of Thugar Brood.

The westernmost section represented the ideal of sustenance. All farmland. Ren's vantage point showed the pristine rows running north to south. These had once fed the Brood family, and she knew it had been designed to produce the ideal rations if they ever faced a siege. The Broods had decided to maintain the fields long after they were functionally unnecessary, because they were the perfect symbol of the brutal efficiency that had built their empire.

The easternmost quarter represented strength. Where the Broods kept their barracks. Every great house had a private army. None rivaled the Broods'. She could see the training grounds. Even now, there was a series of duels unfolding. Practice bouts and training exercises. According to Theo, there was always a minimum of one hundred soldiers on hand to defend the estate, but the full complement could be as high as five hundred, depending on rotations.

Lastly, the ideal of rule. The northernmost quarter was dotted with dozens of smaller houses. The servants' quarters. Each building was meant to demonstrate how many people depended on the Broods for their livelihood. All of their gardeners and their cooks and their physicians lived here. Ren knew many of the men and women occupying those homes had inherited them from their own parents. Some were loyal servants of House Brood and thought of Theo's family as *their* family. Others simply could not find occupations with better benefits and gladly took what they could from the most powerful people in the land. Ren faulted none of them.

"We must set down outside the gates," the driver called back. "Hold on to something, my lady."

As the descent began, Ren realized she didn't know the spellwork that enchanted carriages used for operation. It was a surprising gap in her studies. There had been a magical dynamics class her sophomore year that would have undoubtedly covered it, but she'd opted for Anatomical Magic to round out her resume. There was something marvelous about not knowing. A great reminder that there was more out there for her to learn. She sat in quiet wonder as the driver's spells guided them down with such precision that Ren felt like she was walking down a flight of giant stairs. A final halting charm had the carriage skidding quietly to a stop just outside the looming gates of House Brood.

She might not know how her carriage worked, but she knew why they'd set down outside the walls instead of inside. The

Broods possessed a sophisticated defense system. All the great houses did. What else was there to do, once you'd gathered generational wealth? Obviously, one had to invent clever ways to protect it. She'd heard rumors, of course, but it was Landwin himself who'd confirmed the truth. The Broods were more guarded than their counterparts in one very specific way. The four gates, built to represent the cardinal directions, were only accessible by the direct line of House Brood: Landwin, Marquette, Thugar, Tessa, and Theo.

Theo's access had been stripped from him. His father had claimed it was a part of being the watcher—that historically, they would not allow that person access, in case they were compromised in the course of their duties. That was the ironic part of the whole situation. Theo *had* been compromised. The Broods' suspicious and outdated tradition was working. Theo could not get them inside.

Ren would only be allowed to enter as bait.

The great stone gates groaned open. Ren stood there, wondering who would come down to meet her. Thugar was the primary resident. Landwin was the one who'd actually arranged to meet with her. But as the shadows parted, Ren was surprised to see Marquette Brood. A little chill ran down her spine. This was the Brood she knew the least about. The one who had the vaguest records. Like a star whose brightness was predicated on the larger star it had been fated to be set next to in the sky. Her face was unreadable. Even if she'd married into the family, Ren felt as if she were a Brood in truth. She supposed the passing decades would have bent the woman toward her ruler.

Marquette gestured for Ren to enter. This was the first step. Nestling herself inside the walls. She walked through the gates and actually felt all that waiting magic that was prepared to destroy her. But she'd been waved in by a Brood. Given permission by one of the only gatekeepers. That was enough to keep the magic at bay.

"I am glad you came so early," Marquette said. "I wanted a word with you before your conversation with my husband— and I did not think that I would have the opportunity."

Once more, Ren was surprised. First, that was the longest phrase she'd ever heard Marquette utter. Even at the few family dinners she'd attended, Theo's mother had a habit of curt answers and sharp one-liners. She'd never once heard the woman tell a story or offer a theory about anything at all. The other surprise was that Marquette Brood was sweating. A quiet trickle that was running down her forehead, barely noticeable at all. Except for that it was crisp and chill today, with a fine breeze out of the west. She was nervous about something.

"I came to make a very simple request of you," Marquette said.

The two of them began walking up a beautifully paved road. On their right, the gray castles, brightened by sunlight. Ahead, a small battalion of soldiers running sprints.

"I am always grateful for the opportunity to prove myself. What can I do?"

"Do not sever your bond with my son."

Nothing could have been more startling. Ren actually tripped over her own feet and had to throw out both hands to keep from falling. Marquette looked at her with quiet, pleading eyes.

"Do not break his heart. Do not listen to any of them. Have courage, dear."

With those seditious words in the air between them, Theo's mother turned and began walking up the path again. Quietly she led Ren straight into the heart of the Broods' kingdom. It was a mark of bravery that she'd said what she'd said. A clear departure from Landwin's own plans and a sign that she actually did love her exiled son. Ren almost felt bad. Marquette thought she was playing a risky game by undermining their coming conversation. She had no idea that another game was already halfway finished and that she'd just led the wolf in through the front door.

34

DAHVID TIN'VORI

A son of House Brood met them at the mountain gate.

Dahvid marked him as the youngest. Ren Monroe's bondmate and their supposed confidant. Theo Brood was tall and gaunt, handsome in a way that felt tragic. It reminded Dahvid of the tale about the old dragon, Promethean, who was cursed in the stories to become a wild, ravenous creature for just a single minute of each year. The curse was that he could not know *when* that minute would come—and no matter how he prepared, the results were always devastating. All the good he'd done, unwound and destroyed in less than a breath. Theo had that look to him. A man who was in perfect control until he wasn't.

There was a girl striding a few steps behind him. She had very short hair and very large eyes. Dahvid nodded to her and could not help looking back a few times as the expressions on her face shifted. Brood walked forward and extended a pale hand in greeting.

"I'm Theo Brood. This is my castellan, Dahl Winters. We've been hard at work preparing the way for you and your soldiers."

Dahvid felt soured as he reached out and accepted the handshake. Agreeing to work with a Brood felt like a trap—or at the very least like a dirty sort of compromise. On that fateful night all those years ago, the Broods had not planned to spare any of them. Ware was taken to their estate by Thugar Brood, where he was killed and buried. The other three children—the youngest of which was just seven years old—were assumed to be on the escape boat with their parents. The one that had been burned out at sea. There were no survivors on that ship. They had not shown any mercy then, and it felt strange to leave Theo alive in this mountain castle. The idea stirred uneasily in his mind, but his father had always taught him to not ruffle any feathers until he had both hands around the chicken's neck. For now, he would play nice.

Introductions were in order. He brought Cath forward, and then the acting generals he'd appointed. They were a merciless lot. A bunch of hardened veterans who'd do anything for the promise of more wealth, and there was nothing quite so tempting as sacking a major Kathorian house. Dahvid only wished he'd been there to oversee the fulfillment of Darling's granting of his wish.

He'd awoken on the warlord's estate. Cath had been asleep on a corner cot. Darling visited him once, to inform him the soldiers were stationed and ready to march, down on one of his private beaches. He informed Dahvid there would be no exchanges, no bartering, nothing at all. He was to march the chosen soldiers out before dawn. It was clear that Darling had carefully held back his favorites and his own captains during the selection process. All the men were from the correct companies, at least, but they weren't the soldiers he might have chosen. It would have to suffice.

Theo turned to lead them back through the gate.

"I'll admit I wasn't expecting you to win," he said. "The gauntlet couldn't have been easy."

Dahvid's eyes flicked between Theo and Dahl. He wasn't sure how much to divulge.

"No. It wasn't easy."

"Ren asked me to brief you. On my brother."

The snow crunched beneath their feet as they passed through a courtyard and into a mostly defunct hall. The floorboards possessed a long-faded beauty. Cobwebs hung in every corner. He couldn't believe they had lived here for the past few months.

"You would provide information on your own family?"

It was more of an accusation than was strictly necessary. Dahvid didn't care.

"I have always felt that my family could change. That we could learn from our history, correct our mistakes, and begin writing an entirely new legacy. I've believed that since I was a little boy. Thugar believes the opposite. He wants to be a symbol of our past—and all of its cruelties." Theo glanced over to Dahvid. His eyes did not flick nervously away. He held Dahvid's glare with great intention. "On our estate, there is a tree. It has red-tipped leaves and a black trunk. The wind, when it blows from the west, does not touch its branches. Our own hired gardeners are not allowed to prune it. Only Thugar tends to that tree. He visits it often, because it is the tree that grew from the grave he dug nearly a decade ago."

I will plant you in the ground.

Those were the words Dahvid had heard Thugar speak. Rage trembled through his hands and his bones, and it was difficult to resist making Theo pay for the sins of his family. They'd heard of the tree, though he'd always dismissed it as folklore. Now he knew it was true—and he knew that the only man who'd visited his brother's spirit was his worst enemy. Day after day. Year after year.

It was a trespass he would not forgive.

"Your brother will answer for what he has done."

Theo nodded. "My brother has two functionary roles on our estate. First, he's there to grant access to people who need to enter the estate from Kathor. Only a Brood can do that. But the rest of the time, he trains. Dueling with some of the best generals and fighters that have ever walked the earth. I do not have any love for my brother, but I am not fool enough to think less of his talent. I promise you one thing: he will not be easy to kill."

Dahvid said nothing. He'd suspected as much and now felt even more naked without his tattoos properly restored. The scarlet traveler was a shadow on his chest. It probably looked like a proper tattoo to the untrained eye, but it would not be battle-ready for weeks. He would be without his most valuable weapon and without the twins, which had a longer restoration time as well. The rest of the arsenal would have to be enough.

"But you won a Ravinian gauntlet," Theo was saying. "Which means you're a good match for him. A good match for any fighter in the world. Come. There's food waiting for your soldiers in the main hall. We've set up all the waxway candles there. I'm pretty sure we bought every stub and wick within fifty miles. It's all arranged. If you'll come to the library with me, I can walk you through a layout of the estate and what I know of Thugar's fighting style."

Dahvid accepted. He continued to tiptoe warily through their conversation. Never answering a question with two words when one would do. He and Nevelyn had discussed this matter before she'd left for Kathor. Ren Monroe was playing her own game. It wasn't hard to imagine what she'd envisioned for herself at the end of all of this. Landwin, Thugar, and Tessa Brood would all die.

The Broods were ancient creatures. Their ancestral line would demand that the reins of House Brood be handed not to Landwin's wife but to his oldest child. Theo Brood would be the last remaining heir. Ren Monroe wanted to burn down the parts of the house she didn't like but planned on keeping a few of the rooms in proper order, so that she could rule what rose from the ashes. That had never been their plan—and could never be their plan. No Brood would be permitted to survive.

"This map is a little old," Theo said as they sat down at a table in the library. They were alone. Almost. Dahvid sensed the castellan watching from the hallway. "You can see where I've made changes to match the most recent renovations. It's important to know there aren't just wards along the outer wall, but some sections of the interior house are also warded. At least one of those castles will need to be secured as soon as you enter. . . ."

For a time, Theo Brood trotted through everything like a trained hound. He shared insights Dahvid couldn't have learned anywhere else and kept looking up with such great expectation. The boy was hoping for respect. He wanted a fine clap on the back for his betrayal. Dahvid nodded along, making mental notes, but he refused to give Theo Brood the satisfaction of feeling like they were on the same team, fighting for the same cause. Had Theo burned with hatred for the last decade? Did he thrash awake at night, always imagining the smell of smoke in the air? What had he done to earn a seat at the same table as the Tin'Voris?

"Very good," Dahvid said, when they finished. "I would be alone for a time. I'd like to study all of this. I might even sleep for a little, if you don't mind. This chair is more comfortable than any of the beds I've slept in since I was a boy."

It was intended as a subtle blow. The two of them were close in age. While Dahvid had run from town to town, scraping out a survival, Theo Brood had grown up in gilded comfort. On the night his father and brother raided their home, where had he been? Practicing his spells in a family library, safe as the day he was born? Theo simply stood and nodded.

"Of course. I'll see to your soldiers."

Dahvid leaned back in his chair and pretended to close his eyes. The pretense felt so fine, though, that he nearly gave in. He could have slept for a year in that chair. The march had not been kind to a body that was still recovering. His wounds were stitched or healed, but even the best spells in the world could not make a man whole overnight. He would be lucky to feel seventy percent of his proper self by the time they reached the Brood estate.

There was a rustle near the door. He kept his eyes closed, but a smile began to creep over his face. "I heard you a few

SCOTT REINTGEN

minutes ago. Your shirt brushed against one of the outcropping stones. You've gotten sloppy."

A knife slammed down into the wood between his thumb and forefinger, narrowly missing the skin. Dahl was there, glowering down at him. The library door was shut. It was just the two of them. He carefully slid his hand away from the wobbling blade and rose to his feet.

"You've gotten taller, Sister."

She smiled at him. "I was just about to say you looked shorter, Brother."

He snaked forward for a hug. It was a surprise when Ava didn't dodge or elbow him away. Instead, she met his hug with her own fierce embrace. He knew it was a sign of how much she'd missed him, how much they'd missed each other. It had been nearly two years since she'd departed from them in Peska. Prepared to carry out her part in their grand scheme. That had been before Ren Monroe. Ava had been positioned this entire time to take care of their needs in Nostra. She was still well positioned. Clearly, Theo Brood had no idea who she actually was.

When they pulled away, they were both grinning.

"I guess I can finally stop visiting your grave."

"Oh? Was that a terrible burden for you?" Ava snarked back. "You must have been through such an ordeal living in a city with restaurants and theaters and warm showers. I will make sure I pray for your swift recovery, dear Brother. At least you weren't, I don't know, stationed in the most godforsaken castle in existence."

Dahvid smiled. He'd missed her more than he realized.

"Well, we have a change in plans."

"No shit. Theo Brood's been setting up waxway travel for the army that's going to try to murder his family. Feels like a slight departure from what we'd discussed."

"It is. And the next part will be too," Dahvid said. "I need you to remain here."

Ava looked mortally offended. "Why?"

In the quiet of that library, he explained everything.

35

NEVELYN TIN'VORI

N evelyn had overlooked a single detail.

She'd lowered herself into the dress. The installed harness caught her waist and tightened around her hips, and she hung there, completely suspended in midair. The cables were more than up to the task of keeping her aloft. No matter how she bounced or stretched or moved, she could not even come close to reaching the floor with her feet. She hadn't activated the binding spell yet either, which would limit her movement even more. All of her calculations were perfect except for the ladder.

She'd made a small leap to get down into the dress, and that movement left the ladder just out of reach. She was attempting to rock herself in that direction, lashing out with a kick to knock it away, when the door to her apartment stuttered open. Nevelyn stared at the gap, a thousand warnings ready to spring from her lips.

It was Garth who peeked around the corner. His eyes widened as he drank in the scene. A dress dangling from the ceiling would have been odd enough, but to find her dangling inside it was an entirely new level of strange. He edged into the room like someone who'd spotted a rare bird in the forest and didn't want to startle it away.

"Nevelyn . . . are you okay? Do you need help?"

She supposed that it did appear as if she'd been bound by someone. Not to mention her foot was still bleeding a little. Before she could respond, however, a second realization cut through the first, like an arrow splitting a tossed apple.

"What did you just say?"

He looked annoyed at his own slip-up. She could only watch, trapped inside the dress, as Garth turned around and closed the door. The two of them were now alone inside the room. Her heart was beating fast in her chest. She flung the words at him.

"You called me Nevelyn."

He sighed. "Yes. I'm sorry. Though, I suppose it doesn't matter. No one else is here."

"How do you know my name?"

"I was asked to keep an eye on you."

A bright rage filled her. "Asked by *who*?"

"Old Agnes. She said if I didn't watch out for you at the playhouse, she'd tie me to the bottom of a boat and sail it out into the middle of the ocean."

Agnes Monroe. Ren's mother. Nevelyn knew she'd helped secure the post at the playhouse, but she had no idea her involvement had gone beyond that. She couldn't resist asking the question that had the most potential for hurt. The one that nestled into the center of her deepest fears.

"So all this time . . . you were just pretending?"

Garth started forward. "Of course not. I thought you were a friend of hers. A niece or something. New to the city. She didn't give me much information. I promised her I'd keep an eye out for you, and then the day we met . . ." He shook his head, like he was clearing away cobwebs. "I've never been so taken with someone. Ask my friends. I'm picky about people. There aren't many folks who I think are worth spending time with . . . but you . . ."

Nevelyn hated how easily that made her blush. Especially when she was still feeling the initial sting of imagining he might not care for her at all. She still wasn't sure what to believe.

"I like you," Garth said simply. "I am admittedly confused about why you're dangling from a dress in the middle of a room, but I can promise you that all the flirting and the notes . . . all of that was real."

His words brought her attention swinging back to the task at hand. Garth's honesty would have to be enough for now. She did not have time to ask him questions or to root out a proper confession. Every minute that passed invited more risk into her plan.

"If that's true, I need your help. Move this ladder away."

He frowned. "Don't you need it to get back out?"

"No. I'm staying in the dress. Please, Garth. Move it to the corner."

In spite of his confusion, Garth obeyed again. He carefully set the ladder aside. Nevelyn knew she had no more time to waste. She cut straight to the point.

"I am about to perform magic. When the spell begins, I will not seem like myself. It is very possible that I will scream at you. I might curse you or beg for you to release me. Do not listen to a word I say. Do not move. Do not do anything at all. If you truly want to stay here, you will sit in that corner and obey those commands. Do you understand?"

She was prepared for him to run for the door. To leave, before everything could become even stranger than it already was. Instead, he sat down in the spot she'd pointed to. Nevelyn glanced down at her necklace, briefly worried she'd used magic on him. But the darker heart was facing outward. Garth was obeying because he liked her. He wanted to be here. She found that she was comforted by his presence. If this was to be her end, at least she would not be alone.

"Here goes nothing," she whispered.

The spell was written into the threads of fabric. Layer after careful layer. If a member of the Weavers Guild were there as a witness instead of Garth, she'd be named an expert artisan instantly. With a steady push, the magic woven into the fabric roared to life. It punched out from her like a great gasp of air. Nevelyn instantly felt the dress tighten around her. Like a great, coiled snake. It squeezed her hips and her shoulders and her chest.

Across the city, Tessa Brood's dress would be doing the same.

The second wave of the spell was more of a whisper. Both of her powers were hidden inside it, braided together in the most powerful version of the spell she'd ever created. One half of the magic would convince her to forget herself in this dress, in this moment, in this place. At the same time, the other half of the magic would beckon her to *behold* herself in that other dress, that other moment, that other place. Bound as they were by the twin dresses, Tessa Brood would feel that same push and pull. Nevelyn set both of her mental hands on the magical thread between them—and she unleashed all her strength into the dueling spells.

Her mind shattered.

The very smallest piece of who she was remained in that room, dangling from the ceiling. But the rest of who she was vaulted through the city, shoved headfirst through stone walls, danced past crowds of all the wrong people. Her mind was flung into the distance, and she could only hope the tether worked, that she landed in the right one.

She came gasping to life.

Backstage at the Nodding Violet. One of the other actresses— Nevelyn couldn't recall her name—was at her side. She set a hand on Nevelyn's shoulder, concern lining her face.

"Hey! Are you all right?"

Nevelyn righted herself, still struggling to breathe evenly. It took a long moment to accustom herself to an entirely different body—to control the mind she'd invaded.

"I . . . I think I need a moment to catch my breath. Please excuse me."

Nevelyn turned. Everyone gathered behind the stage watched her go. She walked back to the second makeup room on the right. *My makeup room,* whispered another voice. She did not rush or hurry, as that would draw unnecessary attention. But there was a quickness to her step as she crossed the room to look in the mirror. The girl who stared back at her possessed a cold beauty. She was tall and blond and had cheekbones that looked quite capable of severing an artery.

Nevelyn stared at herself for a moment and then smiled.

Tessa Brood smiled back.

36

REN MONROE

They were intercepted before they reached the southern-most castle.

Marquette Brood fell abruptly silent. Ren looked up to see Thugar Brood crossing the family's manicured lawns with impatient strides. Theo's brother was broad-shouldered and built for war. He possessed all the features she'd once enjoyed about Devlin. Muscled and confident and eye-catching. It was a facade. Lurking beneath was a ravenous creature who had nursed a reputation around Kathor for having an endless appetite. Nothing sated him. He picked fights for no reason. Openly flirted with women in front of his own wife. Ren had witnessed his dark bravado a handful of times. Apparently, that sort of reputation was better than Theo's sin of falling in love with a commoner.

"Ren Monroe. I'm glad you arrived in one piece," Thugar said. He was speaking to her, but his eyes were locked on his mother. "And what a surprise to see you, Mother. I was finishing up some work and was just about to come down and let Ren inside the gate when Beck told me that someone already had. I didn't know you would be here on the estate today. I thought you were attending the commerce briefings in the city."

Marquette's lips pursed. "I see now why I was asked to attend them."

"You were asked to attend them because they might provide vital information for our house and its holdings," Thugar said in the most tongue-clicking way ever. "It's not too late. You could always catch the latter half of the meeting. . . ."

"We have a guest," Marquette replied, stone in her voice. "Let's get her some tea."

It was nice, Ren supposed, to finally have them fighting for her attention. Before she could follow them inside the castle, she glanced north. The hills in that direction tumbled upward, straight into a great veil of trees. Ren knew that just beyond the forest's edge—and just beyond the magical sensors of the Brood estate—there existed a field of ankle-high grass. The space was walled off on all sides by the surrounding forest. The perfect place for a small army to gather, unseen by the rest of the world. Theo had admitted that he used to sneak away to the place as a child. He didn't say why, but she got the sense that it was where he went whenever his older siblings bullied him. What had once been his shield was now the tip of their spear.

Ren marched inside the castle like an honored guest.

They settled her in one of the fancier sitting rooms that overlooked the rest of the estate. She sipped honey-flavored tea and could vaguely hear Thugar and Marquette arguing down the hallway. Whatever the argument was, Marquette lost. When the door opened once more, it was Thugar who returned.

"My father has been informed that you are here. He's in the city, conducting an important meeting, but he will be back as soon as time allows."

Ren nodded. That was expected. She'd learned that from her interviews and her time at Balmerick. The wealthy and powerful rather enjoyed making people wait.

"Thank you."

"For what it's worth, I agree with my mother."

His confession startled Ren. A second Brood family member was ready to give their blessing? It was hard to imagine she'd misjudged them so much. Maybe the shadow of Landwin Brood simply loomed over all their previous encounters?

"You do?"

Thugar smiled, all teeth. "Yes. I think you and Theo should get married. And then you should be allowed to live out your boring lives in that cold mountain pass for the rest of time. Theo is a spoiled prat. He always has been. And you? You're just the girl who stumbled upon the weakest member of the family. The great flaw in our armor. I suppose you deserve credit for being smart enough to drive the knife home when you had the chance."

Ren nearly smiled. This was the reception she'd actually expected. The pretty room and the tea and the pleasant greetings had felt so strange. This was much more the Brood way.

"I'm not sure what you mean. Theo and I fell in love."

"In love?" He laughed without mirth. "He's not here. You can drop the act. I'll admit that I didn't think much of you. I expected Theo would eventually get bored. I mean, look at you."

His eyes casually roamed her up and down.

"But my father read me your letter. Such a clever girl. Positioning yourself this whole time. Wrapping pathetic Theo around your finger. I can respect the strategy. You'll get a fine payout for your efforts, and you deserve it." He scratched idly at his beard. "It's funny. I told Father that we should just . . . kill you. Bury you out in the hills where no one would ever find you. He told me that wasn't very 'diplomatic.' Whatever that means."

Ren had been on the verge of taking another sip. Thugar's words—so casual and cold and cruel—left her frozen, the cup a few inches from her lip. Her hand itched to reach for the horseshoe wand tucked in at her waist. It wasn't time. Not yet. She stared at him over the rim of her cup until he broke out another forced smile.

"Let that be a reminder. When I run House Brood, we will not suffer a slight like this from a girl like you. Come knocking at our door again, and I will show you what the Broods of old were like. None of the stuffy politics and handshakes. I will gut you like the greedy pig that you are. Understood?" He did not wait for a response. Instead, he turned his back to her and started walking away. "Make yourself comfortable. My father will be back from the city before long. I think your payout will depend quite a bit on what he's discovered. Goodbye, Ren Monroe."

His footsteps quietly faded. Ren settled back into her chair, teacup abandoned on the nearest table. She'd never felt more certain of herself. Landwin Brood was an evil she knew. Thugar was an evil in waiting. All this house would ever do was feast on those below them. Ren could feel that familiar anger stirring deep within. A storm thrashing at the gates of her heart.

Soon, she promised herself. *It will not be long now.*

Across the valley, she felt an answer. A matching emotion hummed through her bond. Theo's anger was raising its head to lock eyes with her anger. The hunt was on. Ren felt they had one important advantage. Creatures like the Broods—who had been predators for generations—often forgot what it was like to be hunted. If a new animal was introduced into their food chain, one capable of killing them, it often took years for them to react to the threat. Sometimes it was too late. There was a threshold that, when reached, could lead to only one possible outcome:

Extinction.

37

DAHVID TIN'VORI

Dahvid sat with his legs crossed in meditation.

It was difficult to concentrate. There wasn't much space. Theo Brood had oversold this empty glade. His soldiers were crowded and starting to grow restless. Theo had said it was the perfect spot to hide, but Dahvid was starting to feel like it was the perfect place to be trapped. Trees surrounded them. They had almost no visuals at all and could not risk being too aggressive with their scouts. If a single person was spotted in these woods, there would be a Brood battalion riding out to investigate. They could not be seen before Nevelyn arrived.

Waiting also made him more aware of his own weaknesses. There was a distinct tightness around his still-healing wound. He'd tested it out as they marched. A sharp, shooting pain came any time he reached too high above his head. He knew it would make raised parries difficult to hold. There was his right shoulder, too, which kept threatening to slip from the socket.

He'd apparently popped it out completely during his blurred fight with Agatha Marchment. His face was a constellation of bruises. Blue here, black there. Mostly from the hits he'd taken during his third fight in Darling's gauntlet.

Against the other image-bearer.

His breathing hitched a little. Cath was seated beside him. The two of them had not talked about that yet. She had looked ready to bring up the subject a hundred times but retreated each time they were alone. Dahvid had quietly seethed about it. Now, however, he was knocking on death's door again. When the time came, he would sprint down through the forest with hundreds of strangers. Their loyalty to him was no stronger than the offer of promised gold. He remembered his own thoughts right before the start of his gauntlet. Realizing he could die without telling Cath how he really felt. Was he really fool enough to repeat that mistake?

"I love you," he whispered. "I have loved you for some time now."

When he opened his eyes, he saw that Cath was watching him. The attentive eyes of an artist. He'd always like this about her. The feeling that when she looked at him, she saw more than he could even see in himself. She reached out a hand. He took it in his, raised it to his lips, a kiss.

"The past cannot touch us."

He saw the comfort she took from those words. He understood, too, the irony that he could speak those words to her but not accept them for himself. Was the past ever truly forgotten? He was crouched in a field on his enemy's doorstep because the past was a merciless god. It demanded to be visited, to be worshipped, to be feared. If Dahvid did not give it attention during his waking hours, the past would creep into the world of dreams and claim him there. It had always been that way for him, and he did not want it to be that way for Cath. He kissed her hand again.

"You forgive me?" she asked.

"There is nothing to forgive. I can't ask you to give me your past, Cath. It does not belong to me. I can only ask that you give me today and tomorrow and the next day after that."

She brought his hand to her lips and kissed it in return.

"They are yours."

It was silent for a time. Dahvid closed his eyes again and willed himself to believe that all of this could still work. Even without the scarlet traveler at his disposal, he could walk through those gates and could finish this dark work once and for all. He nearly fell asleep sitting upright, until word echoed back from one of the scouts.

"Carriage."

Dahvid followed the man, crouching low, to the thickest patch of the forest. The two of them peeked through a small gap in the great curtains of leaves. He marked the carriage as it cut through the gray, descending toward the estate. His stomach turned as he waited and waited. The carriage went to the most natural landing point. The southern entrance.

"It's not her," he whispered. "That . . . is Landwin Brood."

The outer walls cut off their view. The carriage vanished from sight. He crept back through the forest and took his place beside Cath.

Where are you, Sister?

38

NEVELYN TIN'VORI

There was a delicate mental balance.

She needed to access some of Tessa's knowledge, but without inviting the part of Tessa that was still there—deep in the recesses of her own conquered mind—to take back control. She could feel the scion like a freshly trapped lioness, stalking from end to end, waiting for the first chance to strike at her captors. Nevelyn was too careful for that. She found the easiest way to acquire the knowledge she needed was to ask.

How do I get back home?

There was a small touch of resistance. And then the answer: *A hired family driver is always on call at Ockley Square.*

Nevelyn navigated down roads she'd never seen. They were foreign to her but second nature to Tessa Brood. The remembered path led her into the heart of the Safe Harbor district. A few people waved as she passed. Nevelyn would wave back, certain they were acquaintances of Tessa Brood, but never daring to risk an actual conversation with any of them.

Around the corner of a great monastery, she found herself walking through the politest market square she'd ever encountered. No one was hawking their goods. There was no hustling or bickering about prices. Just tables full to the brim with beautiful things, and rich people perusing at their leisure. Nevelyn spied the waiting carriage across the way. When she arrived, however, there was no sign of a driver. She circled once, eyeing the nearest pubs, starting to feel a little panicky.

"Looking for Len, Miss Brood?"

A man came striding over from one of the vegetable stands. He knew her name, but Nevelyn had no idea what kind of familiarity existed between them. She decided to go the safest route: a touch of entitlement. She lifted her chin.

"I wish I could say I wasn't."

The man nodded. "Of course. It's just bad luck on the timing. I saw him step away for a quick lunch. Not too long ago. He's never derelict when it comes to his duties."

"Except right now. Will you please find him for me?"

There was a touch of surprise on the man's face. Nevelyn thought maybe she'd overstepped. After all, the other man was no servant of House Brood. She saw no indications or markings that would give him any reason to obey her command. Except for the fact that people in Kathor always obeyed their rulers.

"Of course. Wait right here."

Waiting was not ideal. There was something about stillness that threatened to draw Nevelyn's mind back to the room. Back to the other dress and the body inside it. A small piece of her mind was still there. She felt it was like standing in a room, drinking in all the décor, and then catching sight of another world through one of the mirrors. Briefly, she saw Garth. Crouched right where she'd left him. A look of horror had bloomed on his face. The great black cords trembled with movement. The truth was clear. Tessa was currently occupying Nevelyn's body. After all, the spell was an exchange. It appeared that Tessa was screaming at Garth.

Nevelyn's mind lurched, lured in by that other reality, and she shook herself free of the image. She paced in the market square, trying to stay focused on these surroundings.

You are here. Not there. You are here. Not there.

Mercifully, the man appeared.

"He's coming, Miss Brood. Just a moment."

Len shoved through the doors, wiping at the corners of his mouth. He was an older gentleman with a bald head and quiet, blue eyes. Nevelyn hated the way he bent and groveled and begged her forgiveness. But Tessa Brood would expect such treatment. Len opened the door for her, and she did not bother to thank him as she climbed inside.

In a few moments, the poor man had the carriage moving. Lifting from the ground, rising over the tops of the nearest buildings. Nevelyn kept her face smooth and unbothered, but she hated heights. Her stomach churned uncomfortably. She suspected it would be breaking character to vomit in the back of a carriage that a person supposedly took with regularity.

The city shrank beneath them. It was a sweeping and breathless view of the place that she should have known so well. Street names and neighborhoods and favorite restaurants. It all would have been familiar to her if the Broods had not taken everything from them.

Len tried to make small talk, but Nevelyn kept her answers short and crisp. Nothing that would betray that she was very much not Tessa Brood. As soon as the estate loomed into view, Nevelyn made the one request that she knew was a risk. A very necessary risk.

"Could you please take me to the northern gates? I'd prefer to enter there."

Len reacted as expected. Clear hesitation. This was a departure from their normal practices. It was likely that Tessa Brood had never once approached the estate from that direction. Nevelyn looked out the window, though, pretending to study the trees below. Acting as if her strange request should be treated as law, simply because it had come from her lips.

After a moment's hesitation, Len directed their carriage that way. He brought the floating vehicle lower and lower. Nevelyn could not resist looking north. Her eyes combed the great forest there for any signs of movement. There wasn't a single flicker of sunlight on metal. She could not decide if she was thrilled by her brother's caution or frightened by the possibility that they were not there, that something had gone terribly wrong with the plan.

"Hold on to something, my lady."

The carriage shook, so much that she was nearly thrown into the seat across from her. She caught herself just in time. Len's eyes flicked back to her as the vehicle skidded to a halt.

"Apologies, Miss Brood. It's been some time since I landed here. The ground isn't quite as well maintained on this side of the estate. . . ."

She waved a hand, dismissing the subject without a word.

"You can leave now, Len. Thank you for your services."

He stared at her for a long, uncomfortable moment.

"Is there something else you need?"

He fumbled awkwardly. "It's just . . . we usually wait? For you to come back to the gate after you're done with your family matters. And I . . . I'm sorry, my lady, but you've never called me Len before."

A clear slip of the tongue. Nevelyn knew it would take a great deal more for him to believe the reality of the situation. Who would guess that their normal heiress was being mind-controlled by someone using a set of magical, matching dresses? That was quite a leap to make, but Nevelyn knew there were plenty of stories about manipulation magic. Wizards who specialized in the art of steering the actions of others with quiet bursts of powerful magic. It was not a far cry that the Broods' hired employees would fear such a thing. Either way, she could not afford for him to do exactly what he was doing right now: study her more closely.

She did her best to channel the Tessa Brood she'd witnessed earlier that morning. "That was clearly a mistake, because it seems that using that name has granted you some imagined permission to question my commands." She tilted her chin, ever so slightly. "I will repeat myself for the last time: you are to leave. If I have need of your services—and you should hope with all your heart that we *do* indeed require your services in the future—you will be summoned back to the estate. Is that clear, or shall I recite it a third time?"

Len actually averted his eyes. His response was mumbled.

"Of course, my lady."

She could tell he was genuinely hurt. Maybe his relationship with Tessa was a positive one. Nevelyn could not spare time to consider it further, as she began her descent of the carriage steps. It was a struggle to keep the edges of her long dress from dragging in the mud.

As soon as she was clear, Len had the carriage moving. It glided up and out of sight, and Nevelyn found herself standing outside the looming gates of the Brood estate. She waited there for as long as she dared. Making sure that she was visible from the forests to the north. Her eyes darted briefly that way. There, between the branches, she saw a single, bright slash.

Nevelyn smiled to herself and turned.

Guards watched her from the ramparts. All of them would instantly recognize Tessa Brood. The great heiress to the unspoken throne that was House Brood. She adjusted the straps of her black dress and started walking forward. But now came the final test of her magic.

This had been Ren Monroe's only fear. The magic protecting the Broods' estate was ancient. Layered and harvested over centuries. Magic like that often moved past its original designs. It took on a sort of sentience. Ren's fear had been that the magic would know Tessa was no longer Tessa. Nevelyn could show no hesitation.

She walked straight up to the waiting gates. In the very center, binding them together, was the great emblem of House Brood. An image of four hawks, all facing outward, circling a smaller emblem that represented the city. Their wings and talons had been drawn at such an angle that there was no gap in their ranks. The perfect emblem for the house that had long been Kathor's first defense. *But who will defend you from us?*

Nevelyn reached out with a hand she did not recognize. She whispered a prayer and set her palm to the waiting stone. The door rumbled to life. The magic was actually *working*. All of this plotting and practice, the sleepless years in a dozen different homes, and it had actually worked. The impregnable gates of the Brood estate groaned open. Nevelyn stood there in triumph.

Her part of the plan was finished.

She did not look back. She did not want to give away the surprise. But as a pair of guards came forward to greet their heiress, she knew hundreds of soldiers were sprinting down the forested hills. They would undoubtedly use the trees to cover their approach until the very last possible moment. Nevelyn walked forward, pretending to be Tessa Brood, chatting loudly enough that she would draw the attention of all the surrounding guards.

Not one of them knew the wolves were inside the house.

Time to feast.

39

REN MONROE

R en had been watching the sky.
So far, she'd seen two carriages arrive. One landed by the southern gates, where she'd entered. A second was landing to the north. She had no way of confirming who was inside either of them. Thugar had not returned, though a servant had been tasked with meeting her every need. Ren suspected this was partly to do with good manners but mostly to do with having someone keep an eye on her. Maybe they thought she was going to steal a golden paperweight on her way out. The servant vanished, however, when they heard the sound of boots echoing down the hallway.

Landwin Brood had arrived.

In the carriage that landed to the south.

"Apologies for my delay," he said, crossing the room. "I had matters to attend to in the city."

He slid out of a coat, draping it over the back of his chair. He was holding a lone satchel that appeared to be empty, except for a few papers. He set it down in his lap.

"I don't mind the wait," Ren answered. "I know you're a busy man."

"I am. Like you, I've been so very busy." He patted the satchel in his lap. "Now. I understand that you've been rethinking your position. It's also my understanding that you visited my son in Nostra."

Ren's throat bobbed only slightly. She'd known there was a possibility that he would figure that out. His spies were good at what they did. Not to mention the Hairbone Valley was very much Brood territory. Most of the locals in those towns would see them as one of their main benefactors.

"I visited him, yes. I needed to really know what there was between us. We met in the middle of a tragedy. One that we barely survived. And when we got home, I had just a few months with Theo. Most of them full of various obligations. We were not given much time to enjoy a normal relationship." Ren heaved a pretend sigh. Like it was all so very difficult. "At the Collective, I met other people my age. It was . . . easier to imagine another life. I felt like I needed to go visit Theo and really figure out if we were meant to be with each other. Especially considering what being together would mean. I was in Nostra for a few days. Long enough to make up my mind."

Landwin Brood snorted. "And what? You found my son to be lacking? Gods above. I wish he was here to witness the reward for this kind of foolishness. He stoops to bond with you. He stubbornly resists a severance. A boy who is destined to be matched with any number of princesses, and he chose you. But *you* will not choose *him*. What a humbling moment this will be for my son. Good. He is long overdue for such a lesson."

Ren knew it would not serve the show she was putting on, but she felt a burning need to defend Theo. She liked him too much to let his father talk that way about him.

"You make it sound like this is his fault. I would choose Theo if that meant I was just marrying him, but to marry him is to marry your family. The choice isn't between Theo and some other person. It's between him and enough money to secure my entire future. What father bids against his own son's affections?"

That drew a real smile out of him. It was as if Ren had finally struck a chord that Landwin Brood liked. He reached for the satchel, extracting a few papers. He set them on the table.

"I'm glad you brought up the subject of your payment. After all, we are here to negotiate the terms of your severance. Your letter mentioned that you hoped I might find it in my heart to be a little more generous. I was willing to do that—until some of my own research finally came through. I had a full magical analysis run on the waxway room at Balmerick. Borrowed a friend of yours, actually. A boy named Pecking? He's fully synesthetic. Quite a gift."

Ren had felt so in control. Now the conversation turned— and it was not turning in her favor. "Pecking is no friend of mine."

"That's true. He's not. Which made him even more eager to help me. Remarkable that you could make such an enemy in such a short span of time. Bravo. Now, while the results were not perfectly conclusive, we did manage to determine that someone cast a coil spell in that room. Do you know what coil spells do?"

Ren nodded. She could feel the heat crawling up her neck. "Of course I know what they do. I was the one who cast that spell."

Landwin looked surprised by her admission. "You admit to it?"

"Yes. When I went back to visit the room. After everything that had happened. I don't know. It was silly, really. I was trying to . . . bind the memory of them all. I cast a coil spell. It didn't really do anything. Just fizzled in the air. I guess it was more symbolic than anything else. I just didn't want to forget the people we'd lost. But yes. I was the one who cast the coil spell."

This was a prepared lie. Ren had performed these actions for precisely this moment—so that she might have an explanation at the ready. Unexpectedly, Landwin began to laugh. She'd never really heard him laugh. It was a brittle and lifeless sound. "See, that's the best part. According to Pecking, there were *two* coil spells. Do you know why there would be *two* coil spells, Ren Monroe?"

She said nothing. Of course she knew why. She always knew the answers to their stupid questions. Landwin was leaning forward in his chair, like a predator preparing to strike.

"Not only were there two coil spells, but they were both cast in the same direction. Both cast in the same general area. Pecking had his theories, but you just provided an even better answer. The final piece of the puzzle, really." Landwin tapped the documents on the table. "There were two spells because *you* cast the first coil spell. On the day of the accident. That's why all of your travel distances merged in the waxways. You know, I looked back at the report. Everything you and Theo said to the authorities. There are descriptions from him about *every-one else* in the room. Where they were standing. What they said or did. But Theo didn't describe you at all. He couldn't stop talking about what you did *after* landing in the forest. All your brilliant magic. But not a single word about how you behaved in the waxway room on campus."

Landwin's eyes were boring into her. Ren was trying to summon explanations, but each one felt less and less likely. She could not possibly trust herself to speak.

"Curious, isn't it? That he didn't see what you did. It's almost like you were smart enough to wait until no one was watching. And then, for some unthinkable reason, you cast a coil spell in a teleportation room. The travel distances merged. You got all of your friends lost. Subsequently, you got most of them *killed*. And then when you saw the chance to bind yourself to my son, you took it. And ever since then you've been tugging on that survivor's guilt to make sure he stays in love with you. But I have to wonder, Ren Monroe. If he knew about *this*, what do you think he would say then?"

Distantly, Ren was aware of Theo. There was that familiar pull across their bond. He could probably sense what she was feeling. The numbness that was spreading. A sort of helpless fear. She ignored the pull and focused on the task at hand. She could not risk Theo witnessing this moment.

It would ruin everything.

Landwin Brood looked perfectly satisfied. Ren couldn't believe he'd actually figured it all out. She thought she'd been so clever to cast the spell again and cover her tracks. That no one could possibly perceive the difference between those two spells, cast as they were, perfectly overlapping each other.

She'd made an error, and her professors had always been fond of telling her that errors in the real world had consequences.

"My new proposal," he said. "You can work for Seminar Shiverian. I'll write a letter to them myself. In exchange, you will sever your bond with my son. Immediately. And you will get nothing else. If you accept this offer now, you have my sworn goodwill in recommending you for their house."

Ren sputtered. "But . . . that's way less than before. . . ."

Landwin smiled. "Indeed. That is precisely how a negotiation works. It is called leverage. Maybe they don't teach this down in the Lower Quarter. But when one person has more power than the other, they are better positioned to negotiate. I hope the alternative to this course is obvious. If you do not accept my terms, I will take all of this information to Theo. I will tell him *exactly* what happened and the part that you played in it. And then I will ask him to sever the bond himself. You're right. It's possible he'll say no. It's possible he'll still trust you. But how much confidence do you have that he'll keep you around?"

Ren sat there, pretending to be shocked by it all. It wasn't hard. She actually was a little shocked. True, she was not here to actually sever herself from Theo. It was all a ruse. But now there was a small satchel full of information that could ruin her future. Even if she won today, she might lose tomorrow. Theo could not be allowed to learn any of this. She was trying to figure out what to say when a servant shadowed into view by the entrance. Landwin Brood waved them away, too busy relishing the moment, only to watch his servant ignore the command and enter the room without permission.

"Sir, it is urgent. At the gates."

He looked annoyed that his victory over her would be interrupted. Ren did not smile. She did not gloat. That part would
come later. She was doing her very best to continue to look
stricken by this turn of events. Landwin stood impatiently.

"You have until I return to decide what you would like to
do."

Ren nodded, watching as he departed. As soon as he was
out of sight, she darted over to the window. In the distance,
there was movement. Dust rising over the hill. She could see
soldiers running. Great flashes of magic. Could it really have
worked? Had Nevelyn actually gotten the army through the
gate? Ren's next duty was to make sure the Brood family didn't
seal themselves in the main houses. It would be hard for them
to do it now—they'd already allowed one of the wolves inside
the walls.

She started walking toward the hallway, trying to remember the layout of the house, when the bond between her and
Theo roared to life. It hammered into her like a two-ton anvil.
Ren stumbled sideways, colliding with a bookshelf, and had no
choice as she was ripped away from the sitting room. . . .

No, no, no . . . Theo . . . what are you doing?

Her feet set down in snow. She expected to see the castle or
maybe Nostra. Instead, she found herself in the heart of a forest. At first, it looked unrecognizable. And then she noticed the
tracks in the snow. This was the trail that Theo's predecessors
had built. The same slopes she'd witnessed him sledding down
when she'd first visited. But where was he?

Footsteps crunched in the snow behind her. Ren whipped
around. Dahl Winters was walking down the trail. The thin
girl stalked patiently forward. She looked utterly transformed.

This was not the mousy servant girl who always hunched her shoulders and avoided eye contact. Dahl stood tall, walked confidently, and held a wicked-looking wand. Ren could not help feeling like she was watching an ancient huntress stalking its . . .

Prey. She's looking for Theo.

The girl walked right past her. Of course. Ren was there but not there. She turned, following, and saw the obvious signs of an accident. One of the sleds had veered off the path. Ren stumbled to the edge at the same time that Dahl arrived there.

Below, through gaps in the trees, she saw Theo. He'd fallen a long way, though the snow where he landed was thick and untouched. Likely it was the only reason he wasn't dead. He was staring up at the ridge where Ren stood. His eyes looked unfocused, and blood was running from his nose. Dahl made a disgusted noise and then started making her patient way down to him. It was clear that she was not going to help him.

"Hey!" Ren shouted. "What are you doing?"

The girl didn't hear. Didn't even turn. Ren felt helpless. She reached for the horseshoe wand on her belt. She took two steps forward and aimed a spell at Dahl's back, but no magic came.

"Shit."

She followed Dahl down the hill. What else could she do? It felt the same way that moving through Theo's memory had—last year, when they'd faced Clyde on that bridge. There was a resistance. A thickening of gravity that made Ren feel like she was walking underwater.

"Please," Theo said. "Please help me."

He was reaching out. She realized he was not looking at Dahl. He was staring just over the girl's shoulder, at Ren. He could sense her presence. Ren raised her horseshoe wand again and attempted another spell. Nothing happened. Not even a fizzle of magic.

Dahl navigated around a larger snowdrift and stopped a few feet away from him. Ren waited for Theo to raise his own wand. Anything to defend himself. It took her a second to remember that Vega was on her shoulder, not his. Theo did not reach for his waist, either. Ren saw there was nothing there. He didn't have his other vessel for some reason. He had no way to defend himself at all.

"Help," Dahl repeated. "Look around, golden boy. There is no one here to help you. It's just the two of us. Gods, you have no idea how *long* I've been waiting for this. All of the damn chatter. All of your ceaseless conversation. Having to pretend to enjoy the company of a *Brood*. Finally, your time has come. Just had to wait for my brother to get through the pass first."

Theo's breathing came in uneven gasps. "Your brother?"

"Oh. Yes. That's right. We have not been properly introduced." She made a mockery of it, seizing his hand and moving it forcefully up and down. The motion dragged a painful hiss from him. "I am Ava Tin'Vori. A survivor of House Tin'Vori. You know, the one that your family tried to burn to the ground. You should have made sure we were all dead. Huge mistake."

She kicked him in the stomach. Ren felt that pain flick across her bond. She could not believe what she was hearing. Nevelyn and Dahvid had claimed their sister was dead. Mat Tully had even reported that Nevelyn visited the graveside once a week. This revelation explained their initial reaction to the news that Theo had taken the post in Nostra. They'd already had someone on the inside.

"I've always wondered what death would feel like. Ever since that night. Down in the tunnels. We could smell the bodies burning, you know." Ava knelt down beside him. Ren's own breathing hitched slightly. She didn't want Theo to die, but at the same time, she could hear her own pain in Ava's words. "That's not a smell you forget. And it wasn't even the worst part. The end of the tunnel led to the canal. We had the best view of the harbor from there . . . and the three of us got to watch our parents' ship as it burned. As they burned with it. I was seven years old."

Ava traced an idle finger through the snow. Theo wasn't looking at her. He was staring at the spot where Ren stood, his lips moving, struggling to form words.

"Seven. You see shit like that when you're that young and you become fascinated with death. What's on the other side? What comes next? How does it *feel*? Does your soul leave your body? Is there even such a thing as a soul? I had so many questions about it. My brother and sister would get annoyed by them, so I used to sneak out at night and talk with priests. Random strangers. I'd ask everyone I could. What did they think? What comes *next*?"

Ava took her feet again. She pointed her wand down at Theo.

"You'll have to tell me when you get there."

Theo and Ren both cried out at the same time. They both mentally reached for their bond. Theo gave a heaving, desperate pull. Ren gave a frantic, final shove. Vega was the unexpected answer. Ren watched as the stone bird flew from her shoulder and landed on his. An impossibility. Ava startled back at the bird's sudden appearance. Her wand tip was already igniting with a spell. Vega's flight created a path for Ren to travel.

Impossible, breathless, but real.

Ren Monroe moved through space and time. As if she had her own private waxways. This time, her feet truly set down in the snow. She felt the cold and the wind of that dark forest. It was all real. She raised her wand at Ava Tin'Vori and cast the first stun spell that came to mind.

But what roared out of her wand was something more. Powered by all that emotion and desperation. Powered by her bone-deep fear of actually losing Theo. Her spell lit the entire hillside up with blinding light. It struck the girl right in the chest. Like a backhand from a god. There was a great clap of thunder, and then Ava Tin'Vori was thrown through the air. With so much force that Ren lost sight of her vaulting through the trees. No one could survive a drop like that. Ren collapsed at Theo's side.

"Are you okay? What hurts?"

"You're here," he gasped. "Actually here. How did you do that?"

"I traveled across our bond."

He closed his eyes for a second. "That's . . . not possible?"

"It's bond magic. Historically—"

"Ren. Not now. No history right now." He offered a small smile, and then his eyes widened. "Wait. You're *here*. You can't be here, Ren. You have to be there. At the estate. My father . . ."

"Your father."

They had the same realization. She could not simply leave Landwin Brood to his own devices during the attack. Ren was supposed to be there. She was supposed to limit his options, forcing him into certain actions. She could not do any of that from this wintry pass.

"Push me back," Ren said.

Theo nodded. "The opposite . . . okay. You pull. I'll push. Get ready."

It had to work. They could not take down House Brood and allow Landwin to survive. If he found refuge with one of the other houses, nothing would change. Ren stood.

"I'm ready."

Theo was groaning with the pain. After a second, though, he nodded to her.

"All right. Vega. Go."

With all her mental strength, Ren pulled. She could feel Theo pushing on the other end of their bond. Vega fluttered through the air, landing on her shoulder, and Ren's vision of the surrounding forest was snatched away. The world vanished. She vaulted between here and there, and the magic set her back down in Landwin Brood's office. Something was wrong, though. Ren felt like she was still falling. Almost like she'd overshot the landing somehow. She could feel the magic *burning* and she was briefly afraid she'd end up like Clyde, seared from the inside out.

Instead, Theo stumbled into the room with her. He fell straight into Ren. The two of them collapsed together. His weight was too much for her. Theo let out a guttural cry of pain.

"No, no, no . . . I pulled you too hard. Theo, you can't . . ."

He wasn't supposed to be here. Ren had wanted him to be in the mountains—somewhere safe while they finished burning everything down. They were meant to come back together and sift through the ashes. But now he was here.

Ren reached for their bond, hoping she could push him back

across, but it felt like setting her hands inside an inferno. She pulled back, hissing with pain. Their connection was on fire. All scorched earth. Not dead, she knew, but certainly unusable for now. They'd pushed the magic too far already. Ren helped Theo stumble over to the chair she'd been sitting in. Outside, there were skirmishes happening everywhere. Individual fights. Smaller units working together. Ren could barely tell who was who.

"Your father . . . he was just . . ."

Footsteps echoed down the hall. The shadows stretched and flickered. Landwin Brood appeared. He took three strides into the room before realizing there was a new guest. He held a polished dragon's tooth in his right hand—a unique choice of vessel. Ren had only seen him use his signet rings for spells.

"Theo? What are you . . ."

Ren saw no benefit to talking him through the sequence of events. Far better if they used the element of surprise. She'd waited long enough for this. She raised her horseshoe wand and cast a thundering projectile. As expected, the counterspells built into Landwin's clothing activated. They devoured most of the impact, so that the only effect was a slight sideways stumble. He steadied himself on a nearby bookcase while Ren let loose another spell, and another, and another. She was going through her list with calculated efficiency. Physical magic, fire, acidic. Anything she could do to eat away at the edges of his shields.

She was about to call for Theo to help her when a concussive blast rushed past her from the left. Her bond-mate stood there in proper battle stance, even though he was clearly hurt. They locked eyes for a second and then began to move forward.

Spell after spell struck home, pinning Landwin Brood in on both sides. This was one of Able Ockley's favorite tactics. A barrage of successful strikes would activate defensive magic. And if defensive magic was active, offensive spells were nearly impossible to cast.

Ren circled to the right and timed a barrier spell with one of Theo's offensive castings. It webbed the entryway with invisible magic. Landwin could still run, but passing through that barrier would cost him now. She swung her wand back, mentally preparing her next casting, when Landwin Brood spoke again. His voice echoed strangely. As if he were elsewhere, and his voice could not fully carry the distance between worlds.

"My son," he said. "You have made a grave error."

He raised the vessel in his off-hand and snapped his fingers.

Ren cast a shield spell at the very last moment but realized she wasn't the target of Landwin's wrath. Vega shot instinctively across the room to Theo. The bird dragged Ren's summoned shield across that distance in her claws. Theo's eyes went wide as his father unleashed a spell that shook the entire castle. Darkness pulsed out from him.

All the light in the room—all the light outside, too—briefly blotted. Ren's shield made it to Theo just in time. It caught the direct blast before splintering inward. She could only watch as Landwin's spell unmade the world around them. The back wall exploded outward. All the windows vaporized instantly. The tables and the chairs, reduced to nothing. Theo was writhing on the ground. Ren knew if he'd taken the full spell, there'd be nothing left of him but ash and bone. There was no time to rush to his side. Landwin Brood was turning. In her direction.

His wand tip ignited as he cast a second spell.

40

DAHVID TIN'VORI

The fighting was everywhere.

He saw soldiers dueling up and down rows of unpicked strawberries. Others were rolling in the dust of the central crossroads, kicking and biting and wrestling away weapons. Great bolts of magic kept hissing overhead, stray shots from the more long-distance dueling.

His army's initial rush through the northern gate had been a tidal surge. Five hundred strong met by just a dozen guards. Most of those guards had looked to Tessa Brood—who was not Tessa Brood—for their orders. His sister had called for them to surrender. It was strange to see Nevelyn's expressions written on another face. She'd shot him a meaningful look before sprinting toward the distant castles. As long as she was in control of Tessa Brood's body, the plan was for her to do as much damage as possible.

The insurgents spread across the estate like wildfire. Until they hit the central crossroads. The very heart of the Broods' property. An organized counterattack met them there. That was the group they were still fighting now. Some fifty of House Brood's soldiers and spellcasters. Dahvid could tell they'd taken more damage than the enemy. There were nearly twice as many of his hired swords on the ground. But in the end, their numbers were overwhelming the other side.

Dahvid joined a duel with one of his generals. The two of them made quick work of it before turning to face another soldier. *Block, stab, cross-strike, dead.* He'd intentionally forged a path through the lines and was making his way over to the tree Theo had described to him. The one with the red-tipped leaves. The trunk that was as dark as night. He felt certain this was where his brother had been killed. Where he was buried.

"Incoming!"

A blast of fire nearly scorched them all. It burned a path through their ranks, soldiers dodging aside at the last possible moment. Dahvid pointed to the ramparts where the spell had come from. "Get someone up there now!"

"Incoming on foot! Turn! Turn!"

Dahvid still had some two hundred men left, though they looked tired from the first melee. Now a second unit was coming up the hill—at least one hundred strong. Dahvid suspected Thugar Brood would be amongst them. He settled into his stance. This is what he'd been waiting for.

"To me! Everyone to me!"

His mercenaries weren't new to battle. They joined ranks, raised shields, and waited for the inevitable crash. They had the higher ground. At the very last moment, he shouted to his men.

"Counter now!"

They'd feigned a defensive position. Bracing for impact. Now they drove forward. It was just enough to catch their enemy by surprise. Dust spun into the air, brief and blinding, and then both armies were in the thick of each other. Dahvid's command won them the initial push, but once they were through the front lines, everything fell to chaos. In that great press of bodies, he searched for Thugar Brood. He cut down two men, then nearly had his head taken off by a hacking swing from a third. The soldier was bull-rushed from the side before he could even answer.

No matter how deep he pushed into the enemy's ranks, he could not find the fight he really wanted. He spied a trio of wizards doing damage along the back lines, launching projectiles every few seconds. He forged a path to them and cast his null tattoo. It rippled outward, cutting away their magic. Some of his men swept in to finish them off. The fight felt like it went on without an end in sight.

Exhaustion was coming far faster to Dahvid's already tired bones. He started to feel desperate to find Thugar. *Where are you? Why aren't you fighting with your men?*

Dahvid tried not to use any of his combat tattoos but had to burn the elixir to heal a nasty cut along the back of his calf. He still had his golden rings, the rope spell, and Ware's reaching hand tattoo. He retreated into a small pocket of calm. Near the tree. As he looked around, he saw his army had won the second round, though their numbers were significantly reduced. He counted fifty solid fighters still standing. A small group of Brood soldiers were making their retreat.

Finally, he saw Thugar's plan.

Another battalion waited near the barracks. Thugar stood at the front. He had been waiting all this time. It was the same tactic he'd used the night he killed Ware. He would not risk entering battle against someone who was at full strength. Instead, he'd allowed his hired hands to strike the first blows, so that he could step in and finish the fight. Dahvid had no more healing spells. His scarlet traveler was useless. But the true fear came from the exhaustion spreading across his entire body. He felt just as weak as he had after four rounds in the gauntlet.

Still, he raised his voice. "Form up ranks again!"

His remaining soldiers circled back. Some plucked weapons from the fallen, trading nicked blades for something better. It smelled horrible—like the arena. Death was kind to no one. Dahvid watched as Thugar called out commands to the final group. The third wave began to march.

Halfway up the hill, their march became a run. Dahvid let out a war cry as the two sides collided. But this time, they lost ground. He could feel their lines being shoved back, worn down from too much fighting. Individual duels broke out everywhere.

Thugar Brood came for him now. "Hello there, image-bearer."

His enemy had grown. Far bigger than Dahvid remembered. More polished looking than any version of Thugar he'd ever dreamed of. It was as if he'd spent all his days shaping himself into an instrument of pain and suffering. The man stalked forward wielding a massive broadsword.

"My name is Dahvid Tin'Vori. Brother of Ware Tin'Vori."

Thugar nodded. "I know who you are. Came all this way to be buried beside him?"

Dahvid snaked forward. His only advantage now was speed.

He feigned a side-sweeping blow that twisted into a cross-handed backswing. His blade slit Thugar's exposed right shoulder. Blood trickled down as Dahvid pressed him, darting in and out of his steps, as quick as a man who'd fought a hundred battles in just a few days could be. He wounded Thugar once more before the bigger man adjusted. Switching into an entirely new stance.

"My turn," Thugar grunted.

He cut away Dahvid's quickness through pure strength. Sweeping blows that left no room for counters. All Dahvid could do was backpedal, parry, deflect. The two of them danced in and out of the surrounding duels until it was too much. His body was on the verge of collapse.

He raised his arms to parry a brutal downward cut and felt his sword rattle away. Thugar lashed forward with a brutal punch to the throat. Dahvid stumbled, on the verge of falling, and saw his end coming in a bright flash of silver. The cleaving blow swung from left to right. Dahvid activated his golden rings a breath before the sword reached him.

Golden light spilled outward. A circle inside a circle inside a circle. It entrenched him in a breath, whispering safety. He slumped down within its protection. His hands shook. At least he had time to calm his breathing. Thirty seconds to recover, though he was not sure what would change when the golden light fell away. He needed to make sure . . .

. . . a resounding crack filled the air. Thugar's sword hit the side of his shield with impossible force. Dahvid watched the damage from that impact spread, splintering his most powerful protective magic into a million pieces. He rolled to his right just before the golden light winked out entirely. *That is not possible.* Thugar pressed him again, and Dahvid had no sword to answer with. He ducked and dodged and desperately activated a second tattoo.

His rope spell.

The invisible magic lashed out, coiling twice around Thugar's right arm. Dahvid took the other end of the magical rope and drove it straight down into the ground. He felt the magic anchor there. When Thugar raised his sword again, the invisible rope went taut. His right hand jerked down to the ground. It was forceful enough that he nearly fumbled his sword.

Dahvid took advantage. Darting around the bigger man, rolling to collect his fallen sword. He spun back, hoping to turn the tides of the fight while Thugar was still trapped, but his opponent didn't panic. He lifted his massive sword, set it against the spot where the invisible rope was, and cut through it with a single strike.

That's a sever-sword. He can destroy magic. Shit.

That realization broke Dahvid. He did not have the physical strength. His magic could not turn the tides. Thugar Brood began to wear him down with merciless efficiency. A cut here. A slit there. An unexpected kick to the chest that sent Dahvid backward. He hit the ground so hard that it felt like he was still falling, like the earth itself was devouring him.

There was dust and the blue sky and his sworn enemy looming overhead. When Dahvid tried to jab upward with his sword, he realized it wasn't there. He'd been disarmed again.

Thugar spat down in the sand beside him. The bigger man made a show of collecting Dahvid's blade, abandoning his own. When he came back, he knelt down close.

"Do you want to know how Ware died?"

Thugar grabbed the back of his neck. With incredible strength, he wrenched Dahvid up into a sitting position. He held the summoned sword in his opposite hand.

"I held him like this," Thugar said. "The same way he held my wife. Dancing with her. Flirting with her. In front of everyone. I held him so very close to me. And then I whispered the final words he heard in this life. The same ones you will hear."

Thugar leaned forward. Dahvid thought his breath smelled like a graveyard.

"No one will remember you."

Before he could plunge the sword, Dahvid dismissed the spell. The metal vanished a second before it could find flesh. Thugar instinctively dropped him, and as Dahvid fell, he reached for his very last tattoo. The two hands that Ware had drawn just before he died. One reaching from below the water and one from above. He did not know what would happen. Power thundered out from him.

A forceful wave that threw back anyone within twenty paces. Dahvid could feel his entire body vibrating with an almost painful surge of energy. The magic latched on to something in the distance. He couldn't tell if it was Thugar, or the trees around them, or some other source. But his guess had been right. The spell was an exchange. His weakness for that waiting strength. His wounds for that offered wholeness. Whatever the source, he felt it flood his veins with pulsing life.

Dahvid snatched an abandoned sword and stood. Thugar Brood was scrambling away. The entire world had gone mute and colorless. He saw everything moving in slow motion. Brood was shoving his own men forward, urging them to fight in his place. Dahvid cut them down one by one, all without adjusting his stride. Navigated through them with a strength that was not simply restorative but an evolution of his power. A perfecting. He'd never been so strong.

Thugar was forced to turn. He swung once, backpedaled, and Dahvid began a sequence of his own. He did not need the scarlet traveler to know how it would all end. He swung low to high. Two darting lunges, a spin move, and then his borrowed blade found the belly of the dragon that had haunted his entire life. Thugar choked out blood. Dahvid held him close, twisting the metal, and then ripping it free. Their eyes met as Dahvid prepared the final blow.

"I will remember Ware. Long after you're gone, his memory will live on."

Dahvid plunged his sword into Thugar's heart.

When he pulled it back, the man fell. It was done. There were a few skirmishes left, but his mercenaries held the hill. He knew he should oversee their entry into the family castles. Make sure that no one killed the servants or looted before the time to divide the spoils came.

But he didn't care. He wanted Cath. He had left a small ring of guards with her. Back by the northern gate. He ran, fueled by the pulsing energy of Ware's spell. He felt like he could sprint all the way back to Ravinia in this state. As he closed in on their location, he saw something had gone wrong. The guards weren't watching for enemy approaches. They were all turned inward. Looking down. Muttering to one another. Dahvid shouted and they moved aside, allowing him through.

"Cath?"

She was on the ground. Wounded and bleeding and paler than he'd ever seen.

"Who did this to her?" He seized the collar of the nearest guard and dragged him down to eye level. "Tell me who did this! You were here to protect her. Who did this?"

He realized none of the men looked as if they'd seen battle. There were no signs of sweat or dirt or blood. Had they betrayed him? But the man stumbled back a step.

"Sir . . . I'm sorry, sir. There was no one. We were just . . . we were all standing here. She just fell, sir. She collapsed. All of those wounds appeared. I've never seen anything like it."

Dahvid collapsed back beside her. He pulled Cath in close and stroked her hair and could not admit that she was already gone. His eyes traced her wounds. That pulsing fury was building in his chest. They were lying to him. He'd kill them all for betraying him.

"These are *sword* wounds. If no one came, how could she . . ."

His voice trailed away. There was a strange bruise along her throat. A great thicket of black-and-blue skin. Like she'd been punched with a metal gauntlet. Looking down, he saw a horizontal gash across her thigh. Exactly where his wound had been before the magic healed him. His hands traced the lines of her body, finding each cut, remembering each of his own. It was like following a trail up a mountain to learn a truth that he could not bear actually knowing.

He began weeping. Into his hands. Into her hair. Crying over the body of the only person he'd learned to love since that horrible night. He knew what had happened, even if he didn't know why. No one else had done this to her.

It had been the magic. It had been him.

41

NEVELYN TIN'VORI

Nevelyn glided through unfamiliar halls.

At least unfamiliar to her. Tessa Brood knew them well. The three connected castles felt endless. She could not even begin to fathom why one family could ever need all of this. She moved through the gilded rooms with great caution. She was unarmed. She'd intentionally removed Tessa Brood's vessels and left them outside the gates. If she lost control of the girl, she didn't want Tessa to have a way to defend herself.

A weapon wasn't necessary. She was granted access purely because she was Tessa Brood. If a door was barricaded, the servants would quickly open it to allow her inside. Others peeked out from behind upturned furniture. Each time, she offered the same advice.

"Put down all of your weapons. Do not resist them. If someone comes, surrender."

Everyone stared back in disbelief. She kept moving. There

was no time to explain. She could only hope it was enough to save them from wasting their lives in defense of the Broods. Nevelyn was following Tessa's internal compass to get to her father's favorite study. She hoped to find Landwin there, and Ren Monroe with him. It was impossible to know how their part of the plan had progressed. Too many moving pieces. Too many variables.

She arrived at the second glass bridge.

Her mind stumbled over what she saw. It wasn't what Tessa remembered, and Nevelyn understood why. All of the glass had shattered. As if an explosion had gone off. In the distance, where the bridge should have connected to the third castle, Nevelyn saw a gaping hole. Debris was everywhere. Some kind of duel had broken out here.

She picked her way carefully through the glass, but her mind stuttered again. The briefest of flickers. She saw her other self. The empty room. Garth was standing for some reason. She saw him pacing back and forth like a caged animal. He said something to her, but she could not make out the words. Could not afford to focus on them, because her grasp on the other world might slip.

Settle down. Stay in the moment. You have more to do.

Nevelyn shook the cobwebs of her mind. The bridge appeared. She crossed most of the way and was forced to leap over the spot where the foundations had split. There were shouts ahead. Great bursts of magic echoed down the hallway. She followed their sound and came upon a room that was in utter ruin. Theo Brood was there on the floor. She stared in disbelief. Why was he here? Had Dahvid brought him? Had their initial plan changed? He was struggling to sit up, one hand nursing an injured rib. His eyes landed on her.

"Tessa?"

A snatch of magic sounded farther down the hallway. Nevelyn ignored Theo. She slid on through the shadows. The hallway opened up to a landing. There was a wide stairwell that fed down into a large reception area. There, a battle unfolded. Nevelyn stumbled to the railing and saw Ren Monroe. Their confidant was pinned behind an obnoxious statue. One of the Broods of old glared out, though half of his face had been blasted off. Landwin Brood was halfway down the steps. He showed no concern for his ancestor's legacy as he unleashed another devastating spell. It sent the stone head rolling away. Ren Monroe ducked out, answering with her own magic. A bolt of arcane light that Brood swatted away with no more than a wrist-flick. It was clear. The girl was losing.

"Stop!"

Nevelyn started down the stairs. Landwin's head whipped around. Ren was staring at her, clearly trying to figure out which version of Tessa Brood was about to join the fray.

"Tessa?" Landwin's attention swung back to Ren. "Good. Help me finish this traitor. And then we can attend to your brother."

He turned his back to her. An unthinkable mistake, except for the fact that he saw his daughter coming down the stairs to help him. She reached for the knife along her belt and took the steps two at a time. At the very last moment, some instinct forced him to turn around.

Nevelyn's lunge became a tackle. It was the most bone-crushing physical hit she'd ever felt in her life. There was the initial blow, their breathless flight, and then a second devastating crunch as they collided with the hardwood floor at the base of the steps.

The two of them slid together and Nevelyn landed on top. Landwin's wand—or at least she thought it was a wand—skidded into the shadows on their right. Her knife was closer. She snatched it off the ground, struggling to keep her balance, and then drove it down into his throat.

It caught impossibly in midair. An inch away from actual flesh. Magic hissed between them. She saw a translucent shield, surrounding his entire body. But as she kept driving the knife down, the spell trembled with movement. It was breaking. Underneath all that pressure. The knife had to work. This man needed to die. She drove it down again.

But Nevelyn flinched back when Landwin Brood's face transformed beneath her. His features melted and shifted. She still held a knife, though the heft of it was heavier. The face beneath her was Garth's. Lovely Garth with his broad smile and his toss of brown hair and a great red slash across his neck.

"Garth!"

She was back in her own body. Her temples pulsed with pain. Her entire body reeled, threatening to collapse sideways, but she fought off the feeling. Garth needed her. One of the cords must have ripped. She looked up. No, it had been severed. The knife. Garth had come to help her, against her wishes. He had come forward and cut her down. Thinking it was Nevelyn.

And Tessa Brood had made him pay for it.

Nevelyn ripped the fabric of her dress. She balled it up and pressed it to Garth's neck, but so much blood was already on the ground. It spread out from him, forming dark tributaries.

"Garth," she begged. "Wait. Please, Garth."

His lips were moving. He reached up to her, his hand trembling violently.

"Stay with me! Hey! Stay with me, Garth."

The blood had already soaked through the fabric. It was staining her hands. Garth tried to say something, but the noise guttered back down his throat. A sickly rattle. Nevelyn watched as the light left his eyes.

She screamed. A noise that began deep down in her chest. It was so loud that it didn't even sound human. She thought they would hear it echoing over the city, louder than anything that had ever split the air. But then she remembered the walls were enchanted. Layer upon layer upon layer.

As she cradled Garth in her arms, she knew no one could hear her.

42

REN MONROE

Ren was shouting for Nevelyn to move out of the way. One of Landwin's protective shields was on the verge of shattering—and she had just the right spell to finish it off. Before she could shout again, the girl slumped sideways. She rolled clear of her father and came to rest on her back. With great heaving breaths, she stared up at the ceiling.

The magic reverted. That's really Tessa Brood now. Time to finish this.

She unleashed her spell—a three-headed projectile that screamed from her wand with a high whistle. It struck Landwin Brood as he pushed up to a knee. His flickering shield spell shattered. That was the third one she'd burned through. Theo had told her that the shields were built into special trinkets he always wore on his person. She could see that the face of his watch had shattered. One of his golden rings had dulled to black. The items were destroyed when the shield finally broke.

According to Theo, his father wore at least four layers of protection at all times.

One more to go.

Ren had not been outdueled so far. It was just hard to beat a person four times in a row. She'd taken several wounds herself. Her entire left side would be a pattern of bruises tomorrow, but only if she actually survived today. Landwin's last shield activated. A subtle flicker in the air. He was trying to get back to his feet. He lurched slightly, eyes searching the ground. Ren wasted no time. She hit him with one spell. And then another. Always a rotation. Bolts of fire. Pressurized blasts of air. Arrows of honed steel. Few people had an arsenal that was quite as expansive as hers. Theo had explained that the more the shields had to protect against, the faster they'd drain.

"Ren!"

At the top of the steps. Theo limped into view. Vega was on his shoulder. She watched as he began his own casting. Her next spell struck Landwin first, lighting up the shield. Theo's hit a few seconds later. There was a subtle whine in the air. Already, the last shield was starting to falter.

"The dragon's tooth!" Theo called as he struggled down the steps. "Don't let him get the tooth."

Three things happened at once: Tessa Brood finally stood. The girl wobbled on unsteady legs, looking drunk. She stumbled unintentionally into Ren's sight line. Behind her, Landwin dove for something in the shadows. And a second later Theo's next spell soared overhead, missing its mark by mere inches.

Tessa blinked at Ren. Took one look around the room. And then darted into a shadowed recess on their right. Ren hadn't even realized it was a door. The girl vanished—and was replaced a moment later by her father. Landwin had the tooth clutched in his hand. Ren raised her wand. Theo did the same. Both of them were closing in on where he stood.

"There's nowhere to go," Ren said. "Put down your vessel. Surrender to us."

Landwin smiled. "And then what? What do you think will happen? Do you really think that *you* get to run House Brood?" He was looking at Theo. The smile darkened into laughter. "Gods, Theo. Show some intelligence for once. If you kill me, they'll feast on our entire house. Everything you have. Every comfort you've enjoyed. The other houses will come and they'll take it all. You're not ready. You're not cunning enough to run a house. You never were."

"I'm cunning enough to know you're buying time," Theo said, lifting his wand. "Hoping someone else will join the fight and come to your aid. They aren't coming, Father. Tessa just left you. Thugar is dead. It's just us now. I'm also cunning enough to know that three of your four shields are already destroyed. You've used your best magic. This is over."

Landwin's eyes darted between them. He snorted with derision.

"Just us. Fine. I want you to remember that I gave you a chance. By this time tomorrow, I will be back in this hallway. All of the houses that serve our house will rally to *my* banner. And when we come back here to root out all of the *rats*, I'm sure you'll be gone. On the run. Maybe you'll flee to one of the freeports. But when I find you—and I promise, I will find you—what I do to you will make Nostra seem like the most pleasant of dreams."

Theo swallowed. They'd arrived at the final act of the play.

"You're bluffing, Father. There's no way to escape."

Another heartless laugh. "Gods, you know so very little. There are secrets that belong only to the head of our house. Passed down through generations. One day, those secrets might have been yours. Now you'll never know them."

He raised his dragon's tooth vessel. Ren put on a fine show, casting one more desperate bolt of magic. It crackled helplessly against the shield. Theo raised his own wand, but before he could cast anything, Landwin Brood ported from the room. The air whispered around them and went still.

It was silent. Ren and Theo exchanged glances. For a while, neither one of them said a word. And then Ren smiled in triumph. Theo smiled grimly back.

"I told you," Theo said. "I told you he'd do it."

This was one of their great secrets. Long guarded by all the great houses. Knowledge that belonged only to the head of the house. The safest way to travel had always been with a waxway candle. It was the proven, known method. But the very first travelers had apparently ported by using the fangs of dragons. The Shiverians had wisely hidden that knowledge. The great houses quietly collected every dragon's tooth in existence. The cache was well protected—and each head of house was gifted one when they ascended their unofficial throne. Theo had learned all of this one night when his father had far too much to drink. He'd shared the secret he wasn't supposed to tell anyone else.

A method for instant teleportation. It was far faster than any waxway candle, but it also came with its own limitations. Theo's father had told him that it could take the possessor to a single, fixed point. That place had to be designated well in advance. Theo had never brought the subject up after that, for fear of earning more of his father's displeasure. But he had quietly wondered where his father would choose to travel if his life was ever truly in danger.

He'd never learned the answer. But Ren had.

For a moment, it was just the two of them. Standing in the eye of the storm. Theo's smile faded first. There were signs of damage all around the room. Broken statues and shattered vases. One spell had completely obliterated the wooden railing running up the stairs. Ren knew this could not be easy, knew that he'd feel some measure of guilt for being the one who let the wolves inside his family's house. She was trying to think of the right words to comfort him, but he spoke first.

"It doesn't feel the way I thought it would."

Ren nodded. "I know. I'm so sorry, Theo . . ."

"No. That's not what I meant. It feels like I finally did something right."

He cast one final look around the room, then met Ren's eyes.

"We should secure the castle. I don't want any of the servants killed."

Ren could not help it. She swept across the room and hugged him. All this time she'd wondered who he might become. If he could really transform into someone other than a Brood. For the first time, she felt certain he could. She allowed herself to imagine their future together. One that did not involve plots or revenge or any of that. This future existed well beyond the shadows that the last decade had cast over their lives. Theo hugged her back before wincing with pain.

"Oh. Your ribs. Sorry," Ren whispered as she pulled away.

"Don't be. You saved me again. What are we at now? Five times?"

"Honestly, I don't bother keeping count anymore."

He offered her that lovely smirk. She would have kissed him if their faces weren't quite so covered in blood. Instead, the two of them quietly adjusted their cloaks. A quick straightening of collars and tucking in of shirts. Vega settled on his shoulder. Ren regripped her wand. Armed and ready, they started walking into the next hall, together.

43

DAHVID TIN'VORI

Cath was covered with a black cloth someone had found.
He set guards to watch her body and then started across
the estate. He felt as if he'd lived and died a hundred times.
Like a ghost who could not leave the world, even after the ones
he'd loved had vanished from it. Ware was gone. Cath too. All
he had left were his sisters, and right now he had no idea what
fate had befallen either of them.

Fires had broken out. His mercenaries were getting out of
hand. Some of them were picking their way across the battlefield. Only a few were helping the wounded. Most were gathering valuable weapons and armor and piling them on a crop
wagon that had been commandeered. For the survivors, it
was as perfect a mercenary run as they could have imagined.
They'd won but with enough losses that their cut of the reward
would be far more substantial. Dahvid had nearly reached the
back entrance to one of the castles when he heard it.

Screams. The screams of children.

He rushed inside without hesitation. He was no longer afraid of dying. The sound led him past four different rooms and up a flight of stairs. There was a pair of his soldiers in the hallway. Laughing together. They'd barred a set of double doors with an ancient-looking sword. Something they'd plucked from one of the displays. Smoke whispered out from the crack at the bottom of the door. The screams were coming from inside.

"Who is in there?"

Both guards reached for weapons, then realized who'd asked the question. Their temporary commander. "Just some Brood runts," one answered. "Don't worry. They won't scream for much longer."

Dahvid swiped the tattoo at his wrist. His sword hummed quietly into the air. His fingers closed around the grip. He saw the look the two men exchanged, a silent agreement reached. Their pact did not last for long. Three quick moves, and both slumped to the floor. Death always felt nearby now. Maybe it would feel that way for the rest of his life. Maybe it was the only thing he was good at in this world. He set his sword down and slid away the makeshift lock. A shove had the doors opening. Smoke flooded out.

A man stumbled free with three children in tow. Dahvid did not know who they were, and he did not care. They could have been Thugar Brood's children. It did not matter. They would not die here today. He picked up the smallest one and walked them back through the halls. Outside, where the smoke could not keep blacking their lungs. The man thanked him but fell quiet when he saw the bodies piled in the distance. The strangers picking through pockets. His eyes cut back to Dahvid.

"No one will harm you. Or them. You have my word."

He knew he needed to go back inside. Find out if there were other survivors who needed help, but he worried what might happen to the man and the children. He paced instead. His eyes kept flitting back to the little ones. The oldest couldn't have been a day over ten. There were two brothers and a sister—or maybe cousins. It was like looking into a distant mirror. Being shown his own past, played out all over again. He realized that he had patiently and methodically done exactly what he'd promised to do. He had crossed the world. Summoned an army. Defeated the looming villain of his story. All so that he could shove the same chain of events back into motion. Would these children grow up as he had? Hating a name they whispered into their pillows each night? Dreaming of the day when they might find him and revenge all that they'd lost today?

This is what he'd done. And for what?

Cath was dead. His sisters' fates unknown. Ware's ghost had not thanked him. His brother had not come back to life as Thugar Brood fell to the ground. Dahvid had dreamed and dreamed and dreamed, and never once considered that he might be walking into a nightmare of his own creation. Yes, Thugar was dead. That much he knew was right, but the rest of it? How could he ever live with the rest of it?

He sank down to the ground. The children were watching him. Concern lined their small, round faces. The man approached. He had Ware's face. Long hair, bright eyes. He looked like he would live forever.

"Are you all right?" he asked in the wrong voice.

Dahvid nodded.

"I just . . . I just need to sleep."

And he did.

44

REN MONROE

The other great houses began to arrive.

From the ramparts, Ren could see banners flying for the Shiverians, the Graylantians, and the Winterses. There was an old joke that the Proctors were always the last to arrive, as they'd been on the last ship to reach Kathor. Their battalion could be seen snaking up the valley, just a step behind the others, almost as if they wanted to live up to their family reputation. She noted that they'd kept their companies deliberately small. Tactical units that she knew could do some serious damage, but none so large as to draw attention. That was expected. The leaders of the city would not want to advertise what was happening at the Brood estate until they knew exactly how it might help or hurt their own houses.

Theo took his place on the ramparts. He reached out, briefly squeezing her hand, before straightening his shoulders. He looked breathless but ready. There'd been a great deal of commotion. Putting out the fires inside the castles. Negotiating a reasonable amount of spoils for all the remaining mercenaries, so they could begin counting their rewards instead of hunting innocent servants. Tessa Brood had been captured. Thugar Brood was confirmed dead. It was finally quiet inside the gates, just as it grew noisy outside them.

Marquette Brood strode up the steps. She'd agreed to the transfer of power. Theo Brood would officially be named as successor. He would lead their house forward. Offered the chance to swear loyalty to him, Tessa Brood had spat on the stones. Then she'd cursed Theo's children, his children's children. She likely would have gone on cursing successive generations if he hadn't ordered her to be taken away.

A group of emissaries came forward from the larger army. Ren saw Seminar Shiverian with them. Able Ockley was with them, too, his eyes tracing the ramparts carefully. Most likely he was searching for some weakness in the magic. Ren didn't know the others by name, but she knew there was at least one representative from every major family. That wasn't surprising. After all, the last coup had been during the War of Neighbors. Everyone would want to have a say in what happened next, because they all stood to gain or lose a great deal.

"Care to let us in?" Seminar called. "We'd like to assess the damage. Begin negotiations."

Ren smirked. How casual of them. Theo answered.

"I can hear you just fine from there."

The protection around the Broods' estate still held. Theo and Marquette Brood were the only ones who could open the gates. What had been an obstacle now became a shield, holding the grounds from outside invasion. For all their power and magic, the other houses could not simply force their way inside, because none of them were Broods.

"I'd figure out a way inside eventually," Seminar said, her eyes on Ren now. "There's a key for every lock. All it would take is time. A few months maybe."

"Let us spare you the trouble," Ren said.

Theo nodded. "We think our way is easier."

He gestured. Marquette Brood stepped forward so that the emissaries could all see her from below. "I have accepted Theo's request. My husband is gone. My firstborn son is dead. My daughter has abdicated her rights. Theo Brood will officially take control of House Brood until he finds a worthy successor of his own."

She choked out the last words and fled back down the steps. Some of Theo's guards were waiting there. Ren knew she cared for Theo. Their last conversation proved as much. But she was certain that did not make it easy to bury another son, to lose a husband.

Theo stepped forward in her place. "You're all witnesses. I have assumed leadership of this house. There is no need to negotiate anything. It would be far more beneficial to everyone if House Brood resumed its activities, maintained its status, and upheld the integrity of your rule. Don't you agree?"

Seminar nodded. "That would be in our best interest, but with all due respect to the Lady Brood, she is not qualified to pass on the mantle of your house. Only Landwin Brood can do that. I noticed that your mother did not say he was *dead*. She didn't say that he was *captured*, either. No, she used a very different word. She said, 'My husband is *gone*.'"

"He is gone. He will not return."

There was a small, whispered exchange in their party.

"We ask for proof. We can't approve your ascension without it."

It was Ren and Theo's turn to trade glances.

"Three days," she called back. "And we'll bring it."

"Bring what?"

"You said you wanted proof. Give us three days, and we'll bring you his body."

45

NEVELYN TIN'VORI

Nevelyn was being haunted by ghosts.

She saw them moving around her like vengeful spirits. Talking and pointing and she could not hear anything they were saying. Surely, they had to be ghosts. One of them tried to take Garth from her. She bit and scraped and cursed and fought. When she tasted copper—someone else's blood—she realized that the ghosts weren't there to hurt her. They were there to help. Heavy hands pulled her away. A pair of women brought her to the bath. They quietly undressed her, patiently washed away all the blood. Nevelyn said nothing as her skin turned pink and wrinkly. In the other room, she could see people scrubbing at the blood on the floor. Cutting away the dark cords she'd spent so much time measuring and installing. There was a discussion of what to do with the body. It was so short that Nevelyn did not even hear what they agreed to. There was a far more thorough debate over the dress. No one seemed to want to touch it. Could they burn it? Was it still dangerous? Eventually they left. Everyone except for the two women. Both of them had matching, half-faded bruises along their arms and collarbones. They helped her get dressed, led her over to her bed, and tucked her under the covers like a child.

And like a child, she fell straight to sleep.

When she woke, Dahvid was there. His was the only voice she ever cared to hear again. His and Ava's. Why risk speaking to anyone else? She'd just have to watch them die eventually. She was starting to feel like their life was just a long, winding curse.

"Your plan worked," he said.

Nevelyn nodded. "Why doesn't it feel that way?"

She thought he might understand her bitterness. Surely he'd been told about the man they'd cleaned up from her apartment floor. She hoped for empathy. Instead, her brother's expression broke. He began weeping. She'd only seen him cry one other time. The night they'd left the estate.

"Cath," he whispered. "Cath is dead."

Nevelyn wrapped her brother in a hug. She'd always been the comforter. For little Ava and all her tantrums. For Dahvid, too, when the days felt long and the way home impossible. It was a part of why she'd never had any time for herself. No pursuits of her own. Not until Garth.

"How did it happen?"

"It was me." He shook his head, wiping away tears. "I used Ware's tattoo."

The reaching hands. They'd talked about it so many times over the years. Dahvid had always viewed it with a certain mysticism. She'd begged him to test out the magic, but he'd always felt destined to use the tattoo in his great moment of need. Apparently, destiny really did not care much for the Tin'Vori family. It always did its best to spite them.

"And what happened?"

"It was clever," he said sadly. "Ware was always clever. It's an exchange. My physical condition for his physical condition. I think he assumed that he would always be my favorite. Activating the tattoo was intended to draw on his life force, and only enough to restore my energy for a battle."

"But it drew on Cath," she whispered. "Because she was your favorite. And the tattoo's power had grown over the years. It would have been impossible to control how much you drew on her. Oh, Dahvid. I'm so sorry."

She found herself telling him about Garth. Not just the end, but the entire story. As if she needed to convince someone else that it had really happened. That it was not what it felt like—an already-fading dream. "He's gone."

There was silence. What else could be said? Words would not bring them back.

"What happens now?" she asked.

"House Brood will publicly admit to the fact that the raid of our houses was done on illegal pretenses," Dahvid said. "They will condemn it and ask the governors of Kathor to reinstate our house to its previous status. We are to be paid restitution. Restored."

Nevelyn nearly choked on that final word. How could they ever be restored? She remembered seeing Theo Brood on the floor when she was walking around the estate. Obviously, he had survived. Who else would accept public disfavor to help a long-broken house like theirs? It had to be him—and Ren Monroe.

At least the girl was good enough to keep her promises.

There was only one question that mattered.

"Have you heard from Ava?"

Dahvid's expression darkened. "No. I am making inquiries."

Her jaw clenched. It would be one more reason to feel guilty. It was their fault that she'd been in Nostra. They'd sent her there, knowing all the potential risks. Nevelyn wished she could convince herself that they'd all decided to accept the risk at the outset of the plan, but Ava was the baby sister. She was always going to agree to do anything they asked her to do.

"We'll find her."

She did not believe her own words. Dahvid nodded as if he did. After a moment, he stood.

"Come."

"What? Where?"

He looked back. "We still have to bury them."

They were escorted to their former residence. Nevelyn had never dared to come anywhere close to the old house, for fear of being recognized, and she was shocked to see how it stood. A literal castle, nestled between the busy sprawl of other houses and businesses, and it had remained vacant. All this time. No one had ever moved in after them.

Apparently, every carpet and painting and spoon had been claimed in the aftermath of the raid. All divvied up. But there had been some difficulty in litigating the actual residence. Who should be allowed to claim the property? It was quite valuable, but making a claim demanded that someone put their official name on the deed. That kind of official documentation would unmask one of the culprits. Everyone knew who'd raided the house, but rumors would not hold up in a court of law the same way a signature on a house deed might. And so it had sat all this time. Empty.

Nevelyn followed Dahvid through halls that were so empty, rooms so barren, that she nearly started laughing. Even their house was a ghost. They aimed for the run of glass windows along the back of the house. There were cobwebs and broken glass and decrepit stains. Even in such a state, the view over their back gardens of the harbor was breathtaking. Like looking through time and into her own childhood. She followed her brother outside.

"I had them dig up Ware's body," Dahvid explained quietly. "And the tree that had grown over his grave—I burned it. It was a cursed thing. Fed by Thugar's hatred for him. Our brother's spirit was restless there. Now he's home. He will hear our voices instead."

There were three fresh graves. Dark pits waiting to take the dead from them one more time. One for Garth, one for Cath, and one for Ware. She looked at the three bodies under their black-mesh burial shrouds and thought of all they had lost. Dahvid signaled. The gravediggers quietly set down their shovels, murmured their condolences, and left.

Nevelyn looked around the empty courtyard and the surrounding gardens. All of this had once been a pretend land for them to conquer. They would imagine themselves as famous spellcasters or marauders or pioneers. Such bright imaginations, and all they'd managed to do in real life was turn it into this: a graveyard.

She was about to ask Dahvid if he wanted to say anything when magic rippled in the air before them. Both of them tensed as a girl appeared in midair. She was reaching out, her fingers pinched together, as if she'd just extinguished a candle. She floated above the ground for an impossible moment. And then gravity snared her.

She fell straight into one of the waiting graves. Dahvid hissed one of his rare curses. Nevelyn rushed forward and fell to her knees. Ava Tin'Vori was there. She let out a horrible groan, rolled onto her back, and stared up at them. She was covered in dirt and dried blood and gods only knew what else. After a long moment, she grinned up at them.

"I don't remember the graves. Are they new?"

"You insensitive, crass little creature . . ."

In spite of her scolding, Nevelyn reached down with Dahvid to help their sister up.

"Not a single word from you. Even though you *knew* the plan. Not a whisper! We've been worried sick, Ava. We thought you'd . . ."

"Died?" Ava laughed as they finally pulled her out of the grave. The irony drew out a smirk from Nevelyn, too. Her heart was pounding with relief. So many terrible things had happened. There'd been no reason to smile. Not until now. At least the three of them had survived. But she saw that it had been a near thing for Ava. Her sister's entire body was covered with bruises. She'd bandaged a gash on her left arm, but the blood had soaked through and the wound looked infected. There were a dozen other smaller scrapes and wounds.

"What happened to you?"

"It's a long story," Ava answered. "And I will not tell it without a glass of wine in hand."

Dahvid snorted. "You're insufferable."

"Good to see you, too. Hey. Who are we burying?"

Their brother's smile fell away. "Cath, Ware, and Garth."

Ava navigated past the open graves to look down at the bodies. They followed. She knelt beside Cath's slender form first. "She was so very good to you. I'm sorry, Brother."

He nodded solemnly. She turned to Ware next, setting a gentle hand on his skeletal foot.

"Ware . . . you look a lot thinner than I remember. Good on you for staying fit."

Nevelyn laughed. It hurt to allow the sound out into a world that felt so joyless, but she could not keep it in. Dahvid was grinning, looking more like his old self. Ava stepped around Ware to the last of the three bodies.

"Garth," she said, her voice thick with emotion. Then she turned back. "Who the hell is Garth?"

All three of them were laughing then. Loud enough to wake the dead. It was only later, after they'd finished the burials, that she found herself wishing it worked that way. That a smile or a joke might bring them back. The three siblings gathered together in the empty kitchen that looked out past the back gardens and offered a glimpse of the distant harbor. Nevelyn procured some wine from a shop on the corner of their street, as well as a few cups. She poured a healthy measure for each of them as Ava recounted what had happened.

When she finished, the quiet held.

Dahvid was pacing back and forth. Nevelyn could see that little crease between his eyebrows that meant he was quietly raging. Angry about how close they'd come to losing her. Ava poured herself a second glass. All three of them stared through the windows at the distant harbor. The last time they'd seen it was from a very different angle. Down in the tunnels beneath the house. Watching their parents' ship burn like a lantern in the endless black of night.

Between then and now, they'd lived a hundred different lives. Pretended to be messengers and war orphans and farmer's daughters. Anything they could do to keep themselves clothed and fed and alive. Each of them had sacrificed. Each of them had given everything to make sure, one day, they would return to this place. And each one of them had lost so much to come back.

Nevelyn knew that now was the time to begin again. A season of restoration. Maybe that would mean restoring the castle or selling the place to start new lives elsewhere. Thugar Brood was dead. He could haunt them no longer. They'd just defeated one of the greatest houses in the world. Unbidden, the old dream of living in the mountains returned to her. Reading books on a porch at dusk. It would be a quiet life—one that she'd more than earned.

That was the right decision to make, but Nevelyn's thoughts kept drifting to Ava. The thought of her baby sister alone in that mountain pass, leaving tracks of blood in the snow as she crawled down to Nostra for help. She could not stop the words she spoke next. Even if some small part of her hated to say them.

"I think I might have a plan."

Both of her siblings smirked. Nevelyn always had a plan.

This one was simple: House Tin'Vori would rise again.

46

REN MONROE

On the third day, Ren went hunting.

She thought it would be hard to wait that long, but truly, they'd needed every grain of sand in the hourglass. There was so much to arrange. She'd underestimated just how vast an empire the Broods controlled. The amount of payments that moved between them and their vassals, even on a daily basis, was staggering. Theo had barely slept. When she asked him if he wanted to come with her to see the conclusion of their plan, he'd quietly shaken his head.

"I said goodbye to him a long time ago."

And so Ren traveled alone. First, an arranged waxway candle to her mother's apartment. From there, she was guided by some of her mother's closest confidants. Through the nighttime alleys and shadow-spun streets to a very small apartment building. The address on the outside of the building read: 47 Farthing Road. There were twelve total living spaces.

All of the aboveground units were occupied. There were families who'd lived there for years. Bachelors who thought highly of a location so close to so many taverns. Many of the occupants, if they had lived there long enough, had noticed that the building should have had a very large basement. The front of the building sat at the top of a hill, overlooking the rest of the street, but the hill sloped down on the backside. It seemed as if the architect had wasted a great deal of space. They all had different reasons and explanations for it. Special plumbing or foundational concerns or utility installations. Reasonable guesses, even if each one was incorrect.

When Ren first visited the building on 47 Farthing Road, it had taken her almost an hour to find the secret door that led down into an empty basement space. But magic *always* leaves a trail. She found the place to be in flawless condition, sustained by powerful magical charms. There was a sealed pantry full of dried goods that might allow a person to survive for a year. Longer perhaps. A closet full of clothes and other necessities. There was even a stack of books to read, in case the occupant grew bored.

Now Ren entered for the second time. Down the basement steps. She found her mother waiting there. Harlow was with her. He looked as tall and thin as she remembered, but down in the semi-dark, he looked like a far more serious person. All the levity stolen by the slightest shadow crossing his face. There was also a pair of bruises along his neck that made him look more dangerous. He shook Ren's hand and went back upstairs. The two of them were alone.

With their captive.

Landwin Brood was in a cage of Ren's own design. It was a

null spell wrapped inside a disarming charm wrapped inside three layers of oppositional coating. The very moment he'd ported from the estate, he would have appeared right here. Her trap would have sprung. All his magic would have been stripped away before he even opened his eyes. Someone had removed and destroyed his vessels. He'd been fed scraps of food, but three days in prison had slowly drained him. She thought this version far more accurately represented the man she'd come to know. It was a glimpse at the cruel, pitiful creature that lived within.

Ren went to her mother first. She leaned in close and asked a quiet question. Her mother looked her in the eye for a long moment and nodded. A permission granted. Agnes Monroe stepped back as Ren Monroe stepped forward.

"I thought I might find you here."

Landwin looked up at the sound of her voice.

"47 Farthing Road. It was not easy to find this location."

He stared at her, trying to comprehend. His right hand itched for a vessel that was no longer there. He said simply, "You knew about the dragon's tooth."

"Theo knew. You told him about it when he was a boy. But I was the one who figured out where you would go. Anywhere in the world. Dozens of properties to your name. Some of them with hundreds of potential rooms. And yet . . . a poor girl from the Lower Quarter—the one who you believed was unworthy of your son—figured out exactly where you'd travel. You must be shocked."

He did not smile. "I've always admitted you were good at magic."

"I am not good at magic," she replied. "I am *exceptional*. And now I have orchestrated the downfall of one of the five most powerful men in the world. Here you are. At my mercy."

"So I am," Landwin said. "Why don't we skip past all of this and go straight to the negotiation?"

Ren lifted an eyebrow. "Is that what you think this is?"

"I know how all of this works. Better than you could imagine. I've captured people before, you know. I've even been captured. When I was a little boy. Someone wanted my father's attention, so they took me. You are playing a game that I am intimately familiar with. If you were going to kill me, you would have already done it. People keep prisoners alive this long when they want to negotiate. So, why not skip to that part?"

"Gods." Ren shook her head. "He doesn't remember, Mother."

Behind her, Agnes Monroe spat on the stones. "Remind him."

"I am Ren Monroe—daughter of Agnes and Roland Monroe. I have to imagine you learned that from your research. You had people following me. You conducted magical examinations of places I'd visited. I have no doubt there was a file on me somewhere with all of the relevant information. Including my father's name. But you actually forgot who he was. Didn't you?"

Landwin looked like a man who'd been thrown overboard into dark waters, unsure how deep it went or what else might be swimming there. "I'm a public figure. I meet many people. . . ."

"Roland Monroe. Ten years ago, he helped form a union that inconvenienced your progress on the canals. You arranged a meeting with him on the bridge by Crossing Street. And you also arranged for that bridge to collapse. He and four others died that day. You attended his funeral." Ren pointed back.

"That is his wife." And then she set one hand to her chest. "I am his daughter."

Now he looked like a man who was craning his neck, doing his best to keep his head above the waterline. A man who knew how dangerous it might be if he slipped down any farther.

"This is not a negotiation," Ren said. "Aside from your life, what could you give me that I have not already taken from you? Theo has assumed control of your house. Thugar is dead, Tessa imprisoned. Your wife signed our transfer of power and most of your guards have already sworn their loyalty to Theo. Those who didn't had their contracts sold to other houses. All of the minor houses are coming around to his banner. You have nothing left."

Landwin shook his head. "I am not without allies. I have cousins who will not like the idea of having Theo in charge. People will come looking for me."

"No one is coming," Ren said calmly. "If they are looking for you, they're looking in all the wrong places, because no one else knows this place exists. I had to get the *stones* to tell me about it. You didn't tell your wife. You didn't tell any of your children. It is the one secret that you kept from the rest of the world, because you wanted a perfect fail-safe. Which is what also makes it the perfect trap."

Now he was a man whose head was being held underwater. His mouth moved, but no sounds came. Ren did not care to hear him speak again.

"You know, I did my research too. I found out that the architect who designed this building is dead. So are the three builders. Every single one of them died in a tragic accident. A lot like the bridge that collapsed to kill my father. Almost like someone wanted to get rid of them."

Landwin Brood's face was pale and bloated. His eyes desperate. A drowning man.

"As I said, this is not a negotiation. It is an execution."

Ren almost always used her wand. The horseshoe grip that had gotten so comfortable over the years. Now, however, she set it aside. The dragon-forged bracelet began to glow on her wrist instead. A gift from her father to her mother—long before Ren had even been born. She felt it was the appropriate vessel to store the spells that would kill the man who'd killed her father.

"You know what I love about magic?" Ren said. "There's a spell for *everything*."

She'd imagined this day for a long time. She used to practice the spells and the motions and the steps. All the pretend countermoves he might try. There were a lot of different ways a person might use magic to destroy another person, but Ren had eventually decided on the most practical one: a killing spell.

Landwin Brood started begging for his life right as she dispelled the null trap. It vanished in a breathy whisper. Her first blast struck a moment later. Killing spells did not kill the entire person. They could only kill one part of him at a time. The first blast hit his neck. Ren heard his voice gutter out. Dead. Her second blast hit him directly in the chest. He clutched at his shirt and let out a wordless cry. Black streaks were spreading under his skin, creeping up his neck. Dead. Ren hit him again. His right hand shriveled into nothing. Again, his left eye burst within its socket.

Ren destroyed Landwin Brood, piece by piece by piece.

It ended with him slumped on his knees. No voice to beg

mercy. No eyes to look out with. Everything about him had been reduced to nothing. She'd always thought of her own father as a king without a crown. A man who ruled his small world with great intention and care. Landwin was the opposite. The golden hair and the fine suits and all that polish. He wore those bright crowns to hide the rot that existed underneath.

Now Ren saw him as he was.

She looked back once more to her mother. One more request for permission. Agnes Monroe offered a tight nod.

"For my father," she whispered. "For Roland Monroe."

She carefully adjusted the iron bracelet, lifted her hand, and cast a final killing spell. It caught Landwin Brood right in the chest. Where his heart should have been. The force of it sent him sprawling backward. Ren did not need to check vitals or listen for the sound of his breathing.

The magic had done its dark work.

Landwin Brood was dead.

EPILOGUE

Agnes Monroe carefully removed her clothes.

She folded her pants and shirt. Coiled her leather belt and jammed it into the heel of one of her boots. There was a small recess along the wall of the canal, and she shoved the dry clothing inside the nook for later. It was dark out. All the lights in this section of the canal were broken, casting a shadow the length of several ships. City workers were regularly assigned to replace the lights—and were surprised when they found them broken again a few weeks later. It was the kind of peculiarity that made them mutter about curses or vandals, but it was not so dire that it warranted an actual investigation. They'd simply fill out another form and ask someone to replace it again.

In those shadows, Agnes leapt into the canal. The water claimed her like a child returning home. She knifed downward, hands feeling along the wall. She used the subtle grooves to keep herself from floating upward—guiding herself deeper and deeper into the dark instead.

Her hands found a metal wheel. Patiently, she began cranking it. The process took nearly a minute of patient turning. Enough that anyone who had not worked on the docks for years would grow uncomfortable. Nervous that their lungs might actually run out of air. Agnes wasn't afraid.

There was a subtle rumble beneath her hands. She pulled and the wall gave way. Water filled the space instantly. She swam forward, closing the door behind her, and felt the room pressurize. It was still full of water, but a single pull of a nearby lever opened drains at the bottom of the chamber. The small room began to empty of water. Agnes waited until it was no more than a puddle, and then she began turning a second wheel. The inner door opened to an underground.

A lamp glowed at the heart of the space. That central room honeycombed out into smaller quarters. Each one had a defined purpose. She paused to grab one of the spare robes they always kept on hand, then marched across the room. Harlow was still here. Pacing nervously. Their master stood with his back to them, eyes fixed on a map of Kathor.

"Landwin Brood is dead," she announced.

Harlow's eyes darted back and forth. "We'll have a small window. The buildings won't be occupied during a transfer of power. A few days at least."

Their master made no response. Instead, he carefully lit a candle. The flame flickered like a miniature sun in front of him. They watched him step forward, tilting the candle sideways. He pressed the tip to the place on the map where the Brood estate was marked. There was a subtle hiss as the flame went out, but it left the spot blackened.

Then, one by one, he used the still-hot wick of the candle

to mark black Xs over twelve other locations on the map. Agnes knew each one. She could picture them in her mind. She'd researched every building. Memorized guard rotations. Assessed weaknesses and written up reports. Every one of those dark marks represented a city defense that was run by the Brood family. The secret pillars on which the rest of Kathor had stood for centuries.

All vulnerable now.

"Well," Agnes said. "What do you think?"

Their master turned.

"Let's gut the rest of them."

ACKNOWLEDGMENTS

Being an author is a rather unsettling occupation. You work for months at a time with almost no sounding board. When you finally hand your work off to someone else, there is trepidation. How will this thing that's been rattling around the walls of your mind be received? After all of that time and energy, what will other people really think? Will your instincts be validated or not?

The first person to read *A Whisper in the Walls* was my editor, Kate Prosswimmer. Thank you so much, Kate, for being the calm validation that this book was worthy. Your words were an echo of my own confidence. A quiet reminder that this book was taking our beloved characters in the right direction. I am eternally grateful for that.

The second person to read *Whisper* was my mom. I printed out a copy just for her, in fact. One of the few perks of being an author: you have the opportunity to give some seriously cool

Mother's Day gifts. Mom, I'm honored that you always read my work. I did remove all the cuss words from your version, though, so consider this my sheepish apology about the real book.

I dedicated this novel to my agent—Kristin Nelson—and she could not deserve it more. Kristin, you have been my constant champion. Never wavering once. I couldn't ask for a better person to have in my literary corner. Thank you.

As always, a thank-you to my wife, Katie, and my kiddos. Henry, you were five when I wrote this book and just diving into your love for building Legos. Thomas, you were two when I wrote this book and obsessed with trains. Scottie, you were six months old. Still new to the world, but delighting us every day. Thank you for giving me a reason to create and for letting me practice my stories at bedtime. There's no critic in the world more terrifying than a two-year-old.

My work team: Justin Chanda, Karen Wojtyla, Eugene Lee, Jen Strada, Greg Stadnyk, Nicole Fiorica, Alissa Nigro, Sam McVeigh, Emily Ritter, and so many more. Ren Monroe could never have set off for revenge without you. There would be no story at all. Thank you for your efforts—seen and unseen—to bring this book to the world.

Nothing brings a book to life more than art. I am indebted to Juhani Jackson for his work on this breathtaking cover. I thought it would be hard to follow in the footsteps of the first novel, but you delivered beyond my wildest dreams. Another deserving shout-out has to go to Chris Brackley. Every young kid who writes a story begins by drawing a map of their imagined fantasyland. Chris brought that dream to life for me with one of the most detailed and gorgeous maps I've ever seen. He also asked some really good questions that forced me to think more deeply about my world. Thank you for that.

Finally, thank you, dear reader. It's one thing to read the first book in a series. That's almost like taste-testing. Trying a dish for the first time and seeing if it suits you. Reading the sequel means you enjoyed my work enough to come back to the world and see what was going to happen next. I genuinely believe this is the best book I've ever written—and I hope you feel the same way. Always honored to have you along for the journey.

Spire

Ravinia 1

Oft Isles
2

23

Iron Plains 4

Generous Valley

3

5 Nostra

14

THE DIRES

Harbone Valley

Brood Estate
7

Portal Landing
x 12

19

The Eyeglass

Watcher Mountain

10

KATHOR
8

The Footsteps River

HEARTH

21

6

11

9

20

Darktide River

22

13

15 The Whispers

Morningthate River

Straywhite River

Northern Citadels
17

The Three Forests

24

Southern Citadels

18

16

NORTHERN SEA

Horned Coast

TUSK

DELVE

AN ACCURATE MAP
OF

DELVEA

Miles
0.   10.   20.   30.   40.

1. Ravinia — The largest free port along the northern coast. It is famous for its gladiator pits, but it was also where I first met the Tin'Vori siblings.

2. The Oft Isles — A travel destination for Kathor's wealthiest families.

3. The Generous Valley — The most fertile valley in all of Delvea. It is responsible for producing 90 percent of the food Kathor consumes.

4. The Iron Plains — A brutal stretch of land that has historically been viewed as a natural barrier between Kathor and any northern armies.

5. Nostra — A mountain town that sits in the shadow of the Broods' most famous castle. Once their greatest shield, it became our greatest weapon when Theo was exiled there.

6. The Hairbone Valley — A sparsely populated valley with towns mostly loyal to House Brood.

7. The Brood Estate — The only primary estate for a major house that is located beyond Kathor's outer walls. It was once known as one of the most impregnable fortresses in the world.

8. Kathor — The capital city of Delvea. Reverend Ockley famously described it by saying that "every road leads here, even the ones that haven't been built yet."

9. The Straywhite River — The most prominent river system on the eastern seaboard.

10. The Eyeglass — Famous for its severe peak, it remains the only mountain on record that has not been summited.

11. Watcher Mountain — The tallest mountain in Delvea and the most visible peak from Kathor.

12. Portal Landing — The place where all of this began.

13. The Morningthaw River — The primary river system in the Dires.

14. The Dires — The last home of the dragons. One of the most dangerous places in the world. There are still sections that remain uncharted.

15. The Whispers — The continent's largest desert. It is mostly unpopulated.

16. Delvea — The name Kathorians use when referring to the entire continent—though it more appropriately refers to just half of the continent.

17. The Northern Citadels — A group of cities that were built during the first expansion north along the coast of Delvea.

18. The Southern Citadels — The very first cities established and built by the Delveans after they made land on the continent.

19. The Footsteps — A small chain of mountains that reduce to foothills as they lead into Tusk.

20. Hearth — The capital city of Tusk. It is established, like Kathor, above a vast network of magical veins. The Tusk people refer to the entire continent as Hearthland.

21. The Darktide River — The most prominent river on the western seaboard of the continent.

22. Tusk — The name most Delveans use for the land on which the Tusk people live. A conflation, of sorts, with the people themselves.

23. The Horned Coast — A notoriously treacherous coastline on the Tusk side of the continent.

24. The Three Forests — The region where magic was first discovered—at least by the Delvean people.

25. Spire — A coastal Tusk city in the northwest.